WHERE EVIL DWELLS ...

"I didn't know the library was such an exciting place," Faith said, smiling.

"You'd be surprised," Land said.

The elevator arrived, and they took it down. Faith stared at the descending lighted numbers above the door. She wasn't worried about weirdos. Those she could handle. Her father had taught her self-defense at an early age, and she had no doubt that, physically, she was a match for anyone her size or smaller. Or larger. Her father's technique had been to attack first, ask questions later.

No, if she was worried about anything, it was earthquakes, fires, the building itself.

The sixth floor.

No, that was stupid.

But it was true.

The sixth floor.

She didn't want to admit it, but something about the top level of the library gave her the creeps.

UNIVERSITY

BENTLEY LITTLE

A SIGNET BOOK

SIGNET
Published by the Penguin Group
Penguin Books USA Inc., 375 Hudson Street,
New York, New York 10014, U.S.A.
Penguin Books Ltd, 27 Wrights Lane,
London W8 5TZ, England
Penguin Books Australia Ltd, Ringwood,
Victoria, Australia
Penguin Books Canada Ltd, 10 Alcorn Avenue,
Toronto, Ontario, Canada M4V 3B2
Penguin Books (N.Z.) Ltd, 182-190 Wairau Road,
Auckland 10, New Zealand

Penguin Books Ltd, Registered Offices:
Harmondsworth, Middlesex, England

First published by Signet, an imprint of Dutton Signet,
a division of Penguin Books USA Inc.

 REGISTERED TRADEMARK—MARCA REGISTRADA

PUBLISHER'S NOTE
This is a work of fiction. Names, characters, places, and incidents either
are the product of the author's imagination or are used fictitiously,
and any resemblance to actual persons, living or dead, events, or locales
is entirely coincidental.

ISBN 0-7394-2559-5

For my grandmothers,
Fay Dobrinin and Herma Little

ONE

1

California felt a million miles away.

Jim Parker set the brake on the rototiller and cut the engine. His back hurt like a mother, a dull, throbbing pain just above the belt line, and he stretched, pressing both hands against the small of his back, bending first to the left, then to the right. He'd pay for this exertion tonight. It had been a long time since he'd done this much physical labor, and his body wasn't used to it.

Still, there was something good about the pain. It made him feel as though he'd accomplished something, as though he'd done something real, something worthwhile.

He'd put off expanding the garden until now, spending most of this summer hiking and hanging out, being with his friends. His mom hadn't minded. She'd told him when he'd come home in June that she wanted him to pull the manzanita and create some space for corn and zuchini next year, but this year's garden was already planted, and she'd made it clear that there was no hurry.

Time was running out, though. The summer had gone by much faster than he'd expected, the days and weeks speeding past in what seemed to him to be record time, and exactly a week from today he'd be going back. He'd already received his dorm assignment and registration materials in the mail, had already been assigned a walk-in registration hour, and this morning, when he'd awakened, he'd decided that he'd better get to work.

Jim wiped the sweat off his forehead with the back of his hand. Leaning against the raised handle of the rototiller, he looked across the low skyline of Williams toward the San Francisco Peaks. The mountains above Flagstaff were purple in the distance, the dark, smudged color contrasting sharply with the cloudless blue sky and the green pines closer in.

He did not want to go back to college.

It was a strange thing to admit, but it was true. He'd spent his entire high school career working his ass off to get good grades, following the advice of Frank Zappa, who on an old album cover had said, "Forget about the senior prom and go to the library and educate yourself if you've got any guts." He'd found the album one day in a long-forgotten pile of his dad's old stuff in the storage shed, and while he hadn't forgotten about the senior prom, he had been motivated enough to go to the library and seriously dig into books and subjects that were well outside Williams High School's regular curriculum, a practice that had served him well come SAT time.

When he'd gotten the scholarship to UC Brea, it had been like a dream come true.

But college life had not been as great as he'd thought it would be. It wasn't that anything bad had happened. He hadn't flunked out or discovered that he was out of his depth. Quite the opposite. He'd done well in all of his classes and over the past four semesters had worked his way up through the ranks of the school newspaper to the position of editor. He'd made friends.

He just . . .

didn't like UC Brea.

That was it exactly. He didn't like the school. It wasn't anything specific, not anything he could put his finger on. There was just a vague sense of unease that he experienced when he was there, a feeling of dread he felt when he even thought about the place. It was not the teachers he disliked, or the curriculum, or the students, or the campus. Not precisely. It was . . . all of them.

And none of them.

He knew he was being irrational. Hell, he couldn't justify his feelings even to himself. He was going to be the editor of the *Daily Sentinel* this semester. It was what he'd been working toward the past three years, the culmination of his academic career, and in addition to looking great on his resumé, it would virtually guarantee him a job upon graduation. UC Brea might not be Columbia, but it was pretty well regarded in the field of journalism, and the last editor had gone on to become a first-string reporter for the *Los Angeles Times.*

Yet he wanted to chuck it all and stay here in Williams with his mom and just get a job at the Tru-Value and never look back.

Something was definitely wrong with him.

A jet flew high overhead, its vapor trail spread all the way to the horizon, where it was already dissipating into cloud cover.

Jim straightened, twisted his torso first one way, then the other, and bent down to start up the rototiller engine. Enough of this self-indulgence. He'd think about it later, maybe talk about it with his mom. Right now he had work to do.

He pulled the rope, the engine roared into life, and he disengaged the brake.

He pushed the rototiller through the rocky soil away from the storage shed.

He brought it up at dinner.

His mom had made steak and apple pie to reward him for his labors, and the two of them sat on the couch in the living room, watching the news. During a laxative commercial he took a big drink of milk and cleared his throat. "I'm thinking of staying here," he said.

She frowned at him. "What?"

"I'm not sure I want to go back to school this semester, Mom. I'm thinking maybe it'd be better if I took some time off, worked here for a while, decided what I wanted to do with my life."

"This is a joke, right?"

He shook his head.

Slowly she put her plate down on the coffee table. She faced him. "I oughta smack you." Her voice shook. "You talked about nothing but going off to college all through high school. Now you're there, a year away from graduation, getting good grades, editor of the paper, and you want to quit? Your father and I did not raise you to be a quitter. You know your father wanted more than anything for you to get an education. You got a chance here that he didn't have, that none of us ever had, and now you want to just throw it away?"

"I'd go back. I think I just need some time off—"

"If you took time off, you'd never go back. Look at your father. Do you think he wanted to be a mechanic all his life? You think he didn't want to be doing something else? He didn't have a chance. You do. An education will give you a choice, an opportunity to be what you want to be, not what circumstances force you to be. You'll be able to choose your profession and not just take whatever job comes along."

"I know, Mom. I just—"

"You just what?"

He looked away, unable to answer her, unable to meet her gaze. She was angry, he realized. Really angry. Angrier than he had seen her since he'd backed into a parked pickup and dented the fender of her Buick when he was in high school. He had not known until now how much she had been counting on him to graduate, how much it meant to her. It was not something she had ever mentioned to him, not something he had even thought about, but he understood now how proud she was of his academic career and, even under these circumstances, it made him feel warm and good.

And ashamed of himself for wanting to bail.

But how to explain to her this . . . this dread, this heavy, nameless feeling in his gut? He was still unable to adequately explain it to himself. He thought of Howie. His friend had promised to come to Arizona for a week this summer but had canceled out at the last minute. There'd been a few phone calls since, a few raunchy postcards, but he hadn't seen Howie since May.

That had bothered him.

That had been the start of it.

But his mom was right, he knew. It would be thoughtless and ungrateful of him to drop out. A slap in the face to the memory of his father.

Besides, when it really came down to it, he knew that, trite as it sounded, clichéd as it was, education was his ticket to a better life, and despite his feelings, despite his talk, he would no more quit school than commit suicide.

But he did not want to go back to UC Brea.

"Well?" his mom demanded.

He tried to smile at her over his plate. "Good dinner."

"Jim?"

He sighed. "I was joking. It was a joke. I'm sorry."

"You told me it wasn't a joke."

"It was."

She looked at him for a moment, and he knew she knew that he was lying, but, thankfully, she decided to let it ride. She picked up her plate, started to eat. "Change the channel," she said. "*Entertainment Tonight*'s on." Her voice was flat, still angry, but he knew she would not bring it up again.

2

Faith Pullen edged her VW to the left in order to give the homeless woman pushing a shopping cart through the gutter a wide berth. The Bug's left front tire dipped into a deep pothole, and the car swerved instantly into the next lane, the steering wheel pulling so hard and sharply in her hand that it took almost all of the strength in her arms to steady her course. A car honked at her, a loud, sustained horn blast, and she glanced over to see a red lowrider with black tinted windows pull next to her on the right. She slowed, letting it pass, hoping it wouldn't stay even with her, hoping she wouldn't see a window roll down, and she breathed a sigh of relief as it turned off Seventeenth Street and hung a right at Grand.

She signaled, moved carefully back into the right lane.

It was dusk, and in front of her, above the houses and buildings, the sun was a huge orange ball, its usual indistinct brightness dimmed to visibility by the filter of smog that lay over Southern California. She glanced at it, glanced away. She was never sure if it was safe for her to look at the sun like this. During eclipses people were always warned not to look at the sun, even though it appeared to be safe. Wasn't this the same thing? She didn't know. But she kept sneaking quick peeks at the smog-filtered globe, compelled to look but afraid to stare.

A red light on Main stopped her for what seemed like an eternity. Then she was driving past Bud's Meat Hut, the lifesize steer on the roof of the butcher shop now little more than a bulky silhouette. A few blocks beyond, she passed the street corner where Julio had been gunned down last year in a drive-by.

Then she was turning left and no longer facing east, and the light dimmed considerably as she drove down the narrow street into her neighborhood. She checked the Swatch watch hanging by a bracelet chain from her rearview mirror. Six-thirty. Six-thirty and the sun was already setting.

Good.

She couldn't wait for summer to end.

She couldn't wait to get out of this hellhole.

She slowed the car as she approached her block. She was looking forward to the beginning of school, but not as much as she'd looked forward to the beginning of junior college the past two years. She supposed it was because she felt a little intimidated. High school had been a breeze—but then everyone attended high school and nearly everyone made it through. Orange Coast College had been a little tougher, but still not a major challenge.

Now she was in the big leagues.

A four-year university.

She'd survived junior college—that buffer between the elite and the rank and file—but now she was entering the ivory tower, joining the upper ranks, and though she would never admit it to another living soul, the prospect frightened her. It shouldn't, she knew. She'd had an easy time of it in grammar school, and she remembered her parents telling her that junior high would be much harder. It hadn't been. Her mom had told her the same thing about high school. Again, not true.

She hadn't been good enough to get a scholarship, though, and she supposed that was why she was a little apprehensive now about going to a university.

Still, if Brooke Shields could get through Princeton, she should be able to hack UC Brea.

She pulled into the driveway, grateful to see that her mother's car was gone, and got out of the Bug, sorting through her keys until she found the one that unlocked the front security door.

"Keith!" she called as she opened the door and walked inside. "You home?" No answer. Her brother must be gone too. She locked the door again, reached down to pick up the mail that had been dropped through the slot.

And there it was.

An envelope from the UC Brea Office of Financial Aid.

She licked her suddenly dry lips. It was bad news. She knew it. Good news didn't arrive so anonymously, so casually. She fingered the envelope. Her hands were sweating, her heart pounding. She hadn't expected to be so nervous. She hadn't thought she'd put so much store on this. But she had. Getting a loan or grant was the only way she'd be able to get out of this house. She could work full-time and she'd still make barely enough to cover books and tuition. A loan was the only thing that would enable her to move out on her own.

With trembling fingers she tore open the envelope.

The form letter inside was short and succinct: "We regret to inform you that your application for Cal Grant A has been denied. It has been determined that your family income does not meet the eligibility qualifications...."

She crumpled the letter, threw it down. What the hell did you have to do to get a grant these days? Be homeless? Blow someone in the Financial Aid Office? It wasn't as though she was asking for a handout. She was asking for a *loan*. A loan that she would repay. It would not cost anybody anything.

"Shit," she said.

Now she was stuck here. In this house.

With her mother.

She left the rejection letter on the floor and carried the rest of the mail into the living room, wrinkling her nose as she dropped the envelopes on the battered coffee table. There was the faint redolent odor of pot in the room. The windows were all open and there was an overlay of strawberry air freshener to hide the scent, but it was still there, the pungent smell unmistakable. She glanced around. A small battery cable roach clip lay in the ashtray on the end table, and the unicorn coverlet which normally covered the couch was pulled down and messed up.

Her mother had picked up a guy again.

She'd fucked him there on the couch.

Disgusted, Faith walked through the small dining room into the kitchen. She opened the refrigerator, the freezer, looking for something to eat, found only an old macaroni and cheese pie. Someone in this damn house was going to have to go shopping one of these days and it sure as hell wasn't going to be her. Not this time. Not again. She unwrapped the pie, popped it into the microwave.

Where was her mother now?

No, she didn't really want to know.

She could imagine.

She got a glass from the cupboard, poured herself a drink of water from the bottle next to the sink. On the sideboard she saw a stack of books her brother had picked up at some used bookstore and had purposely left behind for her to see: John Barth, *Giles Goat Boy*; Thomas Pynchon, *Gravity's Rainbow*; William Burroughs, *Naked Lunch.* She shook her head. She felt sorry for Keith in a way. He tried so hard to impress people, was so desperately and pathetically intent on proving to the world—and to her in particular—what a deep and profound thinker he was. If he spent half as much time learning as he did posing, he might get somewhere in life. But he'd bought into the myth of the disaffected urban intellectual lock, stock, and barrel. For the past year, since he'd graduated from high school, he'd dressed the part, acted the part. He wasn't stupid, and she'd told him more than once that he ought to get off his dead ass and sign up for some community college courses at the very least, but he'd ridiculed her belief in the value of traditional education, quoted some old Pink Floyd song at her, and with an air of smug superiority, proclaimed himself to be free from such mundane materialistic concerns.

He was going to end up one of those sad pseudo-intellectuals, part of the detritus of bohemia that littered the retail world of Southern California—a record store clerk who looked down on his customers, convinced that he was hipper and more intelligent than everyone else, yet still earning minimum wage at thirty-five years old.

The bell on the microwave rang, and Faith took out her food. She ate it quickly, leaning against the sink, then dumped the package in the garbage and went into her bedroom to watch the news, not wanting to be in the front of the house when her mother got home.

Keith came in around ten, going directly to his room and locking himself in, but her mother did not return until nearly midnight. Faith was lying in bed, reading, and she heard her mother enter the house, trying to be quiet and failing.

She quickly turned off the light, put down the book, pretended to be asleep.

There was a siren outside—police car, fire truck, or ambulance, she couldn't be sure which—growing louder, coming closer, then cresting and fading once again into the background noise of the city. From somewhere in the darkness came the sound of gunshots, but she wasn't sure if they were from a too-loud TV or a neighborhood across town.

From the kitchen she heard the sound of the refrigerator door opening. Coke, she knew. Her mom was getting out the Coca-Cola.

Other sounds, familiar sounds: footsteps across the floor to the bathroom, the door closing, the cupboard under the sink being opened.

Fizzing.

And the sickening squelching sound of douching.

God, she'd be grateful when school started. When she could stay at school and study in the library and not come home until after her mom was dead asleep.

She closed her eyes more tightly, forced her breathing into an even, regular rhythm.

She drifted off to the sound of her mother washing sperm out of her vagina with the world's most popular soft drink.

3

"I'll need to see some ID."

Vicki Soltis made a show of rummaging through her purse. She had not brought along any identification save last semester's student body card, a fact she had discovered a half hour into the line, but still she pretended to look, praying that ignorance and intent would see her through this crisis. It was not really her fault. By the time she'd discovered that two forms of identification were needed to cash a check for registration and parking fees, it had been too late for her to run back home, return to campus, and get in line again. So she'd decided not to give up her place in line, to take her chances, hoping that the registrars would be too tired and too eager to go home themselves after a long day's work to stick with the full procedure.

She gave up her sham search, preparing to beg for mercy.

The Hispanic woman behind the counter smiled. "You don't have any ID?" she asked in heavily accented English.

Vicki shook her head miserably. "Just my student body card."

The woman looked over at the clock on the wall. It was five to nine. At least fifteen other students still stood waiting behind Vicki. "Okay," the woman said. "I'm supposed to make you go home, get some ID, line up, and go through the whole process again. But it's the last day, it's late, and I'm going to let you slide."

"Thank you," Vicki said, giving her a genuine smile of relief. "Thank you. You saved my life."

The woman laughed. "We're not all monsters here. But you do have to come into the Registrar's Office sometime in the next two days and bring ID. If we don't see your driver's license and at least one other form of valid ID, we can't cash your check and you won't be enrolled."

"Okay."

"I'll keep your check separate. If you don't see me by the cashier's window, ask for me. My name's Maria."

"Thank you. Thanks a lot."

"No problem." Maria handed Vicki her registration materials and student ID, smiling good-bye. "Next!" she announced to the line.

Vicki pushed past the other students going through late registration and stepped outside the Administration building. The night was dark, with no moon, and the campus lights that were supposed to illuminate the walkways had not been turned on. That was stupid. Didn't they know there were still people here registering? She looked down the long walkway that led toward the parking lot, where a few half-powered streetlights shone dimly on a row of shiny cars.

A chill passed through her.

This deserved a letter. A complaint to the president. The school had upped fees a hundred and fifty dollars this semester, had increased parking prices by fifteen bucks, and was still too cheap to adequately light public areas at night.

A slight breeze blew an old candy wrapper past her feet. The breeze was warm, but it did nothing to relieve her chill. She looked back at the lighted doorway of Administration and considered waiting for other students to come out, so at least she'd have someone to walk with. But she figured they'd probably be going out to the parking lot. She was going the opposite way, across the street to her apartment.

Besides, you couldn't be too careful about anyone these days.

Not even students.

She'd just run for it.

She folded her registration materials, inserted them between the pages of her class schedule, rolled up the schedule, and started jogging down the cement path toward the information booth in front of the campus and the streetlight beyond.

It happened fast. Too fast for her to react. Too fast even for her to cry out. From the shadowed murk next to the information booth rushed a blur of a man who pushed her to the pavement, shoving hard. Before she could put out her arms to protect herself and stop her fall, she hit the ground, registration materials flying. Her head snapped against the asphalt, and her nose was broken, a sudden wash of blood streaming from the center of her face. Her hands and knees scraped across the rough ground, the skin tearing.

Then a hand was clamped over her mouth, her head jerked back, and she could not breathe for the blood in her nose and throat. She tried to struggle, but she was too scared, too hurt, to fight effectively, and her body would not cooperate, would not do what her mind wanted it to do.

A hand was shoved up her skirt, and rough, brutal fingers grabbed her panties, yanking them down, pulling pubic hair with them, and she realized that she was going to be raped.

She still could not breathe, could not spit or even make a sound, and her vision was becoming blurry, getting dark. Then the hand on her mouth disappeared, her head fell forward, and she was vomiting, vomiting blood, trying not to swallow as she instinctively gasped for air.

Her legs were shoved apart.

Please, God, she thought, her cheek falling hard into the bloody vomit. Please let it be quick.

It was not.

TWO

1

Dr. Ian Emerson stood in front of the room and looked out at the faces before him, trying not to let his disappointment show. The class was even smaller than it had been the last time he'd offered the course, three semesters ago, and that had been the lowest enrollment ever. He opened his briefcase and took out the notes for his opening lecture, placing them on the podium next to the desk. Time was when the room would have been filled, each seat taken, the doorway and the hall outside crowded with hopeful petitioners. But times had changed, and today the crowds were in the business courses. Even "fun" classes like this one were dwindling in popularity.

When Kiefer saw the enrollment figures, he might lay the course to rest altogether.

Ian looked up again. The students were scattered throughout the room. Front and center was the groupie contingent: four or five students from his American Moderns class last semester, young men and women who had liked either him personally or his style of teaching and had volunteered for another tour of duty. Next to them were the high achievers, a well-dressed, bright-eyed group with straight posture and attentive expressions. The professional students—older guys with beards and anachronistically long hair, efficient-looking women in business suits—filled out the sides of the class, and in the back of the room were the weirdos, those who looked like they not only read horror stories but lived them. This time the group consisted of two girls with white faces, black clothes, and spiky hair; one skinny, nervous guy with glasses wearing clothes about four years out of style; and an overweight kid with a Miska-tonic University T-shirt.

There was one student near the door, however, who defied such quick and easy categorization, and Ian let his gaze linger a little longer on this one. The man was in his early to mid-fifties, wearing a tweed jacket over a casual shirt. He was too old to be a traditional student but too young to be a retiree embarking on a second career. He had a bushy gray-black beard and piercing blue eyes which stared unwaveringly at Ian and made him feel more than a little uncomfortable. On the small, almost child-size desk before the man was a stack of loose-leaf binders and paperback books. He looked like a scholar of some sort, a fellow professor perhaps, definitely an unlikely candidate for the course.

The clock at the back of the room said three past nine, and Ian decided it was time to start. He cleared his throat. "Welcome to English 360," he said. " 'Supernatural Literature.' I'm Dr. Emerson. If that isn't the name written on your schedule, you're in the wrong room."

There were a few perfunctory laughs from the students up front. The rest of the class stared at him blankly.

"Okay, I'm not real big on calling roll, so I'll probably just do it this once. When I call your name, I want each of you to stand up and tell a little bit about yourself."

Students looked around at one another. He heard muffled whispers of outrage and complaint. The kid with the glasses looked panicked.

He smiled. "Just kidding. Don't you hate teachers who do that?"

The tension was broken. He could feel the students relax, and now there was no longer a group of blank faces before him. He had aligned himself with the students; they were now on his side. Several of them were smiling and nodding; all of them seemed as though they would be open to anything he had to say. Out of curiosity he glanced over at the Professor, but the bearded man was unsmiling and unresponsive, not interacting with those around him, and he remained unreadable.

Ian looked down at his notes. They seemed stuffy and suddenly inappropriate. He had spoken to none of the students, nor had they spoken to him, but after fifteen years of teaching he was usually able to judge a class, to take its pulse and determine where he should go with his discussion. Each class had a personality of its own, the chemistry of individuals was different each time, and somehow that personality was communicated nonverbally. He usually did best when he trusted his instincts. Right now his instincts told him to scrap the notes.

He walked around the podium and sat down casually on the top of the desk, feet swinging, facing the front row. "All right," he said. "Let's start off with a simple one: What is horror?"

One of the high achievers raised his hand.

"High school's over," Ian said, smiling. "You don't have to raise your hand in this class. If you've got something to say, just say it."

"Horror is the literature of fear," the student said.

"What's your name?"

"John."

"Good answer, John. The textbook answer, the approved English department answer, but a good answer nonetheless. Horror stories do indeed address the subject of fear and often inspire fear in their readers. That is without a doubt part of their appeal, but there's more to it than that. Anyone else? What is horror?"

"Tales of terror," Miskatonic said.

" 'Tales of terror.' A variation of 'the literature of fear,' but still a good answer. Anyone else?"

There was no answer.

"None of you know what horror is?" He scanned the room. Several pairs of eyes looked away, as if afraid he was going to call on them. Some students shook their heads. "Good. Because if you knew, there would be no reason to take this class." He reached behind him and pulled a book from his briefcase. "This semester we are going to look at the history of horror, from Poe to King, examine various types of horror stories and try to determine why they are horror, what makes them horror—or 'dark fantasy,' as it is euphemistically called today."

"Are we going to be discussing the work of the magic realists at all?" a girl in the front row asked.

Ian looked at her. She was well dressed in a tastefully trendy skirt and blouse and was wearing large thin-rimmed glasses. He chuckled. "Obviously an English major."

"Yes," she admitted.

"Well, we'll see how much time we have. I don't know if we'll be reading stories by any of the so-called 'magic realists,' but we may discuss the impact of their work in regard to the legitimization of the literature of the supernatural. Right now I am going to read you a short story by H. H. Munro, better known as Saki. It's short, only a few pages long, and afterward I want you to tell me first of all if this is a horror story, and if so, why."

He began reading and, as always, he lost himself in the words. He had read the story a hundred times, but it never failed to affect him, and even here, in a well-lit classroom in the middle of the day, surrounded by people, he felt the delicious slight shiver of goose bumps on his arms. After he had finished, there was a lively, intelligent discussion. Janii Holman, the girl who had asked about the magic realists, tried to read into the work Christian symbolism which obviously wasn't there, and Kurt Lodrugh, the kid with the Miskatonic T-shirt, thought the story made oblique references to Lovecraft, which it did not, but on the whole the discussion went well. Although he still didn't know most of the students' names, he marked in his mind who said what, and by the end of the period he had a pretty good bead on the various levels of literacy and interest of the individuals in the class.

The discussion was winding down when Ian looked up at the clock. There were five minutes left to go, and he thought he'd give the students a head start on their next class. "Okay," he said. "I expect each of you to go to the bookstore today and pick up this book." He held up *Classic Stories of the Supernatural*, the anthology he had chosen as the basic text for the course. "For Wednesday, read 'The Black Cat' and 'A Cask of Amontillado' by Poe, and be prepared to discuss the themes of paranoia and premature burial. If you're good boys and girls, I'll let you in on some gossip about Poe's sex life."

There was laughter and conversation as he put his notes and book into the briefcase, a signal that the class was over. Most of the people began to file out, but one of the professional students, a woman in her late twenties or early thirties, approached his desk. She waited patiently until he had closed and locked his briefcase. "Excuse me," she said. "My name's Marylou Johnson, and I won't be able to be here Wednesday. I have to take my husband to the airport. Could you tell me what I should have read by Friday?"

Ian chuckled. "The old husband-to-the-airport routine this early in the semester, huh? You'll run out of excuses by October."

The woman did not smile; the expression on her face was serious. "I really do have to take him."

"I believe you. But I haven't made out a syllabus yet and, to be honest, I haven't decided what I'm going to assign next. I was going to work it all out tonight. But I'm flexible. Just read those two stories, and you can make up the others later."

"Thanks." She turned and walked out the door, and it was then Ian noticed that the Professor had not moved from his seat. That made him slightly nervous. He smiled noncommittally at the man, preparing to leave.

"Dr. Emerson?" The words were spoken in a tone of familiarity. The man's voice was low and gruff, with a definite East Coast accent. He stood up, moving forward.

Ian felt a tremor of apprehension pass through him as he looked at the grim face. "Yes?"

"I need to talk to you."

"About what?"

"About the evil in this university."

Ian's eyes moved toward the open doorway. The hallway outside was starting to fill up; other classes were getting out. The man was between himself and the door, but he could yell for help if the guy turned out to be crazy. Right now that seemed a distinct possibility. He kept his voice calm. "What's your name?"

"Gifford," the man said. "But that doesn't matter. Time is running out, and we need to work fast."

"Work fast at what?"

"We have to kill the university." Gifford's blue eyes stared unflinchingly into his own. "Before it kills us."

"Is this a joke?" Ian asked, but he knew even before he asked the question that Gifford was not the kind of man capable of joking.

"It is no joke. The evil grows stronger each day."

Ian could feel adrenaline pumping through his system. Jesus. Crazies were everywhere these days. The hairs on his arms were prickling. In the back of his mind he recalled reading a story about a psychotic student who had tortured and mutilated his professor when the professor didn't agree with his theories. Ian took a deep breath. He had to put a stop to this now, to lay things out for the guy. "Look," he said, "just because I teach horror fiction, it does not mean I subscribe to this kind of crap. Horror is art, it is entertainment, but it is not something which overflows into the rest of my life. I do not go to church, I do not spend my spare time visiting graveyards or attending seances, I do not believe in channeling or the healing power of crystals—"

"I came to you because I thought you would understand. The evil—"

"I do *not* understand," Ian interrupted. He'd heard an undercurrent of doubt, perhaps fear, in Gifford's voice, and that made him more aggressive. "I don't remember seeing your name on the roll sheet, Mr. Gifford." And he hadn't. He had noticed as he'd taken roll that the man had responded to none of the announced names. "When I asked if there were any names that had not been called or if there were any petitioners, you did not come forward. Are you planning to enroll in my class?"

"No. I just wanted to talk to you, to tell you what is happening."

"Then I suggest you get out of here before I call the campus police." He pressed past Gifford and started toward the door.

"Wait!" The strength of the rough cry caused Ian to turn around.

Gifford's face, which until this point had been nearly expressionless, was now a mask of fear. His blue eyes seemed haunted rather than piercing, and the lips beneath the thick beard were trembling. "I didn't expect you to believe me right away," he said. "But I had to try." He moved over to his desk and withdrew a notebook. "Just read this. That's all I ask."

"What is it?"

"It's my dissertation. It concerns the evil which is attacking this university and the way in which it can be combatted."

"Dissertation?" Ian looked surprised. "You're—"

Gifford picked the rest of his books up off the desk. "I'm an arsonist," he said. He started toward the door, then turned back. His face had regained its composure, but the fear was still there. "My number is on the first page. Call me. Any time. I'll be waiting to hear from you." He walked into the hall and was carried away on the tide of bodies pressing toward the stairs and elevators.

Ian looked down at the document in his hands and turned to the first page. "A Study of Patterned Supernatural Phenomena in American Universities," he read. "Conclusions and Recommendations." The name below the title was Gifford Stevens.

The anthology he was using for this class had been edited by a Dr. G. Stevens.

No, he thought. It can't be.

He quickly opened his briefcase and looked at the book. He flipped it over to the back.

"Dr. Stevens received his Ph.D. in comparative literature from Princeton University," the blurb read. "He is an expert on arson and demolitions, and currently lives in New Mexico with his wife, Pat."

He thought over what had just occurred as he closed the briefcase and stepped out into the hallway to go to his next class, but the more he mulled it over, the more certain he was that the man who had handed him the dissertation had not been wearing a wedding ring.

2

It was a full two hours after reporting for work that Faith finally received her introductory tour of the library.

She'd found the job through the Career Center, had seen the notice for it on the Work-Study bulletin board, and had immediately rushed over to apply. That had been last week, when she'd been on campus for early registration, and a few days later she'd received a notice in the mail telling her that she'd been accepted for the position of library assistant.

She hadn't even had to go for an interview.

The mailed acceptance letter had asked her to report

to Phil Lang at the circulation desk after her last class on Monday, and when her Cultural Anthropology instructor dismissed the class at one-thirty, fifteen minutes earlier than scheduled, she headed directly for the library.

Phil Lang turned out to be a tall, red-haired Ichabod Crane lookalike: bow tie, wire-framed glasses, and all. He was behind the front counter in the lobby when she arrived, explaining something to three other students who obviously worked in the library, and Faith waited until he was finished before introducing herself. He looked her over, nodded, and asked her to step around the counter and into his office in the back.

She'd assumed that she would just show up and start working. But Lang made her fill out a slew of forms, including a W-2 and work-study verification. She then took the forms to the Financial Aid Office, where, after waiting in a seemingly endless line of other students, a bored middle-aged woman scrawled a cursory signature on the bottom of one of the forms, tore off a yellow carbon, and directed her to the Payroll Office, where once again she waited in line behind other work-study students until medical waivers and the proper authorization papers were typed out.

Then she returned to the library for her tour.

Lang was waiting for her behind the front desk when she got back. "All set up?" he asked.

She nodded, handed him the copies of the forms she'd been told to return to the library. He gave the papers a cursory glance, then took them into his office, emerging a moment later. "Okay," he said. "I'm going to take you through all the floors of the library. I don't expect you to remember everything I show you and tell you today, but you do need to familiarize yourself with the building and learn where everything's located so you'll be able to answer patrons' questions without having to ask for help all the time."

"Okay." His condescending attitude was already grating on her, but she forced herself to smile.

"Let's go, then."

Lang took her through the administrative offices on the first floor, then backstage through Circulation, where student assistants were retrieving books from bins underneath the book drop and scanning their bar codes through a computerized check-in machine. Other students picked up the piles of books, sorted them, and placed them on holding shelves.

Back in the lobby, he led her to a computer terminal situated on a low metal desk. "We're on the OCLC system here, which means that patrons look up materials on-line instead of using the card catalogue. Are you familiar with OCLC?"

Faith shook her head.

He explained the system to her, in anal-retentive detail, and though she wanted to pay attention, she found herself tuning him out, her mind wandering. Was it going to be this boring every day?

The old fry station at McDonald's suddenly didn't seem quite so bad.

"Got that?" Lang asked.

She nodded.

"Then let's go upstairs."

"Okay."

They went up the elevator and walked through Records and Documents on the second floor, Newspapers and Periodicals on the third floor, Reference on the fourth floor. Lang spent quite a bit of time walking her through the fifth floor, which housed Special Collections as well as books with call letters A through P.

"UC Brea has the largest collection of Holocaust literature in the United States," Lang said. "We have documents, diaries, and the most extensive assemblage of German atrocity photographs anywhere. Access to this, and to the other single-subject rarities that make up Special Collections are off-limits to students and can only be made available to tenured professors for specific research purposes." He smiled. "But if you last here long enough, you may be assigned to work in Special Collections, and you will be able to view the collections yourself."

Faith forced herself to smile back.

They took the elevator to the sixth floor.

She noticed the difference immediately.

The floor was completely and utterly silent.

Before, on the other levels, there had been noise. Not even a library could be completely quiet, and though the sounds hadn't really intruded upon her consciousness, her mind had registered them as they'd gone through the building: the rustle of papers, whispering between friends, books being dropped, change being jingled, the tapping of shoes on tiled floors.

But there was no noise on the sixth floor.

When the elevator door slid shut with a muted click and the whirring machinery slowed into dormancy, the floor became perfectly silent. For that first second even her own breathing sounded loud.

Then Lang started in on his speech.

He seemed oblivious to the atmosphere here, and he pointed out to her, as he had on the other levels, the map of the floor, mounted in a glass case opposite the elevator. It was an overhead diagram of all of the book-cases, showing where books with each call letter were located. The books moved, clockwise from the elevator, from Q through Z. He then led her through the real thing, and they walked away from the elevator and into the aisles. The bookcases here were huge, well above the top of her head, and she had the sensation of being in a giant rat's maze. The aisles seemed to stretch forever.

Faith was surprised to discover students bent over books and writing on papers in the long row of study carrels that lined the north wall. She wondered how they could remain so silent, refraining from making even those small noises she'd heard on the other floors of the library. She found herself thinking that they, too, were probably intimidated by the heavy atmosphere here, compelled to be quiet by the obvious oppressiveness.

"The books on this floor," Lang was saying, and even his voice was barely above a whisper, "are often disturbed. Students come up here and take them off the shelves, leave them in the carrels, put them back in the wrong places, sometimes even throw them on the floor." He paused. "Part of your job will be to take care of those books."

He led her to the west wall, where a wire-mesh gate opened between two outward-facing bookshelves. Using a key, he opened the gate and motioned for her to step inside. "This is the sorting cage," he said. "This is where you'll be taking the books you collect. You sort them by call letter, then put them on these trucks." He gestured toward several metal carts lined against the cage wall. "Then you take them out to be reshelved."

They walked out of the cage, and he closed the gate behind them.

"Don't worry. For the first few weeks you'll be paired with someone. They'll walk you through everything until you get the hang of it."

They walked again through the seemingly endless aisles until they reached the elevator. Lang pushed the call button. "One more thing," he said. "We've had some trouble up here with . . . with people bothering our assistants. Because of the nature of the library, because it is open to everyone, because people can walk in and stay until closing, for free, it tends to . . . attract some weirdos. I thought I'd better warn you. We get all kinds in here. Every so often someone will . . . expose himself." Lang absently pushed the call button again, though the little plastic Down arrow was already lit. "One guy last semester wore mirrors on his shoes so he could look up women's dresses. Another guy, a few semesters back, used to crawl underneath study carrels to do the same.

"Most of the time you'll be working with other people, shelf reading and what have you, so you won't have anything to worry about. But if you're ever up here by yourself, be careful. And immediately report anything that happens."

Faith nodded, smiled. "I didn't know the library was such an exciting place."

"You'd be surprised."

The elevator arrived, and they took it down. Faith stared at the descending lighted numbers above the door. She wasn't worried about weirdos. Those she could handle. Her father had taught her self-defense at an early age, and she had no doubt that, physically, she was a match for anyone her size or smaller. Or larger. Her father's technique had been to attack first, ask questions later, and she knew that a quick kick to the balls could take out even the toughest he-man.

No, if she was worried about anything, it was earthquakes, fires, the building itself.

The sixth floor.

No, that was stupid.

But it was true.

The sixth floor.

She didn't want to admit it, but something about the top level of the library gave her the creeps.

"I'm going to start you off today shelving books in Circ," Lang said. "That way I can double-check your work. Rennie and Sue are checking in books, and Glenna's stacking them on the holding shelves, so I'll just let you help Glenna. . . ."

She nodded, but she had already tuned him out. She didn't really care what she would be doing or who she would be working with. But she felt an unexpected sense of relief that she would not have to work on the sixth floor.

The library closed at ten-thirty, but Faith's shift ended at eight. Tomorrow she had no classes, and she'd work from seven in the morning until one in the afternoon.

That was the good thing about having a job on campus. The hours were completely flexible. She could even change them if she had to study for a test.

She drove home on the freeway. Traffic was still crawling, though the rush hour was technically over, and it was nearly an hour later before she finally hit the Seventeenth Street offramp.

A gang of teenagers was encircling a flower seller at the head of the incline by the stoplight, and she quickly made sure both car doors were locked before speeding past.

A few minutes later, she passed Santa Ana College, her old alma mater. It looked smaller to her, though she'd only graduated in June, and she had the feeling that if she went back there now, it would be like returning to grammar school, with little desks and little doors and little drinking fountains.

She felt good, happy to be attending a university, a real school. She had no doubt now that she would be able to handle the curriculum, and even though it was only the first day, she felt as though she'd gotten a pretty good feel for the place. She liked the school.

Well, most of the school.

The sixth floor.

She pushed that thought out of her mind.

Across the street, on the right, was the spot where the

old Mitchell Brothers Theater had stood. She glanced at the empty plot of land, and she remembered how, as a child, Keith used to read aloud the titles of the movies on the marquee as they'd driven past—"Bodacious Ta-Ta's," "Debbie Does Dynasty," "Love Goddesses."

If the porno theater was still there, she knew, Keith would be patronizing it.

The thought of her brother made her feel slightly sad. What had happened and when had it happened? They'd been so close when they were little. Even after their father had died, perhaps more so then, they'd hung out together, they'd been there for each other, they'd shared secrets, they'd told each other everything.

Now she couldn't even remember the last time they'd had a simple conversation.

What was going to happen when she moved out on her own? Would all ties be cut? Would they drift apart and never see each other again? She didn't care if she never saw her mom again, but she did not want to lose contact with her brother.

What could she do about it, though?

She turned onto their street. A small child in his underwear who was standing on the lawn of one of the houses threw a dirt clod at her car and yelled something at her. She honked her horn at him, flipped him off.

God, she hoped her mom wasn't home.

Ahead, she saw, the lights of their house were on. In the driveway: her mom's car and a strange motorcycle.

She'd brought someone home with her.

Faith slowed the Bug, thought for a moment, then hit the gas and continued on past the house. She'd grab some food at El Pollo Loco, then hit the public library. It was open until nine. She could catch up on her reading there, and maybe by the time she returned, her mom's new "friend" would be gone.

Maybe.

She turned around in a dark driveway, then headed back down the street toward Seventeenth.

THREE

1

Richard Jameson took his time about getting to the *Sentinel* office. That's what he liked most about being on the paper. The freedom. He could show up late, leave early, go out for a burger. As long as he did the work, he was allowed a lot of leeway.

And he did the work.

He had no illusions about himself. He wasn't a great student or a scholar. He was getting through most of his classes by the skin of his teeth. But he was a good photographer. All of his interest and energies were focused on his photos, and it showed. He might not remember who Archduke Ferdinand was or how to find the cosine of an integer, but he knew his way around a Canon, and he had the awards to prove it.

He did have good technique: an artistic eye, solid editing sense, and extensive darkroom experience. But he attributed most of his success to being in the right place at the right time. He could dodge, burn, and crop to his heart's content, but if the subject he had to work with was crap, all the technical expertise in the world wouldn't save the picture.

That's why he always carried his camera with him. If something happened, if he ran across an event worth recording on film, he was prepared.

That's why he got the good shots.

That's why he won the awards.

Two-thirty classes were already in session, but here and there a few students were walking through the quad, and ahead Richard saw a gorgeous blond girl, obviously a freshman, coming out of the Social Sciences building. He shifted the camera strap on his shoulder, ran a quick hand through his hair. He was not unaware of the effect the camera had on women. Its presence elevated his status in some way, lent to him an exoticism that was not otherwise there. It automatically tagged him as an "artist," and he found that gave him a head start when it came to picking up babes.

And this one was definitely a babe.

He moved a little to the left and quickened his pace so that he would meet her on the steps of the building. She noticed him, took in the camera he was shifting on the shoulder strap, their eyes met, and he saw The Look. She was impressed.

He cleared his throat loudly. "Excuse me? Miss?"

She stopped, turned, faced him. God, she had beautiful eyes.

He smiled. "I'm the head photographer for the *Sentinel,* and I need to get a sort of generic 'first week of school' shot for the front page tomorrow. I was wondering if I might get you to pose for me. All you'd have to do is walk down those steps you just came down and look like you're heading toward a class."

The girl was already shaking her head before he finished speaking. "No. I don't think so."

"Why not? You'll get your name in the paper. By the way, what is your name?"

"Marcia."

"Well, Marcia, your picture and your name'll be on the front page of the *Sentinel.* You can get twenty copies and send them to all your relatives. What do you say?"

She shook her head. "I don't like to have my picture taken. It never comes out good."

"It will when I take it." He gave her a winning smile. "Come on. I really need to get this shot. I have a deadline to meet."

She was wavering. "I don't know."

"Please?"

It fell between them. There was no warning, no scream, no sound, only the body, speeding past them in a blur, and then the blood, flying instantly up in a single splattering wave as the body slammed into the concrete.

In the space of those first few seconds, he saw that the body was male, saw that it had landed not on its head, not on its feet, not flatly horizontal, but knees first in some strange twisting manner that had forced the contents of its abdomen out through its side. Organs were still moving, still jiggling, flopping onto the concrete though connected by bloody tissue to the body. The head was smashed, pulp, even the side that had not hit the ground shattered by the impact, distorted into unrecognizability.

Marcia was screaming, standing in place, unmoving, staring down at what was left of the body, entirely oblivious to the blood that had splashed up onto her bare legs and white shorts. Droplets of crimson spattered her face and light hair, were smearing on her screaming lips.

Richard was stunned into immobility for a fraction of an instant. Then he was looking up, looking down, looking around, getting perspective, weighing options. He stared at Marcia, at her white clothes and white skin, at the red blood.

This was going to look great in black and white. The contrast was perfect.

He did not even hesitate. He backed up, crouched down, took off the lens cap, swung the camera into place.

He started shooting.

2

Production was even busier than it had been the week before school started. The ad people had already finished their work and gone home, but the small room was crowded with editorial staffers: copy editors jostling for position as they proofed the paper, the production manager sitting in front of the VDT typesetting last-minute corrections while her two assistants pasted up. The radio was on, an obnoxious heavy metal station, and, standing in the doorway, Jim Parker had to shout to be heard. "Ten minutes!" he announced. "We have to be finished in ten minutes! The printer says we have to be there by eight!" No one gave any indication that they heard him, but he knew that they had, and he walked over to the nearest light table and looked over the sports page. There were two stories and no photos, and at any other time he would have been furious. He'd laid out the photo policy for each section editor in the first staff meeting last week, and they knew that he wanted no gray pages—each news, feature, entertainment, and sports page had to have at least one photo, and the editorial page had to have a cartoon. But he had more important things on his mind today.

Jim shouldered his way through the crowd of editors and began examining the front page. There was still a small hole at the end of the lead story, but Tony was busy with an X-acto knife, spacing out paragraphs to fill the empty spot. "Geography Student Jumps to Death from Social Sciences Building." Jim read the headline aloud. It wasn't brilliant, but it did its job. Beneath the two-deck banner was an upper-body photo of freshman accounting major Marcia Tolmasoff staring downward in shock at the unseen body, the ledge from which the suicide had jumped visible behind her.

"Good shot," he said.

Richard was somewhere in the back of the room, behind the crush of people. "Thanks!"

In the darkroom hung the white and black negatives of the other photos Richard had taken—the ones they couldn't use. The photographer had snapped an entire roll of film, and Jim could still see many of the powerful images in his mind. Clots of irregular viscera offset against the precise lines of the concrete. A close-up of the suicide's smashed head, a small segment of whitish brain squeezed out through a skull crack that matched a still-extant part in his hair. Marcia Tolmasoff, screaming, her face lightly freckled with blood, the lower half of her body dark with huge patterned blotches of it. And, perhaps the most disturbing of all, a shot of the entire body—crumpled, crooked, bloodily messy—with a crowd of *enthusiastic*-looking spectators staring at the unmoving form, waiting for the police to arrive.

Richard himself seemed a little too undisturbed by this, Jim thought.

Jean and her assistants finished pasting up the last of the corrections. "Done!" she announced.

Jim sighed. "Let's put it to bed. Who's going to take it in?"

"I will," Richard volunteered. He adjusted the camera strap on his shoulder. "I live out that way anyway."

"Thanks." Jim picked up the front page, examining it. He shook his head as he put it into the box with the others and handed it to Richard. "We'll make out a schedule for taking in the paper. We should all take turns doing it this semester."

Richard left, and Jean and her assistants began scraping wax off the light tables with their X-acto knives, cleaning up. Jim turned to face the remaining staff members, who were looking at him, as if waiting to be dismissed. "Good job," he said. "I'll see you all tomorrow." He nodded toward Stuart. "Find out what you can about this tomorrow morning. Maybe assign a sidebar of some sort to one of the reporters."

"Reporters?" Stuart said with mock incredulity. "You mean we have reporters?"

Everyone laughed. The first issue had been written and put together entirely by editors during the week before classes. This second issue had also been written entirely by editors.

"Hit the road," Jim said.

The staffers began to leave the room. Jim turned toward Jean, ready to apologize for keeping her so late, but from the hallway he heard the familiar click-hum of Howie's motorized wheelchair. "Shit," he muttered. In all the excitement he'd completely forgotten that he was supposed to pick his friend up at the Bookstore. He stepped into the hall, expecting Howie to be pissed, knowing he deserved whatever he got, but his friend's face was calm, his demeanor as unflappable as always.

"Sorry," Jim said before Howie could utter a word. "I had to extend our deadline because of the suicide, and—"

Howie smiled, waving away the apology. "Forget it. I understand. No harm done. I figured that's what happened. That's why I came over here." He was wearing his old flannel jacket, as usual, but Jim noticed instantly that there was a new button added to the collection on his friend's right breast. He leaned forward to read it.

" 'Eat Shit and Bark at the Moon,' " Howie said, grinning. "Some guy was selling them outside the Student Center. I couldn't resist."

"Sounds like something you'd buy," Jim said. "Come on. I'll pick up my stuff from the newsroom, then let's grab something to eat. I'm starving."

"Roger." Howie pushed the small toggle switch on the

wheelchair arm, and he followed Jim through Production into the newsroom, nodding hello to Jean and her assistants as he passed through. "So what happened?" he asked. "I heard it was a boyfriend-girlfriend thing."

"Don't know yet. No note's been found, but the guy's parents haven't been contacted. Maybe he left a note at home or something."

"It can't be grades. It's only the first week."

"No one knows." Jim grabbed his backpack from the top of his desk, shoved some papers inside it, and zipped it up. He flipped off the lights in the newsroom. "Let's hit the pavement."

The campus was quiet as Jim walked and Howie rolled toward the parking lot, the only noises audible the shuffle of Jim's heels on the concrete and the mechanized whirring of Howie's wheelchair. The day students had all gone home, the night students were in their classes, and the only person they saw was a lone fraternity member manning the coffee-and-donuts table outside the Physical Sciences building. Summer was not yet officially over, but the air was chilly and there was dew on the grass.

Jim found himself thinking again about why he hadn't wanted to come back to Brea. When he'd arrived last week, signed up for classes, moved into his dorm room, he'd thought his reservations about returning stupid. They'd seemed foolish, babyish, damn near idiotic. But here, now, with Richard's suicide photos in the back of his mind, with the campus dark and cold and silent, they once again seemed legitimate. There was something about this school that bothered him, that made him feel ill at ease. Even now, though he wanted to blame it on the unsettling photos of the dead student, he knew it was something else that disturbed him, something he could not pinpoint but that was as real to him as the darkness.

A shiver moved up his spine, over the skin of his neck.

"Where're we going?" Howie asked. "Bill's Burgers?"

"What?" He looked down at his friend, blinked. "Oh. Yeah. Sounds good."

"I haven't been there since last semester."

"Me either."

Howie pressed harder on his wheelchair's toggle

switch and pulled ahead, swerving to the left and rolling down the cement wheelchair-access ramp off the sidewalk onto the lower asphalt of the parking lot. Jim watched his friend. When he'd returned to Brea last week, he'd been shocked by the way Howie looked. Howie had seemed even smaller and frailer than he had before, his face so thin it was almost skull-like. A stab of pain had slashed through Jim when he'd gone to his friend's dorm room and Howie had opened the door: a sick queasy frightening feeling. The two of them never really talked about the muscular dystrophy—Howie was not one to dwell on his illness—and Jim had more or less assumed that it had been arrested. He had not really taken into account the fact that it was a degenerative disease, that Howie would get worse.

For the first time he'd realized that his friend might die.

He'd wanted to mention it, wanted to bring it up, wanted to talk about it, but instead had found himself stupidly asking, "How was your summer?"

Howie had grinned, shrugged. "You know."

He hadn't known. But he'd wanted to. He'd taken a deep breath. "Is that good or bad?"

"A little of both. Hey, did you hear that Simmons resigned over the summer? Harassment charges, I heard."

And they'd been off on another topic and the chance was lost.

Now he watched his friend's wheelchair bump across the asphalt toward the van. Again he felt that weird, sick feeling in the pit of his stomach. Of course Howie would have to spend the rest of his life in a wheelchair. That was a given. And his physical condition would obviously keep him from living a so-called "normal" life. But within those already set parameters, couldn't things remain stable?

Apparently not.

Jim stepped off the curb, strode forward to catch up to his friend. He tried not to let his feelings show on his face, tried to appear merely tired from the long day he'd put in, but obviously he failed.

"What is it?" Howie asked. "What's wrong?"

He shook his head. "Nothing."

"Bullshit."

"I'm just tired."

Howie looked skeptical, but he said nothing.

Jim's skin was creeping again, he had the unsettling feeling that someone—

something

—was watching them, spying on them, but he resisted the impulse to turn around, and the two of them continued silently across the parking lot to the van.

3

It was after dark when Ian arrived home. He was late, but it didn't really make any difference. There was no one waiting for him, no one to lecture him, no one who gave a damn when he came home. Or if he came home. That was probably why he'd taken to staying so late at school, spending so much time in his office. Even before the semester had started, he'd found himself just sitting at his desk reading, daydreaming, staring into space. His office was not comfortable. It was tiny, cramped, shelves along one wall filled with textbooks he had never read, shelves along another filled with classics and horror novels he had. His desk was piled high with papers and journals, things done and things to do, and his chair, a squeaky swivel seat, sat amongst the mess like a small cockpit. The room had only one small window, and that had always made him feel a trifle claustrophobic; he had generally kept strict office hours and had tried to be away from the room at all other times. But lately he'd been using his office as a hideout, eating his breakfast there before school, staying late after his classes were done. He rationalized it to himself, pretended there were papers to go over, work to be done, preparations to be made for classes, but that was all bullshit.

He just didn't want to go home.

He parked the car in the driveway and sat there for a moment. The timer he'd put on the living room lamp had obviously broken again, and the house was dark, the blank black windows reflecting the dim, silent street scene outside. Time was when each of the windows would have been blazing with life and light, the healthy yellow brightness spilling out even onto the lawn. But that was when Sylvia had been here, and those days were gone for good.

He reached behind him, pulled his briefcase from the backseat, and got out of the car. The porch light was not even on, and he had to fumble a few minutes through his collection of keys to find the ones for the door lock and dead bolt.

He turned on the living room light the moment he stepped through the doorway. In literature, empty houses, the hollow shells of homes which remained after a death or divorce, always seemed much too big, the lifeless rooms cavernous after the departure of a loved one. But in reality the opposite was true. Sylvia's presence had seemed to open the house up, to expand its boundaries outward, and each new antique acquisition or decorative modification she had made underscored the limitless possibilities of the dwelling. But since she had left, the house seemed so much more diminished, almost stifling in its smallness. He had tried getting rid of some of their furniture and replacing it that first week—donating their bed and dresser to the Goodwill, exchanging her china cabinet for yet another bookcase—but the confines of the house continued to shrink with each passing day, and the walls continued to close in on him. He now knew intimately every inch of space within every room, whereas before he had been acquainted with his home on only a general and superficial level, and the more he knew the house, the more he hated it.

Tonight it seemed worse than usual. He quickly walked through the front of the house, flipping on the lights in the dining room and kitchen, turning on the TV in the living room. In the old days he had seldom watched television, save for the odd movie or PBS special. He had spent most of his leisure time reading or writing, listening to music. But now he was grateful for the tube, and at night he found himself sitting in front of the TV more often than not. The effect was soothing; he didn't have to think or dwell on the past or contemplate the future, and the house was filled with the comforting sounds of conversation, the voices of people talking. He'd found, to his surprise, that he enjoyed much of what he watched, that there were usually one or two programs each night that he liked. Either television was getting better, his standards were lowering, or the medium itself had been receiving an unfairly bad rap in academia all these years. Probably a little of each, he suspected. Last semester, in an interesting role reversal, he had even found himself defending television to one of his more pompous students, arguing that an ignorance of popular culture was not something to be proud of and was, in fact, an anti-intellectual attitude at heart. He'd made a good case, he thought, and lately he'd been toying with the idea of putting his thoughts into a paper and submitting it to a journal.

God knew he needed to beef up his list of publications.

Of course, his life was not as empty and pathetic as he sometimes made it out to be. He did have a tendency to overdramatize things, to invest the small aspects of life with the gravity and import they received in literature. He was going through a rough time right now, and though emotionally he felt as though this state would be permanent, intellectually he knew that this too would pass. He was not unhappy. Not really. And he had a lot to live for. He had a fine job, a career he enjoyed, good friends, and there was not enough time if he lived to be two hundred to read all the books he wanted to read, see all the movies he wanted to see, do all the things he wanted to do. Still, on nights like these, when he had things to say and no one to say them to, he felt lonely and hopeless and wished he still had Sylvia.

Sylvia.

He recalled with perfect clarity the way he had come home unannounced for lunch last November and had found the both of them on the floor of the living room, she on the bottom, with her legs spread impossibly wide, he on top, the muscles in his sweaty back and buttocks rippling as he pumped away inside her. Sylvia had not merely been moaning but had been screaming, short, involuntary cries of passion which echoed throughout the house. She had never screamed with him, never, not even in the early days, and the expression of blind ecstasy on her face was one which was entirely unfamiliar to him.

His first thought had been that this was a nightmare, that the empty vacuum which had suddenly sucked out his guts would go away when he awoke and that Sylvia would be sleeping soundly beside him, dreaming of him and only him.

But he'd known it was no nightmare.

The expression on her face changed instantly from ecstasy to horror as she saw him, a fluid flowing, shifting, and rearranging of her features which reminded him of nothing so much as a lycanthropic transformation. She had, with wildly clutching fingers, pushed the man away, up, off her. He had rolled over as he pulled out, and Ian had seen the man's glistening erection, and it was this more than anything which had cemented his resolve, which had led him to kick Sylvia out once and for all. She had pleaded with him, cried, assured him that the other man meant nothing to her. She had met the man in a class, had gone to lunch with him a few times as a friend, and today they had come back here and . . . things had just happened. It was the first time, she said, and the last. She hadn't planned on sleeping with him, and she hadn't even wanted to.

If the circumstances had been different he probably could have, would have, forgiven her. But when he closed his eyes, he saw again that foreign look of ecstasy on her face, heard her cries of uncontrollable passion, saw again the man's shiny penis, and he knew that he would never be able to put behind him what had occurred. Each time he made love to her and heard her familiar quiet moans, he would think of the shrill cries the other man had elicited. And he would know that he was unable to satisfy her.

So he had told her to get out, had changed all the locks. She'd moved in with the guy, he'd heard from a friend of a friend, and the two of them were now living down near San Diego somewhere.

He pulled a beer from the refrigerator and popped open the tab, taking a long drink. He was not really hungry, but he looked through the refrigerator anyway, searching for something to eat, trying to take his mind off Sylvia.

It had to have been something more than sex that she'd been after. He knew that, had reassured himself of it a thousand times. She'd hinted about it more than once. She'd even tried to spell it out to him during their fights. But her dissatisfaction had been vague, not something he could focus on or dissect, and he still couldn't figure out exactly what had gone wrong or where.

Lately, he'd been bored and dissatisfied with himself, although he was not sure why. He'd become what he wanted, a university professor. His house was lined with bookcases, their shelves filled with books, most of which he had not yet read. And yet ... And yet he couldn't help feeling that he had made a wrong turn along the way, that somewhere after his marriage and before his divorce, personally, irrespective of any relationship, he had taken the wrong road and it was too late now to go back and correct his course.

But what did he want? Did he want to chuck it all and live in Tahiti? Not really. Did he want to live the simple life as a construction worker or truck driver? No. He had no aptitude whatsoever for physical labor. That had been one of Sylvia's complaints, that he hadn't even been able to do a decent job of maintaining the house.

He still enjoyed teaching, still liked the exchange of ideas in a classroom, but in the past year or so he'd become increasingly annoyed with the other half of his role: the petty office politics, the intellectual one-upmanship, the required publication of meaningless articles in unread journals. He'd begun to feel that he did not fit into this world, that he did not belong, that this life did not suit him. But he knew that he really did fit in, that this *was* his world—and that depressed him even more.

Perhaps that was why his focus had shifted, why he now preferred to read and discuss mysteries and horror novels rather than Jane Austin and John Milton. It felt more legitimate, more meaningful, more connected with real people and the real world.

He walked back into the living room and checked the answering machine. The light was on and blinking. He'd received two messages.

He rewound the tape, played the messages back. The first one cheered him up. It was from Phillip Emmons, one of his old creative writing students and the only one who had ever amounted to anything within the literary world. Phillip had always had talent, had in fact worked his way through grad school selling porno stories to what were euphemistically referred to as "men's magazines," but it had not been until after he graduated, until after he had escaped from the confining preciousness into which he had been straitjacketed by the well-meaning but myopic members of the English department, that he had really come into his own.

Now he was in town and wanted to get together. He'd left the name of the hotel and his room number.

The second message on the machine was from Eleanor, his current "girlfriend," if she could be called that, and her message made Ian's spirits immediately sink. They'd tentatively planned to have dinner together on Friday, and she was sorry, she said, but she had to take a rain check. Something had come up.

Ian stood there for a moment, unmoving. He suddenly didn't feel like being alone tonight. He took a deep breath, then lifted the receiver, and dialed the number of Buckley French, his only real friend within the department and one of the few unmarried friends he had.

Buckley answered the phone with his customary greeting. "Yeah?"

Ian felt better just hearing his voice. "It's me. Why don't you come over?"

Buckley groaned. "Don't do this to me. I've got a seven o'clock class tomorrow."

"Come on."

"Fighting with ghosts?"

"Yes," Ian admitted.

"I'll be there." He hung up abruptly, and Ian listened to the dial tone for a few seconds before setting the receiver back in its cradle. He had intended to spend this evening reading the dissertation Gifford had given to him, but he had glanced through it during his lunch and free period, and it had seemed pretty dry going, despite the subject matter and the rather spectacular way in which it had been delivered. Besides, this was one of those nights when he needed company. He could read the dissertation tomorrow.

Buckley arrived around ten minutes later, peeling into the driveway, the squeal of brakes on his old Thunderbird loud enough to hear over the TV. Ian stood up, turned off the television, but Buckley had already opened the door without knocking and was walking across the threshold, a huge bag of potato chips in one hand, two videotapes in the other. "I have arrived!" he announced, bumping the door shut with his rear end. "Bringing potato chips and porn!" He walked into the living room and dropped the bag of chips on the coffee table. He held up each of the tapes. "We got your *Hong Kong Honey.* We got your *Babes in Boyland.* Take your choice." He grinned hugely. "If this doesn't cheer you up, nothing will."

Buckley was a full professor and a respected Chaucer scholar, but outside the classroom he was an overgrown perpetual adolescent. Six-five, weighing well over two hundred and fifty pounds, he had a white doughboy face and favored faded jeans and T-shirts with obscene slogans. He also had a voice loud enough to cut through distant conversations, and one of the foulest mouths Ian had ever encountered. His non-academic tastes ran to smut and cheap horror flicks, a love which Ian shared. When Buckley had joined the staff five years ago, they had hit it off instantly.

Ian smiled, picking up one of the videotapes. The cover photo featured a gorgeous, well-endowed Latin woman suggestively licking the tip of a strawberry. "Where did you get these?"

"Stopped by the Wherehouse earlier today. I was going to check out *Women in Love* for my Twain to Moderns class. I haven't made any lesson plans for this week, and I thought I could fake my way through it with a film, but no such luck."

"*Women in Love,* huh?"

"Yeah, the little girls in my classes always wet their seats when they see Oliver Reed's wang bouncing around. Besides, I look a little bit like Oliver Reed, and I figured the subliminal effects of that visual metaphor would not have been lost on my brilliant fourth-year students."

"You're a sleaze." Ian laughed.

"Yeah, but a happy one."

"What do you say we hit the videotape stores and see if we can find a copy for you before they close?"

"What about *Hong Kong Honey*?"

"Some other time. I don't feel up to it right now."

" 'Up to it?' " Buckley grinned. "You been cuffing your carrot? Pulling your pork?"

Ian grinned feebly. "You caught me. Come on, let's go." He put an arm around Buckley's shoulder, leading him out.

"Where are we going?" Buckley looked at his watch. "Most of the videotape stores close at nine."

"That gives us a half hour. Besides, the record stores stay open until eleven."

"What a pal."

They walked outside. Ian locked the house and Buckley got into the T-Bird, starting and racing the engine. He reached over the seat and pulled open the lock on the passenger door. "Hop in, pardner!"

Ian got in, fastening his seat belt.

The car backed up, brakes squealing horribly, then they were off, speeding down the residential street toward Harbor. Buckley pushed in a tape. Led Zeppelin. *Houses of the Holy.*

"How come in movies they always show people our age listening to old soul and R and B hits?" he asked. "They think all of us Big Chillers, all of us middle-class white boys, sat around listening to fuckin' Motown?"

Ian grinned. "Hell, no. We were rockers."

"Still are." Buckley hit the power booster and Jimmy Page's guitar soared to ear-splitting volume. "Metal!"

"Those were probably the only songs they could get the rights to," Ian shouted.

"What?"

"That Motown crap!"

"What?"

"Never mind!" Ian shook his head, signaling that it wasn't important. Buckley obviously couldn't hear him, and he couldn't hope to compete with the volume of the stereo.

The song ended a few minutes later, and Buckley turned down the sound. He looked over at Ian. "Did you know the boy?" he asked.

"What boy?" Ian stared at him blankly.

"The suicide."

"Suicide? I didn't hear anything about it."

"Didn't hear . . . ? Shit, you got your head up your ass or what? Geography student. Took a swan dive from the Social Sciences building. Didn't you see the cops and the ambulance and everything?"

Ian shook his head. "I was in Neilson Hall all day."

"It's been all over the news. I don't know how you could've missed it."

"Come to think of it, a lot of people in my classes were talking about death."

"Jesus, you're out of it. A bomb could fall on the fucking school and you wouldn't have a clue."

"What do you expect from an absentminded professor?"

They drove down Brea Boulevard, and Buckley sped through a yellow light, barely making it. "So where should we try?"

"Blockbuster Music?"

"Blockbuster Music it is."

They turned right on First Street, then turned left on White Oak, driving past the campus on their way to the record store. There was no buffer zone here as there were around campuses back East, no sedate, classy neighborhoods of red brick colonial houses surrounding the school, no wrought iron gates blocking the road at the entrance. The school simply appeared on the side of the busy street, rising behind a small shopping center.

Ian stared out the window as they drove past. The parking lot was full, a sea of glass and metal reflecting the light from strategically placed streetlamps. There was no sign of any people, not even an after-class couple talking over the hood of a car, and despite the full lot the university seemed empty, abandoned. Juxtaposed against the warm, flat suburban homes surrounding the campus, the tall buildings of the university seemed impossibly cold and distant, vaguely menacing.

Ian looked away, staring instead at the street before them.

"I sure hope I can find this," Buckley said. "If not, I'm up shit creek."

"Yeah."

Buckley looked over at him, frowning. "You okay?"

Ian forced himself to smile. "I'm fine."

"All right, then. Let's find Oliver Reed's cock."

FOUR

MAINTENANCE PURCHASE ORDER #3499–02

PART NO.	ITEM DESCRIPTION	QTY.	UNIT PRICE	REASON
1076–VS	Window Glass	16	45.25	Smashed windows on east-facing third floor of Physical Sciences, Biological Sciences, Social Sciences, and Administration buildings

FIVE

1

If this wasn't her last semester and she hadn't needed the class to graduate, Cheryl Gonzalez would not have added Dr. Merrick's marketing course. She'd heard that he was hard-core, that he was humorless and completely inflexible, that his lectures were numbingly dry, his tests ultra-long and filled with unimportant minutiae, but she had not realized to what extent his sadistic bent manifested itself until she'd attempted to petition his class. Instead of adding the petitioners after he'd taken roll and signed off the drops, he'd made all of the petitioners wait until the end of the session before deciding whom to add. There were only four open spaces and six students were petitioning, but he hadn't had the decency to approve four and let the other two go. He'd made all six sit through his lecture.

That first night he'd talked until nine-fifteen. The class was scheduled to end at nine.

Nine-fifteen.

The first night.

She'd known then that it was going to be a long semester.

Tonight he'd droned on until after nine-thirty. Some of the braver souls had departed before the end of the lecture, leaving shortly after nine, but Cheryl could tell from Merrick's eyes as he watched them exit that he was keeping track, keeping score, and that revenge would be exacted through grades.

So she stayed in place with the rest of the cowards, waiting until he officially dismissed them, even though she desperately had to go to the bathroom.

As soon as Merrick announced the reading assignment for the coming week and said they could go, she was out the door and down the hall, rushing into the women's rest room.

She studied her face in the mirror as she washed her hands afterward. It was a weird sensation, but she felt old this semester. Not old as in grown up—she'd felt grown up since her first year in high school—but old as in over the hill. She was still a student, but she was also rapidly approaching thirty. When her mother had been her age, she'd already been married for six years and had had a five-year-old kid.

Cheryl dried her hands on a paper towel. Two freshmen had laughed at her this morning as she'd walked up to the *Sentinel* office. That was nothing new. She'd often been snickered at because of the way she looked. But this time the laughs had not been directed at a threatening fashion statement the jeerers could not understand. No, this time she'd been laughed at by someone more hip, ridiculed as a practitioner of a dying subculture, and that really made her feel old. She'd suddenly realized that the "alternative" movement which had blossomed and flourished during her high school years was as passé to the younger generation coming up as long hair and hippies had been to her and her peers.

It was a bizarre sensation, this realization that somewhere along the line she had passed from trendy to out of date, and it was not something with which she felt comfortable.

At the same time she was committed, she could not back down. It had always been all or nothing with her, and she could not change the way she looked now. It would be like ... like admitting that she'd been wrong. Like admitting that none of it had meant anything.

She threw the paper towel into the metal wastebasket and gave herself one last look in the mirror before picking up her books, notebook, and purse.

When she emerged into the hallway, it was deserted. Dr. Merrick and her classmates were gone, and the floor was silent. She started walking toward the elevator, and the sound of her boots echoed through the empty corridor. She glanced to her left as she passed a classroom and saw through the open doorway a glass case filled with human bones and skulls and archeological artifacts.

She quickened her step.

She had never liked this building. Particularly at night. It gave her the creeps. There was something about the closed crampedness of the classrooms, the archaic dustiness of the visible display cases that made her feel uncomfortable and ill at ease. It was all psychological, she knew, but somehow the thought of all those ancient fragments of dead people and lost civilizations sitting in empty rooms in an empty building at night, while she had to walk past them, caused goose bumps to pop up on her skin, caused her heart to beat faster.

She might be getting old, but she'd never grown out of her childhood fears.

She reached the elevator and instinctively raised her arm to push the Down button, but she saw that the control panel had been covered with a taped-on sign that read OUT OF ORDER.

"Shit," she said.

She'd have to take the stairs.

She walked over to the stairwell door, pushed it open, and started down. The cement steps were slippery and her boots didn't exactly have the greatest traction in the world, so she shifted both her books and notebook to her right hand, and grabbed the metal railing with her left, descending carefully. The stairs wound down to an intermediate landing, then on to the next floor below.

She walked from the sixth floor to the fifth, from the fifth floor to the fourth. She was staring down at the steps beneath her feet to make sure she didn't trip when, out of her peripheral vision, something caught her eye.

A person.

A man.

Cheryl glanced up.

On the landing below her stood a· janitor. He was looking up at her and grinning, and there was something in that grin that made her pause. She held tightly to the railing and slowed her steps. The janitor was holding a push broom as though he was going to sweep the landing, but she realized that he hadn't moved a muscle since she'd seen him. He just stood there.

Unblinking.

Grinning.

She wanted to go back up to the previous floor, knew she should, but that same stubborn impulse that would

not let her turn her back on the alternative cultural
movement to which she had committed her youth now
forced her to walk forward, down the steps.

Toward the janitor.

Who still had not moved.

Don't be an asshole, she told herself. Get the hell out
of here. Go back up to the fourth floor and take the
elevator. Or take the stairs on the other side of the
building.

But she kept walking down.

She stepped onto the landing.

And the janitor moved.

She screamed. She couldn't help it. All he did was
push his broom forward a foot or so, and she jumped a
mile, nearly falling backward onto the cement steps.

Then he was laughing and moving toward her, still
pushing the broom, and his laugh was low and manic
and not like anything she'd ever heard in real life. She
tried to turn around, tried to start back up the stairs,
but the broom was already sweeping hard against her
feet and she was pushed down, books and notebook flying as she stumbled against the bottom step. She put her
hands out to catch her fall, trying to twist around at the
same time, but the broom was pushing against her back
and she could feel its hard bristles stabbing her skin
through the thin material of her top.

"Help!" She screamed as loud as she could. "Help!"
Her voice echoed in the empty stairwell, already coming
back to her, mingling with the low, constant laughing of
the janitor. She scrambled for a foothold, a handhold,
trying to crawl up and away from the stabbing bristles,
but the broom was shoved into her back. Again. And
again. And again.

She was crying. Sobbing. She was not the crying type
and could not even remember the last time she'd shed
tears, but she was positively blubbering now, the combi-
nation of fear, rage, humiliation, and frustration conspir-
ing to undermine her usual emotional equilibrium.

She screamed again for help, but there were no words
this time, only an inarticulate cry of anguish, and somehow through her sobs and the reverberation of the echoes she realized that the laughing had stopped.

The pressure of the broom disappeared.

She stood, fumblingly grabbed onto the rail, tried to start up the steps, but a strong, sinewy hand closed around her wrist.

"Gonna fuck you," the janitor whispered, and, like the laugh, there was no end to it. He kept repeating the phrase over and over again, like a mantra, until the stairwell was filled with the echoes of his whispering. "Gonna fuck you gonnafuckyou gonnafuckyougonnafuckyougonnafuckyou . . ."

She cried, screamed, struggled, trying to get away, but the hand was strong and would not let go. His penis was out and it was hard, emerging from between the folds of his open zipper, and she tried to kick it, acting instinctively, but he punched her sharply in the left breast and she doubled over, sucking air in a single prolonged gasp, the sudden pain unbearable.

Still holding her wrist with one hand, he unbuttoned and jerked down her pants with the other.

He turned her around, bent her over.

She wanted to scream, but the pain in her breast was excruciating and it hurt to even breathe.

And he shoved it in.

2

The quad was crowded with booths and tables, as it always was during the first two weeks of classes. A blond, clean-cut, humorless-looking young man was standing stiffly behind the Campus Republicans' table, which was decorated with red, white, and blue crepe paper and piled high with several perfect stacks of professionally produced pamphlets. Black fraternity members, wooden crescent moons dangling from loops of string around their necks, clustered about a green booth, laughing loudly at some private joke. The bearded student manning the Young Democrats' booth was chatting happily with a top-heavy girl in a halter top.

Ian always liked these first few weeks of the semester the best. Although university officials liked to refer to the faculty, staff, and students as the "campus community," this was really the only time when the school actually felt like a community to him. The recruiting booths for school organizations, the overly busy and slightly chaotic crowds, the general hubbub to be found in the quad at the semester's outset, all gave him the sense that they were in this together and that he was a part of it all.

It was a good feeling.

He was already late for his first class, but he stopped for a moment in front of the Bulletin Board. A covered four-sided column in the center of the quad, it was empty save for a single yellow flyer, last semester's notices for rallies, seminars, money-making opportunities, and travel deals having all been taken down, leaving only white corkboard punctured with staples and tacks and pinprick holes.

The lone flyer was for this semester's Associated Students Film Festival, and Ian grinned as he saw the familiar ASFF logo. He should've known. Brad Walker was the most efficient committee chairman on campus. He might be a little dull, a little predictable, but he was a great organizer.

He'd make an excellent PR man when he graduated.

Ian scanned the list of films planned for this semester.

The Devils. A classic.

Henry: Portrait of a Serial Killer. Good movie.

Salo.

Snuff.

He frowned.

Cherry Popping Poppa.

Little Girl, Big Donkey.

Was this a joke?

These sure as hell weren't the types of movies that Walker and his people would pick. Walker's taste ran more toward *Ghandi, The Color Purple, Malcolm X.* Serious, mainstream, socially relevant movies. Even before his tenure, the trend over the past half decade had been away from so-called cult films toward "nice" movies. Date movies. Movies that had been popular a few years back but that still worked better on a big screen than on video.

Little Girl, Big Donkey?

Something was wrong here.

Around him, the noise of the campus continued unabated, the conversations of the newly enschooled students still fresh and excited and enthusiastic, but for him the tenor of the day had been changed, the tone irrevocably altered, and even the liveliness of the quad now seemed tainted.

On the board, in pencil, next to the flyer, he saw a bizarre piece of graffiti: "Katherine Hepburn Whipped His Ass!" Something about the complete incongruity of that statement unnerved him even more, and he moved away from the Bulletin Board and hurried through the crowds toward Neilson Hall.

Ordinarily, Creative Writing was his best class. There were always a few phonies in the bunch—pseudo-intellectuals with intricately conceptualized ideas that they never would get around to writing; people who wanted to write, planned to write, thought about writing, talked about writing but never actually wrote—but for the most part the class was filled with interesting, self-motivated individuals who had legitimately artistic impulses.

This semester, however, the class looked like it was going to be a dud.

Things could always improve—that was one of the nice things about Creative Writing, its unpredictability—but he had asked each member of the class to submit a writing sample, not for public consumption but simply for his own edification, so he could get a quick handle on who was interested in what, as well as determine the various writing levels of the students, and the samples were, with one curious exception, either very bad or very boring. Among the "serious" students, Updike seemed to be the model this year. There were a lot of sensitive studies of relationships set in bland New York apartments or colorless middle-class suburbs along the Eastern seaboard.

The lone exception was a boy named Brant Keeler, who hadn't come to class today and whose face he couldn't recall.

And who had submitted a single page of pure porn.

Keeler's writing was clear, polished, and effective. A description of a teenage boy's lust for his prepubescent sister, it was genuinely erotic. But the tone of the piece, and the easy familiarity Keeler seemed to have with his subject matter, was more than a little disturbing.

Little Girl, Big Donkey.

He'd hoped the student would show up for class today, but when he finished passing back the writing samples, he had two left over and one of them was Keeler's.

It was going to be a long hour.

He leaned against the edge of the desk and faced the class. "All right," he said. "Today we're going to talk about structure ..."

After class, Ian walked down the long hallway to the stairwell, following a group of students wearing identically rolled-up T-shirts that exposed the tattoos on their arms. The tattoos were all variations on a theme—the names of currently hip underground bands.

What kind of person would use their own body, their own skin, as an advertisement for obscure local musicians?

The seriousness with which these students took their music depressed him. He recalled the days of progressive rock and punk rock and new wave and heavy metal, and he remembered the students who had made of the music not just a listening preference but a lifestyle. Where were those students now? *What* were they? Had the leather and the mohawks been replaced by business suits and receding hairlines?

The problem was that his memory had no depth perception. Everything seemed recent. The safety pins of punk seemed as current to him as the flannel of grunge.

He thought of T. S. Eliot. *Hurry up now, it's time.* He supposed that was what made him feel so depressed, the fact that time was speeding by, running out, that there was now more time behind him than before him. It seemed like only a few years ago that he had been in grad school himself.

He looked away from the students, concentrated on the floor in front of him. One thing he'd discovered over the years was that he'd become increasingly less tolerant of fads in fashion. In the heady hippie days of the late sixties, he had defended long hair and blue jeans, beads and buttons, against the criticism of his more reactionary professors. Students in those days were making a statement with their hairstyles and modes of dress, he'd argued, there was meaning behind their fashion movements. But when the punks had come along in the late seventies, he'd found that his allegiance had subtly shifted to the establishment. The kids then had seemed dumber than those of his generation, their styles and poses pointless and artificial.

Now he could no longer hope to keep up with the

subtle intricacies of hipness, and the whole thing seemed silly and nearly incomprehensible to him.

He was old.

He reached the stairwell entrance, pushed open the door, and began trudging up the stairs to the English department office on the fifth floor, the briefcase heavy in his hand. He was like a slow-moving log in the river of students rushing up and down the stairs, and the young men and woman wound around him, swirling past, talking loudly and excitedly about relationships, weekend plans, and other subjects entirely unrelated to school. The stairwell was hot with the warmth of so many bodies, smelling sickly of perfume and sweat, aftershave, and breath, and the echoing sound was deafening. He caught only the briefest snatches of conversation as students passed him, and then individual words were enveloped in the collective roar and the stomp of feet.

Then he was on the fifth floor and through the door and in the quiet sanctuary of the English department. Here there was only the hushed tones of individual conversations, low words from offices in which students and instructors discussed literature and course requirements. Unlike communications, the most popular and active department in the school of humanities, the English department seldom had office visitors, and the ratio of instructors to students here on any given day was usually three to one. It had not been that way in the sixties and early seventies, when the study of literature and the arts had been de rigueur for anyone daring to call him- or herself a college student. But those days were long gone, and he was now part of a dying department, destined to go down with the ship.

What the hell was wrong with him today?

Little Girl, Big Donkey.

That was part of it. That damn flyer. It had screwed up his mood, affected his outlook.

Disturbed him.

It had disturbed him, though he didn't want to admit it. Hell, here he was, a horror fan, a porno fan, a tireless supporter of First Amendment rights, and a little announcement for a film festival had sent him into an emotional tailspin. He knew the word Buckley would use: "Pussy." Maybe that was right. Maybe he was a pussy.

But there was still something about that movie lineup that bothered him.

He glanced at the wall clock as he walked into his office and dropped the briefcase on his desk: 11:10. The department meeting wasn't supposed to start for another twenty minutes. That gave him plenty of time to go down to the Hunger Hut and grab a burger or something, but, though he was hungry, he wasn't in the mood to fight the crowds, and instead he slumped into his swivel chair and took a swig of the flat, warm Coke from the half-filled can on his desk. He picked up the textbook for his horror class.

Gifford.

Was the loon who'd accosted him in the classroom really the same guy who'd edited this book? It seemed so. He flipped through the pages. It was a hell of an anthology. The guy really knew his stuff. He'd picked only the best and most representative works from each period and from each of the major authors and had produced a collection that was at once shorter and more comprehensive than nearly all of the other horror anthologies currently in print.

We have to kill the university. Before it kills us.

Ian put down the book and opened his briefcase, searching for the "dissertation" Gifford had given him, but it wasn't there. He'd left it at home. He'd tried to read it a few nights ago, had gotten about ten pages into the work, but it was a rambling mess, bordering on incoherent, and seemed to have no point. It was not structured like a true dissertation, it had no thesis, but it was written in an intricately convoluted, pseudo-scholarly style and was pretty dry going. He'd had a tough time getting into it.

He was in the mood to read it now, though—

Little Girl, Big Donkey

—and he was curious to see what Gifford had to say.

Ian closed the briefcase and leaned back in his chair, staring at the wall of bookshelves before him. He sighed, took a deep breath. Maybe he'd been reading too much horror lately. He was actually sitting here in his office, planning to read some purported "dissertation" concerning an evil university written by a man who claimed that the school was trying to kill him. And all because he'd seen a flyer for a student film festival of cult movies.

Maybe he needed to get a life.

No. There was no "maybe" about it. He definitely needed to get a life.

He hadn't called Eleanor since she'd left the message on his answering machine. She'd tried to call him, leaving messages with the department secretaries, but he hadn't returned her calls, instead attempting to punish her with his silence.

How pathetic could you get?

He looked at his phone, thought of calling Eleanor now, but he figured she was probably at work and he wouldn't be able to reach her anyway.

"Hey, bud."

Ian swiveled around. Buckley was standing in the doorway, munching Doritos. He held the bag out. "Want some?"

Ian shook his head.

"Busy?"

Ian shrugged. "Not really."

"What say we have a short strategy session?"

"Strategy? For what?"

"The meeting." Buckley walked into the office, shut the door, sat down in the extra chair. "Kiefer just got back from the faculty council. He wouldn't look at me, pretended he didn't even see me when he passed. You know what that means."

"He bent and spread 'em."

"While he handed them the dildo."

"So what's your strategy?"

Buckley popped another Dorito in his mouth. "Confront him, make him squirm. The guy's a pussy and a half. We'll put a little pressure on the old boy, force him to go to bat for us next time, whether he wants to or not."

"Bullying tactics."

"Works every time."

Ian nodded. "I'm in." He reached over, into the bag. "Give me some of those. I'm starving."

The department meeting was held, as always, in the conference room, and Buckley and Ian walked down the hall together, gathering recruits from the other offices: Joachim Perez, Lawrence Roget, Midge Connors, Elizabeth Somersby, Todd Crouse, Francine Ashenton. They walked into the conference room en masse, and although Kiefer and a few of the old guard were already there, seated around the oversized table, they ignored the entrance.

Ian sat down across from Kiefer. Buckley took up a seat farther down the line. The others filled in the seats in between.

"How goes it?" Buckley asked. He held up a hand. "Don't answer. That's a rhetorical question. I don't want a quote from antiquity from one of you overread, under-socialized misfits."

"Overread?" Todd Crouse said.

The others laughed.

Kiefer, the department chair, said nothing, merely looked at the blank wall of the conference room, fiddling absently with his tie.

Chair, Ian thought, watching him. What a stupid word. An attempt to find a neutered noun for the head of the department was fine—although he personally saw nothing wrong with "chairman" and "chairwoman"—but at least a new word, a word with no previous connotations should have been chosen. As English instructors, they ought to respect the sanctity of words, be more aware of and alert to nuances of meaning than other people.

Chair.

A "chair" was an inanimate object, something upon which people sat, not the head of a department.

Although if any member of the department could be compared to an inanimate object, it would have to be Kiefer.

Ian looked over at Buckley, caught his eye. Buckley nodded.

Kiefer nervously cleared his throat. "Well, we're all here. It's not exactly eleven-thirty yet, but I guess we might as well start. As you all know, budget cuts have hit us hard the past few years. We've had a moratorium on hiring, we've lost a few instructors to attrition, and with our declining enrollment we've had to sacrifice some of our part-time lecturers. I don't want to sound like the voice of doom here, but once again state funding has been cut for this fiscal year. We went over a tentative financial outline in the faculty council meeting today, and while there were no decisions made, it looks like our department budget is going to be even more limited than it was last year."

"And you didn't say a word about it because you couldn't justify alloting more money to our department, right, Kiefer?" Buckley shook his head disgustedly.

"Of course I protested their proposals. Vigorously. As department chair, it's my duty to look after the interests of the English department."

"But ..." Buckley prompted.

"But frankly, no, I can't really justify alloting more money to English when there are other departments facing the crunch as well, departments with increasing enrollment that need more instructors, more equipment. The faculty council has to look at the whole picture, at the entire school, and decide what's in the best interest of the university community."

"Come on," Ian said. "That's a crock and you know it. The budget for the athletic department is way out of proportion to its enrollment."

"The university's sports teams—"

"—are nothing. No one's ever heard of them. No one ever will hear of them. Brea? Football? Basketball? Wake up. What little notoriety we have comes from academics. That's where our strength is. We should be building on it."

"Yeah," Midge Connors said. "Why are we always relegated to second-class status?"

"Because the alumni like sports."

Buckley shook his head. "Jesus, Kiefer, pull your head out of your ass and smell the coffee."

"Well, what would you suggest?"

Buckley grinned at Ian, and Ian smiled back. "We thought you'd never ask."

3

Faith hated her Twentieth Century American Lit class.

It had taken her over a week to discover it, but it was true. It wasn't the fault of the instructor, Dr. Roget, who seemed pretty cool. It wasn't the curriculum, which consisted of books she'd planned to read one day but just hadn't gotten around to yet.

It was the students.

Never in her life had she met a more insufferable group of pretentious assholes. She thought Keith was bad? He was positively down to earth compared to some of the people in here.

What made it even worse was that most of these jerks were bright. Really bright. Intimidatingly bright. For the first time in her life she honestly felt out of her league. Some of these students had read detailed interpretations into the short stories they'd had to analyze that she could not have come up with if her life had depended on it. And they'd been able to substantiate their ideas under heavy questioning from the instructor.

Maybe that was why she hated this class so much. It made her feel stupid.

No, that wasn't it.

It was part of it.

But not all of it.

Luckily, her other classes were better. Creative Writing was a no-brainer. She was breezing through Physical Anthropology and World History. Algebra and Principles of Botany were no problem.

But American Lit ...

Although most of the class had settled into a regular seating arrangement, there were more desks than students, and she'd moved each session, trying to find someone she could talk to. Today she'd gotten herself stuck next to the most obnoxious and pretentious guy in the entire class, an effeminate man a few years her senior who wore his thinning hair in a short ponytail and who spoke as if all of his words were pronouncements from on high. He'd spent the time before class officially began pontificating, holding court, giving his assessment of a foreign film he'd seen the night before to two other students who seemed equally smitten with themselves.

"All right," Dr. Roget said. "Let's get into it. *Deliverance.* How many of you read it like you were supposed to?"

All hands went up.

"Good, good. I know some of you are lying, but at least you're smart enough to lie. In my book, that shows initiative." He scanned the room. "So what did you think of the novel?"

"Better than the movie," someone said.

The students laughed, but Faith looked around to see who'd made the comment. She'd seen the movie as a kid, cut-up on regular TV, and she'd seen it again a few years back, on cable. She hadn't liked it much. The macho bonding routine hadn't appealed to her, and she'd found the violence offensive. But, to her surprise, she'd enjoyed the novel. The same elements were present, but the people were real, their feelings and actions understandable. She'd found the work effective.

Mr. Pretentious spoke up. "I found the overly detailed nature descriptions somewhat overdone. They don't seem to have any real symbolic or metaphoric meaning, and I think they make the novel overlong. It would have been much more effective as a novella."

Jesus.

"I liked the descriptions. I thought they were perfect."

The voice came from the rear of the class. Faith turned in her chair to look at the speaker. Tall, thin, with tangled, longish hair and an open, intelligent face, he was sitting straight in his chair. He looked vaguely familiar, though she could not recall noticing him before.

"Go on," the instructor said.

"That's what it's like when you're camping. You notice those little details. They become important. You become familiar with the knothole patterns on trees, with individual clumps of grass, with the shapes of lichen on the rocks. That's your world, for the amount of time that you're camping in that spot, and you get to know it. I thought Dickey captured that feeling perfectly."

Mr. Pretentious turned slowly in his chair. "Don't you feel that he could have done the same thing in half the time? We, as readers, do not need to read detail for detail's sake."

"I thought it worked."

"But what's the point?"

Faith took a deep breath, gathered her courage, spoke: "I think what Dickey was trying to do was provide verisimilitude, to make this world he'd created real. Not everything in a novel is a symbol or a metaphor. Not everything should be."

"Exactly," the student in the back said. "*That's* the point."

Faith looked back at him. He nodded at her, smiled.

*   *   *

His name was Jim Parker and he was editor of the school paper.

She talked to him for a few minutes after class on the way to the elevator. He seemed nice—intelligent but not phony—and she liked him immediately. He disliked Mr. Pretentious and some of the other students in class as much as she did, and as classrooms emptied out around them and refilled with new students, she found that she did not want to stop talking to him. The Up elevator arrived, the metal door opening. Her Principles of Botany course was next, but she pretended as though she had no other classes and asked Jim if he wanted to get a cup of coffee and continue the conversation.

He said he had to get over to the newspaper office, that he was the editor and had a lot of work to do to put out tomorrow's issue. "I'll take a rain check," he said.

She couldn't tell if that was a real excuse or just a polite way to say that, no, he wasn't interested, so she smiled, said good-bye as he stepped onto the elevator, and waited for the next elevator going down.

Whether she'd been rebuffed or not, she felt jazzed as she walked across the quad toward the Biological Sciences building.

She liked this guy.

She hurried across campus, walking quickly, almost jogging, but she was late nevertheless, all of the other students in class seated, the instructor already lecturing.

Although the class itself was not particularly large, it was conducted in a huge lecture hall, one of the three theaters built specifically to provide scientific demonstrations to groups of up to two hundred students. Until now the stage had not been fully utilized by the professor. He had used the overhead projector once, but that had been it; the rest of the time he had stood at the podium unmoving and talked. Today, however, the front of the lecture hall was crowded with wire cages of various sizes, spread out on the stage on both sides of the podium. Within the cages were animals ranging from rats and gerbils at one end to dogs and cats at the other. Beakers filled with dried plants were set on a long table in front of the left-most cages.

Faith found a seat near the door and sat down as unobtrusively as possible, taking out her pen and notebook.

"... and I will be demonstrating the effects of these toxic plants on various animals," the professor was saying.

One of the dogs barked loudly.

The professor pulled on a white surgical mask he took from his coat pocket. His voice when he spoke was muffled, but he spoke at a volume loud enough for the words to carry. "We will begin with a little monocotyledoneae, of the order Scitamineae." He removed a dried flower and stem from one of the beakers. "This herbacious subtropical specimen grows naturally in certain areas of the Amazon basin, although it can also be successfully cultivated in North America. When ingested by the rat, as we see here"—he pushed the stem between the wire of the first cage and the rat began nibbling on it—"the plant has a toxic effect not unlike that of the poison xantic chlorethelene."

The rat suddenly began flinging itself at the side of the cage in a violently spastic manner, apparently heedless of the effect of the wire on its body. With each assault the wire pressed into its fur, into its flesh, and it continued to throw itself at the unyielding side of the cage, deeper cuts appearing on its face until its tiny head was crisscrossed with dripping red.

Breathing heavily after one last powerful lunge, it expired.

"Even more interesting is the effect this campanulatae from southern Georgia has on the gerbil." The professor took a twig from one of the beakers and pushed it into the gerbil's cage. The animal immediately moved away from the dried plant, as though sensing its toxicity, but the professor maneuvered the twig around, forcing it into the gerbil's mouth.

The animal immediately began vomiting blood.

Faith looked away, sickened and outraged. This wasn't legal, was it? A teacher couldn't just kill animals to demonstrate something to a class, could he?

The professor sounded almost amused. "Our friend Mr. Pussycat is not exactly enamored of this specimen of the order sapindales, as we shall now discover."

The cat screamed, and Faith looked up for a brief second to see the animal gnawing crazily at its own stomach.

She again glanced away. Around her, the other students were dutifully taking notes, acting as if nothing was wrong, as if nothing out of the ordinary was occurring. She heard the professor say something, heard the cat cry out in agony—a short, sharp, searing burst of sound—and then there was silence. The girl to her left did not even flinch.

It might be legal to kill these animals, but it wasn't right. This could not be considered, by any stretch of the imagination, legitimate scientific research. This was merely a needless demonstration of gruesome trivia that could have been explained just as well through a lecture or a textbook. This was cruelty for cruelty's sake.

She felt sick, and she forced herself to take a deep breath. Someone had to put a stop to this. Someone—Jim.

Yes, Jim. She could tell him about this. Maybe he'd print an exposé in the paper. If the general student population found out that animals were being tortured and killed en masse merely to show how their bodies were affected by toxic plants, there'd be protest. Maybe the science department, maybe the entire administration, would be embarrassed into changing the policy on this.

"Note how the feline's stomach ruptured," the professor explained. "This is why it was attempting to bite open its own abdomen. The blood you see here ..."

Jim.

Faith stood, took her books and notebook, and walked out of the class.

SIX

1

It was a typical smoggy Southern California day. The hills to the north were hidden behind a wall of white, and even the gym at the far end of campus was lightly obscured by haze. He had a headache from breathing the air.

Staring up at the pale sky, Jim thought of Williams, of the massive cotton white clouds that spread endlessly across the expansive blue all the way to New Mexico.

He wished he was there now.

A group of female students walked by, dressed almost identically in the short, form-fitting fashions of summer.

Although there *were* a few advantages to being here in California.

His stomach rumbled loudly, and he looked over the shoulder of the guy in front of him to see if the girl at the front of the line had gotten her food yet.

Of course not.

In the four years he'd been going to Brea, through countless shifts in personnel, service at the Hunger Hut had never changed, had never improved. It still took ten minutes just to get a simple cup of Coke.

He looked behind him, at the growing line for the snack bar. Blank faces stared back at him, and he realized for the first time that no one in line was talking, that he heard no conversations. The students waiting to buy lunch were completely silent.

The unease he'd been feeling on and off since returning to California reasserted itself. This wasn't normal, this wasn't right. College students did not wait in line silently. He looked from one face to another, seeing nothing there but hard, unthinking passivity, and he felt suddenly chilled. He forced himself to face forward.

Nothing had happened, nothing concrete, but he sensed an undercurrent of violence in the blank faces and body language of the people around him. It was the same feeling he'd experienced when he'd gone to a concert at the Forum right before the L.A. riots. Nothing had happened then either, but there'd been a tension in the air, a sense that something *could* happen, probably would happen, and that feeling had lingered, affecting his enjoyment of the concert. He had not felt safe until he'd driven back to Orange County and was safely ensconced in his apartment in his suburban middle-class neighborhood.

This was like that, on a smaller scale.

He was suddenly uncomfortable with all of those silent students at his back, and he considered giving up his place in line, grabbing a frozen burrito from one of the vending machines, and going back to the newsroom. But he'd put in too much time here, and he was only one person away from the order window. Besides, it was broad daylight. On the grassy knoll to the left of the Hunger Hut, two students were loudly attempting to teach a black labrador to catch a Frisbee in midair. On the walkways, crowds of students walked to and from classes and cars.

What could possibly happen here?

He didn't know, but he was still not able to relax until, ten minutes later, he had gotten his plate of nachos and his Dr Pepper and had left the snack bar behind him.

He walked slowly back toward Neilson Hall, trying to finish all of his nachos before he returned to the newsroom so he wouldn't have to share. In front of the library, he stopped for a moment and looked inside, through the sliding glass doors. Faith Pullen, the girl from his American Lit class, was inside there somewhere.

Again he felt chilled.

She'd come by the newsroom earlier, furious at what she'd described as the "animal cruelty" that was being conducted in her botany class. She'd said that rats and gerbils, dogs and cats, were being exposed to poisonous plants and killed for no reason at all. She'd said that the instructor had merely wanted to show his students that the plants were toxic to animals.

Animal torture in a General Ed science class?

He'd believed it instantly. That was the frightening thing.

She'd sat down with him, given him the instructor's name, described exactly what had happened. "I don't think it's legal," she'd said. "And even if it is legal, it's ethically wrong. I think people need to be informed about it."

"I do too," Jim had agreed. "I'll get someone right on it."

For the first time since she'd entered the newsroom, she'd smiled. "Thanks."

He'd asked her if she'd wanted to grab a bite to eat, since it was nearly lunchtime, but she'd told him that she worked at the library and she was late already. He wasn't sure if that was a real excuse or one she'd fabricated because she wasn't interested, but he'd let her go without suggesting that they get together some other time.

He'd see her in class Wednesday anyway.

He stared through the glass doors into the library, and he found that he was disappointed that he couldn't see her inside.

Finishing off his nachos, he drank his Dr Pepper as he walked back to Neilson Hall. In the newsroom, Stuart, Ford, and Eddie had apparently decided to try to use their press passes to get into a Rams' game.

"We should probably go there around four or so to beat the crowd and make it look like we're official," Ford said.

Stuart looked at the clock. "Maybe I'd better call my mom."

Eddie grinned. "Hey, how much is it to talk to her now? Two-fifty a minute?"

"Yeah, what's her number? 976-BLOW ME?"

"Very funny."

"You can't go until your pages are all done," Jim said, walking by. "That means pasted up and put to bed."

Eddie jumped to his feet, gave a robotic Nazi salute. *"Jawohl, mein commandant!"*

Jim shook his head, grinning. "Dick." He glanced over at Cheryl Gonzalez as he headed toward his desk. The entertainment editor was slumped in her chair, staring dully out the window at the campus below. She'd been unusually quiet the past few days, and while it was pretty obvious that something was wrong, he didn't really know her well enough to feel comfortable prying into her personal life. She was the newest member of the staff, on board because Howie had declined the job and had recommended her in his stead.

She'd probably just broken up with her boyfriend or something, but it couldn't hurt to have Howie ask and see what was the matter.

"Cheryl!" Jim said.

She looked up, frowning.

"Your page all set?"

She forced a smile. "I'm set for the next week. I have a backlog of reviews."

"Good." Jim didn't know what else to say, so he turned to Faruk Jamal, the news editor. "Who has the Greek beat?"

Faruk looked at the typed list taped to the top of his desk. "Ron Gregory."

"When he checks in, tell him to cover the Theta Mu rush. I think tonight's the last night. Last year I had one of their officers in my American Studies class, and he pissed and moaned the entire semester about how the paper favored the other fraternities and gave them short shrift."

"Gotcha."

There was a clicking and humming from the hallway outside, and Howie rolled into the newsroom. He was smiling, but the smile seemed out of place, inappropriate on his overthin, pain-ravaged face, and although Jim waved a greeting, forced himself to smile, he found himself noticing again how much his friend had deteriorated.

"How's it hanging?" Howie asked, rolling up to Jim's desk.

"Heavy and low. I'm a mighty meaty stallion of a man."

Eddie snickered. "That's not what Cheryl told us."

The entertainment editor did not even rise to the bait.

Jim leaned forward, close to Howie, whispering. "What's with Cheryl? She seems kind of out of it the past few days."

"I've picked up on that myself."

"Any idea what's wrong?"

"No."

"You think you can find out? You know her better than I do."

Howie nodded—or tried to nod, his head moving too far down, not far enough up. "Let me talk to her." His fingers, which had never left the wheelchair control, pushed the small joystick to the left, and the chair rolled across the room toward Cheryl's desk.

Jim tossed his empty cup into the wastepaper basket on the side of Stuart's desk, and sorted through the small pile of articles in front of him. Submissions were down this semester. More people had enrolled in the two journalism classes from which the paper drew its talent pool, but they were either less ambitious or less talented than their predecessors of the past few years and were not writing enough articles.

He'd speak to Norton when the adviser came in after his one o'clock class.

He found the notes he'd taken on Faith's botany story. He read over what he'd written, considered assigning the article to someone, then decided that he'd tackle this one himself. He folded the paper, put it in his pocket.

Howie returned a few minutes later. Cheryl was no longer staring out the window, was now proofing an article of some sort, scribbling over typed text with a red pen, but the expression on her face had not changed. Jim looked quizzically at Howie as he rolled forward across the floor, but his friend's eyes told him to say nothing, to not ask any questions until Cheryl was well out of hearing distance.

Jim nodded slightly, to show he understood.

Howie tried to smile. "Jan Anderson's giving a concert tonight at the Club. I'm going to be reviewing it."

"I've heard the name, but I don't think I've heard the music. What's she play?"

"Folk-country-pop. Like Shawn Colvin or Lucinda Williams or Mary-Chapin Carpenter. She's good. I have her CD if you want to borrow it."

"Sure."

"I thought you might want to go with me tonight." Howie twisted, straining, in his chair, craning his neck in an obviously painful position in order to meet Jim's eyes.

It hadn't taken that much effort for him to look around last semester.

"All right." Jim almost made a joke about his being a poor substitution for a real date—*would* have made such a joke last semester—but somehow it now seemed to hit a little too close to home.

"You'll like her."

"You want me to stop by and pick you up?"

"My four-thirty class doesn't get over until six," Howie said. "The concert's at eight. I'll just hang until then, go to the library or something, and I'll meet you outside the Student Center."

"Okay."

Howie grinned. "I'll be the one in the chair."

"I think I'll recognize you."

As promised, Howie was waiting outside the Student Center, his chair parked just to the right of the smoked glass doors. On the left side of the doors, next to a planter, a leather-clad couple was feverishly making out. Jim saw a portion of exposed breast, heard the sound of a zipper.

Howie grinned. "It's always a party at UC Brea."

"I guess so." Jim held the door open for his friend, and the two of them headed across the lobby of the center to the elevator that led down to the Club.

The Club was a lot more crowded than Jim would have thought, and the audience looked rough and rowdy, not the type of people who would ordinarily be expected to come and hear a female folkie. He and Howie flashed their press passes, got their hands stamped by the bouncer at the door, and made their way through the overdressed guys and underdressed girls, through the leather and spandex and hair, to a spot near the stage where Howie's view would be unobstructed.

"Get my pen and notepad out of my backpack," Howie said.

Jim did so, glancing around as he handed Howie the items. Two identically ponytailed men in identically studded black jackets were getting into a shoving match at the far end of the room. In the dark opposite corner, a big-titted blond girl was kneeling before a biker-looking guy. The air was hazy with smoke. He smelled marijuana.

This was not the Club he knew.

"Quite a crowd old Jan draws," he noted.

Howie nodded. Or tried to. "Weird."

"So what's up with Cheryl? You never did tell me."

"I don't know."

"You don't know? Then what was with that hush-hush routine?"

Howie craned his neck, trying to look toward Jim. "She wouldn't say. Not exactly. But something happened to her. Something bad."

"Broke up with a boyfriend?"

"More like . . ." He thought for a minute. "Raped."

Jim stared at him. "Cheryl? If that had happened to her, she'd be all over the police's ass, making sure they caught the sucker and put him away."

"You can never tell how people will react," Howie said quietly.

The lights darkened, the crowd began clapping and cheering and stomping feet, and a lone spotlight lit the stage as Jan Anderson came out, acoustic guitar in hand. She stepped up to the mike, grinned shyly, and nodded her thanks.

"Take it off!" someone yelled.

There were hoots and catcalls.

"Maybe later." She strapped on the guitar and started playing, an uptempo bluegrass-tinged song about traveling across country.

It was as though that was the cue for everyone to start talking. The conversation volume increased instantly as people began shouting to be heard over the music. From somewhere near the bar came the tinkling of broken glass. Jim looked over at Howie. His friend was frowning, obviously annoyed by the behavior of the crowd, but his eyes were on the performer and he was trying his best to filter out the background noise and concentrate on the music.

The song ended. Howie, Jim, and a few others at the front tables clapped, and Jan Anderson said a sarcastic "Thanks, you're a great audience" into the microphone.

"Show us your tits!" a man yelled.

"Yeah!" A woman seconded the request. "Let's see what you have!"

The singer grinned wryly. "They're A-cups," she said.

"I don't think that's what you're looking for." She turned toward Howie, Jim, and the few other people who had obviously come to hear music. "This one's called 'Jessica.'"

She started singing, playing to the front rows, trying to pretend as though the rest of the people in the Club didn't exist, but the crowd seemed to be getting louder and more obnoxious.

"Let's see your bush!" someone screamed.

"I have a chunk of choda here for you, babe!"

Midway through the fourth song, a beer mug flew into the spotlight, bouncing on the stage at the singer's feet. She stopped playing. "Listen," she said angrily, "I'm here to play. You're supposed to be here to listen. If that's unacceptable to you, I'll leave right now."

A drunken Ted Nugent lookalike waltzed between the tables to the foot of the low stage, pretending to play a heartbreaking violin.

"I'll cut off the concert right here," she said. "I don't have to put up with this. I don't get paid for being assaulted."

"Tight-ass cunt!" a woman yelled.

The singer took a deep breath, obviously deciding that the show must go on. She looked down at Howie. "I wrote this song when I was—"

A baseball flew out of the darkness and hit her shoulder.

She cried out in pain, reeled back, and the crowd erupted into spontaneous laughter and applause.

"Wanna ball?" someone shouted out, and the cheers grew.

"Fuck you!" she shouted into the microphone, then stormed off the stage, through the side door where she'd entered.

The boos started. A bottle was thrown and smashed against the wall behind the stage.

"Food fight!" a man yelled.

Jim leaned over, so Howie could hear him. "Let's get out of here," he said.

Howie adjusted his control, backed up his wheelchair, and the two of them made a quick exit. Luckily, they were already near the door. They passed the bouncer who had stamped their hands on the way in. He was grinning as he shoved his hand up the short skirt of a giggling redhead.

The elevator door was already open, and the two of them got quickly inside, Jim punching the button for the ground floor. Not speaking, they hurried through the Student Center lobby until they were safely outside.

Jim breathed deeply, even the smoggy night air feeling refreshing after the closed, smoky crampedness of the Club. "Jesus," he said. "Have you ever seen anything like that? Do those people actually go to this school?"

"Things are changing here," Howie said quietly.

Jim looked down at his friend. He'd been thinking exactly the same thing, but it was disconcerting to hear it spoken aloud by someone else.

"I know you've noticed it too," Howie said.

Jim stopped walking. "I don't . . ." He trailed off, then nodded. "Yeah," he said.

Howie shifted painfully in his chair, trying to adjust his position, his entire body contorting in an effort to move a few inches up on the seat. He took a deep breath, looked up. "It was a tough summer, dude."

It was the first time he'd spoken of the time they'd been apart, and Jim felt an awkward tightening in his chest. "Tell me about it," he said.

"Nothing to tell."

"Come on."

Howie sighed. "It started with the M.D. It started coming on really strong right after school ended. The worst it's ever been. It's let up quite a bit now, but . . ." His eyes looked away. "Thank God my parents were there. I thought I was going to die when it hit. I honestly thought, 'This is it.' "

"That's why you couldn't come to Arizona?"

"Yeah."

"Why didn't you tell me?"

Howie continued to look at the ground. "I don't know. I . . . Summer was just starting . . . I guess I didn't want to worry you."

"What do you think I am, a fucking stranger?"

"No, but . . . It's my problem, you know?"

Jim licked his lips, took a deep breath. "I thought . . . I thought it was, like, arrested. I didn't think you'd get worse."

"The doctors told my parents when I was first diagnosed that I was not expected to live past twenty-one. Even if I beat the odds, for sure I would be dead by thirty." He stated this in a matter-of-fact manner, in an even, reasonable voice, and Jim marveled at his friend's strength and self-control. As if reading his mind, Howie smiled. "I've known it since I was little. It's a fact of life. You get used to it after a while."

"But you don't have to like it."

"I don't like it. But I accept it. I have to. I have no choice."

"But ... how can you just go on with your normal life? How can you pretend that school, homework, tests, even the paper, how can you pretend it means anything? I mean, shit, if I had a—a fatal disease I'd quit school immediately and try to do as much as possible. I'd try to cram as many experiences as I could into the time I had."

Howie smiled philosophically. "You're under a death sentence too. Everyone is. Why do *you* bother? Why do you waste your time doing things you don't want to do?"

"But unless some freak accident occurs, I'm going to live out a normal life."

"That's the point. I want to live a normal life too. While I can. And a normal life for a guy my age is going to school, studying, hanging out, being with friends. That's what I do."

"But don't you want to—"

"What? Run a marathon in my wheelchair? Climb Mount Everest?" He shook his head awkwardly. "I don't have anything to prove. This is who I am, this is what I am. I just accept it and live with it and—"

"Roll with the flow."

"Exactly."

Jim smiled and nodded as if he understood, but he didn't understand, and he found himself wishing, absurdly, that *he* had been stricken with muscular dystrophy instead of Howie. He wouldn't feel so bad if he was the one with the disease. He wouldn't feel so helpless and useless and so filled with pity.

But that was stupid. Howie was handling the disease far better than he himself would ever have been able to do. Despite what he might like to believe, there was no way he'd be as strong as Howie.

"It wasn't just the M.D.," Howie continued. "Things here started to deteriorate too. I was supposed to work in the Career Center over the summer on work-study. The M.D. got so bad that I had to drop out, but even before I did, I could sense the change. People seemed meaner, you know? Different. I ... I don't know how to describe it."

"Like the people we saw in there." Jim gestured back toward the Student Center.

"Not that extreme, but, yeah, like that." He tried to glance back at the building but only ended up twisting his neck into an uncomfortable-looking position. "Even the job openings and the job requests we got seemed ... weird."

They were silent for a moment.

"What's with this place?" Jim asked finally.

"Fuck knows." Howie pressed the toggle switch on his wheelchair. "But if we don't get out of here, our fellow concert goers are going to be out and we'll get caught in their stampede."

"Let's go." Jim put his hand on the back of the wheelchair, to the right of Howie's head, and the two of them headed across the campus to the student parking lot.

2

Fraternity Row was a shambles.

Ron Gregory sat in his car, looking out the window. He had never before been in this neighborhood, and he was not sure exactly what he had expected. Perhaps, because of the tanned, blond athletes manning the fraternity booths in the quad, he'd thought that the frat houses would be well-manicured homes with sweatered guys and gals sipping white wine while mingling on lawns.

No way in hell.

The five Greek houses were converted apartment buildings situated right next to one another. In front of each, attached to peeling walls, hung gaudy homemade signs tackily proclaiming the houses' initials. Cars were parked along both sides of the street, and frat rats were running around the small, ill-kept yards, jumping over low bushes, harassing the few unattached females. A cop car, lights flashing, was parked halfway down the block, and its red and blue lights illuminated a short, wiry boy pissing in the gutter.

John Belushi would have been proud.

Ron grabbed his notebook from the passenger seat next to him and got out of the car. He patted his right front pocket, made sure he had a pen. When he'd talked to Theta Mu's president over the phone, the fraternity head had told him that the Theta Mu house was the first one on the street. Thank God he'd been given directions. There were no address numbers on the curbs or on the buildings—and, he thought wryly, the bannered letters were all Greek to him.

He stepped over a teenager passed out in a fetal position on the lawn and knocked on the decorated door of the fraternity house. A friendly-looking guy with a few days' growth of beard mirroring his own answered it.

"Hello," Ron said. "My name's Ron Gregory. I'm covering your rush for the *Sentinel*."

"Oh, yes. Come on in."

Inside, the fraternity house was surprisingly well furnished. The semi-bearded student introduced himself as Luis, said he was a philosophy major, and led Ron into the living room, where small groups of people were sit ting on couches and futons, talking quietly. Several oth ers were clustered around a television screen, watching rock videos. "Matt made those videos," Luis explained. "He's a comm major. Right now he's working with a local reggae band called New World Order. He's trying to get them some airplay on one of the local cable-access channels."

There was another knock at the door, and Luis excused himself. "Make yourself at home," he said. "There are Cokes and beer in the fridge. Just take whatever you want. I'll be back."

"Thanks." Ron scanned the room. Near the TV a girl was sitting by herself, watching the videos, and he sat down next to her, notebook out, hoping to get a quote he could use. "Hi," he said.

"Hi."

She smiled at him.

They hit it off immediately. Her name was Ruth and, like Luis, she was a philosophy major. She'd come to the party, she explained, because her brother had asked her to.

"Oh," Ron said. "Which one's he?"

She smiled. "He's not here, of course. He's dead."

The expression froze on his face. It was a joke, he thought. It had to be. He continued smiling stupidly, saying nothing.

"He said he could be reached through the Den Mother," she explained. "The Adversary allows them to speak through the Den Mother." She shook her head. "God, I miss him."

Ron continued smiling, nodding idiotically. What the hell was this? Was the videotape student doing some kind of *Candid Camera* routine? Was this some sort of fraternity gag or initiation ritual?

"Do you want anything to drink?" Ruth asked suddenly. "I'm dying of thirst."

"Sure," he said, getting up.

She put a hand on his shoulder, gently pushing him back down. "I'll get it. What do you want? A beer?"

He shook his head. "Just a Coke."

"All right. Be back in a sec."

She walked into the kitchen, and he looked quickly around, searching in vain for Luis, trying to find someone to talk to about this. Maybe old Ruthie was emotionally disturbed, maybe—

Then he heard it.

"The Den Mother told us to have it on Friday. We had our choice of Wednesday or Friday, but she said have it on Friday."

Ron turned around. Two guys were sitting on the couch behind him, talking.

". . . is what the Den Mother said."

In front. A group of four people.

"The way to get through to the Adversary is . . ."

He felt suddenly chilled. They were all around him.

"Here." Ruth returned, handing him a cold can of Coke.

"Thanks," he said. He took a sip, looked at her. "Who's the Den Mother?"

She laughed. "You don't know?"

He shook his head.

"The Den Mother's a—a den mother. I don't know how to explain it any better than that. You know how your newspaper has an adviser? Well, it's the same sort of thing. The fraternity members run the fraternity, but she oversees things and gives advice. They ask her opinion on controversial subjects, and she kind of guides them in the right direction."

He could not resist a touch of cruelty. "And Theta Mu's Den Mother is also a psychic?"

A look of shock crossed her features. "You don't believe?"

"No." He shook his head.

"Then why are you here?"

"Why am I here? I'm here to cover the rush for the paper. I'm here to give Theta Mu some free publicity. I'm not here to chat about den mothers, about adversaries, about talking to dead brothers!"

They were staring at him now, Ron realized. The room was quiet. Only the low buzzing of the rock videos on the television made any noise. He must have been louder than he'd thought. He scanned the room. The faces focused on him were neither hostile nor amused, only mildly curious.

Luis came in from the front room. He looked from Ron to everyone else, his gaze finally settling on Ruth. "What's going on here?"

No one spoke.

Luis shrugged. "Well, then. The Den Mother is ready."

The Den Mother is ready.

His instinct told him to leave, to get the hell out of that fraternity house and never look back. But he found himself following the crowd into the kitchen. Luis led the way past an old gas stove, past a refrigerator, to the broom closet next to the breakfast nook.

But it was not a broom closet.

Luis opened the door to reveal narrow wooden steps descending into the building's basement. It was dark below, but he did not turn on a light, he merely started down the steps. Four or five guys followed. Ron and Ruth walked down the stairs. Another ten or twelve people were behind them.

At the bottom they stopped.

The Den Mother was at the opposite end of the empty basement. Although the room was otherwise dark, a series of lights were trained on her, and Ron could see her perfectly.

He closed his eyes, opened them.

She was still there.

He stared, unable to look away. The Den Mother was ancient, hideous, and her wrinkled skin had caved in on itself to conform to the contours of her bones. The muscle, the fat, the meat, the juices, had been sucked out of her along with her life, and the dried and shriveled body was propped up against two crisscrossing wooden poles in a kind of makeshift shrine. The wall behind the Den Mother was covered with dried brown palm leaves, and several plastic dolls and cornhusk fetishes had been nailed to the wall, forming an obscene halo around her head. An orange spotlight was trained directly on her face, and Ron could see her grimacing smile, the dead, dried skin pulled taut across the overlarge teeth.

He looked away, looked toward Luis. The fraternity leader's face was transformed, lit up with an expression that could only be called rapture. Luis looked back at him triumphantly. "Bow down," he said. "Show your respect to the Den Mother."

Around him, people began dropping to their knees, and Ron did the same, afraid to do otherwise.

Luis remained standing, and he walked up to the Den Mother. He stood before her, head bowed. "Den Mother," he said. "We thank you for a successful rush this year."

The mummified figure did not move, but a cracked voice whistled from between the parchment lips: *"Welcome."*

The room grew suddenly colder, but Ron could see, even in the darkness, even through his fear, that all eyes were now trained on the Den Mother, and that everyone was smiling.

"You are our guardian," Luis continued. "You are our liaison. May we speak today to the Adversary?"

The whispering came again: *"Yes."*

And something shifted.

Ron took a deep breath. The air seemed suddenly heavy, rough, thick. It was difficult to breathe, even more difficult to see. A new darkness appeared to have descended upon the existing darkness.

The Den Mother's head moved slowly to the right with a sound like crumpling cellophane. There was a loud crack of bone. Dead lips flickered over the rotting skull teeth.

"ASK."

The voice issuing from the shriveled form was rumbling, powerful, terrifying.

"ASK AND YOU SHALL RECEIVE."

The room was silent after the hideous booming of the voice. A young man crept slowly forward. "I have to get all A's this semester," he said in a blubbering, desperate tone. "I'm already on academic probation, and my old man said if I don't get A's this time—"

"YOU SHALL."

The young man was now openly crying. "Thank you. Thank you."

Another student crawled forward. "I've been working out all summer, and I've tried really hard to get on the football team, but I'm only second-string . . ."

The requests came fast and furious. Ron remained on his knees, watching this spectacle, not daring to look away, held in a kind of stupefied trance. Each new petitioner had something he wanted, and the Adversary promised to grant all of the wishes.

He should have brought a tape recorder.

Finally Ruth moved forward. "I'd like to talk to my brother Jason," she said. Her voice was timid and tentative.

"Hey, how's it going?"

"Jason!" The worry left her voice with an audible whoosh, and her features relaxed, the tension in her body dissipating. She smiled. "How are you?"

Ron watched in horror as she carried on her conversation for a good five minutes, talking to the shrunken husk of a woman propped up on the crossbeams, the dead woman answering in the voice of a teenage boy.

Luis turned to him after Ruth and Jason had said their good-byes. "Now you," he said.

"What?" Ron looked up, confused, more than a little frightened. "I—I don't have anything to say."

"All new pledges must ask for something from the Adversary."

"Go to hell," he said, standing. "I'm not one of your pledges, and I'm not asking for anything. I'm getting out of here." He stormed up the stairs and out of the basement.

No, he didn't.

He wanted to, but he didn't.

He crept slowly forward on his knees, keeping his eyes on the ground in front of him, avoiding the sunken orbs of the Den Mother, aware that the gaze of everyone else in the room was upon him. His mind was blank, he could not think of anything to say, but he could feel the pressure from the fraternity members and other students behind him. He could feel the hideous suction of anticipation coming from the Adversary.

"ASK AND YOU SHALL RECEIVE."

He had nothing to ask!

"ASK."

"I—I want a . . . girlfriend," Ron muttered.

"IT IS DONE."

And the room shifted back.

After the horrible intensity of the previous moments with the Adversary, the Den Mother seemed almost benign. Luis and some of the older fraternity members consulted with her awhile longer, talking in low, respectful tones while she answered in crinkled parchment whispers, before allowing everyone to stand up and leave.

Once safely upstairs, Ron hurried through the kitchen, through the living room, past the still-playing television, and out of the fraternity house. Outside, from the other houses, he could hear screams and laughter and loud bass-heavy music. A second police car had joined the first, and two cops had four jocks spread against the side of the vehicles.

There was a heaviness in his chest, a fuzziness in his head, and in some small, responsible portion of his brain, he was thinking that he hadn't gotten any quotes for his article.

He walked over, around, through the chaos of rush and to his car. He got in, tossed his notebook on the seat next to him, turned on the ignition, and took off.

He drove home in silence, and before he went to sleep

that night, he closed his eyes, folded his hands, and prayed. For the first time in ten years.

But he knew that no one heard him.

He was awakened in the morning by the sound of the telephone.

It was Ruth, asking him for a date.

SEVEN

From the *Brea Gazette,* September 29:

A committee of self-described "angry local residents" petitioned the City Council Monday to ban public parking in residential neighborhoods near UC Brea.

According to Brett Samuels, chairman of the unnamed ad hoc citizens' committee, vandalism, graffiti, and other forms of property damage have increased dramatically since the start of the university's fall term on September 11. Samuels blamed the increase in crime on the influx of college students.

"They have no regard for privacy or property," Samuels said. "One woman caught a young man defecating on her front lawn in broad daylight. When she confronted him, he screamed obscenities at her. It's getting so bad that some mothers are afraid to let their children play in their own front yards."

A spokesman for the university stated that complaints like this are nothing new and have been made by irate residents each year.

"Sure, there are some bad apples," said Cliff Moody, Public Liaison Representative for UC Brea. "But that holds true for both sides. Students are not at the root of all of these complaints. Some of these incidents have been exaggerated way out of proportion, and some have been made up by nosy neighbors with too much time on their hands who don't like people parking on their street."

While Samuels admitted that there have been minor disagreements between homeowners and students in the past, particularly between residents and fraternity members, he said that this semester things are different.

"There's a new attitude these kids have," he said. "An I-can-do-whatever-I-want-and-you-can't-stop-me attitude. Well, they're wrong. We can stop them. And we'll do whatever we have to to reclaim Brea's streets for Brea citizens."

The City Council has scheduled a public hearing on the matter of public parking in residential neighborhoods for next Wednesday. The hearing will be held in the council chambers at city hall. Members of the public are invited to share their views.

EIGHT

1

They were fighting in the kitchen when she arrived home, Keith and her mother, having a knock-down, drag-out, screaming at each other at the top of their lungs. Faith thought of turning back and leaving, thought of going straight to her bedroom and hiding, but instead she forced herself to walk through the living room, through the dining room, and into the kitchen.

They were facing each other: Keith standing in the open doorway to the backyard, her mother at the sink opposite, leaning against the counter to steady herself.

Her mother's eyes were red, her face flushed, and the kitchen smelled strongly of tequila.

"I don't care if you are my mother!" Keith yelled. "I don't have to listen to you! You can't even take care of your own life!"

Their mother's eyes narrowed. "I never wanted you anyway," she said. "You were a fucking accident, and it's been downhill from there."

Keith stared at her for a second, looked toward Faith, then slammed the door and was running through the back yard, toward the side yard, toward the front.

"You shouldn't have said that." Faith confronted her mother. "Can't you tell what to say and what not to say?"

She shrugged. "He'll get over it."

"Maybe he won't."

Her mother waved her hand dismissively. "Actions speak louder than words," she said.

But that was not always true, Faith knew. Sometimes words spoke louder than actions.

And sometimes there was no difference between the two.

The phone rang, and her mother lurched over to the wall phone next to the refrigerator to answer it. "Yeah?" She was silent for a moment, then held the receiver out to Faith. "For you. Hart."

Hart? Again? It had been nearly a year since they'd broken up, and he still tried calling her at least once a month. Didn't he have a clue?

"Tell him I'm gone. Tell him I'm out on a date."

"Tell him yourself." Her mother spoke into the receiver. "Here she is."

Faith took the phone from her mother's hand, slammed it down in the cradle. She turned and left the room.

Her mother laughed. "What should I tell him if he calls back?"

Fuck him yourself, bitch, she almost answered, but she held her tongue, went into her bedroom, and closed the door.

What the hell was wrong with her mother?

And what was with Hart, still calling her after all this time? She recalled their very first date, the night after she'd met him in her American Studies class at Santa Ana College. He'd taken her to a sex shop. Well, it was not exactly a sex shop. It was called an "adult toy store," and it catered to the same pseudo-hip, secretly chauvinistic "new men" who considered *Playboy* the height of sophistication. He'd wanted to impress her with his open-mindedness and intellectual daring. He'd spent ten minutes ogling the silicone-enhanced breasts of beautiful naked women, then had pouted for the rest of the date because she'd jokingly turned the tables on him for a second. They'd been getting ready to leave—finally—and he'd pointed toward a comically oversized rubber penis. "How'd you like that one?"

"Ooooh," she'd said, licking her lips.

And he'd pouted.

It did no good to tell him that the idea of a chunk of rubber shoved into her vagina did not thrill her in the least, or to explain that the thing was at least a foot long, which meant, with her short body, that it would reach all the way to her lungs. His pride was hurt and his masculinity threatened, and he'd taken her joke as a personal insult.

She should have known it wouldn't work out right there.

But they'd gone together for an entire semester before finally splitting up after a bitterly acrimonious argument in the middle of Main Place Mall that had attracted quite a crowd of onlookers.

And he still tried to call her.

That was kind of creepy.

She glanced at the alarm clock on her dresser. It was getting late. She had to get ready. She opened her closet door, started sorting through the hanging clothes. She hadn't exactly been lying when she'd asked her mother to tell Hart that she was on a date. She really did have a date tonight, although she was not looking forward to it.

It wasn't her date's fault. She'd met him that afternoon in the library. She'd been shelving, he'd been looking for a book, and he'd asked her for help. Her first thought, shallow and immature as it was, was that he was a hunk. It was the type of observation her mother might have made, and she immediately felt guilty for even letting it cross her mind. But it had gotten his foot in the door, they'd started talking, and he'd ended up asking her out. His name was John, John Taylor, and he was a junior and a history major. He'd seemed nice, he'd seemed intelligent, he was definitely attractive, and when he'd asked if she'd like to go out with him, she had not been able to say no.

But she'd immediately regretted it. Weird as it was, she felt as though she was betraying Jim. That was ludicrous, of course. He had not really given her any reason to suspect that they would ever be more than acquaintances or casual school friends, but he *had* asked if she'd wanted to get something to eat after she'd told him about her botany class yesterday, and that might mean that he was interested.

Might.

It was enough to make her feel bad for going out with someone else.

She chose a pair of designer jeans, pulling them off the hanger.

Her botany class.

The thought of that still disturbed her. She had already made up her mind to drop the course, but she had not yet done so because she had to get the instructor's signature on her drop form.

And she was afraid to see him alone in his office.

Even thinking about him now caused a ripple of cold to spread down her arms and the back of her neck.

She'd go to class tomorrow, get him to sign her drop while all the other students were there. He couldn't do anything to her then.

Why would he do anything to her at all?

She didn't know. But she didn't like the thought of seeing him alone.

She chose a white blouse to go with the jeans. Dressy yet conservative, it would make her look nice but at the same time make it clear that she was not willing to just automatically spread her legs. She'd play this one by ear. She did not rule out the possibility of things working out, but she was acutely aware of the fact that John was really her second choice—and that was not the best way to begin a relationship.

Wisely, she'd told him that she would meet him at school, at the Student Center. He lived on campus, and they had tentatively agreed to check out *The Devils* at the Associated Students Film Festival. She'd told him that it was too far and too inconvenient for him to drive all the way to Santa Ana to pick her up, drive back to Brea to see the movie, drive back to Santa Ana to drop her off, and drive back to Brea again to go home. That was true. But it was only part of the reason she hadn't wanted to give him her address.

She was ashamed of where she lived.

And she was afraid he might meet her mother.

Those were the real reasons she hadn't wanted him to pick her up, and as she thought of her mother leaning drunkenly against the sink, yelling obscenities at her brother, she was glad she'd made that decision.

She took a shower, washed her hair, put on her makeup, put on her clothes. Her mother was on the phone in the kitchen, talking loudly to some guy, by the time Faith was ready to go, and she used the opportunity to sneak through the living room and out of the house.

She wondered where Keith had gone, but she knew he could take care of himself. He would probably stay with a friend tonight. Or wait until their mother had passed out on the couch before returning home.

A year ago, last semester even, she would have told her mother where she was going and when she'd be back. But she'd come to realize that her mother did not care where she was or who she was with or what she was doing, and now she didn't even bother to leave a note.

Talk about dysfunctional.

John was seated in one of the couches in the Student Center lobby when she arrived, and once again she could not help noticing how good-looking he was. He'd told her that he worked at Circuit City on weekends, selling stereos on commission, but she thought that he could have easily gotten a job as a male exotic dancer if he so chose.

She was thinking like her mother again.

She rubbed her tongue over her teeth to make sure there was no lipstick there, and smiled as she approached. "Hi," she said.

John looked her over, grinned appreciatively. "Hello."

There was something wrong with the date from the beginning. She didn't know what it was and didn't know how she knew it, but she did, she could sense it, and if there was any way she could have cancelled the date or bailed out of it, she would have done so after the first ten minutes.

In the library they'd gotten along fine. He'd seemed charming and friendly, and she'd enjoyed talking to him. But something had changed. He did most of the talking as they walked over to the Scopes Theatre, so she didn't have to maintain the conversation, but there was still an undercurrent of awkwardness, and she felt uneasy being with him.

And she definitely didn't like it when, in the middle of the movie, as a group of nuns went into a sexual frenzy on the screen, the hand he'd had around her shoulder reached down to cup her right breast.

Politely but firmly she moved his hand back to her shoulder.

Afterward, John suggested that they grab something to eat at the Leaning Tower, the pizza parlor closest to campus. She didn't really want to, but she agreed, and he drove them to the restaurant, praising the film and talking about the historical event that it was based on as he sped too quickly down the underlit street, while she nodded, smiling, saying as little as possible.

The pizza parlor was crowded. And noisy. In one corner a group of jocks was watching Monday Night Football, coaching the teams on the TV between beers, yelling excitedly when their team scored, cursing loudly when the other team pulled ahead. In the back of the darkened room, five or six younger kids, high school students, were playing video games, and the games beeped and whirred and electronically exploded as the players fought their way through alien landscapes. Music, loud dance music, was coming from everywhere, and throughout the restaurant conversations were pitched at shouting level to compete with the noise.

But she was happy it was noisy, happy it was crowded.

She didn't want to have to talk to him.

She didn't want to be alone with him.

She found herself thinking of Jim, wondering what he was doing right now, wondering what this date would have been like had he been the one she was out with.

Jesus, she had to knock off this teen romance novel crap.

The booths were all taken, but a group of John's friends were holding court at one of the sports tables near the TV, and she and John ended up sitting with them. His friends were obnoxious and he was obnoxious when he was with them, but she was grateful that the two of them did not have to be alone together.

They stayed for about an hour, until the game ended and the pizza parlor started to empty out. She herself had had only one beer, nursing it, but John had been keeping up with his friends the entire time and had to have had at least four or five mugs. She did not really feel comfortable letting him drive back to school, but she sensed a new belligerence in his bearing as he walked across the parking lot, holding tightly to her hand and pulling her with him, and she figured it was better to remain quiet, quickly get back to campus and quickly leave than to get into any sort of argument with him.

They drove back to school, and she directed him to

where her car was parked. He pulled next to the Bug, turned off the ignition.

And slid next to her on the seat.

Her mouth felt suddenly dry. She hadn't expected this, had thought she could maneuver her way through the evening without having to deal with it, but, lo and behold, here it was.

"I had a good time," she lied. "Thank you." She pulled up on the door lock, reached down for the handle, and his right arm slid along the back of the seat, coming to rest on her shoulder. She turned to face him. He pressed in closer, his breath smelling strongly of already stale beer.

"I had a good time too," he said.

He leaned forward.

She allowed him a quick no-tongue kiss, then tried again to reach for the handle, but the hand on her shoulder held her fast. It moved down to her breast, squeezing, the arm pinning her back into the seat.

Then his other hand was between her legs, rubbing her through her jeans. She stiffened, beginning to panic, wondering how she had let things get this far, wondering how she could get away. It was not as if she'd never been in this situation before. In fact, had she met John a month ago, even a week ago, this probably would've been her idea of a perfect end to their first date.

But there was something about his unyielding strength, the hint of roughness beneath his insistence, that frightened her and made her wish that she had put an end to the date immediately after the movie, the way she'd wanted to.

His hand pressed harder against her crotch, beginning to hurt. She tried to close her legs, tried to push his hand away, but he continued rubbing her there, following the seam of her jeans, pressing in with greater pressure at the spot where he knew her hole was.

"Come on," he said. "You know you want it."

"No," she said. "I don't. I want to go home." She tried to make her voice stern, forceful, the voice of a person in command of the situation, but she was aware that it came out weak and pleading, a captive begging a captor for a favor.

She grabbed his wrist, but his arm was strong, and his

hand moved up to her belt. She squeezed as hard as she could, tried to pull his arm away, but he laughed, easily resisting her efforts, and his fingers unfastened the belt clasp.

"Knock it off!" she ordered.

The button of her jeans popped off as his hand pushed down into her pants, into her panties, rough fingers rubbing against her pubic hair. She struggled, hitting at the arm that was pinning her shoulder against the seat, digging into his other arm with her fingernails.

"You know you like it," he said.

She was dry, frightened not aroused, and she yelped in pain as a finger forced itself into her opening anyway. She bit his arm.

He pulled out instantly, screaming, and it was only when she saw the half ring of teeth marks and the stream of blood that she realized how hard she must have bitten him.

She didn't care, though. She was just grateful to have this window of opportunity, and she opened the door by touch and scrambled backward out of the car.

"You frigid bitch!" he screamed. "You fucking frigid whore of a bitch!"

She wanted to scream back at him, wanted to spit on him, wanted to rip out his eyes and kick in his goddamn balls, but she took out her keys as quickly as she could and, with trembling fingers, opened the door of her Bug and got in, locking it. She did not look to see if he was coming, but inserted the key in the ignition, started the car, and took off.

She was still shaking a half hour later when she pulled into the driveway of her house.

2

"How's that?" Sindee asked.

Riley tried moving his arms, tried moving his legs, couldn't. "Uh, fine, I guess."

"Good," she said.

And began stripping.

He watched her as she slowly removed her shoes, her socks, her shirt, her pants, his erection growing harder with the discarding of each item of clothing.

It had started out so innocently. She'd been in Dr. Emerson's Creative Writing class with him, sitting two seats away, though he hadn't even noticed her that first week. She'd volunteered to be the first student to have her work critiqued by the class, and the professor had told her to make copies of her poems or play or short story and pass one out to each student.

At the next meeting she'd walked up and down the rows, passing out paper-clipped copies of her poetry, and she'd paused for a moment in front of his desk, fumblingly attempting to take a sheaf of copies from the bottom of her pile. Her hand had trembled, shaking as she handed him the paper. She'd moved quickly on to the student behind him, and he'd looked down at the Xeroxed sheets in his hand.

"I think you're interesting," feminine script at the top of the sheet had said. "I would like to meet you. Call me at 555–9087. Sindee."

Interesting?

He'd refolded the note and turned to look at the girl. She wasn't a centerfold or anything, but she was definitely attractive in a wholesome, blond, girl-next-door way. She'd glanced at him, seen him looking, and reddened, turning away.

He'd reread the note. It was stupid. High school time. But it was also very flattering.

They'd critiqued her poetry aloud in class, with most of the students finding it emotionally honest and effective, and Dr. Emerson had told them to write comments on their copies and return them to Sindee.

He'd written only six words: "I'd like to meet you too."

He'd called her that night, and they'd talked for nearly three hours, covering his rotten childhood, her happy sitcom childhood, their previous girlfriends and boyfriends, their interests, their plans for the future. They didn't have a lot in common, but somehow that didn't seem to matter, and they'd made plans to go out on Saturday.

The date had gone well. They'd made out a bit afterward—kissing and necking, with a little squeeze here, a little feel there—and on Monday, as he'd passed her seat on his way into class, she'd handed him another note. He'd opened it at his desk.

"Fuck me raw."

His penis had stiffened instantly, and he'd looked toward her.

And she'd smiled.

That had led here, to this motel, to this bed. He'd never done it in a motel before, had never done it anywhere besides his car, but she'd insisted, and he'd borrowed money and called in a few markers in order to raise the cash.

He'd expected champagne, maybe a romantic bubble bath, but the second they'd closed the door, she had opened her purse and taken out the silk handkerchiefs and said, "Okay, big boy, drop your drawers. Let's see what you've got."

He'd taken off his clothes, and she'd knelt before him and used her mouth for a few minutes before convincing him to let her tie him to the bedposts.

Now he watched her take off her bra, pull down her panties. Her vagina was bald, recently shaved, pink lips protruding from between an unusually white fold. Smiling, she picked up the panties, trailed them over his face, letting him smell her on the silk.

"Do you like that?" she asked.

"Yes," he managed to get out.

She let the panties drop to the floor and climbed onto the bed, straddling his face. He could see her opening, could smell her arousal. Then she was crawling over him, down him, moving slowly, sensuously, like a panther or cat. She bit his big toe, lightly, gently, then turned around, arching a leg over his body and crawling back up.

He heard a hissing sound, felt hot wetness splash over his crotch.

Something wasn't right. He craned his head forward. Jesus Christ! The crazy bitch was pissing on him! He struggled, tried to disengage himself from the bonds as she continued to crawl up the length of his body, urine spraying out from her shaved vagina and onto him. The stench was horrible, and he breathed out, trying not to vomit.

"What the hell are you doing?" he screamed.

The piss was soaking not only him but the bed, and now he could see it and it was red, bloody. Was she having her period?

"Untie me!" he ordered.

The flow stopped. "I thought this was what you wanted."

"Wanted?"

"It's what I wanted."

"Untie me right now!"

She crawled backward, sat on his knees, grabbed his penis. One long fingernail scraped against the underside of his now soft organ, and a line of red welled forth.

"Jesus," he said. "Jesus . . ."

She reached down, picked her panties up off the floor, used them to wipe the bloody urine off his stomach. She shoved the panties into his mouth, stuffing them all the way in.

He threw up instantly, but his mouth was filled and there was no place for the vomit to go and it backed up into his throat. He tried to cough, tried to breathe, tried to suck in air, but his air passage was blocked, and he knew at that instant that he was going to die.

She squeezed his testicles tightly, dug in with her fingernails.

He felt his left testicle pop.

"Fun time's just starting," she said.

If he could have, he would have screamed.

NINE

1

"That's the beauty of horror literature," Ian said, leaning forward on the podium. "Horror lives. Horror speaks to people. Even many English majors have a tough time placing the names Paul Morel or Gavin Stevens. But everyone knows Frankenstein. Everyone knows Dracula. Charles Dickens' most memorable character, Scrooge, comes from a ghost story. Unlike Mann and Proust and other authors whose works are kept alive through the artificial life support of academia, the works of horror authors survive on their own, in the real world, living, growing—"

"Like a monster," Kurt Lodrugh offered.

"Yes. Like a monster." Ian grinned. "The fact is, horror has been with us from the beginning. The first recorded examples of Western literature—*Beowulf, Sir Gawain and the Green Knight*—are horror stories. There are horror stories in the Bible, in ancient Chinese literature. Nearly all of the world's great authors have turned their hand to horror stories. Academics may consider those stories the weeds of literature, but they have withstood the test of time and their power remains undiminished."

Perry Magnuson, a smug-looking student in the front row, a thin-lipped young man with the superior air of a grad student who had shaken his head derisively at the mention of Mann and Proust, raised his hand.

Ian pointed at him. "Yes."

"The problem is that horror fiction is popular literature, not serious literature."

"The problem, huh? That's a very anti-intellectual stance you're taking, Mr. Magnuson. Are you implying that literary worth is determined by subject matter?"

"Uh, no," the boy said.

"Then how can you make a blanket statement like that? The fact is, there is no strict dividing line between what constitutes 'popular' literature and so-called 'serious' literature. Dickens and Hardy were the popular fiction writers of their time. So were Tolstoy and Dostoyevsky. Are you going to tell me that their appreciation by the masses deprives their work of literary merit?"

"Of course not."

"Then how can you automatically dismiss all horror fiction that way? Only time can decide whether a work will survive. For all we know, Saul Bellow will be forgotten in ten years and the works of Sidney Sheldon will live for eternity."

The class laughed.

"I'm being facetious, of course, but I do think it's a very dangerous attitude to have, this elitist idea that we in academia are the ones who determine whether a work of fiction is Art with a capital A."

"But someone like King," Janii Holman said. "Don't you think all those popular references, all those brand-nameisms are going to date the work?"

"You know, that's the same problem I have with Steinbeck. His work is so dated. All those references to the Depression. And, God, that Hemingway . . ."

The class laughed.

"That's what a lot of people don't understand. Placing a novel in a specific time period does not date it. It merely provides a setting and context for the work. In a larger sense, all fiction is a product of its time. Often, it's because of that fact, not in spite of it, that certain works are still being read and studied today. Addison and Steele, Samuel Johnson and Alexander Pope, are valued as much for their historical documentary value as their literary worth. More so, perhaps.

"As to the 'brand-nameisms,' I suggest you take a look at the work of Thomas Pynchon. Pynchon, hardly a literary lightweight, is English department-approved, and his work is chock full of pop cultures references. That doesn't seem to hurt his credibility or the artistic value of his fiction." Ian glanced up at the clock. "All right," he said. "It's getting late. Let's call it a day. By next meeting I expect you to have read the two M. R. James stories and *The Turn of the Screw*. Be prepared to discuss the James gang, similarities and differences. A helpful hint: this may be on the mid-term."

As always, a small group of students hung around after class to ask questions, to give the comments they were too shy to state in front of everyone else, or to do a little lobbying for their grades. Today, though, Ian politely excused himself and hurried back to his office, where he had to dump his books and papers on the desk before heading out to Acapulco, the restaurant where he was supposed to meet Eleanor for lunch.

Eleanor.

The emotionally unstable character at the center of *The Haunting*.

Why had he thought of that?

Why hadn't he thought of it before?

It didn't matter. He closed his office door, took the stairs down, and walked out to the faculty parking lot.

Eleanor was already there and waiting when he arrived. Of course. She had gotten a booth and had given the hostess such an accurate and detailed description of him that before he even gave his name he was being led to her table.

It had been over two and a half weeks since they'd seen each other—the longest time they'd been apart since they'd started going together—and he found that he was a little nervous. He slid in the booth next to her, put a hand on her leg as the hostess placed a menu on the table in front of him.

"Our specials today are tortilla soup and shrimp fajitas," the hostess said.

Ian gave her a perfunctory nod, waiting until she had left before speaking.

"I missed you," he told Eleanor.

She gave him a wan smile. "Did you?"

"You know I did." He pulled back, looked at her. "I thought this was all over. I thought we weren't going to fight."

She shook her head. "I'm sorry. I was just sitting here waiting, thinking about you not calling me back, going on with your normal life as if nothing had happened, and I found myself wondering if it made any difference if I was a part of your life or not. I thought you could probably just go on without me and not even notice I was gone."

He hoped the hurt registered on his face. "You know that's not true."

"Do I?"

He paused. "I don't know. Do you?"

She smiled at him, nodded. "Yeah, I guess I do."

He looked into her eyes, and he found himself remembering something Ginny, his girlfriend before Sylvia, had said when they'd finally decided to split up for good. They'd been going through the contents of their apartment, dividing up the accumulated material manifestations of their life together, and had started sorting through a box of photographs that they'd never gotten around to putting in albums. "Mine are the ones with people in them," Ginny had said. It was an offhand remark, made casually, with no thought behind it, but he'd instantly seen that she was right and he wondered why he'd never noticed it before. Her photographs were of him, of them, of friends and relatives in the various locations to which they'd traveled. Snapshots. His pictures were never of people; they were always of places. His were landscape shots, sterile and purposefully composed. He'd remembered, in Monument Valley the summer before, shooing Ginny out of the frame because she was blocking the view of one of the peaks.

She had not said anything more, but the implications of her statement had hung in the air between them as they divided the photographs. And more than anything else she'd said about him or about their relationship, he remembered that sentence: "Mine are the ones with people in them."

It still bothered him.

He forced himself to smile as he took Eleanor's hand. "What do you say we play hooky for the rest of the day? I'll skip my last two classes, you call your office, tell them you came down with something, and we'll go to the beach. Or we'll hit a movie."

She laughed.

"I'm serious."

"Good afternoon, I—oh, hi, Dr. Emerson!"

He looked up at the waitress who had arrived to take

their order. She looked vaguely familiar and was obviously an ex-student, but he couldn't put a name to the face. "Hi," he said.

"Marianne Gale," she said. "I had you two years ago for Comp 101."

"How are you doing?" He still didn't remember her, but he pretended as though he did, and she told him she'd be graduating this semester and was planning to pursue a career in advertising and had just landed an internship at McMahan and Tate.

After she'd taken their order and gone, Eleanor shook her head. "They're everywhere."

He shrugged. "You get used to it. Now, what about my hooky idea?"

"I'd like to, but—"

"Come on."

She thought for a minute, then nodded. "Okay," she said. "It's a date." She slid out of the booth, stood. "I'll be back in a minute. I'm just going to call."

They spent the day at Laguna, going through the shops and galleries, and by the time they drove back to Brea, it was almost dark. She decided to spend the night, and it was as if nothing had ever happened between them. They sent out for sandwiches, took a shower together, made love.

Afterward, in bed, watching *Body Heat* on HBO for the hundredth time, she asked him how the semester was going.

He was tempted to tell her, tempted to put into concrete words and sentences the vague sense of strangeness he'd felt, the indefinable weirdness that had seemed to him to be hovering over the campus since the start of the school year, but it was too difficult, and he decided that this was neither the time nor the place.

"Fine," he said.

"How's your horror class?"

"Bigger than I thought. Initial enrollment was low, but I got quite a few adds by the end of the first week. Horror's supposed to be in a slump right now, but I guess there's still a demand."

"Or it sounded easier than Milton."

"Or that."

"Is Kiefer still coming down on you?"

He snorted. "Are you kidding? Nor only do I have to rejustify myself every time I want to offer this class, now he's telling me that next time around he wants to change the name. Apparently 'Horror Fiction' does not look prestigious enough in the catalogue. He wants to call it 'Fantastic Themes in World Literature.'"

She laughed, shook her head. "Kiefer."

"Yeah."

"What an ass."

Ian lightly slapped her backside, grinned. "That's just what I was about to say to you."

She rolled slowly onto her stomach, looked coyly up at him. "It's here for the taking."

He looked at her quizzically, eyebrows raised.

"You don't want to?"

"You mean you're serious?"

She nodded, slightly embarrassed but trying not to show it.

"Really?"

"I thought we might try it. I'm sort of curious, too, you know."

"But you—"

"I changed my mind."

"I'm not complaining. It's just that I thought—"

"You don't have to if you don't want to."

"No, it's not that. You know I do."

She smiled up at him. "Then get the Vaseline."

He gave her a quick kiss on the lips and rolled out of bed. He smiled at her. "I love you."

It was the first time he'd said the words, and they both knew it, but she didn't make a big deal out of the occasion. She simply smiled back at him. "I love you too," she said.

2

"Fifteen people injured?" Jim, cradling the telephone receiver between his head and shoulder, glanced over at Howie. His fingers continued to type. "Three hospitalized? Hold on a minute." He stopped typing, straightened his neck, and picked up the phone with his hand. "There was a riot at the football game at UNLV," he told Howie.

Howie looked at him. "We started it, didn't we?" he asked quietly.

Jim nodded. "Yeah. The Sentinels lost after a bad call by the ref, and people in the stands started protesting. I guess it turned into a regular soccer situation, crowds stampeding onto the field, pushing people, fighting. Ford says it's pure luck there weren't more injuries."

"Jan Anderson," Howie said. "The Club concert."

Jim placed the phone back in the crook of his neck. "Okay," he told the sports editor. "Keep going. Three hospitalized?"

Ten minutes later, after reading the story back to Ford over the phone and making corrections online, Jim hung up. He leaned back in his chair, put his feet on top of the terminal. "Jesus. Rapes, suicides, riots. This semester's like a journalist's dream come true."

"Or a normal person's nightmare." Howie's wheelchair clicked and hummed as he rolled around the center table and over to where Jim sat.

Jim turned toward his friend. "You heard about the child-molestation charges, didn't you?"

Howie tried to shake his head, managed only to twitch a little to the right. "No."

"Steve's working on it. It'll be in Thursday's issue. Two sets of parents claimed, independently, that their kids were molested over at the Children's Center. I don't know if there's any truth to the charges—after the McMartin case, the school instituted very strict child-care guidelines, and there seems to be no time at which the kids were left alone with any of the teachers or students—but the parents claim one boy was fondled and one girl was forced to perform oral sex in a closet."

"Is there any sort of crime that hasn't been committed at Brea this semester?"

"If there is, it'll probably happen before December."

"Doesn't all this strike you as being a little . . . suspicious?"

Jim put his feet down, sat up straight. "Suspicious?"

"Yeah. I mean, all of this at one school, in such a short period of time. Doesn't it seem just a little bit unusual?"

"Of course."

"I mean, even the city council's noticed." Howie motioned jerkily toward a copy of the *Brea Gazette* sitting in his lap. A headline just above the fold stated that the council had passed a resolution to increase the number of policemen assigned to the campus.

"What's your point?"

"I don't know. I just have a bad feeling about this."

Jim felt a cold shiver move up his sine. "Crime's up everywhere."

"Not two thousand percent or whatever it is here." Howie rolled backward as Jim stood. "You know, there's a theory that there's a time for certain ideas and inventions, that advances are made not because one genius comes up with an idea on his own but because that genius was the first one to synthesize what was already in the air. If Thomas Edison hadn't invented the light bulb, someone else would have. It was in the zeitgeist. It was time for that invention. This feels like the same thing to me. Like maybe this is the time for violence. We just don't *happen* to have violent students here this semester. It's . . . it's in the air. It's time."

The chill had turned into full-fledged goose bumps. "That's crazy."

"Is it? There's not one person we can pin all this on, not one centralized cause. But all of these things are connected, they're all part of a trend, a pattern."

"Not necessarily."

"Come on."

"We'll discuss it later, okay? Right now I have to print out this story, redesign the front page, and paste it up. The printer expected the paper forty-five minutes ago. I have to call and tell them that it's going to be another hour."

"Want me to see if anyone's in the newsroom?"

"No. They're all gone. I even sent Jean home."

"Faruk has a night class. I can get him out."

"No, I'll do it myself. It's a one-person job. You hit the road too. I'll see you back at the dorm."

"And we'll discuss our school's sudden propensity for violence?"

"To your heart's content."

Howie chuckled. "Okay, Lou Grant. Later."

"Later." Jim walked with Howie to the door, then watched his friend roll down the corridor to the elevator.

He walked back into Production alone.

It took longer than he thought.

He'd estimated an hour, told the printer an hour and a half, but it was closer to two hours later before the paper was finally put to bed. Ford's story hadn't been that difficult. And he'd even rearranged the page layout fairly quickly. But he'd kept noticing errors as he worked—misspellings, typos—and he'd been forced to go back and retype, and repaste up several lines in each story.

He'd then double-checked the other pages.

And fixed those errors.

The copy editors were in for a major lecture tomorrow.

They'd missed the printer's deadline by a good three hours, but he called and explained, and the pressman said that their load was light tonight, it shouldn't be any problem, the paper should still be printed and ready for distribution by six in the morning.

Jim quickly cleaned off the paste-up tables, turned off all the machines, shut off the lights, and locked the door. He walked into the newsroom to pick up his backpack.

It was after eleven, and he'd been on campus since seven o'clock this morning. Sixteen hours. He was so tired that he almost fell asleep in the elevator on the way down, lulled toward slumber by the small cubicle's gently rocking motion. Then the elevator stopped, pulled up, and he jerked awake as the metal doors slid open.

The bottom floor of the building was silent and deserted. Even the donut sellers had gone home. Recessed fluorescents in the high ceiling illuminated the lobby, but the light reflected against the wall of windows and made the world outside seem black and featureless. He walked across the tiled floor, his footsteps loud in the stillness, and reached the door, opening it. Cool night air blew against his face, sucked in by the difference in air pressure, and he pushed the door all the way open and stepped outside.

He had never been on campus this late before. Always when he'd left, there'd been at least a few students about, lone studiers walking from the library to their cars, couples sitting on the stone benches surrounding the flower enclosures. But tonight even the library had already closed, and all of the night classes had long since been dismissed. The lights in the quad were at half power, and the windows in the buildings were dark.

The sight of the dark, empty campus was more than a little creepy, and his grip tightened on the box of page dummies. His boots sounded loud on the cement as he hurried toward the parking lot, the only sound competing with them the far-off rush of car noise from Imperial Highway.

"Nice night."

He jumped at the voice, nearly stumbled and fell. From the shadows next to the side of the building emerged a man, a short, stocky man with a thick, bushy beard.

"Or maybe it's not such a nice night, mmm?"

The man moved into the half-light, and Jim saw that he was a professor. Or at least he looked like one. An older guy, with a tweed jacket. But there was something wrong with him. His eyes looked bright even in the darkness, and they did not seem to blink. They remain focused unwaveringly on Jim's face.

"Uh, yeah," Jim said, trying to hurry by. "Whatever."

"I know what's happening here," the man said.

Jim stopped, turned to look at him.

"It's an evil thing, this university. And it's going to get worse. We need to destroy this son of a bitch to save it. We need to blow this fucker to kingdom come." The man grinned, but there was no change in the dead-serious intensity of his eyes, and the grin disappeared as quickly as it had arrived.

"I'm late," Jim said. "I have to go." He started walking toward the parking lot.

"Ask Dr. Emerson. He knows," the man said. "It's not too late."

Jim continued walking, not looking back, staring straight ahead. Before him, the parking lot was dark. Too dark. In an effort to cut down on maintenance expenses, the university had installed energy-saver bulbs in the street lamps that bookended every other aisle of the parking lot. The lights periodically winked off and on, and even when they were on they shone at half power. Instead of pools of shadow, the parking lot was broken by pools of light, weak, fuzzy circles of illumination that receded into the darkness and distance.

He could see his car from here. He'd driven over from the dorm at lunch and had parked during the peak hours. He'd been lucky to find the spot he had, but now his Hyundai sat alone in an otherwise empty aisle, one of a small handful of vehicles left in the entire parking lot.

He licked his lips as he stepped off the curb. He felt exposed walking across the empty asphalt, and he could not shake the feeling that the man, the professor, the whatever-he-was, was watching him, staring at him. He tried to maintain his usual pace, to act as though nothing was wrong, but the more effort he expended to keep things normal, the more he felt them slipping away. His steps felt awkward, the swinging of his arms as he strode across the lot unnatural. He kept trying to glance around casually, to see if the man was still there, still watching him, but the shadows were too dark and he was too far away.

To his left, he heard a cracking sound, like a twig being snapped.

He jumped. And ran the rest of the way to his car.

TEN

1

There'd been a power outage sometime during the night, and instead of waking up to the sounds of the radio and the darkness of pre-dawn, Faith awoke to the sound of the Martinez's mufflerless Chevy next door and the bright light of mid-morning. She sat up immediately in bed, glanced at the clock, saw 12:00 flashing on and off, and hurriedly threw on her bathrobe and ran to her mom's room. As she'd expected, her mom was gone. The wind-up clock on the dresser said 9:35.

She'd already missed two of her classes.

Damn it, why hadn't her mom awakened her? She knew that she had early classes on Monday, Wednesday, and Friday.

Or maybe she didn't.

It was hard to tell how much attention the bitch paid to any family-related things these days.

Faith went into the bathroom, started to comb her hair, then stood for a moment looking at herself in the mirror. Did she really want to go to school today? Since she'd dropped botany, she had only one more class this morning. And she could trade her hours this afternoon at the library and work some other time.

Part of her did not want to go to school. Part of her had not wanted to go to school since the first day. There was something about Brea that made her feel ... uncomfortable. She still could not pin down why. Some of it was the students, of course. But American Lit was really the only course filled with out-and-out assholes. And they were sort of counterbalanced by Jim. No, there was something else, and while she wasn't big on hunches or women's intuition, this fell along those lines. She'd always had concrete reasons for liking or not liking things at Santa Ana College, but the ambiguous feelings she experienced toward Brea were entirely different. And that itself made her uncomfortable.

At the same time, what else did she have to do today? Hang around here? Wait for her mom to come home and see who she brought back with her? School, at least, did offer her something constructive to do. Besides, she honestly enjoyed working at the library.

And, truth be told, she did want to see Jim.

She caught herself smiling in the mirror. She tried to tell herself she wanted to see Jim because she wanted to find out about the newspaper's investigation of Dr. Austin and his animal torture, but it was really because . . . well, because she was interested.

That settled it, then.

She was going to school.

She quickly combed her hair, brushed her teeth, slipped into a pair of jeans and an old Greenpeace T-shirt, and grabbed her purse and car keys off the dresser in her room.

She walked into American Lit five steps behind the instructor.

Today's discussion was of Flannery O'Connor's *Wise Blood*. It was a short novel, but she'd gotten only halfway through it, and she purposely kept quiet and did not participate in the discussion. Jim, sitting next to her, had a lot to say about the work, disagreeing on interpretations with several other students in class. She hadn't read enough of the book to know who was right, but she took Jim's side anyway, silently cheering him on, as though this literary discussion was a football game and he was the quarterback of her team.

After class, they walked together to the elevator.

"What's happening with the article?" Faith asked. "Find anything out?"

Jim sighed. "I wish I could say I had, but I haven't been able to substantiate your story. Dr. Austin denies that it ever occurred. I showed up at your class Monday, talked to a couple of students, and they said it didn't happen either."

"Oh, I'm a liar. Is that it?"

"No. It's just that . . ."

"You don't believe me, do you?"

Jim looked at her. "Yes, I do."

They stood for a moment in the middle of the corridor, unmoving.

"Why?" she asked finally. "I mean, I wouldn't if I were you."

"I don't know," he said. "Maybe it's because I think you're honest. Maybe it's because—because that sort of thing doesn't sound that implausible here."

She wanted to ask him what he meant by that. She had the feeling that this was something they both understood and would agree upon, but for some reason she held back and said nothing.

"You know," Jim said, "we could write the article from your point of view, use you as the sole source. I'd interview you, quote you, describe what happened. Our usual policy is two sources minimum, but I could make an exception here. You'd probably catch a lot of heat, though. Everything would come down on your head."

"Do you accept guest editorials?" Faith asked.

"Sometimes."

"What if I write one, do it that way? You won't have to go against your policy or anything, and I could still let people know what happened."

Jim smiled. "You sure you don't want to major in journalism? I'll sign you up right now."

"Who knows?" Faith said. "It may work out that way."

"Our editorial page runs on Tuesdays. You've missed this week, obviously, and next week's deadline was yesterday. If you want to get it in the following week, you'll have to get something to me by Monday. Otherwise, it'd be the week after that."

"I'll have it for you Friday."

"I won't be in class Friday."

"Oh." She tried not to let her disappointment show. "I could bring it to the newspaper office."

"I'm not sure of our schedule Friday. Make it Monday."

She nodded. "Okay."

"Eight o'clock?"

"Monday morning. Eight o'clock sharp."

"That'll give me time to proofread it and have you rewrite it, if necessary."

"Rewrite it?"

"Policy's flexible. Standards aren't."

Faith laughed. "Deal," she said.

They walked to the elevator. He pushed both buttons. "Are you—"

"Yeah, I have to work. I had my hours revised when I dropped the class. I get off earlier at night this way."

The elevator doors opened, a dull bell chiming as the Up arrow was illuminated. The crowd of people shuffled together to make room for Jim. He stepped inside. "Well, I guess I'll see you, then."

"Bye."

"Remember: eight o'clock."

"I'll be there."

The doors started to close.

"Wait!" Faith put her arm between the sliding pieces of metal. "Where's the newspaper office?"

"This building. Third floor. Room 306."

She stepped back, waved. "See you there."

The elevator closed. Not wanting to wait for the next elevator, she turned and walked over to the stairway. She should feel worried about the editorial, she thought. She should feel pressured.

But she felt pretty good.

As far as Faith was concerned, the UC Brea library was a nice place to work. The pay wasn't all that hot, but she liked the atmosphere, the quiet, the studious students and the aisles of books. She especially liked shelving, though it was a job that most of the student assistants avoided. She enjoyed discovering books she would not ordinarily read, looking at their covers, seeing their titles. She would open and read the dust jackets of the ones that looked interesting, sometimes even skimming paragraphs, pages, chapters. In a way, it made her feel intimidated, made her realize how little she knew, how deficient had been her education, how small was her universe. But it also inspired her and made her feel as though anything was possible, as though there was a whole world out there waiting to be explored. There was so much to know, so much that interested her, and there was so much to choose from, all of it literally at her fingertips.

Of course, she'd always loved libraries. Even as a small child she'd loved going there, and during the summers she and Keith used to walk down to the Santa Ana Public Library, to the children's room, where they'd check out huge stacks of ten or twelve books at a time, probably only a fourth of which they actually ended up reading.

The thing that had stayed with her most strongly from those days was the smell, that unique and unmistakeable odor of books. She didn't know what caused it, whether it was the paper, the ink, or the binding, but that lovingly familiar odor always seemed to her to be the smell of knowledge, and even today it made her feel warm and comfortable and secure.

The sixth floor.

That was something she didn't think about.

She picked the next book off the cart and glanced at its title before trying to put it on the shelf. *Pink Velvet: Erotic Lesbian Poetry 1900–1940*. She peeked around the edge of the aisle to make sure Glenna wasn't around before opening the book. She liked Glenna, considered her a friend, but she was pretty sure Glenna was a lesbian. A P.E. major who definitely looked the part, her voice was low and masculine, almost raspy, and she had a square body and a butch haircut atop a plain face. Faith wasn't bothered by Glenna's sexual preference— she didn't care one way or the other—but she did not want to give the library assistant any ideas or have to explain her way out of an awkward situation.

She opened the book randomly to a page in the middle, read a little:

> I unfold her, open her
> Place my lips on her sex
> Softly moist, tasting of salt and honey

Wow. This was written that long ago? Graphic stuff.

From down the aisle she heard footsteps, and she quickly closed the book, placing it in its proper location on the shelf.

Glenna stopped next to the book cart. "I thought I'd find you here. Phil's called a meeting of everyone in Circ."

Faith stood. "What is it?"

"I'm not supposed to say, but ..." Glenna glanced around to make sure no one was nearby. "It's Sue."

"What about her?"

"She was assaulted. Some guy held her down and felt her up until she kicked him in the nuts and got away." Glenna's voice dropped. "It was a professor. A history teacher. Phil wants to talk to us all about it."

"Jesus. When did this happen?"

"About an hour ago," Glenna said. "Upstairs. On the sixth floor."

2

Ian looked around the Club, found Buckley at a back table, and headed over to where his friend was sitting. Buckley waved down a waitress, ordered a second beer for himself and one for Ian.

"Slow lunch hour," Ian observed, looking around.

"Drinking's not the sport it used to be. Everyone's so damned responsible and health-conscious these days. I used to teach classes totally wasted. Now I feel guilty if I even have a brew at lunch. It's a different world out there."

Ian laughed. "It doesn't seem to have slowed you down any."

"Ah, it's my birthday. What the fuck."

"Speaking of that, I have your present back in my office."

"Is it something I can play on a turntable?"

"Maybe."

"What a pal. What a guy. What a man."

The waitress returned with the beers and Buckley took out his wallet, but Ian held out his hand. "This one's on me. Birthday treat."

"I knew there was some reason I kept you around."

Ian paid the waitress, one of his students from last semester, and gave her an unusually large tip so she wouldn't think he was cheap. He wasn't sure why he cared what ex-students thought of him, but he did, and that usually meant that he ended up buying things he didn't want to buy, paying too much for them, and overtipping.

Buckley finished the dregs of his first beer, took a healthy swig from his second. He looked over at Ian, shook his head. "Fuckin' Republicans, man."

"What is it now?"

"I have this student in my 300 class. Right-wing fanatic. Gives me Reagan flashbacks."

"The president misspoke himself."

"No questions allowed during photo ops."

"You've seen one redwood, you've seen 'em all."

"Eighty percent of air pollution is caused by plants and trees."

"Ketchup is a vegetable."

"Ah, the good old days. Blaming the nation's problems on Congress, lawyers, and the media."

Ian grinned. "That's what's wrong with this country. Representative democracy, the American system of justice, and a free press. Get rid of those and we'd have a pretty nice place here."

Buckley was silent for a moment. He took another large swig. "Did you think this was the way things were going to turn out? I mean, when you were twenty, is this the way you saw the country being when you were forty-five?"

"Ah, that's what brought this on."

Buckley stared blackly into his glass. "No. It's that kid. He scares the shit out of me. It's only been, what? two or three weeks, and already I know more about this character than I ever wanted to know." He finished off his beer. "I mean, this guy is armed to the teeth in preparation for the imminent collapse of society."

"Isn't that always the way of it? The ones who claim to be so pro-American never seem to have much faith in the American system of government. They always think it's going to collapse or be overthrown, from within or without. I've always been under the impression that it was pretty stable."

Buckley held up a reminding finger. "Because the Brants of this world have enough weaponry to keep the commies away."

"Brant?"

"Yeah. Brant Keeler."

"That guy's in my creative writing class."

"Shit. That little peckerhead's everywhere."

"He writes some pretty good porn."

Buckley looked up. "Porn? Brant? You're joking."

"No, I'm serious."

"Well, well, well. Maybe there's hope for the boy after all." Buckley waved down the waitress.

"Are you sure you should—"

"No, I shouldn't, but it's my birthday, and I don't give a rat's ass." He smiled at the waitress. "One more, my dear. Put it on his tab."

"Thanks," Ian said.

Buckley leaned forward across the table. "He doesn't put his political views into his porn?"

Ian shook his head.

"Weird. I mean, I have him for 300, and, yeah, there're places to inject political topics, but this kid's wearing it on his sleeve all day every day. I've thought of asking him if he thinks he signed up for a political science course. I mean, I seriously wonder sometimes if he knows that he's in an English class. This guy's out there."

Ian laughed.

"It's not funny."

Ian looked at his friend. "This guy really has you spooked, doesn't he?"

"Yeah. I mean, shit, I've lived here for twenty years. I'm used to your usual garden-variety Orange County fascist."

Ian smiled. He knew to whom Buckley was referring. The type of people he ranted about after every election. The politically unsophisticated and philosophically simpleminded who seemed to have gotten their knowledge of civics from vigilante movies and television cop shows. In their world, honest, hardworking policemen always arrested the right men, and bleeding-heart courts always let the most dangerous criminals go free. Although they passed themselves off as tireless supporters of the American way of life, they exhibited an alarming lack of faith in the American system of justice and seemed to want to adopt the law-and-order techniques of totalitarian states.

And they made Buckley crazy.

Buckley shook his head. "Brant's something else, though. He . . ." He trailed off. "Fuck it. I don't want to talk about that little pissant anymore. Let's change the subject."

"Okay. How about . . . sex?"

"Now you're talking. Did you check out the ass on that waitress?"

"Quiet down. That's one of my students."

"This semester?"

"No, last."

"Then don't worry about it." Buckley grinned. "Remember the old days? Before all this harassment shit? When we used to hold court here and all our little undergrad groupies would hang off our very word, wetting their pants at our brilliance?"

"You mean when you used to unfairly use your knowledge, experience, and position to worm your way into eighteen-year-olds' panties?"

"Yeah."

"You're a sleaze."

"But a happy one."

"So what are your birthday plans?"

"Televised sports, six-pack of beer, outcall massage."

"Seriously."

Buckley chuckled. "Okay. Televised sports, six-pack of beer. Want to join me?"

"I'd be honored."

"It's a date. Speaking of dates, how goes it with Eleanor?"

"Fine, I guess."

"You guess?"

"I guess."

They were silent for a moment. The waitress brought another beer, put it in front of Buckley, Ian paid for it, overtipped. Buckley downed half the glass with one chug and emerged frowning.

"What is it?" Ian asked.

"Ah, nothing."

"What?"

Buckley looked at him. "That kid. Brant." He shook his head, looked away. "He really bothers me."

3

"Slavery was a very profitable institution. If the South had not been so reliant on agriculture and had been able to successfully diversify, to transfer its slave labor force into an industrial labor force, it would have been a very potent economic power, a world-class economic power."

Jim stopped writing notes and looked up at the professor.

Elvin Jefferson, the lone black student in the class, raised his hand. "But how can you have a thriving economy if there are people in that economy who aren't making any money?"

"It depends on your definition of 'thriving.' It depends on whether you're concerned about maintaining a minimum standard of living for even the lowest people in that society, or whether you're concerned about overall output and GNP. True, the slave class was not economically healthy within itself. But having a slave class relieved the pressure on the rest of society, providing a foundation for economic growth that it was simply not possible to reproduce after slavery's demise."

What was this? What was going on here? Jim looked around the small classroom, saw students busily writing in notebooks. Didn't anyone else notice that this lecture was getting a little ... strange?

Elvin did, obviously, and Jim looked over at the black student, met his eyes. Elvin shook his head in disgust.

Jim thought about Faith's botany class, about the animal torture.

The professor leaned against the podium. "From an economic standpoint slavery made a lot of sense."

Elvin stood. "I object to your treating slavery as though it didn't exist outside economics. There was a human element—"

"Sit down, Mr. Jefferson." The professor's eyes were hard, his smile cold. "This is an economics class, not an ethics class, and what we will discuss here is economics." He pointed toward the blackboard. "Slavery, as I have been explaining, was actually good for the American economy. Very good."

A girl seated near the left wall raised her hand. "What

if the South had won the Civil War and the North had been forced to convert to a slave-based economy?"

The professor smiled. "Good question, Miss Powell. In my estimation, and in the estimation of most serious historians and economists, the result would have been a strengthened manufacturing base during the important expansion period of the Industrial Revolution—"

Elvin stood, loudly gathered his books, walked toward the door at the back of the room.

"In the long run, America's economy would have benefited greatly from an expansion of slavery—"

The door slammed.

The professor stared at the closed door for a moment, and a smile spread slowly across his face. "Nigger," he said.

There were grins, low laughter from the students.

"Jungle bunny," someone said.

"Coon."

The professor looked around the class. "Nigger," he repeated.

And giggled.

4

"Here," Ruth said. "Where all the cars are."

Ron pulled in back of a Jeep, parked.

Ruth opened her door, looked down at the paper in her hand. "It's up that long driveway."

"Let's go."

Ron got out of the car, locked the doors, and walked around the hood to take Ruth's hand. Ever since he'd become a Theta Mu, ever since he'd met the Den Mother and talked to the Adversary, his life had changed. He now had Ruth, of course—that was the biggest change—but it seemed that other things were falling into place as well. He was doing better in his classes; his assignments for *The Sentinel* were getting more prestigious; he was making a lot of new friends, becoming more popular; at work, he'd gotten a raise.

Something like *this* never would have happened to him before. He never would've been invited to a party at a professor's house if he had not become a Theta Mu.

Still, despite the upward turn that his life seemed to

be taking, there was something not quite right about it all, something that did not sit well with him, and when he was alone in bed at night, thinking things over, he could not help wishing that none of it had happened, that he had not gone to the Theta Mu rush, that he was still the boring, average, dateless student that he'd always been.

"Are we late?" Ruth asked.

He looked at her, smiled, shook his head. "I don't think so."

The winding driveway ended at a white wooden house situated halfway up the side of the canyon, a forties-style bungalow added on and opened out into a starker, more modern structure. The front door was wide open, the porch and the foyer filled with people, and, not seeing anyone they knew on this periphery of the party, the two of them walked inside.

Like the exterior of the house, the interior had been remodeled extensively, its origins visible only in the arched vestibule and rounded ceilings. The house had been gutted and restructured, a small number of large rooms taking the place of a large number of small rooms, and extensions had been added, providing window where once had been wall. Shiny hardwood floors contrasted with empty white space. Framed Expressionist prints hung in deliberately spaced order throughout the house, and furnishings were sparse: low couches, glass tables, a black Steinway grand on a Persian carpet.

"Glad you could make it!"

Dr. Coulter emerged from the crowd, making a bee-line toward them, pulling along a gorgeous Asian woman who was probably half his age.

Ron smiled at the professor. "Glad you invited me."

"Oh, we like to have these little get-togethers a couple of times each semester. Keeps things interesting." He chuckled. "I don't want you to think it's going to help your grade any, though."

"I wasn't counting on it."

"Oh, I forgot. Have you met my wife?"

Both Ron and Ruth shook their heads.

"This is Miyako. She was one of my grad students a few years back. Met her at one of these parties, actually."

Miyako smiled, nodded. "Pleased to meet you."

Ron nodded back, smiling as well. He caught himself staring at the woman. He tried to look away, but he couldn't. Dr. Coulter was quite an impressive man, intelligent, well spoken, charismatic. But it was still hard to believe that he rated a woman like Miyako. She was, hands down, the single most beautiful woman Ron had ever seen. She looked like a fashion model, only better. There were none of the flawed features that were usually exposed when a model was seen from a different angle. No matter how Miyako turned, no matter how she moved, she was flawless.

Miyako stared back at him, her eyes flicked to his crotch, then back again. Her smile widened.

Ron felt Ruth's fingernails digging into his palm.

She must have noticed.

He looked away.

"Make yourselves at home," the professor said. "There're drinks and appetizers in the kitchen. Take what you want. The festivities won't be starting until a little later." He looked behind them. "More guests. I have to greet them." He gave Ruth a quick kiss on the cheek, patted Ron on the shoulder. "I'll talk to you later."

Miyako also touched Ron's shoulder as she walked by, lightly.

"She sure seems awfully friendly," Ruth said.

Ron grinned. "Jealous?"

"No."

"Good. Come on. Let's get something to drink."

The kitchen was crowded, too crowded. Ron grabbed a Coke for himself and a beer for Ruth and was about to go back into the living room, but Ruth had found a friend of hers and was talking, so he handed her the beer and left the kitchen alone. A quick perusal of the living room told him that there was no one here he knew. He wasn't really in the mood to meet new people, so he moved to the edge of the room and parked himself there, nursing his Coke.

He glanced out the window at the small canyon, at the golden grass on the hillside, shaded red by the setting sun, at the blue-black shadows creeping upward from the floor below. Not a bad view. Not a bad area.

He wouldn't mind living in a place like this himself someday.

Especially if he could have a wife like Miyako ...

There was a light tap on his shoulder, and he turned around, and there was the professor's wife.

He was stunned into silence, not sure of what to say.

"It's going to be starting soon," she told him. She spoke with a very slight Japanese accent. "Do you want to be the first?"

"The first what?" he asked.

"The first to fuck me."

He blinked, thought for some reason of the Den Mother, the Adversary.

"It's better to be first. It is messy later."

The conversation wasn't registering. She was asking him if he wanted to have sex with her, and she stood before him in a tight, revealing gown, the most beautiful woman he had ever met, but she was asking him to be the engineer on a group of guys pulling train, the first guy in a gang bang, and he was hearing this, talking it over with her calmly, but it was as though he was disassociated from it all, as though he was overhearing this exchange, not participating in it.

"I'd love to fuck you," he found himself saying.

"Then get by the piano. That's where the line starts."

Lights dimmed, conversation stopped, there was the sound of a gong. Between heads, over shoulders, Ron saw Dr. Coulter, dressed now in some sort of black Japanese robe, holding a small padded drumstick. The still-sounding gong was on top of the piano.

"It is time," the professor said.

Miyako touched Ron's hand, gave it a small squeeze, then made her way through the crowd toward the professor. A line was already starting to form, and Ron moved forward, pushed his way into it. He wasn't first, he wasn't second, but he was third. He glanced around the room, looked toward the kitchen, searching for Ruth, but she was nowhere to be seen.

He turned back toward the piano, and Miyako was stripping. Naked, she was even more beautiful than he would have thought. Her breasts were small, the dark nipples large and perfectly formed, and the thatch of down between her legs was enticingly, sensuously sparse.

She leaned back onto the piano bench, spread her legs in the air, grabbed onto her ankles with her hands and pulled her legs over her head until her open vagina was facing outward.

Dr. Coulter grinned. "First come, first served," he said. He chuckled. "Or should I say first served, first come."

The guy at the front of the line, a dorky-looking student who could not have been more than eighteen, was already unbuttoning his pants, taking out his penis.

He crawled on top of Miyako.

Dr. Coulter watched, grinning. It was over in a few minutes, and then the second man climbed onto her.

Ron stood there, waiting. Part of him was disgusted, part of him was outraged, but part of him was also excited, and he found himself unbuckling his belt, unbuttoning his pants, unzipping his fly, to free his growing erection.

"Next," the professor said cheerfully.

The man in front pulled out and off of Miyako, and Ron stepped up to the piano bench. He let his pants fall to his ankles. Miyako was smiling up at him from between her knees, and he looked down at her and he suddenly felt empty and sad, so sad that tears were welling in his eyes. He was one of probably fifteen people in line, but he felt alone, more alone than he had ever felt in his life. These weren't his people.

This wasn't him.

He pressed his erection against Miyako's wet opening. His penis slid easily in.

He began pumping.

Two minutes later, it was over, and he was buttoning his pants and moving to the rear of the room, looking for Ruth. All of the other girls and women seemed to be clustered around the kitchen and the largest window, talking, drinking, eating, pretending as though nothing unusual was happening, but Ruth was nowhere to be found.

The bathroom. Maybe she was in the bathroom.

Sure enough, she emerged from the hallway, five minutes and three men later. He waved to her, but she ignored him, and, embarrassed, guilty, he did not make an effort to go after her, to explain.

He looked again toward the scene at the piano, wandered back over.

Miyako, between men, saw him, smiled. She put her legs down. "I am tired," she said to her husband.

"My wife is tired," Dr. Coulter repeated loudly. "Would anyone like to take her place?"

"I will."

It was Ruth's voice.

Ron wanted to object, wanted to tell her she couldn't, wanted to grab her and drag her the hell out of this place, but there were too many people around and he did not want to make a scene in front of them, and he watched as she stepped up to the piano bench, pulled off her top, pulled down her pants.

She knelt on top of the bench, on all fours.

"Get her while she's hot!" the professor announced.

Ron watched as the older man in the front of the line pulled down his pants, took out his unusually large penis, and shoved it into her.

This was not the way it was supposed to be. This was not what was supposed to happen. They were supposed to have come here for drinks and intellectual conversation. They were supposed to—

Ruth cried out.

He did not know whether it was in pain or pleasure, but something within him shrank at the sound. He turned away, went back over to where the women stood talking.

Miyako caught up with him in the kitchen as he grabbed himself a beer. She smiled at him. "Did you like it?"

He wanted to punch her in the face, but instead he nodded tiredly. "Yeah," he said.

She took his hand. "Come on."

"What?"

"They're almost done."

He followed her back into the living room. Ruth was already getting dressed. He saw the glint of wetness on her legs, did not know whether it was sweat or sperm.

Everyone was gathering around now, men and women, and Miyako led him through the crowd to the front, where Dr. Coulter was placing a thick bundle wrapped in Japanese silk.

The pressure of Miyako's hand on his increased. He saw excitement on her features, anticipation.

Ron experienced a sick, almost nauseous feeling in the pit of his stomach. Again he thought of the Den Mother, thought of the Adversary.

The professor unrolled the silk. A collection of knives spread out along the top of the piano.

He turned toward the assembled partygoers, grinned. "Now," he said, "it is time for the bloodgames."

ELEVEN

CAMPUS CRIME STATISTIC SUMMARY REPORT
OCTOBER 10

Crimes Reported	Semester to Date	Year to Date	Previous Year Total
Assault	24	59	26
Auto Theft	22	25	9
Rape	10	25	12
Robbery	256	1,135	903
Vandalism	14,199	25,203	10,087

TWELVE

1

"The bookshelves of the library are stacked row upon row, in endless order, through the top three floors of the building, the rows running parallel to the recessed white bars of fluorescent light in the ceiling. The books themselves are arranged in mathematical progression, letters to numbers to dates. Here history segues neatly into philosophy, philosophy just as neatly into political science, and on and on and on. Everything looks so nice, so orderly, so reasonable. And everything is nice and orderly and reasonable. With the exception of the computer science books, strewn about every which way by overzealous computer freaks.

"And the sixth floor."

Faith stopped writing, reading back what she had written. The words had flowed quickly and easily, her pen fairly flying over the lined yellow paper, and they had come so fast that she was not sure they made any sense. Looking over the paragraph now, she saw that the words fit smoothly together, the sentences creating a sort of natural rhythm.

She was surprised. She had signed up for Creative Writing only because it was a junk course, an easy A, and she'd figured it would balance out the harder classes and give her a decent GPA. Before this she had penned a few poems, started a few godawful adolescent essays with titles like "On Love" and "Art," but the words had always come hard and slowly, the end results only marginally readable even after extensive polishing and rewriting.

But now, for some reason, her thoughts were clear, the ideas coming to her fully articulated, translating instantly and perfectly to the page. It was wonderful, but it was spooky in a way. It was almost as though she was a conduit through which these words were being transmitted, and she wondered if this was how those artists felt who claimed that they were simply a medium for the message, that their works originated not with them but with some divine inspiration.

Equally unnerving was the fact that she had never written anything even remotely horrific before—her poems had been either sweet-and-light sonnets or trendy pseudo-beat free verse reflecting contemporary concerns. This, however, was the beginning of a horror story. No, not merely the beginning. In her mind she had the entire story completed, and as she thought about it, her attention skipped to individual descriptions, individual phrases, coming to rest at the hard-hitting last line of the piece.

She thought of stopping here, going to bed, finishing the story in the morning before going to school, but she knew she couldn't do that. She wouldn't have time. She was scheduled to read her work tomorrow, and she had to make copies for each member of the class.

Besides, she had the creepy feeling that the story would remain in her brain as is, waiting to be tapped, no matter how long she put off the actual act of writing.

She reread what she'd written, then picked up her pen again.

"*I don't know what it is about the sixth floor that first brought it to my attention,*" she began.

And she was off.

Keith arrived home while she was typing the story, pounding away on her mom's old typewriter in the living room. She looked up as he came in. He'd gotten a haircut, shaved off the hair on the left half of his head, combing the long right half over the baldness. It looked ludicrous, but she said nothing to him, only watched as he dumped his latest batch of books on the couch.

"Still running the race, huh?" he said.

"It's called getting an education."

He shrugged. "The education they tell you you should get is not necessarily the one you *should* get."

"Spoken like a true record store clerk."

He looked at her, almost said something, then walked into the kitchen.

Faith was immediately sorry that she'd opened her big mouth. Why did she have to get down on him like that? Wasn't it bad enough that their mom was on his case all the time? She sat there, not typing, turning back toward the kitchen. She'd seen the hurt on his face, and she felt sick inside knowing that she had caused it. He was young, immature, that was all. It wasn't a crime. His pseudo-intellectual phoniness might tick her off sometimes, but she shouldn't overreact. She should be able to handle it.

She thought for a moment, then stood, walking into the kitchen. Keith was drinking orange juice from the pitcher in the refrigerator. He looked up as she entered. "Going to yell at me now for not using a glass?"

She shook her head, wanting to apologize but knowing she couldn't. That wasn't the way things worked between them. She opened a cupboard, took out a can of Pringle's she didn't really feel like eating. "Where's Mom?" she asked.

"Who knows?"

"She's been awful hard on you lately."

"What else is new?"

They looked at each other. Everything was okay.

Keith finished off the juice and put the empty pitcher in the sink. "How many guys you think Mom's fucked?"

"Keith!"

"Come on, you know what she is just as much as I do. How many guys?"

Faith shrugged, shook her head. "I don't know."

"You think she . . . screwed around on Dad?"

"No." The denial was immediate and heartfelt. Many times she'd asked herself the same question, gone over in her mind what life had been like back then, and always she had come back to the same conclusion.

"You think she'd be like this if Dad was still here?"

"I don't know. I don't think so. I think . . . I think she was pretty young when it happened. I don't think she knew how to deal with it."

Keith nodded. He stole a handful of chips from her Pringle's can, then walked out of the kitchen and down the hallway to his bedroom. She heard his door close.

She stood there for a moment, then put away the Pringle's and went back out to the living room to finish typing her story.

She left the house early the next morning, skipping breakfast and stopping by Kinko's to make copies of her story before going to Algebra, her first class.

Walking from the Physical Sciences building to Neilson Hall, she began to get nervous. She didn't like reading in front of people, particularly not something she'd written, and the confidence in her work that she'd felt the night before had fled.

She read as she walked, going over what she'd written, looking down at the top page in her hand, and though she thought she could see where she was going, thought she could catch upcoming obstacles in her peripheral vision, she did not see the student crossing in front of her, and she bumped squarely into him, her outstretched hands hitting his shoulder.

She looked up, embarrassed. "Excuse me," she said. "I'm sorry."

The boy looked at her with flat, emotionless eyes. "Fuck you, bitch."

She watched him walk away, continuing on his path to the Social Sciences building. He bumped into someone else, another guy, and the other guy shoved him. He shoved back. Within seconds they were fighting.

What was it with this place?

She turned away from the fight, tucked her papers under her arm, and hurried across the quad toward Neilson Hall.

Any secret hope she might have held that large segments of the class would be absent today were dashed when she walked into the room, saw that it was full, and took one of the few empty seats in the front row.

Dr. Emerson smiled at her as she sat down. "Ready?"

She shook her head, tried to appear more confident than she felt. "No, but I can fake it."

"Dr. Emerson!"

They both looked toward the rear of the class, where a pale young man in the back row was waving his upraised arm.

The instructor nodded. "Yes, Mr. Keeler?"

"I'm going to be absent next class, and I was scheduled to read then. Could I switch and do mine today?"

"That's fine with me, but it's really up to Ms. Pullen here." He looked down at Faith. "What do you say? Is it all right if we trade, let Mr. Keeler go today?"

She looked back at the pale student in the rear, and she didn't feel the relief she should have at being let off the hook for another session, but she nodded anyway. "Sure."

"Did you make copies?" Dr. Emerson asked the young man.

"Uh, no. I forgot."

"Well, maybe we should postpone you until the class when you return—"

"It's a short story. I can read it now and leave copies in your box and you can pass them out next time."

There was something in the other student's voice, a hint of desperation, that made Faith more than a little uneasy.

Dr. Emerson thought for a moment. "Okay," he agreed. He glanced up at the clock. "We might as well start now. You ready?"

"Yeah."

The instructor nodded. "Go ahead. The floor's yours."

"Do I have to stand in front of the class? Or can I read from my seat?"

"Whatever makes you feel more comfortable."

The student glanced around the room. His gaze settled for a moment on Faith, and her heart began pounding. There was something familiar in his expression, something she couldn't put her finger on, something that set her nerves on edge.

He smiled at her, then looked down at his paper. "The books in the library," he began, "are stacked row upon row, in endless order, through the top three floors of the building . . ."

Faith's mouth felt dry as she heard her own words read aloud. Her hands, on the top of her copies on the desk, were shaking.

". . . The books themselves are arranged in mathematical progression, letters to numbers to dates. . . ."

2

"It was creepy," Jim said.

Faruk shrugged. "So you got a teacher who's a bigot. What else is new?"

"That's not it. It was ..." He tried to think of some way to describe the surrealism of the scene, the horrifying matter-of-factness that had accompanied the wild implausibility. "It was the fact that everyone else just accepted it, that no one noticed that anything weird was going on. Except Elvin. I mean, this guy was off the deep end. And he was doing things that could get him, if not fired, at least in serious trouble. And no one cared."

Steve snickered.

Jim glared at him. "What's so funny?"

"You. All this PC, touchy-feely shit. This is a university. You're a journalism major. Ever hear of freedom of speech?"

"This wasn't a free-speech issue."

"Then what was it?"

"You had to be there. It was ... weird."

Steve snorted. "Yeah. Right."

Jim looked at him. "Are you through with your page?"

"Fuck off, Jim."

"What?"

"It's none of your business. My page is my responsibility."

"None of my business? I'm the editor. I'm *your* editor."

"Eat me."

Steve's tone was not light and bantering but serious, sneering, and Jim had to fight back the urge to haul off and roundhouse him.

What the hell was happening here? He looked around the newsroom at his staff. Most of them had worked together last semester and had gotten along famously. But this semester ... this semester things were falling apart. Cheryl was off in her own world, Steve was becoming belligerent, Faruk's laid-back attitude was edging closer to apathy, and the other editors, when they bothered to show up, were edgy, short with each other and with their reporters.

Things have changed.

Howie was right. Things *had* changed. He didn't know when it had started or why it was happening or even what it *was*, exactly. But he knew it was happening, and it scared him. Maybe Howie was on to something. Maybe there were certain times for certain events. The social upheaval of the sixties had had no single catalyst, it had just . . . happened. Maybe this was the same.

No, that was stupid. He was overreacting.

He looked at Faruk, who shrugged and turned away. "What can you do?"

He could threaten to kick Steve off the paper, that's what he could do. He could talk to Norton, get the adviser to side with him on this, maybe get him to threaten Steve with a lowered grade. They could use authority to restore some order in this newsroom.

He walked past the empty sports desk, past the graphics desk, to the adviser's office. The door was shut, but he opened it without knocking and closed it behind him. "We have to talk," he said.

Norton was seated behind his desk. He looked bad. Really bad. Jim had not noticed the adviser's condition before, but then he hadn't seen him that much this semester. During the spring Norton had been in the newsroom almost as often as he himself had. And he'd been pitching in, rewriting stories that were not up to snuff, redesigning page layouts that had been overtaken by events—working, not merely offering advice. But this semester he'd seldom been found even in his office, and on the rare occasions when he did show, he holed up like he'd been doing this afternoon, hiding from the staff, not talking to anyone.

Now Jim looked at him, concerned. "Are you okay? Are you sick or anything?"

The adviser shook his head, tried to smile, though it looked more like a grimace. "Nah, I'm fine. Just a little tired is all."

Jim nodded. Norton was sweaty and twitchy, like a bad impressionist doing Anthony Perkins. It was disturbing just to look at him, and Jim found himself focusing on a spot above the adviser's head instead of making eye contact. "We need to talk."

"Shoot."

"I, uh, think you need to be a little more involved in the day-to-day activities of the newspaper. You've kind of stepped back a little this semester, and some of the students seem to think that this means they can do whatever they want—"

"They can." Norton grinned.

"But I think they need to see that—"

"What's the matter, Jim? Can't handle it?"

"It's not that."

"What is it, then?"

Jim forced himself to look straight at the adviser. He was still grinning, but the grin had been in place too long and was fading at the edges, disappearing into the taut muscles of the sweaty cheeks. "Norton ..." he began.

"I'm resigning," the adviser said. "I've already told the dean." His grin disappeared, replaced by a more natural-looking tiredness.

"Why?"

"*I* can't handle it anymore."

Now it looked as though the adviser was about to cry. Jim wondered if Norton was having some type of nervous breakdown. "Do you want to talk? Do you need—"

"I need you to get out of my office!"

Jim backed up, found the doorknob with his hand. "Okay, okay." He opened the door, smiled apologetically, stepped out.

Steve was standing by the graphics table, smirking. "Didn't get very far, did you?"

Jim turned on him. "You're fired. Clean out your fucking desk. You're off the paper."

The smirk disappeared. "Hey!"

"You heard me."

"I was just joking! Jim!"

"You're out of here," Jim said.

He did not look back as he strode across the newsroom to his desk.

3

"Hello, Dr. Emerson."

Ian nodded to Maria as he walked past the secretary's desk through the English department office toward the mailboxes. "How's it going, Maria?"

"It would go a lot easier if you'd give me your schedule. It's been a month already. Students keep calling, asking about your office hours, and I can't tell them."

"Sorry," he apologized. "I forgot. I'll get it to you today."

"I've heard that one before."

There were several pieces of mail in his box, and Ian stuck his hand into the cubicle and pulled them out. He sorted through them, standing next to Maria's desk, tossing those that he didn't want into her wastebasket: an ad for a new English textbook on the Romantic period, a brochure about some computer software program, minutes of the last faculty council meeting.

What was this? An overstuffed envelope bearing his name that had obviously been hand-delivered. Curious, he opened it. Inside was a map of the university. Beneath that map were other maps, structural drawings of building floors and plumbing and electrical systems that he could only assume were schematics of the university buildings.

On each drawing there were two or three red X's, clearly marked.

He turned toward Maria, showed her the envelope, the maps. "Who delivered this, do you know?"

She looked, shook her head. "No one's delivered anything here today. Must've been last night."

Underneath the maps, the drawings, was yet another paper, this one a list of chemicals. He scanned the list, read through the short paragraph of text below it. This was a formula, a recipe, and though it didn't spell out what this was for, he assumed from the word *glycerol* that these were instructions on how to make explosives.

He scanned back through the drawings, at the red X's. Was this a bomb threat? Were these places where bombs had been planted on campus?

He quickly folded the pages. He'd have to take this to the police, let them decide what—

"Dr. Emerson?"

He looked up.

Maria pointed toward a small white slip of paper on the floor. "That fell out of your mail."

He reached down, picked up the paper. "Plan for Destroying the Evil" was typed on top of the small square.

Underneath that, in a barely legible scrawl, were three words: "Will call soon."

Underneath that were initials: "G.S."

G.S.

Gifford Stevens?

The bio on the back of the anthology said that the man was an expert in demolitions.

This was too weird. Ian reread the note, looked over the drawings and the bomb recipe. He knew he should still turn this in to the police, tell them what he knew, hand over Stevens' "dissertation." Obviously, the man's plan was to blow up the school. And, just as obviously, he wanted Ian to help him.

But something held him back, something kept him from going to the police, and he refolded the pages, put them back in the envelope, and walked out of the department office to his own office down the hall. He sat down at his desk, thought for a moment, then took out the list of chemical names. From his middle drawer he withdrew his copy of the UC Brea Faculty Phone Directory.

He called Ralph Scofield, in the chemistry department, to find out if this really was a recipe for a bomb.

He stopped at Carl's Jr. on the way home, picked up a western bacon cheeseburger, some criss-cut fries, and an extra-large chocolate shake.

He still felt guilty buying junk food like this.

The Sylvia influence.

He ate his dinner in the car, at the stoplights, and by the time he pulled into the driveway ten minutes later, he was done.

He had not called the police. He had started to—several times throughout the day. But in the end he had not reported Stevens to the proper authorities, and he was still not sure why. The recipe was indeed for a very powerful explosive, and other, more subtle questioning of several maintenance employees had revealed that explosives placed at the marked locations on Stevens' schematics would definitely do the most possible damage.

Yet he had not told anyone.

He didn't want to believe it, didn't want to think

about it, but it seemed pretty obvious that, on some level at least, he bought in to Stevens' theory.

That was scary.

He went inside, tossed his trash in the kitchen, poured himself some cold water from the pitcher in the refrigerator, and went into the living room to call Eleanor. She wasn't home, but she'd left him a note on her answering machine, saying that she was coming over and was already on the way.

The living room was still a mess from this morning—newspapers scattered about, breakfast dish and glass on the floor next to the couch—and he quickly cleaned up, putting the plate and glass in the dishwasher, bagging up the newspapers and placing them next to the garbage cans outside for recycling. He returned to the living room, looked around, straightened a few pillows, then sat down on the couch and flipped on the television, pretending as though he'd been relaxing here in this neatly kept room since arriving home.

Thank God he'd had junk food for dinner.

He looked at the clock. It was on the hour, but it was prime time. He'd missed both the local and national news broadcasts, so he flipped the channel to CNN.

"Tonight's top story," Bernard Shaw said. "A bomb blast at the University of Mexico killed ten and injured at least forty-three others." Videotape showed a multistory building with one wall gone, several floor interiors exposed. Rescue workers were digging through the rubble on the ground, and ladders led to the stories above. It looked like one of the scenes after the earthquake a few years back.

"We have on the line Dr. Gifford Stevens, an American demolitions expert who happened to be visiting the university when the explosion occurred." The screen shifted, and Stevens was standing in front of a crumbling brick wall, a microphone in his hands.

Ian felt suddenly cold.

The screen shifted back to Bernard Shaw. "Good evening, Professor. I understand that you were in the affected building at the time of the explosion."

Stevens nodded, and to Ian it looked as though he was trying to hold back a smile. "Yes, I was, Bernard. And let me tell you, I've never felt anything like it."

"You are a demolitions expert?"

"Yes, I am."

"Do you have any idea what might have caused the blast?"

"It's too early to tell, of course, and we won't know for sure until we examine the point of detonation—"

The doorbell rang, and Ian jumped.

". . . would guess that it's some sort of plastic explosive, perhaps the type used in—"

The doorbell rang again, and Ian got up to answer it, keeping one ear on the newscast as he hurried toward the entryway.

"Thank you, Dr. Stevens. As we said, there are ten reported dead, another forty-three injured. We will continue to update this story as details arrive. In other news . . ."

Eleanor smiled at him as he opened the door, her smile fading as she saw the expression on his face.

What was the expression on his face?

"What is it?" she asked, her hands reaching out to touch his cheeks. "Are you all right?"

He almost told her.

He almost told her everything: Stevens, the "dissertation," the formula for explosives, the map of the university's structural weak points, the newscast.

But at the last moment he pulled back, pulled away, took her hands in his and smiled. "I'm fine," he said. "Just tired."

He closed the door as she walked inside, and led her into the living room.

THIRTEEN

1

After putting the paper to bed and sending Stuart to take it to the printer, Jim thanked the staff for putting out another solid issue and walked alone across the parking lot to the dorm.

Another solid issue.

Another rape. A follow-up on the molestation charges. An AWOL professor who hadn't showed up since the first week of classes and whose disappearance was being investigated by the FBI.

Just a typical day at UC Brea.

It was amazing how quickly human beings became inured to horror, became used to the unusual. He had always seen himself as a caring, sensitive person, and he had never thought that he'd be one of those journalists who was so jaded that injury and suffering would no longer affect him. He had never been able to see himself participating in something like a death pool, betting on how long an assassination target would hang onto life after being shot and placed in intensive care.

But today he'd found himself rearranging the front page to accommodate the late-breaking rape story and not thinking about the rape at all, seeing the assault as only an element of composition for his paper, not as a crime perpetuated on a fellow student.

Even now he could not find it in himself to identify with the plight of the victim.

And part of him was happy that the rape had occurred, supplying the paper with yet another great news story. If things continued this way for the rest of the semester or, even better, the rest of the year, the *Sentinel* might have a whole shelf full of awards to its credit.

What kind of thinking was this?

Practical thinking.

Awards and good work would help land him a decent job after graduation.

Graduation.

It suddenly dawned on him that this would be his last year of school, that after he completed his internship next semester, he would be expected to go out into the world and make a living. The thought was intimidating and more than a little frightening. He had known what he wanted to do with his life since high school, since he'd signed up for journalism class, and all of his subsequent education had been geared toward preparing him for this occupational goal. He was good at what he did—he received easy A's in both the writing and theoretical classes, and he'd been proving for two semesters that he was able to function under deadline pressure and make the right editorial decisions—but he still didn't feel ready to go out into the real world. He didn't feel prepared or qualified enough to take on the responsibilities of working on an actual newspaper. Despite his outward confidence, in the back of his mind was the thought that this was all play, practice, rehearsal.

Real life was different.

But real life was nothing like this. Rapes, assaults, molestation . . .

Well, maybe real life was like this. But though the acts might be the same, the reasons for their occurrence were not.

He thought of the professor he'd met at night outside Neilson Hall—

It's an evil thing

—and he thought about what Howie had said, and he thought about Faith Pullen's botany class animal sacrifices, and he thought about his own economics class and the uneasy feeling he'd had about Brea since even before the semester had started, and he realized that he bought in to it. Howie was right. That crazy old professor was right. His gut instincts were right. These weren't normal occurrences. There was something wrong with this school. There was something weird happening here. Maybe the university was haunted, maybe there was a scientific explanation, maybe . . . well, he didn't know. But something was the matter with this place, and it was affecting the students attending the school and the teachers teaching here.

It was affecting him.

He'd been happy that today's victim had been raped because it might help the *Sentinel* to win awards.

He thought of Cheryl and immediately felt guilty.

Whatever was going on, he had to be on his toes. He had to be aware of what was occurring and fight against it. He couldn't let himself be affected.

There was no one in the parking lot, although quite a few cars were still parked out here, but tonight he didn't feel afraid. The paranoia that had hit him before was absent, and he stopped for a second, turned around, looked at the tall buildings of the campus proper. He could see nothing unusual in the makeup of the university skyline, no hint of malevolence in the lighted windows of the classrooms, no clue that anything was amiss.

He started walking again toward the dorm.

He heard the dormitory before he saw it, a warring mix of rap and rock, underscored by the less rhythmic sound of student voices loudly talking. He walked between the double walls of overtall oleander bushes that ringed the parking lot, and emerged near the garage spaces below his room. He walked over to the stairwell, started up, thought for a moment, then turned back and walked around to the front of the first floor. He headed down the corridor to Howie's room and knocked on the door. "Howie! It's me!"

"Come on in! Door's open!"

He turned the handle, pushed open the door. Howie was seated in his chair in front of the television, Nintendo controls in his lap. Jim closed the door, walked in, looked at the screen. "You any good at that?"

"No, but it's supposed to help my motor control and my small-muscle coordination."

"Bullshit."

"Okay. I like playing games better than doing homework. Satisfied?"

"That's more like it." He glanced around the small, specially equipped room, saw that the bathroom was empty and that both beds were unoccupied. "Where's Dave?"

"A date."

"But what if you have to—"

"Take a shit?" Howie grinned. "I can hold it 'til he comes back. Although, it's good you showed up. I do have to take a wicked wizz."

"Come on. Don't do this to me."

"All you have to do is pick me up and hold me in front of the toilet."

"And take it out and point it."

He grinned. "Come on. You know you've always wanted to grab a handful of my manhood."

"Do you really have to go?"

Howie laughed. "No. I just thought I'd put a scare into you. Had you going there, didn't I?"

"Asshole." Jim plopped down on Howie's bed, leaned back. "I still don't understand why you don't just live at home."

"I told you, I want to be independent."

"But you're not independent. You have to have an attendant. And it seems to me that it'd be easier to have your family help you than a stranger. Cheaper too."

Howie's expression hardened.

Jim sat up. "Sorry. It's just that you said the M.D. was getting worse."

"I had a bad spell during the summer. I'm back to my ordinary old crippled self now."

No, you're not, Jim wanted to say, but he let it go.

"Look, if you just came over to harass me—"

"No, I didn't."

"Then what did you come over for?"

"I just wanted to hang."

The two of them were silent for a moment.

"I think you're right about Brea," Jim said finally.

Howie tried to turn his head, then gave it up and adjusted the position of his chair, backing up and moving forward until he faced the bed.

"A lot of weird shit's been going down."

He told Howie everything, from the beginning, starting with his not wanting to return to school this semester, ending with his feeling today that more violence on campus might make the *Sentinel* a better paper and help his career.

Howie nodded, his head bobbing up and down strangely. "The question is now: what are we going to do about it?"

"What can we do about it?"

"Have you talked to Dr. Emerson?"

Jim shook his head.

"Well, maybe you should. Or maybe I should. That guy you met might be a crank, but he might know what he's talking about. And it can't hurt to talk to Dr. Emerson."

"I had Emerson last semester for 301. He's a pretty good teacher."

"Talk to him, then."

Jim sat up. "What are we talking about here? Really? Is this place, like, haunted? Or is it . . ." He trailed off. "You know," he said, "in Arizona there's a theory that the reason everyone who goes into the Superstition Mountains looking for the Lost Dutchman goes crazy is because there's a high amount of magnetic rock in the mountains and the magnetic fields affect the brain. Maybe this is something like that. Maybe they're doing some sort of covert research in the physics lab. Maybe the government's funding some sort of defense project, and we've all been exposed to something that's making us act this way."

"Maybe," Howie said doubtfully.

"Then what do you think?"

"I don't know. But my mind's open. I'm not rejecting anything."

Jim stood. "I'll see Dr. Emerson tomorrow."

Howie smiled wanly. "In a sick way," he said, "this is going to be kind of fun."

"Yeah." Jim nodded. "It's like the Hardy boys or something, isn't it?"

They looked at each other, but neither of them smiled.

"Then again," Jim said, "maybe not."

2

After Faith's shift ended and she went home, Glenna had the sixth floor of the library to herself, and she sat on the cold tile, shelving art books. On the metal cart next to her were a hundred books with the same call letters which had been checked in during the past week. She hated art books. Many of them were oversized and did not fit properly on the shelves, and there were so damn many of them that the call numbers were very close together and other, stupider library workers were always misfiling them.

But she liked working in this section of the sixth floor. Here the bookshelves were stacked so closely together that there was no room for study carrels or tables or chairs. There were only books. So when people came here looking for something, they usually searched for a moment or so, took what they needed, then went to one of the other floors to read. Which meant that most of the time she was alone.

That suited her just fine.

After the hubbub of the hallways, after the great hordes of students all talking and pushing and forcing their way past one another in an effort to get to class, to get out of class, to go home, to get something to eat, the peaceful quiet of the library was welcome and refreshing.

Taptap. Taptap.

In the silence she heard clearly the sound of footsteps coming up the main aisle away from the elevator. No, not just footsteps. Bootsteps.

Cowboy boots.

She quickly stood up, brushing the dust off her jeans. She felt the muscles in her face tightening. She should have known he'd come by this morning to apologize, to make up. She began pushing the cart back down the row toward the shelving cage, against the far wall, but she was not fast enough. Calhoun caught her as she crossed the main aisle. He was wearing his usual straight-legged Levi's and flannel shirt, and there was an expression of humble apology on his face.

Neither of them said anything for a moment, Glenna looking at him in anger, he begging her with his eyes for forgiveness. It was he who spoke first. "I'm sorry," he said. "I was just—"

"Fuck off," she said coldly. She tried to push the cart past him, toward the cage, but he grabbed the other end with his hand and held it still.

"I was a jerk," Calhoun said. "I admit it. I should have called you and told you—"

"Two hours!" she exclaimed. Her voice, loud, sounded like a scream in the surrounding silence, and she forced herself to keep it low. "Two hours!" she said. "I waited there for two hours. I thought something had happened to you. Maybe you'd been in an accident or had been attacked by a mugger or something."

"I'm sorry."

"Then I call your house and find out that you went to a club with your asshole friends."

"I forgot! What can I say? I did try to get in touch with you later."

"Bullshit. I was home all night."

"Well, maybe you were asleep when I called."

"I waited in front of that damn restaurant for two hours."

"You already said that."

"Yeah? Well, I'll say it again. I waited two hours for you to show up." She peeled his hand from the cart and pushed it forward. "I'll give you a little helpful advice, Calhoun. Next time you ask someone out on a date, try to show up."

"Come on," he said. "You're not going to let a little thing like this ruin our relationship."

"What relationship? We don't have a relationship. We went out once; we almost went out twice." She reached the cage and opened the gate, pushing the cart inside and moving in after it. She slammed the gate shut behind her, locking it. She faced him through the wire mesh. She took a deep breath and forced herself to remain calm. "I don't want to talk right now, please go."

He stared at her for a moment, shaking his head. "I don't believe this."

"Please leave."

"This is the school library, not your house. You can't kick me out of here. You can't tell me what I can or cannot do."

"If you don't leave me alone, I'll call someone to remove you from the building."

He snorted. "Beat off, bitch. Where do you get off being so high and mighty? I have to listen to your fuckin' tirade, and then when you're tired of it, you tell me to get out or you're calling security. I don't believe you." He pushed his fingers through the mesh, pressing close. Glenna backed up. "I was wrong, I'm sorry, what more do you want me to do?"

"I want you to leave me alone."

"Fine," he said. He backed away from the cage. There was a funny pinched look to his face which made it appear as though he was almost smiling, though his voice when it came out was cracked. "I bet you were a lousy lay anyway."

He turned to go, then suddenly came rushing back. His fist slammed against the gate, causing the entire cage to shake. "Fuck you!"

Glenna walked purposefully toward the rear of the cage. "I'm calling the campus police," she said loudly and firmly.

"I'm out of here."

She stopped, listened.

Taptap. Taptap.

Glenna closed her eyes, backing against the far wall of the cage. She heard his boots retreat down the aisle but did not open her eyes until she heard the arrival of the elevator. She was trembling, she realized. Her hands were shaking. She felt like a coward. She had been mad at Calhoun, but not as mad as she'd led him to believe. And she'd waited closer to forty-five minutes than two hours for him last night. She was ashamed of herself, but she had used this situation to her advantage. His thoughtlessness had taken the burden from her shoulders, and she hadn't had to find a nice, kind way to tell him that she no longer wanted to go out with him. She found it easier to finish a relationship with a fight in which both of them ended up hating each other than she did with an "I'm sorry but . . ." story. Fighting made her feel less guilty, less like the aggressor, and it allowed him to feel as though he'd initiated the breakup, which she was sure was easier on his ego.

She didn't like to hurt people.

She was still trembling, and she looked toward the rear of the cage where she'd been heading. Thank God her bluff had worked. There was no phone in the cage, no way she could have called anywhere, and if he'd come in after her . . .

She hadn't expected him to get so crazy.

The question was, why did she keep going out with guys anyway? She wasn't interested. Appearances? Why should she care about appearances?

She did, though. That was the pathetic part. She hadn't even told her parents of her preference. Her parents? She hadn't even told her sister.

The sad thing was that maintaining this facade had kept her from having any sort of real relationship at all. She just playacted her way from one phony date to another.

She heard footsteps outside the cage and stiffened for a moment, listening, but the steps were softer than Calhoun's, tennis shoes, not boots, and she relaxed.

"This is getting to be a pretty violent place," a male voice said.

"Yeah," someone else replied. He chuckled. "Although I've seen a few babes here I wouldn't mind raping and leaving on the beach."

"I hear you."

"Did you ever have Southern for anthropology? Hell, I'd take her down and give her the hot beef injection if I thought I could get away with it."

The first student laughed.

Glenna leaned against the wall, unmoving, her heart pounding. What kind of conversation was this? She heard the two move away, down one of the aisles, and she thought about the professor who had assaulted Sue up here last week. Dr. Nicholson. She'd had him for World History her freshman year. He'd seemed normal, nice. She never would've guessed.

You couldn't tell.

She thought about Calhoun, thought about how far away she'd parked today, and wondered if he might be waiting for her somewhere between the library and her car. He knew what kind of car she drove. It was possible.

She shivered.

She was just being paranoid. She shouldn't think about this stuff. She'd get herself all worked up over nothing, and pretty soon she'd be afraid to step out of this cage.

She *was* afraid to step out of this cage.

She told herself she wasn't, pretended that she wasn't, started packing carts with books from the cage shelves and made herself believe that she was doing this work because it had to be done, but she did not leave until Phil came up a half hour later and told her it was time to take a break.

FOURTEEN

1

Richard saw the flyer at the same time he heard the crowd.

He'd been downstairs in the Club, eating lunch with Angelina, trying to subtly find out whether she'd ever had any secret fantasies about her friend Crystal, and when he emerged into the sunlight outside the Student Center, the bright red paper tacked to the bulletin board caught his eye.

"Rally Today," the flyer said. "ASB Presidential Candidates Will Speak at Noon in the Quad. Be Informed. Attend." At the bottom of the flyer was a small American flag.

From the general direction of the quad he heard the sound of people cheering.

Usually these things were announced way ahead of time, publicized on the campus radio station and in the *Sentinel*. But, to his knowledge, there'd been no advance publicity for this rally at all. He hadn't even seen the flyer when he'd gone into the Student Center earlier.

Jim hadn't told him about the rally, but maybe Jim hadn't known. It wouldn't hurt to go over there and take a couple photos—crowd shots, candidate shots—just in case.

He started toward the quad, taking a shortcut around the back of the bookstore. He unsnapped his lens cap as he rounded the corner of the library. The crowd was much bigger than he'd expected, much bigger than that of any previous rally he could remember, and he stood at its periphery and screwed a wide-angle lens on his Canon in order to capture the entire width and breadth of the gathering.

"*American* universities should be places where *American*

students can get an education," a thin, wimpy-looking speaker was saying. He was standing on one of the steps in front of the Administration building, speaking into a microphone connected to a portable sound system. "But when good, honest, loyal *Americans* are shut out in favor of Japs and gooks and camel jockeys and towel heads who can't even speak our fucking *language* ..."

A huge cheer went up from the crowd.

This was great. Controversy. Jim would definitely want pictures of this.

Richard maneuvered his way through the students until he was about fifty feet in front of the speaker and had a clear shot that would incorporate enough of the crowd to give a feel of its size.

"My name's Brant Keeler," the speaker announced, "and I'm running for ASB president on a pro-American platform. Some of you might be wondering what being pro-American has to do with the office of ASB president. Well, I'm going to tell you. Have any of you been denied student loans? I know a Jap in my algebra class who hasn't. Have any of you had to petition for a class because you could not get in, even though you signed up for it during pre-registration? That happened to me in one of my classes. Yet I know an Iranian towel head who got right in. Does this seem right to you? Does this seem fair?"

"Fuck no!" someone yelled.

"Fuck no!" Brant repeated. He laughed harshly. "These countries don't even have to go to war with us. We already give them everything they can possibly want." He paused. "But it is a war," he whispered into the microphone. "And some of us have *not* given up before we've started."

"Kill gooks!" someone yelled.

"Yes," Brant whispered. "Kill gooks."

"Waste Arabs!"

"Yes," he whispered. "Waste Arabs."

Behind Brant, at the top of the steps, a student emerged from the Administration building, an Asian student carrying an obviously heavy briefcase. Richard shifted his position, knelt down, aimed upward, got a picture of Brant speaking into the mike, the Asian student descending the steps behind him.

"Jap!" someone yelled.

Brant grinned.

"Jap!" the student repeated.

Others took up the cry: "Jap! Jap! Jap!" Fingers began pointing toward the steps behind Brant.

It appeared at first as though he hadn't heard, as though he didn't know what was happening and what was being said, but the second that the Asian student stepped onto the same stair level as Brant, the ASB candidate turned around and, in one smooth motion, grabbed the student's arm and knocked his briefcase to the ground.

The briefcase flipped open and papers flew out, scattering over the steps.

"Where do you think you're going?" Brant asked.

The student looked around, baffled. He took in the crowd, Brant. He tried to bend down and pick up his papers, but the candidate held him fast.

"I asked you a question, Jap. Where do you think you're going?"

The student tried to jerk away.

"I need some help here," Brant announced.

Three jocks rushed up the steps, grabbed the struggling student, held him.

"Kick his ass!" someone yelled.

Others joined in, yelling their own requests for physical injury, but "Kick his ass" had name recognition and a good rhythm going for it, and it soon became a chant, yelled in unison.

Richard changed lenses, putting on his zoom, and began snapping photos of individual faces. The rally was turning ugly, and the change in the crowd was almost palpable. Fervency was edging into fanaticism, and even those individuals on the fringes of the crowd who had merely stopped to watch were beginning to chant the refrain.

"Kick his ass! Kick his ass! Kick his ass!"

The girl next to him, a blonde with the wholesome good looks of a cheerleader, was yelling loudly, her pretty face contorted into a screaming visage of hate. Her eyes, the same eyes that probably misted over at the death of pets in family movies, were bright and glinting, angled into cruelty by her excited eyebrows.

He quickly stepped back, snapped a photo of her face.

He was running out of film, and he let go of the camera, adjusting the strap over his shoulder. He glanced around at the deteriorating rally, at the chanting students. The whole thing made him uncomfortable.

No, the whole thing *should have* made him uncomfortable.

But somehow it didn't.

Somehow it felt . . . right.

The Asian student tried to get away, tried to break free of the grip of the jocks, but the other students held tight.

"Let's humiliate him, the way he and his foreign *friends* have humiliated *us*!" Brant screamed into the mike.

The sound of ripping cloth could not be heard over the roar of the crowd, over the mingled sounds of rhythmic chanting and angry shouting, but Richard thought he could hear it anyway as he saw the jocks rip the boy's shirt. The action was accompanied by a loud cheer, and then the bullies were yanking his pants off, pulling down his underwear. The cheer grew in intensity as the Asian student began to cry.

"Cut off his cock!" the girl next to Richard yelled.

"We could do that," Brant agreed, answering her. "Or we could . . . *string him up!*"

"String him up!" the crowd roared.

Someone handed forward a rope, which was passed through the hands of the crowd until it reached the candidate. He tied it into a quick, makeshift noose and placed it over the naked boy's neck, holding the other end himself. The student was screaming for help now, kicking out at the jocks holding him in place.

Brant laughed. Holding his microphone by the cord, he swung the mike into the Asian student's crotch. There was a thump that was magnified through the speakers. Brant picked up the mike again. "Not much there, Jappo, is there?"

The crowd laughed.

Richard laughed. He didn't want to but . . . but, damn it, this was funny stuff. He glanced down at his camera. Four photos left. If he was lucky, they would hang the student. That would be a great shot. But there were no branches or beams overhanging the stairway, nothing over which the rope could be thrown. Either they'd have to move somewhere else, off the steps, or else they'd have to settle for a visually uninteresting strangulation. That would really fuck up his photo opportunity—

"The pigs!" a woman yelled behind him.

Richard turned to see a line of five policemen striding through the crowd toward the steps.

"Break it up," one of the cops was saying.

A rock hit the cop on the forehead.

The batons came out, the police marched forward, and suddenly things were being thrown from all directions, people were being pushed, punched, jostled.

A riot!

This was even better than a hanging.

Multiple injuries.

Blood.

Richard moved, climbed atop a concrete planter so he'd be able to get an above-angle shot of any downed students or policemen.

He saw a man punch one of the cops, saw the policeman swing out with his baton. He caught with his camera the exact second at which the baton struck the student's cheek.

God, this was great.

If only he'd had another roll of film with him.

2

"I thought we'd lead with the story on the new fences on Neilson Hall, maybe run a before and after photo, talk about the suicides over the years."

"Hey," Jim said, "that's good news judgment. We practically have a riot, police are brought in, and you want to lead off with a story about fences. I'm glad I picked you for this job."

Faruk reddened. "Okay, okay. I just thought that since we had a photo for this story, it'd look better as the lead, from a graphics standpoint—"

"We don't have any photos from the riot? You didn't send someone down there when you heard what was happening?"

Faruk licked his lips. "I was going to, but no one was around—"

"No one was around? If no one's around and something like that's happening, you get a camera from Photo and go out there and do it yourself."

"I'm sorry."

Jim shook his head. "Fuck."

Richard rushed into the Production office, grinning hugely. "I got 'em!" he announced. "Photos! And damn if there isn't a Pulitzer Prize winner in there."

"Photos?" Jim hurried over, pretended to hug him like a long-lost brother. "I love you!"

"That's 'cause you're a girly man." Richard pulled away. "How much space do I get?"

Faruk looked at Jim.

"Front page, seven by five, three columns, boxed." Jim quickly scanned the pages laid out on the light tables. "Another three inside."

"What size?"

"One three-column, two two-column. Four inches each."

"You got it."

Across the room, the production manager finished what she was typing and removed her disk from the machine, handing it to her assistant. "Look," she said. "I don't know what your plans are here, but the production deadline is in a half hour. Period. I have a lot of reading to do, and I'm sure other people do too. We don't want to spend the whole damn night working on the paper."

Jim looked at her. "You knew the hours were irregular when you signed up for this job."

"An hour I can understand. Every once in a while. But three hours? Four times a week? Come on! This isn't a real newspaper here. This is a school paper."

"This *is* a real newspaper. And it's the only newspaper that covers this community, the university. It's our responsibility to make sure that our readers receive timely news."

"You don't think this is going to be in the *Times*? The *Register*? Be serious. People can read about it there. Besides, it doesn't matter whether you have—"

"It matters to me," Jim said. "And I'm the editor."

"Maybe you need to get a life."

"Maybe you need to get a new job."

"Maybe I do."

They glared at each other.

"Hey," Howie said from the corner, "ease up, calm down, chill out."

Jim broke the stare-off, turning toward his friend. He sighed, tried to smile. "You're right," he said. He turned back toward Jean. "Look, I'm sorry. We're all under stress here. I didn't mean to take it out on you. If you have studying to do, go ahead. I'll finish up here."

The production manager stared at him for another moment, then slowly shook her head. "I'll do it. I just don't want this to become a permanent thing. I know a lot of shit's been happening lately, and that's great for you guys, and I hope you win a whole truckload of awards, but I really do have other classes."

"I know," Jim said. "So do I. And I've been letting them slide."

The wheelchair hummed as Howie moved into the center of the room. "What are we waiting for, then? We're all friends again. Let's get busy and get this sucker out."

"Within the hour," Jean said.

"Within the hour," Jim agreed. He turned back toward the editors. "If your pages are done, I want you out of here. The rest of you get your asses in gear."

Howie followed Stuart and Eddie toward the door. "I'm heading for home," he said. "My work is done."

"I'll stop by later," Jim told him.

"I'll be waiting."

"You're both girly men," Richard said.

"Get back in that darkroom and don't come out until we have photos!" Jim ordered.

"Later!" Howie called.

Jim waved a hand toward his friend as he turned away, following Richard into the darkroom to check out the shots.

The riot was on the eleven o'clock news.

One of the radio/TV/film students had had enough presence of mind to grab a videocamera when the melee began, and apparently he'd already sold the tape to Channel 2. Jim watched the news in Howie's room. He saw an overhead shot of the large crowd, obviously taken from one of the landings on the Physical Sciences building, then a zoom on one of the policemen being attacked.

"Jesus," Howie said. "I didn't realize it was that bad."

"Neither did I," Jim admitted.

"Four minor injuries were reported," the newscaster read. "Six arrests were made. University officials say that the disturbance was apparently racially motivated."

A small part of Jim could not help feeling envious as he watched the videotape. *There* was a student who was on the ball, who was ambitious enough to be adding to his resumé.

As usual, the paper would be a day late and a dollar short.

But Richard had gotten some damn fine pictures.

And their article had more facts in it than were being given out on the newscast.

A commercial came on, and Jim flipped the channels to see if any of the other local newscasts were covering the riot, but either the stories had already been run or the other channels were not devoting any air time to the incident.

He turned off the TV, staring for a moment at the darkening screen. He felt suddenly afraid for the campus. The fear and uncertainty he had experienced before had been more personal, more immediate, but somehow seeing the school on the news, looking at it through this objective, third-person viewpoint, made everything seem much bigger, increased the scope of it all.

He would talk to Dr. Emerson tomorrow, see if that weird professor was right, if Emerson did know what was going on.

"Still think this is normal?" Howie asked.

"I never said it was normal."

"What do you think it is?"

"I don't know."

They were silent for a moment.

"Turn on some tunes," Howie said finally. "It's too quiet in here."

Jim stood and walked over to the bookshelf, glancing through the small stack of CDs on top of the paperbacks. "What sounds good?"

"Anything."

He picked out a CD by The Judybats and put it on the stereo. Seconds later, the catchy guitar strains of "Down in the Shacks Where the Satellite Dishes Grow" came strumming through the speakers.

"Oh," Howie said, "I almost forgot. When you were in Production, some girl stopped by the newsroom with an editorial she said she was supposed to give you. I put it on your desk."

"Why didn't you send her into Production?"

"Why? All the pages were filled."

"Shit."

"Ah-ha." Howie grinned.

"Did she ask about me?"

"As a matter of fact, she did. I told you her were busy but would get back to her. She said she'd stop by tomorrow."

"Good." He looked over at his friend. "Stop grinning like an asshole."

"How come you didn't tell me about her?"

"Nothing to tell. I'm just thinking of asking her out, that's all."

"Do it," Howie said.

"The only thing is, she's in my English class. If things don't work out ..."

"If things don't work out, you move to the other side of the room. BFD."

"It is a big deal."

"I wouldn't know," Howie said wryly.

Jim was silent for a moment. "How come you never try to ask anyone out?"

"Yeah. Right."

"I'm serious."

"What's the point?"

"What do you mean, 'what's the point?' "

"Because I don't want anyone to get attached to me. I'd only die on them. Is that clear enough?"

"But I'm attached to you."

"I always did have my doubts about you."

Jim tried to smile. *I'd only die on them.*

The school. Howie. The whole world was turning to shit.

"I was only joking," Howie said. "Don't take it so seriously."

Jim shook his head. "I'm not," he said, but he knew Howie knew that he was lying. "I'm not."

3

On her way home from school, Faith stopped for gas at the Texaco station on the corner of Imperial and Campus Drive. There were no cars at any of the other islands, and the owner, a middle-aged Middle Eastern man, walked over to unlock her pump as she unscrewed the gas cap on the VW.

"Good evening," he said.

She smiled at him, took the nozzle from the pump. "Hi."

"You are a student?"

She nodded as she started pumping gas.

"At Brea?"

"Yeah."

"Were you there at the riot?"

She shook her head. "I heard about it, though."

The man sighed. "I do not like that school. There is something wrong with it."

Faith did not respond, but she looked at the attendant's grave expression and felt a lightening within her, almost as though someone had offered to share a heavy burden that had been hers and hers alone. It was creepy to hear someone say that about Brea, but in a way it was good. If it was obvious even to an outsider, then that meant that her own perceptions were not totally off the wall.

"To be honest with you," the man admitted, "I have never liked that school. My daughter went there for a semester before transferring to Irvine, and I found that campus a very uncomfortable place to be. She did not like it either. That is why she transferred."

"I know what you mean." The nozzle clicked, indicating that the gas tank was full, and the attendant took the hose from Faith, placing it back in its pump niche. The price on the pump was nine dollars and forty cents, and she handed him a ten. "This is my first semester, and I don't like it much either."

The man took sixty cents from the cash drawer next to the pump and handed it to her. "Be careful," he said.

"Careful?"

"A lot of accidents happen at that school. A lot of . . . violence happens there." He looked at her, and there was no hint in his eyes that he was anything other than dead serious. "I have been at this location for fifteen years now. A lot of things have happened at Brea during that time. Some years are worse than others, I have noticed. And this is the worst year I have seen yet. You are a nice girl. A nice, pretty girl. Be careful."

"I will," Faith promised, getting into the Bug.

The man nodded. He smiled at her, waved. "Have a good evening. Drive carefully."

She waved back as she pulled onto Imperial and headed toward the freeway.

It was late and there was very little traffic, but there was construction on the 55, and it was nearly an hour later before she finally turned off onto Seventeenth.

A heaviness settled over her as she drove, and she found herself wishing that the library was open twenty-four hours a day, wishing that she could afford to live on campus in one of the dorms.

Wishing she did not have to go home.

She drove past Bud's Meat Hut. It was night, but the smog was still visible: a faint haze, illuminated by the orangish yellow arc lamps, that made the air look grainy, like a photo blown up from a too-small negative. On the sidewalk, a gang of teenage boys wearing matching blue windbreakers were harassing a couple who were trying to get into their car.

God, she hated coming home.

They were arguing again, Keith and her mom. She could hear their screaming, angry voices as soon as she pulled into the driveway and stepped out of the car, though she could not make out the words. From down the street came the sound of another argument, in Spanish, and from the open windows of several houses blared amplified rap music and too-loud televisions. For a split second she considered getting back in the car and driving away, getting out of here and never coming back, heading east, using her mother's gas cards until they were cut off and then finding a job as a waitress or something in a small Midwestern town with white picket fences and happy families who always got along.

Then reality returned with the sound of breaking glass, and she hurried up the porch steps and into the house to see what was going on.

Inside, Keith was standing in the kitchen doorway, his face red with anger, a shattered drinking glass and a spreading puddle of milk on the tile floor at his feet. Her mom had obviously been sitting on the couch but was up now, standing, screaming, "I will not have you talking that way to me in my own house!"

Keith's voice was purposefully soft, goadingly even. "Really, Mom? Is that so?"

"Come on," Faith said, stepping between them. "I could hear you guys all the way outside."

"I don't care!" her mom yelled.

"What happened?" Faith asked.

"I came home and she was sucking some guy's cock."

"I will not have you speak to me like that!"

"Oh, you can do it, but I can't talk about it, huh?"

Faith felt sick. She'd intended to remain impartial, to stay out of it, to merely try to cool off the tensions between Keith and her mom, but she found herself automatically siding with her brother. Didn't that woman have any common sense at all? Didn't she know how to behave in front of her children? Couldn't she do that shit somewhere else?

"He's in the bathroom right now," Keith said. "Wiping off whatever she didn't drink."

"Get out of this house!" she screamed at him. "This is my house and you can't talk to me that way!"

He smiled coldly at her. "Fine, Mom, fine. If that's the way you want it. I'm out of here." He turned, walking through the kitchen and out through the side door.

"Keith!" Faith called. "Come on! We need to talk this out!"

"Not with that bitch!"

"Fuck him!" her mom said. "Ungrateful little shit!"

"Mom!" Faith pleaded.

"Fuck you too!" She threw herself down on the couch.

Was that where she'd been when Keith had come in on her?

Or had she been on her knees in front of the guy?

She stared for a moment at her mom. Why couldn't her mom have died and her dad lived? Things would sure as hell be a lot different now if that had happened.

A lot better.

She knew she should feel guilty for even thinking such a thought, but she didn't. It was true. She almost felt like saying it, like yelling it out loud to her mom, but she knew that right now the woman wouldn't even care.

She'd save it, though. Use it sometime when it would have an impact.

She even had her reply ready for whatever her mom's retort might be: "The truth hurts, doesn't it?"

"What are you staring at?" her mom demanded. "Go to your room. I have company."

Slut, she thought, but she didn't say it aloud, merely turned and started down the hallway toward her room.

The bathroom door opened as she passed it. The man who emerged, wiping his hands on his jeans, had a long blond ponytail and a thin mustache. "Ah, family feuds," he said. He smiled at Faith.

No, not smiled.

Leered.

She continued down the hallway to her bedroom, where she slammed the door and locked it behind her.

FIFTEEN

UNIVERSITY OF CALIFORNIA, BREA
CONTRACT EMPLOYEE ACCIDENT REPORT

Employer:_____

Name of Injured:_____

Age:_____ Married?:_____ Occupation:_____

Date of Accident:_____ 19_____ Time: _____

Nature of Injury:_____

Who Gave First Aid?: _____

Name and Address of Physician:_____

_____

Did Injured Leave Work?:_____ Date and Time: _____

Was Injured Acting In Regular Line Of Duty?: _____

Names of Witnesses:_____

Where And How Did Accident Occur?: _____

_____

_____

_____

_____

Date: _____ Supervisor: _____

SIXTEEN

1

It was supposed to be his office hour, but he wasn't really in the mood to talk to students about extra credit or makeup exams, so Ian closed and locked his office door, leaning back in his chair and kicking his feet up on the desk.

He had not been looking forward to this semester. Even without the weirdness, even without what Hunter Thompson would call the "bad craziness," it would have been a fairly miserable term on its own merits.

Hunter Thompson.

Did students still read Hunter Thompson? Did students still read? He stared at his bookshelves, scratched the growing bald spot on the top of his head. Who were the countercultural heroes of the current generation? In his day it had been Vonnegut, Heinlein, Brautigan. *Slaughterhouse-Five* and *Stranger in a Strange Land* and *Trout Fishing in America*. A few years back, it had been David Lynch. But were film directors now too esoteric for the post-literate generation? Were films too much like reading, too much like work, too difficult to understand?

Little Girl, Big Donkey.

What the hell was his problem?

The weirdness was part of it, definitely. Mixed in with everything, bound inexorably up with his personal problems, was the surrealism of the semester, the unexplained and unexplainable that seemed to have been dogging this campus since the beginning of the term. But that wasn't all of it, might not have even been most of it. A large part of this feeling, this malaise, was due to his own dissatisfaction with academia, with college life—a dissatisfaction that had been steadily growing for the past several years and was probably now nearing some type of crisis point.

But what else was there for him?

He had worked for a year in the real world, as a technical writer for Northrop during the interim period between graduation and the securing of a teaching position. He had seen how the other half lived and he had not liked it. His coworkers had been too busy with the minutiae of their jobs and the financial strictures of their lives to give anything but the most cursory thought to the larger questions and issues that affected their world, their existence. Many had been too busy to be conversant even in current events, though they were as adamant as the legitimately informed about the rightness of their beliefs and their electoral choices.

It had depressed him, that life. And it had scared him. What had scared him most was that he and Sylvia had been so easily able to slip into such an existence. They had fallen almost instantly into a routine: *up at six, in bed by ten; lovemaking on Wednesday night, Friday night, weekends.* The days passed, one like another, then the weeks, and though he knew it was happening, he was caught up in it and did not know how to extricate himself. *Movies on Saturday afternoon; grocery shopping on Sunday morning.*

It was only his belated acceptance at UC Brea that had rescued them from a lifetime of small, unchanging horizons and deadening, unending sameness.

Of course, it was Brea that had led to their breakup.

At first he had truly enjoyed the world of academia. In the beginning his new colleagues had seemed to him brilliant, heroic, alive, part of that vibrant intellectual universe he had thought about so often and to which he had aspired. The first year here, he'd been awed by the fact that his diligence and determination had paid off and that he was now part of the inner circle, invited to plays, to parties, to poetry readings, sipping cocktails with tweed-jacketed men who had met O'Neill and studied under Miller, pontificating with the best of them on Fitzgerald and Hemingway and their sublimated sexual bond.

But his enamoration with academia had been very short-lived. He soon discovered that the other English professors were neither as brilliant as he'd expected nor as interesting as he'd hoped. Like the rest of the world, they were mired in pettiness, bogged down with the smallness of their own lives, their glamorous facades merely a pale reflection, a secondhand acting out, of the same intellectual roles they had read about in novels, seen on screen. Away from the classroom, away from the party circuit, Rose Janeway, the department's resident Shakespearean scholar, was a neurotic mess, barely able to shop for her own clothes without help. Elizabeth Somersby, their D. H. Lawrence specialist, was a priggish, prudish woman who had never been married or, to Ian's knowledge, been on a date.

Only Buckley had survived to become a real friend, his cartoonishly extravagant vulgarity a welcome tonic to the arch pomposity of their fellow professors.

Still, his disdain for his colleagues had not prevented him from becoming enough like them to drive away Sylvia. He looked across his desk at the freestanding plaque she had given him one year: "Academia Corrupts and Absolute Academia Corrupts Absolutely."

Why had he kept that?

The phone rang, and he picked it up, grateful for any distraction from his self-pitying self-indulgence.

It was Eleanor. Her car was dead. She was fine, but she needed him to pick her up at Pep Boys after work. She'd already called Triple A and they were going to tow the car there.

"Pep Boys?" he said disapprovingly.

"You have any other suggestions?"

"No," he admitted.

"Well, since neither of us know anything about cars, and since Pep Boys is close to my office and on your way home, that's what I'm going with."

"Okay. What time?"

"Five?"

"I'll be there."

"Love you," she said.

"Me too."

He hung up the phone. There was a knock at the door, and he remained completely still, not moving, not breathing, hoping that whoever was out there hadn't heard him talking.

The doorknob rattled.

"Ian? I know you're in there."

Kiefer. Shit.

"Your door is supposed to be open and unlocked during your office hours."

Ian leaned back in his chair, unlocked the door. He swiveled toward the department head as the door swung open. "Sue me. I'm feeling crappy, and I've cancelled my office hours for today. I thought I could get some peace and quiet in the privacy of my own office without being harassed."

Kiefer suddenly looked concerned. "Should I come back later?"

Ian shook his head tiredly. "No. What is it?"

"We need to discuss your list of publications."

"Publications? Well, I'm writing an essay on Borges, Marquez, and *Nightmare on Elm Street* for the *Paris Review*."

"Be serious."

"I am being serious. The movie is a perfect example of the mainstreaming of a formerly elitist literary movement. Or, if you prefer, the Americanizing of a South American literary phenomenon."

"I saw that flick with my kids and it's a piece of shit. Get real, Ian. This isn't a joke. This is your career we're talking about."

"The influence of Trollope on *Basket Case*?"

"Goddamn it, Ian."

"All right, all right. What's the problem?"

"The problem is, your list of publications is awfully thin. You promised me last semester that you would try to beef up your output."

"I did try. I failed."

"Come on. What about your novel?"

"What novel?"

"The one you've been working on for the past five years."

Ian looked up at the department head. "You know, Ken, I've begun to think that the key to great art is not talent or ability but arrogance. I think that's why so much of our greatest literature is produced by young men. They have the arrogance of youth. They think they know everything, they're convinced their ideas are totally original. But as one gets older, as one learns more, he begins to realize how little he knows, how similar his ideas are to those that have come before. A great weight is placed on the act of creating."

"How do you explain Joyce, Proust, Lawre—"

"They were arrogant to the end. They refused to see the similarity between their work and the work of others. They thought they were totally original. In other words, they were poor critics."

"What you're saying is—"

"What I'm saying is that I'm a tired old fuck and I'm too burnt out to produce anything worthwhile at all."

"The world could always use another novel chronicling a jaded English professor's midlife crisis."

Ian laughed. "A joke. You actually made a joke. There's hope for you yet."

Kiefer smiled. "We'll discuss this later. But you're not off the hook. Pressure's being put on me, so I'm putting pressure on you. I need you to publish a minimum of two essays or analyses or one short story this semester." He backed out the door. "Think about it."

"I will." Ian kicked the door shut and let his chair fall forward again. He'd been talking off the top of his head, but he found himself wondering if maybe there wasn't something about institutions of higher education that stifled creativity. Or perhaps it was the lack of knowledge that came with youth and innocence that really did provide the impetus of creativity without fear. God knew that his fellow professors who'd started out as poets, playwrights, novelists, had bent and cracked under the weight of their literary forebears, trying in vain to equal the classics they taught, to gain respect from their fellow scholars. If they hadn't known what they were up against, they might have had the guts to produce something worthwhile.

He himself hadn't even tried to write so much as a review since Sylvia left.

Kiefer was right. For once. It was time for him to get off his dead ass and publish something.

"Publish or perish," he said aloud.

He stood, stretching. Through the window he could see, on the lawn below, a fight. Two young men were flailing away at each other on the grassy knoll between

Neilson Hall and the Hunger Hut. Instantly, immediately, the two were joined by other students, rushing in from all directions. One boy tripped the girl in front of him, punching the guy in front of her in the back. Yet another boy kicked the first one in the knees. More students arrived, and from up here it resembled a hockey fight or a baseball brawl, an ever tightening circle of bodies, everyone punching, kicking, clawing at random, wanting only to hurt, to connect with a body, not caring whose.

We have to kill the university. Before it kills us.

He watched the melee for another few minutes, watched the fighting intensify, not dissipate, watched the crowd grow, not disperse, and he turned away from the window, sitting heavily in his chair, feeling cold.

He thought for a moment, then picked up Gifford Stevens' "dissertation."

He leaned back in the chair, turned to the first page.

He started to read.

Ian finished reading and slowly closed the folder, placing it on his desk.

The university was alive.

That was Stevens' contention, that was the crux of his theory. The campus was not haunted, not cursed, not built upon sacred land or ancient burial grounds or any of those hoary old clichés.

The university was alive. It was a living, sentient entity.

The reason for this was not stated, was perhaps unclear even in Stevens' mind, but mixed in with the sophomoric philosophizing and the dull pretentiousness of the writing were some interesting observations and fairly original conclusions. Whether the cited incidents were true or not was debatable, but the events described were close enough to the unfolding situation here at Brea that either way the parallel was more than a little disturbing.

According to Stevens, over a four-year period an escalating pattern of violence had been charted at Sanderson College in New Hampshire, Oakhurst College in Florida, and Springfield State University in Illinois. All three schools had begun with an unusually high rate of crime in comparison with other learning institutions of comparable size and socioeconomic makeup, and each had experienced a sudden, noticeable increase in rapes, assaults, injurous hazings, suicides, and murders approximately two years into the study. During the last two years a combined total of twelve professors, thirteen staff members, and fifty students from the three schools had been placed in mental institutions. Fifteen instructors, ten staff members, and nearly a hundred students had been convicted on felony assault, rape, or murder charges and were serving time in prison. Another eight instructors, twelve staff members, and fifty students had been arrested but not convicted.

Strange statistics, to be sure. Overwhelming. But even more overwhelming, and much more frightening, was the anecdotal evidence that Stevens presented, the firsthand accounts of the horrific events that had supposedly taken place at the schools. At Sanderson College, a tightly knit group of Druidic tree-worshiping English, history, and philosophy professors castrated the male student with the highest GPA each semester for three straight years, nailing the student's severed genitalia to an elm tree in front of the campus in order to ensure health, happiness, and long life to members of the college community. At Oakhurst College, the football team, the basketball team, and two fraternities had conducted weekly human sacrifices in the gym. Enough blood had been gathered from the victims to fill the school's Olympic-sized pool to a depth of three feet, and the president of the college and his wife swam twenty laps in the blood and then copulated standing up at the five-foot mark to the cheers of the students as part of a ritual that was supposed to cure their daughter of Down's syndrome. At Springfield University, a group of fifteen visiting European immunologists attending a conference on AIDS research were gang-raped in the Health Center by a hundred HIV-positive students.

Those were the most spectacular events described, but there were more, much more, everything from reports of ghostly voices in libraries to school vehicles that ran on their own, and Stevens attributed everything to the schools themselves, which were, he claimed, living beings, creatures capable of both thought and action.

"The university," Stevens wrote, "is able to control

all variable factors within its proscribed borders, from class size to building temperature to insect population to rate of plant growth. Students, staff, and faculty invariably find themselves in the position of caretakers, catering to the whims of the increasingly mad and increasingly power-hungry institution: fighting, killing, dying, and procreating for its entertainment; offering themselves as food and sacrifice to a being that requires life for life."

The comparison he made was to HAL, the computer in *2001: A Space Oddyssey*, a conscious entity completely controlling its environment.

This was why, Stevens argued, the university had to be "killed." It could not be allowed to increase in power. It could not be allowed to "graduate" to a higher level. For that was its goal. According to Stevens' calculations, the rate of growth from sentience to independence was four years—the time in which a normal student earned a college degree. At the end of that time period, the university would evolve into something else. It would be on its own, free from the confines of the campus, virtually unstoppable. As a being without a body, an incorporeal personality, it would not be limited by the boundaries of its physical form. There would be no way to prevent it from growing, spreading out, taking over, say, an intersection, a shopping center, a subdivision.

A city.

The three schools in his study, he noted, had all "died" before the end of the fourth year.

Sanderson College had burned to the ground.

Oakhurst College had been destroyed by Hurricane Hugo.

Springfield State had been hit by a tornado.

They were all being rebuilt, but the buildings would be new, the grounds different. Whatever it was, whatever serendipitous intersection of design, location, and environment that had provided the catalyst for "life" was gone and could not be recaptured.

Ian vaguely remembered reading something about Sanderson College a few years back, but he could not recall hearing anything about Oakhurst or Springfield.

At the end of his paper, Stevens listed other schools that were being monitored, that exhibited, what he termed, "sentient tendencies."

One of them was the University of Mexico.

One of them was UC Brea.

Ian stared out his window at the smoggy white sky outside. The theory was ludicrous, of course, wilder than many of the premises in the horror fiction he was teaching this semester, but something about Stevens' stories and numbers gave him pause. There was no proof and very little support given to the central thesis, the idea that the university was a living being, but while the conclusions drawn might be incorrect, the manifestations of the ... evil could not be ignored. Whatever its source, whatever its purpose, evil had thrived at those three schools. And was thriving still at UC Brea.

Evil.

That was a word Stevens had not used in his "dissertation," though he had used it freely upon their meeting. Had something happened in the interim which had altered his objective perspective?

He thought of the man's ringless hand.

Had one of the universities killed his family?

There was a knock on the door, and Ian jumped.

He stood, embarrassed though no one had seen, and opened the door. The student who stood before him looked vaguely familiar, but he did not know if he had had the kid in a class or just seen him around campus, so he put on a bland, generic smile and said, "Is there something I can do for you?"

"Yes. My name's Jim Parker, and I'm editor of the *Sentinel* this semester, and ..."

"Yes?" Ian prompted.

"You probably don't remember me ..." Jim trailed off, shook his head. "I don't know how to say this, so I'll just come right out with it. Do you believe in ghosts, Dr. Emerson?"

Ian frowned. "I believe in them as a cross-cultural sociological phenomenon, as an element of folk tales worldwide, and as a very powerful, effective literary metaphor. But if you're asking whether I believe that there are physically such things as ghosts, I'm afraid I have to disappoint you and say no."

"You've never had any sort of supernatural experience?"

"No," Ian said slowly.

"You don't think something . . . weird's going on at this school?"

Ian looked at the boy, saying nothing, trying to ignore the unfamiliar fluttering in his stomach.

"The reason I'm asking is because I saw this guy, this professor, I guess, the other night outside Neilson Hall. It was late, after ten. I'd just finished working on the newspaper and was heading out to my car, and the guy stopped me and started talking about how Brea's evil and we have to blow it up. He said talk to you, you would know what he's talking about."

Ian's heart was pounding, but he forced himself to remain calm. "And you believed him?"

Jim took a deep breath. "I don't know if you've noticed, Dr. Emerson, but a lot of weird things have been happening here this semester. Like I said, I'm the editor of the paper, and I've pretty much been privy to it all. Rapes, riots, suicides—"

"I've noticed," Ian said.

"And you don't think it's all a little . . . strange?"

"No," Ian said, and the word was out before he was even aware that he'd said it. He'd been half planning to tell the kid everything, everything Stevens had written and said, everything he himself had been thinking. Jim seemed like an intelligent young man, a worthy ally, and, truth be told, he felt somewhat relieved to hear some of his own doubts and concerns voiced by someone else, someone who had made such observations independently.

But at the last minute he closed himself off, retreated. Lied.

He was protecting the student, he told himself, keeping him out of something he should not be involved with.

But he knew that wasn't true.

Jim was obviously caught off guard. "That professor said you knew what was happening here."

"I have no idea who you talked to," Ian lied. "I have no idea who that man is."

Jim looked at him, and he felt the same way he had when he used to lie to his mother as a child: transparent, his lies and motives obvious and completely visible.

But what were his motives? He didn't even know himself. He had no idea why he was lying to this kid. His reputation? Hedging his bets in case his instincts were wrong? He had never before been a hypocrite or an equivocator. Why should he start now?

No, it was something else, something deeper, something he could not understand or explain, something he did not want to face, and again he put on his blank, generic smile. "I'm sorry," he said, "but I have a class in twenty minutes, and I need to prepare my lesson plans."

"Sure," Jim said. He dug through his pocket, pulled out a business card. "If something happens, though, call me. The number of the newsroom's on the front. I wrote my own number on the back."

Ian nodded.

"And keep your eyes and ears open. You might be surprised by what you see. And hear."

"Will do."

"Is it all right if I check back with you? In a week or so? Maybe that guy'll call or come by or something."

"I'll let you know if he does. Thanks for stopping by." Ian waved good-bye and closed the door.

He held onto the knob until he was sure the boy had gone, then, with a long exhalation of held breath, fell into his chair. His heart was pounding, his hands trembling, and he felt as though he was a criminal who had narrowly avoided being found out by a suspicious detective who had used a social pretext to ask pointed, probing questions.

That was a weird thing to think.

Or was it?

He'd read enough horror novels to recognize that he was acting like someone who had been tainted by whatever evil lurked here, someone who was still rational, still sympathetic, still on this side of the fence, but who was being gradually corrupted and coaxed into the self-destructive behavior that had always lain within him.

Jack Torrance in *The Shining*.

He didn't think that was happening here, though. And he wasn't behaving *that* unreasonably or out of character.

Besides, life was not a horror novel. Even UC Brea, despite the weirdness, despite Stevens' claims in his "dissertation," was not Hill House or Hell House or the Overlook.

But strange things were happening here. And he

wasn't the only one who was noticing them. In a way, it did feel as though he was part of an unfolding horror story, and while that scared him, it was also exhilarating in a way. Now that he thought about it, that was probably the reason he had brushed off Jim. He wasn't yet ready to relinquish control, he wasn't yet ready to share. This was still his baby, his theoretical concern, his intellectual plaything, and he didn't want anyone else in on it.

He glanced once more at the window, frowned. He was up here in his ivory tower, playing mind games, while below there were riots. And death.

Jack Torrance.

No, that would never happen.

Besides, if worse came to worst, he could call up Gifford Stevens. And if Stevens was gone, well, he still had the recipe for the bomb.

And he still had the plans for the campus buildings in his desk.

2

Faith stopped by the newsroom just after six.

For once there'd been no late-breaking stories and they'd actually finished the paper on time. The other editors had all left for home or work or class, and Jim and Howie were alone in the newsroom, the battered stereo in the corner tuned to Orange County's lone country music station.

"In Arizona," Jim was saying, "half the stations on the dial play shitkicker music. But out here you're lucky if you can find—" He stopped as he saw Faith standing tentatively in the doorway and knocking on the metal frame.

"I'm sorry. Am I disturbing anything?"

"No," Jim said. "Come on in."

Howie grinned up at him and awkwardly shifted his position in order to reach the control lever of his chair. "I was just leaving." He rolled back from the low table where he'd been stationed and headed toward the door, pausing for a second as Faith moved aside to let him by. "I'll see you tomorrow," he called out.

"Later," Jim said.

Faith walked into the newsroom. In her hand, he saw

now, was a rolled-up copy of today's *Sentinel*. "So you saw it?" he said.

"I'm a big hero at the library."

"What was the reaction in your classes?"

"That's what I came to ask you. What kind of reaction have you had?"

He shrugged. "I've been here most of the day. I don't know what people are saying."

"Not much." She sighed, leaned against the side of a desk.

"No one really cares, do they?"

She shook her head.

"I was afraid of that."

They stared at each other for a moment.

Faith straightened, stood. "I could understand it if I'd written about something trivial, about a club or a sport or . . . or, I don't know, anything. But animals were being killed. Not just killed, tortured." She shook her head. "Maybe it's my writing. Maybe I'm just not a good enough—"

"You're a fine writer. I told you, it was an excellent piece. It's not that. And it's not the headline or the type style or anything else. It's—"

"—this school," she finished for him.

He nodded. "Yes. This school."

"I called the Orange County chapter of the ASPCA, you know. And PETA. They'll be sending people over here to talk to Dr. Austin."

"See? You didn't need us anyway."

"I did." She smiled. "And thanks for the support."

"If nothing else, at least you can lay claim to being published."

"I stole about fifty copies out of one of the news racks. You know, friends, family. I'll show the animal rights groups when they come."

"That's the spirit."

"I'm just . . . disappointed."

"I told you not to expect miracles."

"Yeah, well . . ."

"Wait a few days. Maybe there'll be some fallout. Once other profs read it, once the administration gets a hold of the story, maybe word'll come down from on high."

"Maybe," she said doubtfully.

"These are weird times." He started to say something else, then held up his hand, his face squinting. He sneezed, then sneezed again.

"Bless you," she said.

He held up a hand. "Wait a minute. They always come in threes." He sneezed again.

"Bless you."

He sniffled, wiped his wet mouth on the back of his hand. "You know, the reason they started saying 'Bless you' is because they used to think evil spirits could get into your body while you sneezed and your mouth was open. It was a preventative measure."

"I know that sneezing is a legitimate defense in court. If you're ever the cause of an accident, tell them that you sneezed. When you sneeze, you lose control of your voluntary muscles and you close your eyes. It's an accepted medical defense."

He laughed. "Now that we've both demonstrated our firm grasp of sneezing trivia, what do you say we get a bite to eat?"

" 'Get a bite to eat?' " She smiled, shook her head. "I thought you were better than that."

"What?"

"Come on. You want to go out with me, but you're afraid to just come out and ask, so you pretend we're just going to casually get some dinner. This way there's no pressure, you can bail if you want—"

"Actually," he said, "it wasn't that thought out. It's late, I'm hungry, I'm closing up here, and I thought you might want to come with me and get some food."

She reddened. "Oh, God. 'Faith,' " she admonished herself, " 'leave the psych in the classroom.' "

Jim grinned. "Actually, I was lying just now. You were right. I was just too chicken to ask you out."

"I accept."

He grabbed his backpack from the floor next to his desk and turned out the lights as he ushered her out the door. "We can discuss your editorial."

"Anything but that."

"American Lit."

"Or that."

"Then we'll just play it by ear." He closed the door,

locked it. He felt nowhere near as calm as he obviously seemed, but he was pulling it off.

They started toward the elevator.

"Any food preferences?"

"I don't live around here," she admitted. "I live in Santa Ana. So I don't really know what's around this area."

"Chinese, Mexican, Italian." His expression brightened. "We could go to Bill's."

"Bill's?"

"You've never been to Bill's Burgers?" He seemed shocked.

She shook her head.

"Oh, it's great. It's like that place on *Saturday Night Live*, the original ones, with John Belushi? They'd go to this place where they had, like, these foreign guys cooking and all they knew how to say was, 'Chee-burger! Chee-burger! Chee-burger!' Bill's is kind of like that. They have the best burgers I've ever had in my life."

She smiled. "I pegged you for a health food nut. Maybe a vegetarian."

"Looks can be deceiving."

"I guess so."

"So what do you say?"

"I'm game."

He grinned. "Bill's it is."

The hamburger stand was located in the overlarge parking lot of a rundown shopping center on the border of Brea and Placentia. The only store in the center still open as they pulled into the parking lot was a gun shop. Backlit behind the barred windows, Jim could see the twin proprietors: grossly overweight men dressed in matching flannel shirts.

He drove past the gun store and parked on the side of the hamburger stand. Faith was already out of the car, locking and closing her door, before he could open it for her, and he walked around the hood to meet her. Together they walked to the order window at the front of the stand. Jim looked in vain through the dirty glass for the team of fry cooks he'd told her about, but there was only one man behind the counter, a burly middle-aged Ed Asner lookalike.

She glanced over at him quizzically.

Jim shrugged. "Wrong night."

They ordered—cheeseburgers and Cokes, fries and onion rings—and sat down at one of the two tables. The other, to their left, was ringed with a group of five or six jocks. Jim recognized one of the guys from the P.E. class he'd been required to take during his first semester.

"So let's talk," Faith said.

"All right."

They were both suddenly, awkwardly silent. There'd been no shortage of conversation on the drive over, and Jim had found Faith a relaxed, interesting companion. He'd felt instantly comfortable with her, and there'd been none of the hesitant verbal toe-stepping that usually accompanied first dates. Now, however, the pressure was on, and he could find nothing to open with, nothing to say that wouldn't sound forced and stilted.

Faith shook her head. "Blew it again," she admonished herself.

Jim laughed.

And the spell was broken.

"So I assume you're not . . . seeing anyone at the moment," he said.

"If I was, I wouldn't be here."

"I like that attitude."

Their order number was called. Jim stood and took the tray of food from the pickup window and brought it back to the table. They ate slowly, talking, starting off with the subjects of school and previous relationships, gradually letting the talk spread outward, sink deeper. He told her about his father, about the Frank Zappa record, about getting the scholarship, about meeting Howie.

"My father's dead too," she told him, speaking quietly, not looking up.

"I'm sorry."

"Nothing for you to be sorry about. It happened a long time ago." She was silent, using a french fry to push the puddle of ketchup between them into a square shape.

"What happened?" he prodded.

She looked up, smiled at him, but the smile faded almost instantly. "Killed in the line of duty. The only policeman killed in the line of duty in the Costa Viejo P.D. in thirty years. He was on a pot bust, breaking up a party, and . . . someone popped him."

Jim sucked in his breath.

"They caught him. I mean, there were two teams on the bust, and the guy was right there, but my dad was dead before they even got him to the hospital."

"How old were you?"

"Nine."

"Did you see him?"

She nodded. "My mom didn't want me to, but I screamed and fought and threw a tantrum and she let me. I think it was to punish me. He was in a metal drawer in a metal room in the hospital. The morgue, I guess. They'd cleaned him up, but the hole was still there, right in the middle of his cheek. I could see one of his teeth through it."

"Shit."

"I suppose that's why I'm so anti-violence. I've seen firsthand what it can do."

"I don't mean to get too personal, but I'd think something like that would make you more . . . well, I'd think you'd want revenge against those kinds of people after what happened to your father."

"I do. Or part of me does. But another part of me sees that violence only begets more violence and that the chain has to be broken somewhere." She looked at him. "It might as well be with me."

" 'Think globally, act locally.' "

"Something like that."

"Wow." He shook his head, not knowing what to say.

"To be honest, I think my father wanted a boy. I think he was disappointed when I came along. I mean, he never showed it, and he loved me more than anything. But he was one of these, you know, big, macho guys. He'd been a marine and he was a policeman and he was always teaching me football and baseball and self-defense. Sometimes I wonder what he would think of me now, if he'd be happy with the way I turned out."

"I think he would."

She smiled. "I think so too."

"What about your mom?"

"What about her?"

"Is she still alive?"

"Yeah."

"Are you guys close?"

She shrugged.

He sensed that it would be better if he dropped the subject. "Life sucks sometimes, doesn't it?" he said.

"Sometimes."

Jim finished his Coke, popped a chunk of ice cube into his mouth. He glanced toward the jocks at the other table, and his attention was drawn by a flyer on the metal light pole between the two tables. White against a black background, the square of paper stood out sharply, and he wondered why he hadn't noticed it before. He squinted, trying to read the red lettering.

> GOOKS. CHINKS. JAPS.
> KILL 'EM ALL AND LET GOD SORT 'EM OUT.
> VOTE BRANT KEELER. AS PRESIDENT.

"Jesus," Jim said. He stood, walked around the table, looked closely at the flyer. In the bottom left corner was an exaggerated cartoon caricature of an Asian man about to be crushed by a giant boot. In the upper right corner was an American flag.

"Hey, buddy."

Jim turned. Behind the screen in the pickup window, the cook was pointing at the flyer.

"Yeah?" Jim said.

"Rip that offa there for me, will you?"

"Be happy to." He reached for the piece of paper, tore it off the pole.

"Hey!" yelled one of the jocks at the other table. "What do you think you're doing?"

"Tearing this down."

"What are you, un-American?"

Another stood. "Yeah. Who do you think you are?"

"I told him to tear down that piece of shit!" the cook roared. "This is my place, that's my pole, and I don't want it up there. And if any of you don't like it, you can go to McDonald's!"

The jocks sat down, grumbling among themselves but not arguing.

Jim walked up to the window, handed the crumpled

flyer to the cook through the opened screen. "Thanks," the man said. "I was going to do it myself, but I haven't had a chance to get out there."

"No problem."

The man glanced toward the still-scowling jocks. "Times have changed," he said.

Jim nodded. "Yeah."

"It's that fucking school." He glanced quickly toward Faith. "Sorry."

She smiled, walking over. "I've heard the word before."

"You guys aren't students at Brea, are you?"

Faith nodded. "I'm afraid we are."

"Sorry. I didn't mean to offend you."

"I'm not offended," Jim said, looking over at Faith. She shook her head. There was an interested expression on her face.

"You don't like Brea?" she asked.

"It's not that I don't like the school it's ... well, I guess I don't like the school." He smiled. "Nothing personal, you understand. It's just that the kids there all seem like ... well, like them." He motioned toward the jocks. "Assholes." He glanced toward Faith. "Sorry."

"I've heard that one before too."

The man stuck his hand out through the window. "Name's Bill."

Jim shook the hand. "Jim."

"Faith."

The man nodded. "Pleased to meet you."

"You own this place?" Jim asked.

"Yeah."

"Where are those guys who . . . who usually work here?"

He laughed. " 'Chee-burger! Chee-burger! Chee-burger!'? Those are my sons. They do that as a joke. They don't really talk that way."

"Oh." Jim was disappointed.

"I'll tell 'em to keep it up, though, if it helps business. I bet they don't know they have a fan club out there." He laughed.

Another customer came up, an older man, and Bill excused himself, moving to the order window.

Jim walked back to the table, cleaned off the cups and

wrappers, and dumped it in the trash can while Faith picked up the trays and slid them back through the window. They waved good-bye, Bill waved back, and they walked around the side of the hamburger stand to the car.

Jim took out his keys, unlocked the passenger door. Faith was standing next to him, close, almost touching. She was looking up at him, and he thought she wanted him to kiss her, though he wasn't positive, and he was about to chance it when he saw movement behind her.

The jocks.

"Faggot!" one of them yelled.

"Foreign-loving fuckhead!"

They were angry and heading quickly toward the car, and he yanked open the door. "Get in," he told Faith. "Now." He hurried around to the driver's side, but the first one had already arrived, slamming his fist down hard on the hood.

Faith closed and locked her door, reaching across the seat to unlock his side. At the same time she pressed hard on the horn, causing the jock by the hood to jump. She did not let up but continued to press, the horn honk persisting without pause.

And Bill emerged from the rear of the stand.

He was holding in his hands a metal baseball bat, and he strode purposefully forward, bat upraised. "Get the hell off my property!" he ordered. "I warned you once, you bastards, and I'm not telling you twice!"

Jim was still standing by the driver's door, fists clenched, ready to take on the first jock, but at Bill's appearance, all five would-be attackers started running.

Bill stopped in front of the car. "You all right?" he asked.

Jim nodded. "Thanks."

"Pussies," Bill said. "Need to be in a group to do anything."

"I'm sorry," Jim said. "I didn't mean to cause you any trou—"

"You didn't cause shit. It was those assholes. I swear, if I ever see them around here again, I'm calling the cops and having their butts hauled away." He smiled, waved at Faith through the windshield. "Hello again."

She smiled wryly back.

"Go on," Bill said. He nudged Jim, grinned. "I can tell you have quite an evening planned." He scanned the parking lot, lowered his voice. "Just make sure you aren't being followed."

"If I am, they'll follow me right to the police station."

Bill nodded. "Good."

"Thanks again," Jim said.

"My pleasure." Bill waved good-bye, started back toward the rear of the stand. "See you later."

Jim got in the car.

"You're right," Faith said. "That's quite a place."

Jim laughed as he turned the key in the ignition. "Dinner and entertainment. What more could you ask for on a first date?"

She smiled teasingly. "So, do you have 'quite an evening planned'?"

He reddened. "Heard that, did you?"

"I didn't hear your response, though."

"How should I have responded?"

She smiled, didn't answer.

They drove out of the parking lot, onto Imperial. "You know," Jim said, "I think ... I think maybe you should drop out of UC Brea. You know, leave school for a semester or maybe go someplace else."

"What?"

He licked his lips. "I don't think it's safe here."

She frowned at him. "Why?"

He thought for a moment, then shook his head. "I don't really know. Not for certain. But you saw what happened back there. And your botany class? That was only the tip of the iceberg—"

"I figured that one out for myself."

"I like you," he said. "Ordinarily, we'd meet for lunch on campus, go to some free concerts, gradually escalate, and maybe things would work out and maybe they wouldn't. But everything's speeded up now, and I'm going to put myself on the line here and say that I, uh ... I really like you. I know I don't know you that well— hell, I don't really know you at all—but I don't want anything to happen to you. That's why I think you should drop out, skip this semester, go somewhere else next year."

She smiled. "You 'really like' me, huh? That *is* putting yourself on the line."

"I'm serious."

"I'm not stupid," she told him. "When my botany class started getting weird, I got out. I'm not a plucky little heroine who's going to remain in a dangerous situation just to prove how tough and self-reliant I am. If things get hairy, I'm out of there."

He smiled. "I like that attitude."

"But it's not that bad yet."

"It's—"

"If it gets that bad, I'll leave. I have nothing to prove, and I come from a long line of quitters. I have no problem with it. But right now it's interesting, and I'm staying."

"Okay," he said.

They drove in silence for a few moments.

"Do I have 'quite an evening planned'?" he asked finally.

She smiled at him. "I hope you do." She paused. "I do."

They were both smiling as they drove back toward Brea.

SEVENTEEN

1

Milk, orange juice, or New York Seltzer?

Orange juice.

Glenna picked up the small carton and put it on her cafeteria tray next to the salad. Her hands were still shaking, and she was grateful for the metal runner next to the food display that allowed her to push her tray instead of carry it.

If she'd had to carry her food, there'd be a floor full of salad right now.

She reached the register, paid for her lunch, then found an empty table for one in the corner of the cafeteria. She hurried over to the table as quickly as she could and slouched down on the short, contoured bench seat.

What was she going to do?

She slowly scanned the cafeteria, saw no one she knew, no one from the P.E. department, and gratefully closed her eyes, finally allowing herself to relax.

They'd almost caught her.

Everything had seemed normal when she'd showed up for her badminton class this morning. She'd gone into the locker room, suited up, and gone out into the gym with everyone else. The first indication she'd had that something was amiss was when she was the last person chosen for a doubles team. She was not the best player in class, but she was definitely one of the top five, and it was not only unusual for her to be chosen so late, it was unheard of.

She was surprised and, to be honest, a little hurt, but she didn't dwell on it, and she didn't really think about it as the first game started.

Then things started to get weird.

She was getting ready to serve when a birdie from

another game hit her on the back of the head. She whirled around, startled, and another birdie hit her full in the face. This one hurt, the feathers poking into her eyeball, and she dropped her racket, holding a hand over the tearing right eye.

"Goddammit!" she said. "What asshole—"

A racket smacked her hard on the buttocks.

She yelped in pain, took the hand from her eye, and turned around. Her vision was still blurry, her right eye stinging as though it was filled with sand, and she couldn't see that well, but it looked to her like all of the games in the gym had stopped. The team they'd been playing was moving under the net, toward her, and her own partner was standing way too close.

Someone behind her grabbed the elastic waistband of her shorts and yanked them down.

She bent to pull them up and another racket smacked against her bare buttocks.

"Shove the handle up her ass!" someone yelled.

She pulled up her shorts. She was not scared—not yet—but she was angry, humiliated, and in pain, and at the top of her lungs she screamed, "Knock it off!"

"Shove it up her cunt," a closer voice said, and Glenna grew cold as she recognized the voice of Joyce Elwin, the class instructor.

She held a hand over her right eye and scanned the gym with her left. They were advancing on her, all of the students in her class, their badminton games abandoned. She didn't know what was happening or why, but immediately, without thinking, she ran for the nearest exit.

The gym was filled with sound of yelling, the stomping of feet, the clatter of rackets being thrown and hitting the floor.

She knew what they planned to do to her without being told. She'd seen it before, on an old Linda Blair TV movie. Linda had been a new girl in prison, and the other girls had trapped her in the shower and held her down, raping her with a broom handle or a plunger— the quick cuts had not made it clear which. She'd been in junior high at the time, and a lot of the kids in her school, boys *and* girls, had found the scene somewhat stimulating, but the idea of penetration had been completely repugnant and horrifying to her.

It was no less so now. And that was the impetus that spurred her on, that pushed her to reach the exit door, shove it open and run crying outside, away from the gym, across the wide lawn to the campus police.

They hadn't believed her, of course. They'd taken down her statement, given her a case number, a uniformed officer had even escorted her back to the locker room so she could get her clothes and change. But at the gym everything appeared to be normal. Through the locker room doorway she saw her badminton class innocently playing doubles, and when another officer, notebook in hand, started asking Joyce Elwin questions, she saw the instructor smile, say something, and shake her head.

Thirty people against one. Who were the cops going to believe?

Glenna had thanked the officer who'd escorted her and headed toward the Student Center. She wanted to go home, but she had a test in an hour in her sociology class, and she couldn't afford to miss it. The professor was a hard ass who didn't allow makeups and didn't accept excuses.

She opened her eyes, took a deep breath, and picked up the small carton of orange juice in front of her. She opened the carton, drank. The officer who'd taken the report had said that they'd call her within five to seven days to inform her of their progress on the investigation, but with no hard evidence and no corroborating witnesses, she knew what that would mean.

They'd claim that she'd merely overreacted to being hit in the eye with a birdie.

Maybe she should've shown them the red racket marks on her ass.

No, they would've just leered and then chalked that up to an accident as well.

The sliding doors to the cafeteria opened, and she glanced up nervously, grateful to see that the entering students were not people she recognized.

She felt like she was in grade school again, hiding from the school bullies.

This wasn't supposed to happen when you were in college.

She stared down at her salad for a moment, then picked up the plastic fork and slowly began eating. What was she going to do? Obviously, she had to drop the badminton class. But what about her other P.E. courses? Some of those students were in her other classes.

What would they try to do to her with tennis rackets? With baseball bats?

Glasses clinked on the table behind her, and she jumped, pieces of lettuce spilling from her fork onto her jeans.

She picked up the lettuce, tossed it onto her tray, and closed her eyes.

It was going to be a long day.

2

Johnny McGuane felt different the minute he entered the stairwell of the Social Sciences building. The change was subtle but noticeable, and the lethargy which had enveloped him all afternoon seemed to simply fade away. There was a slight shift in his perceptions, not unlike the effect of alcohol or drugs, and he suddenly felt stronger, smarter, more sure of himself. It was a giddy, heady experience, and the feeling grew in intensity as he ascended the stairs. By the time he reached the eighth floor, he was fairly buzzing.

But there was something else, too, underneath the surface pleasantness, a darker, harsher undercurrent, like the low, ominous hum heard beneath the sound of innocent children's voices on a horror movie soundtrack, a foreshadowing of bad things to come.

No, he thought as he continued up the maintenance stairway above the top floor. He had been mistaken. There was no undercurrent to his elation. He felt good, he felt charged, he felt great.

He had been head custodian at UC Brea for the past half decade, and although he had initially been content with the position, he had grown increasingly dissatisfied with his duties. He dispatched janitors to clean up spilled food in the Student Center cafeteria, he made sure light bulbs were replaced in the buildings and trash picked up in the quad. True, he had been asked to help oversee implementation of the Americans with Disabilities Act, to make sure that classrooms and rest rooms and phones and drinking fountains and elevators all had handicapped access, but for the most part, his job was a no-brainer, something anyone could do.

He deserved better than that.

What really ticked him off was that so many of the instructors here, the so-called "educators," were sooooo fucking stupid. When he'd first gotten this job, he'd found himself intimidated by these people's positions and backgrounds, their educations and reputations. He'd automatically assumed that they were more intelligent than he was, that they could do things that he could not even begin to understand. But he'd learned over the years that they were nowhere near the infallible geniuses he had originally taken them for, that they were, in fact, smug, self-important snobs who used and abused the trust placed in them by naive and unsophisticated students.

He was smarter than those pompous fucks. He was the one who should be teaching those classes, not those panty-waisted pussies who passed themselves off as professors.

Panty-waisted pussies who passed themselves off as professors.

He grinned to himself. It was a good line, a good use of alliteration.

He should teach English. Poetry.

But no. Instead the bastards had kept him down, used his lack of a formal education against him, put him off with condescending smiles, made sure he cleaned the shit out of their fucking toilets and emptied the bloody tampons out of their trash cans.

He'd been angry about that, bitterly angry, and everything had threatened to come to a head within him this semester, but then, suddenly, out of the blue, he had discovered the stairwell and its ... therapeutic effects. The anger had left him, replaced by a youthful exuberance when he was in the stairwell, by a tired calm when he was away from it.

And he'd known what he had to do.

At the top of the stairs Johnny stopped. He pulled the

key ring from his belt, found the gold round-headed key, and used it to open the metal door of the supply room.

She was still there, bound and gagged right where he'd left her, and in the faint, diffuse light that made it around the bulk of the door, the girl's frightened eyes looked comically white and huge.

Johnny grabbed his crotch, hefted it. "You want it, don't you?"

He laughed as she squirmed and fought against her bonds, a terrified and all but inaudible mewling the only sound able to penetrate the tight gag.

"Just joking," he said, patting her head. "Just joking with you."

He pulled the string that turned on the bare bulb and leaned against two stacked boxes of hand towels that were pushed up against the overstocked supply shelf, looking at her, admiring her. She was pretty. She didn't overdress or underdress like a lot of students did these days, and the slight hint of makeup on her face served to accentuate her angular good looks and beautiful eyes.

She'd wet her pants since he'd put her here early this morning. He should've thought of that, should've prepared for it. He felt bad for her, but he saw that the wetness had caused the thin material of her pants to stick to her skin, to conform to the contours of her crotch. He could see the V-shaped outline, the cleft at the tip.

He felt a stirring between his legs.

He looked at her, smiled. Sex would be fun. No doubt about that. But it was not her pussy that he wanted.

It was her hands.

He needed her hands.

He'd noticed her hands on the first day of school. He'd been in the stairwell, bolting a new bulletin board on the third-floor landing, when she'd walked past, waving to someone on the lower stairs. He'd been struck then by the symmetry of her fingers, by the graceful carpal movements, by the pale perfection of her skin, and he'd marked her face, remembering.

She'd been on the stairway often after that. She was a junior, he learned, a geography major, and most of her classes were in this building. By luck, by intention, by observation, he'd roughly learned her schedule, and he'd arranged to be in the stairwell the same times as she, accompanying her, unseen, to different floor landings, listening in on her conversations.

He was not sure now, could not really remember, but it was possible that her hands had been the inspiration for his foolproof plan to enter the world of academia. It was not until recently, though, that he realized he could actually use them.

That he needed them for his experiments.

The problem was, if he took her hands, he'd have to kill her. Even if she promised not to say anything, and even if she kept her promise, her family and friends would all be asking, "What happened to your beautiful hands?" And she'd have to invent some sort of story to explain their disappearance, and somehow, in some way, the trail would lead back to him and he'd get caught.

He'd have to kill her.

He didn't want to. He didn't want to harm her in any way.

But he needed her hands.

Once he had them, he could complete his project. Then . . . then he would get the respect he deserved. The professors here would have to accept him as an equal once he showed them what he could do. Nothing spoke as eloquently as ability. Words paled next to deeds. And when he demonstrated his knowledge and talents, they would come to realize that a diploma, a fucking piece of paper, was not all that important when it came right down to it.

He'd probably have his choice of one of the science departments or the engineering department.

He didn't *want* to kill her, but some things were more important than life.

She squirmed, mewled, rocked back and forth on her chair. He smiled at her. Even wide and frightened, her eyes were beautiful. He had wirecutters in here, and long-nosed pliers. He could take her eyes out, keep them for himself. He remembered seeing an old episode of the *Tonight Show* with Sammy Davis, Jr. Old Sammy had had a glass eye, and as a joke Alice Cooper had come on the panel wearing a glass eye on a necklace.

He could do that too.

Take out her eyes, wear them on a necklace.

No, that was vain. Stupid and vain. He wanted her eyes, but he didn't need them. He only needed her hands.

He was stalling, he realized. Wasting time so he could be with her. He looked down at his watch. He had to meet the second-shift crew in fifteen minutes at the physical plant. He didn't have any time to spare.

He stood. "Sorry," he said. "But I need to get those off you now."

He walked to the back of the supply room, to the portable refrigerator, and took out the bag of ice he'd bought this morning. He opened the bag, dumped the ice on the bottom of the refrigerator and spread it out. He'd store the hands here. The cold should keep them from sustaining too much damage.

He walked behind the girl, kicked over her chair. Her head hit the concrete floor, and while it didn't knock her out, it obviously left her a little groggy, her mind fogged, and he quickly untied her upper arms to take advantage of her temporary disorientation.

He untied her wrists, pulled her arms in front of her on the floor. She was starting to move now, so he retied the wrists together.

From its hook on the wall, he took the big shovel.

"Sorry," he said again.

He raised the shovel high above her wrists.

Brought it down hard.

4

Thanh Lam stayed in the library until it closed, until the library workers came around and told him it was time to leave. He'd intended to go home after his last engineering course at four, but the results of his test had changed his plans.

C He'd gotten a C on his first test.

For a few shocked moments after the professor had handed back the Scantron form, Thanh had simply stared at the paper, at the penciled-in bubbles, at the fat red letter that was scrawled in marking pen over the top of the form.

C Then he'd begun thinking ahead, to what his aunt and his brother would say when he took the test home and showed them his score. The heretical thought had crossed his mind that if he could get perfect scores on the remainder of the tests, on the midterm and the final, and if he could try to work out some extra credit, this C would average out to an A-minus and he wouldn't have to show the test to his family at all.

But he'd already told them about it. He'd told them two days ago, when he'd taken the test, and he'd even said that he thought he'd done well. They were expecting to see the results.

They were waiting to see the results.

They would demand to see the results.

It wouldn't be so bad if all of their hopes weren't riding on him, if there wasn't so much pressure placed on him to perform. But his aunt had saved all of her extra money from the beauty parlor for the past ten years in order to pay for his schooling. His brother had decided not to attend college, to give him a better shot, so he could afford to go to Brea instead of Fullerton. And both of them constantly made him aware of the sacrifices that they had made for him.

He could not show them the C.

Thanh left the library and walked into the quad. His gaze was drawn to the fences on each landing of Neilson Hall. He thought for a moment, then glanced toward the Social Sciences building. There were no fences on the Social Sciences building.

He started walking.

His mind was blank as he rode the elevator to the ninth floor. He got off the elevator, walked down the long hallway to the glass door that led to the smoking area outside.

He stepped onto the landing.

He was not alone. Standing against the low railing, at regular intervals, were other students. Other Vietnamese students. He recognized Cuong Pham and Linh Nguyen and Lu Ngo. Each of them held in their hands test forms or blue composition books.

They'd received poor grades too.

For a brief fraction of a second he considered not going through with it. He wasn't the only one having trouble this semester, so it wasn't that humiliating. Maybe it wasn't even their fault. Maybe there was some sort of academic conspiracy going on, an attempt to sabotage their usually high grades.

But the thought fled as quickly as it had come. It didn't matter if others were doing poorly. It didn't matter if the entire student body was flunking. What mattered was the fact that he had failed. He had let his family down.

A slight wind blew up here. The air felt cool against his face, and he stood unmoving for a moment to enjoy the sensation. From this vantage point he could see almost all of Orange County. He looked to the south, thought he saw Garden Grove, the Asian Palace shopping center in Little Saigon, its oversized bulk setting it apart from the low surrounding buildings.

Mai was probably there right now, hanging out at the music store.

He wanted to cry when he thought of Mai.

How had he screwed up so badly? Why hadn't he spent more time studying, less time with his friends?

No, he could not place the blame on anyone else. His failure was his own fault.

He walked forward, to the edge of the landing, looking over the low rail at the quad below. From this angle he could see what looked like a face in the configuration of plants in front of the building, a round bush mouth and slanted hedge eyes presenting to him a mocking caricature of an Asian face that only served to underscore his inability to live up to expectations.

To his right, on one of the posts connecting the rail to the roof, his attention was drawn by a flyer fluttering in the slight breeze. He could read only the top line of the flapping paper.

KILL GOOKS.

He looked to his left, met the gaze of Cuong Pham, looked right and caught the glance of Lu Ngo.

As one, they climbed onto the edge of the railing.

He took a deep breath, looked down at the concrete sidewalk below. The plant face seemed to grin mockingly up at him.

He screamed, Cuong screamed, Lu screamed, Linh screamed.

As one, they jumped.

EIGHTEEN

1

After they finished making love, Ian went into the bathroom to take a quick shower. When he emerged into the bedroom a few minutes later, Eleanor was sitting up in bed, reading through what looked like a magazine. He sat down next to her, kissed the back of her neck. "What're you doing?"

"I'm thinking of taking some classes," she said.

He groaned. "I'll never get to see you."

"I'll take them at Brea. You'll see me all the time."

"No," he said, straightening up. He looked more closely at the magazine in her lap and noticed, for the first time, that it was next semester's class schedule. "Go somewhere else."

She closed the schedule. "What for? Brea's close, it's convenient—"

"I don't want you going there."

She stiffened. "*You* don't want *me* to go there? I'm sorry. You're my lover, not my father. I will not have you telling me what I can and cannot do."

"You can take classes at Fullerton, at Irvine—"

"Brea's closer." She looked at him, her eyes narrowed. "You don't have some little undergrad cutie stashed away there, do you?"

"No," he said dismissively. "It's not that."

"What is it, then?"

"We've had a lot of . . . violence on campus this semester."

"So? What else is new?"

"This is new. We've had riots, attacks, suicides—"

"Suicides? What does that have to do with me?"

"I just don't think it's safe there."

"I worked for six years in downtown L.A. I'll take my chances."

He looked at her. He wanted to tell her the truth, wanted to tell her what he really felt, what he really thought. But here, in the bedroom, next to her, with the TV on in the background, it seemed foolish, both stupid and childish. An evil university? It sounded ridiculous even to him.

He kissed her cheek. "We'll talk about it later."

"We won't talk about it at all. I want to take some classes, and I'm going to. That's all there is to it. You have nothing to say in the matter."

"There was a mass suicide yesterday. And two girls are missing."

"I don't care."

"Fine," he said tiredly. He turned off the lamp next to his side of the bed. "Do what you want. I'm going to sleep." He climbed under the covers, rolled onto his stomach.

"You're a jackass sometimes," she said.

He did not respond.

"But I still love you."

"I love you too." He closed his eyes. A moment later, he heard her turn off the lamp on her side of the bed, felt her snuggle next to him.

He put his arm around her, held her.

He was still holding her when he fell asleep.

He awoke at six, with the initial hint of dawn creeping through the partially opened window shades, and his first thought was that he'd forgotten to set the alarm and was going to be late for his first class.

He was already halfway to the bathroom, underwear in hand, when he realized that it was Saturday.

He stopped, breathed deeply, rubbed his eyes, looked back toward the bed. Eleanor was still asleep, curled up like a shrimp, completely undisturbed by his frantic attempt to get ready for work on time. He considered crawling back into bed next to her, but she was obviously tired and needed more sleep and he was already wide awake, and he walked into the bathroom, put on his underwear, put on his robe, and headed into the kitchen to make some coffee.

After putting on the coffee and popping two slices of bread in the toaster, Ian went outside to get the paper. It was down at the end of the driveway today, near the street, and he walked past his car, past Eleanor's, and picked up the rolled newspaper. He glanced down at the headlines as he headed back toward the kitchen: U.S. JAPAN TRADE TALKS RESUME, O.C. DOCTOR INDICTED FOR FRAUD, 4 PALESTINIANS KILLED IN SECOND DAY OF FIGHTING.

PROFESSOR KILLS STUDENT LOVER.

He stopped walking, reread the headline.

PROFESSOR KILLS STUDENT LOVER.

A chill passed through him as he scanned the text for the school name he knew he'd find.

UC Brea.

There it was, just as he'd known it would be, first paragraph, first sentence. He looked for the name of the professor. Dr. Thomas Chang. He'd heard the name but didn't know the man. Chang was a new philosophy instructor hired at the end of last semester to take the place of Gretta James, who officially was on sabbatical and unofficially had had a nervous breakdown.

The name of the student was Lisa Harrison. He didn't know her at all.

He walked slowly into the house, into the kitchen, reading the article.

When he finished, he placed the paper, with the article face up, on the table in front of Eleanor's seat.

Maybe she'd get the hint.

They'd planned to spend the day together—or rather, he'd planned for them to spend the day together. But she had some work to catch up on and had to go back to her apartment to use her P.C. and access the database in her office, and he was left with the day before him and nothing to do.

He considered calling Buckley but remembered that Buckley had driven up to Santa Cruz for the weekend to take part in a panel discussion at a Russ Meyer film festival.

So he spent the day hitting his favorite local book, record, and thrift stores. He hit Music Market, Music Mart, and Music Surplus in Costa Mesa; stopped by the

Goodwill As Is Yard in Garden Grove; browsed through Aladdin Books and Book Harbor in Fullerton, and finally ended up at Something Wicked in Brea.

He parked on the street directly in front of the former bank building that now housed the bookstore. The acrid exhaust fumes which permeated the street and sidewalk disappeared as he opened the door and stepped inside, the pollution held at bay by the wall of cool, conditioned air that filled the doorway. Immediately, the harsh odors of the city were replaced by the soft, comforting smell of books.

F.W., the clerk, was busy talking to a young, trendy-looking couple wearing matching black jackets and silver bracelets, so Ian merely waved over the couple's heads and made his way down the far aisle toward the used horror paperbacks in the rear. He stopped before a series of shelves filled with black-spined books and began scanning the titles to see if anything new had been added since the last time he'd been in.

He found the Paperjacks edition of Richard Laymon's *The Cellar*, a British edition of Harry Kressing's *The Cook*, and a copy of the third *Shadows* anthology, which he'd lent to a student long ago and the student had never returned.

Not a bad haul.

He moved to the next aisle, to check out the books on literary criticism and see if there was anything he could use for next semester's European Lit class. It had been a long time since he'd had to teach that course, but the wheel had spun around again, and it was his turn. It would be a lot easier to refresh his memory through criticism than to reread the novels.

At the end of the aisle, the black-clad couple was looking through the ever popular Beat Writers section.

"Burroughs is God," the young man said. "*Naked Lunch*."

The young woman nodded. "Steely Dan."

"Interzone."

Ian smiled to himself as he listened to their conversation. Buzzwords. Literary trivia. He remembered doing it himself in his younger days, trying to amass an encyclopedic knowledge of dust-jacket information—brief plot synopsis, brief bio, list of other works. Then it had seemed important, and, like his fellow English majors, he'd lived in simultaneous fear and anticipation of "literary" discussions, planning out entire arguments ahead of time, storing up the easily referenced details he thought necessary to prove that he'd read a book he hadn't actually had time to read. The words the author had written, the meaning of a work, had not seemed as critical as being able to feign familiarity in a casual conversation.

But he'd learned eventually that buzzwords were not as important as concepts, plot points not as important as themes and ideas, and he'd given up that sort of grandstanding when he'd gone into grad school. It was a trivialization of literature, this pretended knowledge, a sacrilege to art. As he now told his classes, he'd rather have someone read a book and forget everything in it than have someone know the plot and theme of a book secondhand. It was the experience of reading that was important, and even if you didn't remember the details of a book you'd read, it had done its work, it had affected you, it had changed you.

"How about Bukowski?" the young man said.

The young woman nodded. "*Love Is a Dog from Hell.*"

"Hey!" the clerk called from the front of the store. "Professor!"

Ian moved around the end of the aisle and looked toward the register. "Yeah?"

"I got it for you. The book."

"What book?" Ian walked to the front of the store.

"The one your friend said to hold for you?"

He frowned. He'd asked no one to put a book on hold for him.

F.W. pulled a volume from the shelf behind the register and placed it on the front counter. "It was a tough one. I did a computer search and only found two copies. One in North Carolina, and this one in Santa Barbara."

Ian looked down at the title.

Fighting the Supernatural With Firepower.

The author was Gifford Stevens.

Ian picked up the book. It was thin and cheaply produced, obviously a vanity press publication, and it appeared to be at least ten or twenty years old. He opened the cover, checked the copyright date. 1979.

"I was glancing through it," F.W. said. "Pretty interesting."

Ian looked up at him. "Who did you say asked you to find this for me?"

"Another professor. I wrote it down on the card." He took the book from Ian, opened it to the last page, withdrew a three-by-five card. "Dr. John Montague."

Dr. John Montague.

The professor from *The Haunting of Hill House*.

Goose bumps rose on Ian's arms.

Eleanor.

This was getting a little too damn creepy.

"What did Dr. Montague look like?" he asked. He already knew the answer, but he wanted to have it confirmed.

F.W. looked puzzled. "Big beard, jacket, uh, average height."

Stevens.

"Why? Don't you know him?"

"I know him," Ian said. He looked again at the book, started to take out his wallet. "How much is it?"

"Dr. Montague already paid for it. Overpaid, in fact." The clerk looked uncomfortable. "Should I give you the change, or hold on to it until Dr. Montague comes back—"

"How much is the book?"

"Twenty-five fifty-seven, with tax."

"How much did he give you?"

"Fifty."

"Keep the money." Ian withdrew his wallet. "I'll pay for it. Give him his money back when you see him."

He added the book to the paperbacks he'd picked up and paid for everything. The paperbacks he allowed the clerk to put in a bag, but *Fighting the Supernatural* he carried in his hand. He thanked F.W. and started out the door, staring at the cover of the book, at the drawing of a haunted house in the background, a detonator in the foreground.

And he wondered, as he walked out to his car, how Stevens had known that he patronized this store.

2

She had never before worked on a Saturday, and Faith was surprised at how crowded the library was. She herself seldom did schoolwork on Saturday, and it was strange to see that, inside the library, it looked almost like a regular weekday. The Reserve Book Room was crowded with students trying to check out materials their instructors had put on hold, and nearly all of the study carrels were occupied. There were even groups meeting in the larger study rooms on the fourth, fifth, and sixth floors.

She was scheduled to work from eleven to five, from the time the library opened until the time it closed, but she was busy the entire time and the day sped by quickly. In the afternoon she spent most of her time reshelving returned materials in Special Collections.

She had only been in Special Collections once before, during the initial tour with Phil, and ordinarily she would not have been allowed access to this area of the library, but several students had been out sick this week and one of their regular volunteers had abruptly quit, so they were shorthanded. Phil had left notice that she was to be granted access and was responsible for reshelving a collection of Swedish erotica that had been returned earlier in the week by a feminist professor.

She walked slowly through the cramped aisles in the partitioned room. In addition to the Holocaust literature, she'd learned that Brea housed one of the world's largest collections of hardcore pornography as well as an extensive compilation of serial killer diaries, letters and photographs that had been dedicated to the school by the murderers themselves.

Why would a university even want to keep such gruesome memorabilia?

She glanced at the Swedish erotica as she returned the individual books and magazines to their places on the shelves. She came across a magazine titled *Anal Love*, and she quickly flipped through the pages, glancing at the pictures.

She thought of Jim.

They were going out again tonight, and she was supposed to meet him at Spoon's around six-thirty. He'd

wanted to pick her up, to come by her house, but she'd
told him no. She'd explained everything to him, how she
felt, and he'd understood.

She wished now, though, that she'd told him she'd
meet him at seven instead of six-thirty. She needed
enough time to go home and take a shower.

And wash.

Everything.

She closed the magazine, put it on the shelf.

As the senior student assistant, Glenna was in charge
of the library today. Faith had told her about the date
first thing, asking if someone else could close so she
could take off exactly at five, and Glenna had said don't
worry about it. Rennie, Sue, and Daniel would close
today. She could leave on time.

She was signed out and walking by 5:01, and she
waved her thanks to Glenna as she headed through the
lobby and out the door, but her friend did not respond.
Throughout the day Glenna had seemed jumpy, tense,
distracted, and more than once Faith had considered
asking if anything was wrong, if there was anything she
could do to help. But she still didn't know Glenna that
well, and she figured that if the other girl wanted to talk
to her about it, she would.

She walked out of the library. She'd parked in the
faculty lot today, and she hoped she hadn't gotten a
ticket. She didn't think that parking regulations were
enforced on weekends, but she wasn't sure and she
hadn't bothered to check.

She walked through the quad and past the Education
building, cutting across the lawn until she reached the
cement walkway between the Performing Arts Center
and the Biological Sciences building that led to the faculty lot.

She'd been striding quickly, in a hurry to reach her
car, but she slowed considerably as she reached the
walkway. Her mind had been on Jim, and on the upcoming evening, but after the openness of the lawn, there
was something about the narrowness of the walkway that
seemed somehow threatening to her, that made her feel
uneasy. The sun had not yet gone down, but it was situated well behind the Biological Sciences building, and
the walkway was heavily shadowed by the tall foliage on

its sides. The relative darkness made her uncomfortable. She thought about what Jim had said, about what she herself had felt this semester, and she considered, for a second, taking a long cut, going around Biological Sciences to the parking lot. But she told herself that she was merely being paranoid and overcautious. It was still light out, she could see to the end of the walkway. There was nothing there. If she hurried, if she ran, she would be through it in a matter of seconds.

She forced herself to move forward, passing the mirror entrances of the two buildings, looking not at the ground, as she usually did when walking, but forward, ahead, to make sure there was nothing in front of her, that there was nothing—

—moving.

She stopped, sucked in her breath.

Blinked.

The shadows on the sidewalk shifted, swayed, stirred as though by a stiff wind, although their sources remained stationary. Faith looked fearfully around. There was no breeze at all, no wind of any kind, the only movement in the walkway her own. The trees and tall bushes that lined that sidewalk were still.

But the shadows continued to move.

The pace of their motion quickened, accelerated.

Her heart was thumping, her lips dry, her skin flush with goose bumps. She knew now how people in horror movies felt when they were in a haunted house and heard tapping on the walls or saw doors open of their own accord. Distanced, on screen, seen secondhand, those encounters had always seemed to her somewhat ridiculous, and she had never understood why characters had been so frightened by small sounds and movement. But she understood now that it was the context that provoked such a response. Ordinary acts took on a terrifying, fearsome quality when the source was unknown, unexplainable, and when the act itself was unnatural, when something like this happened, when the shadows of bushes moved and the bushes themselves didn't, the fear was compounded by a horrifying feeling of utter helplessness.

On the cement, the shadows were whipping back and forth frenzedly.

She remained rooted in place, afraid to move forward, afraid to move backward, not knowing what was happening or why, not knowing what she could or should do about it. There was no sound to accompany the action, and the incongruity of that only served to highlight the threatening irrationality of the occurrence.

The shadow of a winged creature, a shadow for which there was no real-world counterpart, was born from the whipping trees and bushes, and it separated itself from the mass of moving plant shapes and made a beeline across the sidewalk toward her.

She turned and ran.

She ran from the walkway, away from both the Performing Arts Center and the Biological Sciences building, back across the lawn from which she'd come.

She did not stop running until she was all the way to the sports complex.

Leaning against the wall of the gym, she stopped for a moment to catch her breath—before walking all the way around the perimeter of the campus to reach the faculty parking lot and her car.

NINETEEN

Friendly Computers
1909 Orangethorpe, Suite A
Fullerton, CA 92632
(714) 555-0989

Thomas Olson
Computer Operations
UC Brea
100 Campus Drive
Brea, CA 92590

October 25

Dear Mr. Olson,

I regret to inform you that due to the excessive claims made by your organization during the past year and the consistently poor condition of your equipment, we will not be extending your service contract on repair work.

Your current contract expires on December 31.

We are, however, extremely competitive in our pricing of time and materials and would like to retain your business. We can offer you a government discount of 10 percent, applied to the total price of each service call.

If you have any questions, please call me at ext. 5681.

Sincerely,

Safad H. Ramaal

Safad H. Ramaal

TWENTY

1

Brant Keeler awoke feeling good.

He sat up, breathed deeply, then swung his legs off the bed, hit the floor, and did twenty push-ups. He was straining on the last ten, his arms shaking, ready to give, but he forced himself to finish the exercises before bounding up and jogging into the bathroom for his morning shower.

He emerged from the steaming bathroom ten minutes later, clean and refreshed, face shaved, hair combed, dressed impeccably in slacks, shirt, and tie.

He walked into the kitchen, whistling. "Hi, Mom," he said. "Hi, Dad."

His parents stared at him from the chairs to which they were tied, their eyes bulging and panicked. Blood and saliva had soaked through both of the handkerchiefs he'd used to gag their mouths, and comically identical circles of red stained the white cloth, making his parents look like twin clowns.

He had to laugh.

He patted their heads. "I love you guys." He walked past them to the refrigerator, taking out the butter and jam. From the cupboard above the sink counter he grabbed a sack of Weber's bread, opening it and popping two slices into the toaster. He looked out the window as he poured himself a glass of water from the sink faucet. In the kitchen of the house next door, Mrs. Cray was washing dishes. She saw him, smiled, waved, and he waved back.

He turned again toward his parents. The blood on their faces and upper chests had dried, leaving only dull ruby lines that bisected and intersected and resembled nothing so much as tribal markings. He walked across the linoleum floor, grabbed the back of his mom's chair, pulled on it, and swung it around until she was facing away from the table.

As before, he found himself staring at her breasts. They were heavy and full, not wrinkled as he'd imagined they'd be, but smooth and unblemished, white with prominent brown nipples. He had not seen her breasts since he was an infant—and he could not remember that—but he'd seen them last night when he'd stripped her and cut her and tied her to the chair, and he had longed to touch them, to suckle on them, to roll the brown nipples around on his tongue. He had not known if the University would like that, though. If It would understand or approve.

Now he saw white wetness dripping down her stomach, droplets oozing and issuing from the downward-pointing tips of her large breasts.

She was lactating again. After all these years.

Wonderously, wonderfully, she was producing milk.

The University worked in mysterious ways.

Grinning, he knelt before her, lifted her left breast in his hand, began sucking on it.

She jerked and screamed behind her bonds and gag, obviously trying to move her chair away from him, but he had tied her knots well, and she was helpless before him, forced to submit to his wishes. He reached for her right breast as he suckled on her left, rubbing it roughly, smearing the milk on her skin, feeling the warm slipperiness slide over the ridges of dried blood from her cuts.

Her body was wracked by sobs, tears streaming from her bulging eyes.

He sucked harder.

Next to him, from behind the gag, his dad bellowed, enraged, shoving his chair forward with a powerful lurch, and Brant stopped and stood and smacked the old fuck on the head, knocking him over. The old man lay on his back like an overturned beetle, struggling, crying, and Brant kicked him once in the midsection for good measure, gratified to hear a howl of pain from behind the bloody handkerchief.

He turned back toward his mom.

"A growing boy needs his milk," he said.

He knelt once again, sucking the fresh milk from his mom's titties, and it tasted warm and good.

He continued sucking until his toast popped up.

After breakfast, after righting his dad's chair, after giving both of them a few fresh cuts for the day, he walked back to the bathroom and brushed his teeth. He returned to his bedroom, picked up his shoulder holster from its peg on the back of the door and strapped it on. He lovingly stroked the Ruger on his desk, then picked up the pistol and slid it into the holster. From the top of his dresser he took his switchblade and put it in his pocket.

He looked at himself in the mirror and smiled.

He was ready for school.

2

Jim looked around the newsroom: at Cheryl's empty desk, at Eddie and Ford arguing, at Faruk sitting sullenly in a corner chair. What the hell was wrong? They'd had almost exactly the same staff last semester and everyone had gotten along wonderfully. Now they were constantly at one another's throats. The camaraderie, the sense of family that he had experienced in his other semesters on the paper, had disappeared completely, replaced by this petty backbiting, this jealous bickering. He'd always been laid back, had always run a loose ship, and it had usually served him well. Last semester he'd left people alone to do their jobs, giving guidance, not orders, operating as an arbiter of minor disputes, not a dictator, and that was the same approach he'd tried to take this semester.

But this semester something was different.

This semester everything was different.

He swiveled in his seat, looked toward the adviser's empty office. It was strange how quickly the unusual became usual, how you adapted to things you never thought you'd be willing to accept. The Vietnamese suicides had caused barely a ripple in the newsroom last week. Were they so jaded that suicide had become commonplace, not spectacular enough to warrant a reaction? Or were they just burnt out?

Was this how people handled war? Was this how they were able to endure disasters?

He'd always heard that it was hope that kept people going, that acted as an antidote to despair, but he wondered now if "hope," the intangible quality that writers and philosophers attributed to human beings, that supposedly set humans apart from animals and enabled men and women to keep on going despite staggering odds and horrible conditions, was merely a romantic conceit, a made-up concept. Maybe it was the simple animal quality of adaptability that allowed people to go on.

Maybe people could survive violence and death and horror simply because they were able to get used to it.

He felt like an island of normalcy amid a sea of chaos, and he felt as though he was being slowly but surely eroded away.

He swiveled again, looked out the window at the hordes of students walking from one class to another. Hell, half the campus probably wasn't even aware of what was going on. The administration liked to refer to the "campus community," but there was no real community here. There was a collection of students who attended the same classes—half of whom didn't even talk to the people seated next to them. Too busy to read the *Sentinel*, too apathetic to participate in university-sponsored events, they attended the school but knew next to nothing about what went on here. Brea was a commuter campus, a school of strangers, and while that might make things easier for most people, it only made things harder for him.

To top it all off, Howie was sick. He claimed it was the flu, had asked Jim to drop off a paper to his World History professor, but he'd looked pale and his muscle coordination seemed to be even worse than usual. Jim had played along, had put on a happy face and pretended that he bought the flu story, that it was nothing, a simple illness, and Howie would be fine tomorrow, but he had a sinking feeling in his gut that it was the M.D., and all day he kept seeing the agonized expression on Howie's face as he'd tried in vain to lift his arm and point to where he'd left the history paper.

Maybe Howie wouldn't make it.

The thought kept forcing itself upon him, and he kept pushing it violently away.

Maybe Howie wouldn't make it.

At least there was Faith. Clichéd as it sounded, she was a ray of sunshine in the darkness of this semester. As his father used to say, flowers grew best in shit, and Faith probably appeared to him even more appealing than she would have otherwise against the background of the campus.

She made him glad he'd come back to school this semester.

Was there the possibility of something permanent between them? He didn't know. He thought so—but then again, he always thought so. He'd had lives planned out with Kathy, Rita, Jennifer. And now he was starting to imagine a future with Faith, adjusting the specifics of his general life plan to accommodate her, mentally noting the compromises he'd be willing to make, compromises on where they'd live, what they'd—

A chair clattered noisily to the floor, and Jim looked up. At the far end of the newsroom, Ford threw a punch at Eddie. Jim leapt from his seat. "Goddammit! Knock that shit off!"

Faruk stood as well, hurrying over to help Jim break up the fight.

"He started it," Ford said. "That fucker—"

Eddie swung, and Ford ducked to the right, the fist hitting him in the shoulder. He swung back.

Jim stepped between them, blocking a blow with his arm. "I said knock it off!" he yelled.

The two students glared at each other.

"One of you get the hell out of here. The other stay. If you're still pissed off tomorrow, then we'll have to sit down and talk it out."

"I'm leaving," Eddie said. "I'm tired of looking at his ugly face anyway."

"It beats looking at the top of your mama's ugly head, like I do every time she gives me a BJ!"

"That's your mom you're thinking about." Eddie grabbed a notebook off his desk, strode out the door.

"Eat me!" Ford called after him.

Jim looked at Faruk, who shrugged. He turned toward Ford. "So what was all that about?"

Ford looked at him, then turned away. "None of your damn business," he said. He walked over to his own desk, grabbed his books, and followed Eddie out the door.

Faruk grinned wryly. "God bless our happy home."

"Yeah," Jim said. Sighing, he sat at his desk, slumping down in the chair. He turned on his computer terminal. He'd been dicking away half the morning, staring into space and daydreaming, and there were still five or six articles he needed to proof before lunch.

He accessed the news file for today and called up the first story: a threatened loss of accreditation for the university's school of business administration. He read the lead, chopped the first sentence into two, and scanned the rest of the article, deleting two graphs.

"I'm going down to the Hunger Hut to grab some chow," Faruk said. "You want anything?

Jim looked up, shook his head.

"Be back in a while then."

Jim waved a distracted acknowledgment. He reread the article once more and was about to save the revised version on diskette when the screen went blank.

"Shit," he said.

He reached around the side of the terminal and turned the monitor off, then on again.

Nothing.

He checked underneath his desk. The power cord was still plugged into the surge protector on the floor. He straightened, looked again at the monitor.

Foreign characters and symbols filled the screen. He blinked, startled by the speed with which the characters had appeared. They were unlike anything he had ever seen before, neither Sanskrit nor Chinese nor Arabic, and he thought at first that the characters were merely a random display caused by a computer malfunction, but as he watched, the alien symbols moved, shifted, connected, blended together, circles and curves straightening out, edges flattening, until there was only a tight coil of straight lines in the center of the screen, like a rolled-up ball of string.

And then the string unwound.

Green lines whipped around, wiggling, curving, cornering, forming eyebrows, eyes, nose, lips, chin, cheeks.

A face.

Jagged, frazzled hair grew out from the side of the head.

A background brightened into existence.

The graphics were simple but effective, perspective line drawings like those on the old video game Battle-zone, three-dimensional in a way that more intricate animation could not be.

Jim wanted to look away but could not, his gaze held by the frightening visage before him. He had never seen anything like it, but something about the terrifying face seemed vaguely familiar, struck a chord of memory somewhere within him.

He was suddenly aware of the fact that he was alone in the newsroom, that there was no one else here.

The room's lights blinked off, and the picture on the screen grew correspondingly brighter. The only illumination in the newsroom came from the outside sunlight, filtered through the tinted windows, but even though it was a sunny day, the room's corners were dark, the areas around the desks shadowed.

He stared at the face.

It screamed, its voice a cross between a screeching rodent and a crying baby. The sound, synchronized perfectly with the movements of the overlarge and suddenly befanged mouth, emerged from the speakers connected to the newsroom's stereo.

Only the stereo had not been turned on today.

Jim's heart was hammering away in his chest. He'd jumped when the face had screamed, and the fear continued to grow as the features of the face settled back into placidity. Whatever was at this school, whatever was here—

It's an evil thing

—was powerful enough to create images on a computer, to control the lights in a room, to activate and utilize a stereo that was not on.

It was big, whatever it was, and his first impulse was to get the hell out of here, to run to his dorm, pack up his stuff, and catch the first bus to Williams. This was not something that could be fought, certainly not something that *he* could fight.

But if not he, who? He at least was aware of the

situation, had some idea of what was happening. It would not only be cowardly for him to bail, it would be irresponsible.

He thought of Faith, thought of Howie.

He owed it to the people he cared about—he owed it to himself—to do what he could.

But his resolve did not make the fear go away. His heart was still pounding, the hair on his arms prickling. He was not just afraid, he was terrified. Not only had he never before faced anything like this, he had never even imagined anything like this.

He looked at the face on the screen.

It grinned.

Screamed.

He ran out of the newsroom.

"Dr. Emerson?" Jim opened up the professor's office door without knocking.

Ian looked up, startled.

"I need to talk to you."

The professor nodded tiredly. "Come in, sit down."

Jim stayed standing in the doorway. "I didn't know who to go to. But since I talked to you before, I figured . . ." He took a deep breath. "This school is haunted."

Ian nodded grimly. "I know."

"You know?"

"I lied before. There is something here. I've noticed it. I've felt it. I don't know what it is, but I know it's growing stronger."

"You got that right. It just chased me out of the newsroom." Jim explained what had happened downstairs.

Ian was out of his seat before the story was finished. "Show me," he said. "Maybe it's still there."

The last thing Jim wanted to do was go back in that newsroom, but he did want the professor to see what had appeared on his computer screen. Maybe he would know what to do. At the very least, the event would be confirmed by someone else, someone older, an instructor. Besides, what could happen?

The creature could leap out of the screen and take off both their fucking heads. That's what could happen.

He followed Ian to the stairwell and, once on the third floor, led the way to the newsroom.

Where Faruk was at his desk, eating a hamburger.

Where the lights were on, and there was no sign that anything out of the ordinary had ever occurred.

The two of them walked over to Jim's terminal, which was shut off, the screen blank.

"I swear—" Jim began.

"I believe you," the professor said.

Jim turned on the computer, watched as an innocuous menu screen appeared. He turned the machine off, looked up at the professor, took a deep breath. "Why the sudden about-face? Why do you believe me now?"

"I believed you before."

"Then why did you lie to me before?"

Ian shrugged. "It's not important."

Jim watched his face, wondering if he should let the professor get away without a follow-up, finally deciding to let it slide. "So what do we do now?"

Ian smiled wryly, held up a thin book he'd carried down with him. "According to this, we blow the place up."

"Blow up? You mean, like, explode?"

"According to this." He handed Jim the volume. "It was written by my 'friend,' the guy you saw that night."

Jim licked his lips. "So what do we do? Get some ... dynamite or something?"

Ian shook his head. "That's what *he* thinks needs to be done. I'm not at all sure I agree with him. I'm going to talk to him, though, tell him what's happened, see what he knows."

"What do *you* think needs to be done?"

"I have no idea."

"Maybe there's some sort of ritual we can do, like an exorcism or something."

Ian smiled. "You ought to take my class on horror fiction. I think you'd do well in there."

"What if that ... thing comes back? What if I see it on my computer again?"

"Then turn off the—" The professor paused. "No. Wait a minute. Is there a printer connected to your machine?"

Jim nodded.

"Hit the print screen key. Try to print out a hard copy of the face. It might give us something to work with."

Jim recalled the face, shivered. "I'll try. But that thing scared the crap out of me."

"I know," the professor said. "I know exactly how you feel." He thought for a moment, glanced around the newsroom. "Tell me, do you guys have a morgue, a place where you keep old copies of the *Sentinel*?"

"Yeah."

"It's not computerized, by any chance? It's not online?"

"No. Why?"

"Well, I was wondering if you could do me a little favor. Some research. If you could, I'd like you to look through as many old issues as you can and compile a list of all the deaths that have happened here since the school opened—suicides, murders, accidents, whatever. Anything else you can think of that might be related too. Anything that seems weird or out of the ordinary."

Jim nodded. "I can do that."

"I don't know what it might tell us, but knowledge is power and, who knows, we might be able to discover something."

"So what about now? We just sit, wait and do nothing?"

"If you have any ideas, I'll be glad to listen to them. Anything short of blowing up the school. Other than that, I don't know what to suggest right now. Tell everyone you can—the people you think will listen to you and believe you. Try to get the warning out. Keep your eyes and ears open." He shrugged. "Do what you can."

"That's not very much, though, is it?"

"No," the professor admitted. "But right now that's all we have."

Jim did not manage to put the face completely out of his mind, but he did push it far enough to the side that he was able to concentrate on his afternoon classes and the newspaper. The paper was even finished on time again. If they didn't watch themselves, they might actually start meeting their deadlines and passing themselves off as an efficient, professional, and competent staff.

He had no intention of going back into the newsroom alone, so he'd brought his backpack with him to Production, just in case he was still working after everyone else had left. But most of the editors and copy editors were still around after putting the paper to bed.

He found that he still didn't want to go back into the
newsroom, though.

It was night.

He imagined the lights shutting off, the door slamming
shut and locking, the computers all winking on at the
same time, that green three-dimensional face screaming
at him from all four monitors.

He wanted to tell the other editors what had happened, but he found himself too embarrassed to do so.
Faruk, he was sure, had overheard at least part of his
conversation with Dr. Emerson, but if he had even an
inkling of what had occurred, he gave no sign of it, and
when Jim asked him to close up the newsroom, shut off
the computers, and turn off the lights, he did so without comment.

He felt guilty for sending Faruk off unprepared, and
he breathed easier when the news editor returned a few
minutes later.

"Thanks," he said sincerely.

Faruk looked at him strangely. "You're welcome."

They were all leaving now, packing up their stuff, getting ready to go, and Jim made sure they all left in a
group, so that no one was left on the floor alone. When
Jean remembered that she'd forgotten the folder with
her design project and went back in Production to get
it, Jim made sure that they all waited for her until she
returned. It might have seemed strange to some of them,
but he didn't care and he didn't offer any explanations.

Faruk was taking the paper to the printer, Jean was
going to the library to study, but the rest of the editors
were going to the Club to relax and unwind. They invited Jim to accompany them, but he begged off, explaining that he had to stop by Howie's room and see
how he was doing.

They parted outside the building, heading off in their
separate directions, and Jim made sure that they were
all out of sight before he started running toward the
parking lot.

He did not stop or slow down until he reached the
safety of the dorm.

3

Buckley didn't know whether it was himself or the class, but something wasn't right tonight, and he ended up dismissing his Chaucer seminar an hour early. They were supposed to go over "The Miller's Tale" this session—usually one of the semester's highlights—but tonight the story was going over like a vein in a hot dog, and getting these couch potatoes to respond at all was like pulling teeth.

He finally gave it up, tired of hearing himself talk, tired of having the tale's wonderfully bawdy humor fall on deaf ears, tired of looking out over the roomful of blank faces, and he dismissed the class and, out of spite, told them to write a three- to five-page analysis of the humor in "The Miller's Tale," using Northrop Frye's definition of humor and not C. Hugh Holman's.

The assignment would create more work for him as well, since he'd have to grade the papers the class wrote, but his job would be easier than theirs, and the punishment seemed appropriate.

Besides, he could always have a graduate assistant grade them.

He looked at his watch as he packed up his briefcase. Eight-thirty. Not bad. There was still time to make it home before nine and catch *Killer Klowns from Outer Space*.

There was no better way to end a bad day than by watching a great shitty movie.

He shut off the light, closed the classroom door, and headed down the hallway toward the elevator. The hallway was silent, the only sounds his loud, ragged breathing and the quiet flapping of his tennis shoes on the floor.

He quickened his pace.

Ian had sat him down this afternoon and told him his wild tale, and while Buckley had been properly skeptical, he had not been quite as skeptical as he should have been. He had not said so to Ian, whom he assumed had wanted him to offer rational contradictions and a healthy dose of down-to-earth reality, but he had not been particularly shocked by anything his friend had had to say. Sure, the demon in the computer was a little hard to swallow, but he chalked that up to stress. Everything else, the abnormal behavior, the violence, he'd noticed himself.

Hell, maybe even the creature wasn't that far-fetched. Maybe the kid *had* seen a face on his screen. Maybe some psycho computer science geek had programmed it to do just that in order to put a scare into him.

He wouldn't be surprised by anything anyone did.

Not this semester.

The elevator arrived, and Buckley got on, pushing the button for the first floor. He'd always thought that Brea was kind of strange. He'd never taught anywhere else, and it was possible that all universities were like this, but somehow he didn't think so. His first impression had been that the people here—students, staff, and faculty—had seemed unusually unfriendly. Nothing overt, of course. Nothing he could point to or pin down. But there was a general feeling of hostility he got from those with whom he came into contact, a sense that he was not really welcome here. That feeling had abated somewhat in the subsequent years, as he'd gotten to know people, but there still seemed to him to be an inordinate amount of infighting and backbiting among faculty members, an unusually high percentage of troubled and disturbed students.

And there was just something about the school that made him feel uncomfortable.

This semester, though, everything had kicked into overdrive. Whatever negative qualities had been in evidence before were now magnified tenfold. Tensions that had previously simmered below the surface were now boiling over the top. Weirdos were coming out of the woodwork.

Even Mike, the counterman at Brennan's, the bar he frequented, seemed to have noticed. The last time he'd been in, Mike had complained to him about the rowdiness of the students this year, their willingness, their *eagerness*, to get into a physical altercation over the most meaningless things. He said he'd kicked out more students during the past month than he had in the previous three years, and if things continued this way, he was going to have to hire a bouncer.

Weird shit.

The elevator doors opened, and Buckley got off, walking across the lobby and outside. The night was cool but humid, the air thick. Beneath the lights in the quad, the smog looked orange.

Although it was still early, the campus seemed relatively empty. One couple sat on the bench in front of the library. The student manning the donut and coffee concession stood alone behind his table.

Buckley strode across the quad. To his left, the Performing Arts Center was lit from the inside, the lights in its lobby on at full power. Was there some type of play or concert tonight? He didn't recall having heard or read anything about it. He altered his course, walking curiously toward the building. As he neared the entrance, he could see silhouetted squares of paper taped to the series of double doors. Flyers. He reached the doors and looked at the flyer nearest him: "Trio for Flute, Piano, and Screaming Flagellant. Little Theatre. 8:00." Frowning, he opened the door, stepped into the lobby. From the Little Theatre he heard discordant, atonal piano punctuated by shrill flute—and loud screams.

What the fuck was this?

A joke, he wanted to answer himself. But he had the sickening feeling that it was not a joke.

He walked across the length of the lobby, past the closed doors of the John Downey Theatre, to the open doors of the Little Theatre beyond. The piano and flute were louder.

So were the screams.

He walked inside.

A young female student dressed in a blue usher's jacket tried to hand him a program, but he ignored her and walked through the second set of doors into the darkness of the theater. It appeared to be full, the seats all seemed to be taken. On the stage, a bald, older man in a tuxedo was thumping away on the piano while a considerably younger woman, dressed in a strapless evening gown and facing away from the audience, played the flute. To their left, a heavyset man in black leather S&M gear was studiously reading sheet music placed on a stand in front of him and, at periodic intervals, whipping a naked man tied to a post with a cat o' nine tails.

The naked man was bleeding from an uncountable number of cuts and welts all over his body and was obviously in extreme pain. He screamed when whipped, blubbered and cried quietly between lashes.

Buckley winced with each whip snap, but in the aisle seat directly in front of him, an old woman gently rocked her head in time to the agonizing cries. A man across the aisle tapped time with his rolled-up program.

Buckley felt the flesh creep on the back of his neck. Maybe this was performance art. Performance artists did shit like this, hurt themselves on stage, tattooed themselves in front of an audience, gave themselves enemas. Maybe that's what this was.

But the makeup of the audience said otherwise. These were alumni. Conservative patrons. Older men and women with season passes.

That's what made it all so creepy.

In the beam of the stage lights, red mist sprang into the air as whip hit wound, and Buckley thought he could see each tiny microscopic droplet of blood fall slowly through the air to the stage.

In a pause between flute and piano, the flagellant screamed again as a portion of whip snapped his already bleeding genitals.

The man could not be a wiling participant in this, Buckley thought. He was obviously in real agony. He had to have been forced into doing this. That's why he was tied to the post—

He jumped as a finger tapped his shoulder.

He turned around. It was the usher. "Excuse me, sir. I'm afraid you'll have to sit down . . ."

"I'm leaving," Buckley told her.

The usher grinned up at him. "I thought you would."

He grabbed a program from her hand and stormed out of the theater, hoping he did not seem as rattled as he felt.

Behind him, in time to an out-of-tune arpeggio, the flagellant screamed.

4

It was her turn to help close, and Faith volunteered to take the first, third, and fifth floors.

Anything to avoid being alone on the sixth.

She had hinted around about the sixth floor, had indirectly asked Glenna and Sue if they felt as uneasy and uncomfortable there as she did, but as far as she could tell, her reaction was unique. No one else seemed to detect anything unusual on the library's top story.

At one time she probably would have believed she was overreacting, being overimaginative, being a baby. But after what Jim had said, and after what she herself had experienced on the walkway the other night, she had no doubts about the veracity of her feelings.

The walkway.

She had not told Jim what had happened there, and she was still not sure why. She felt guilty for not confiding in him, as though she was somehow betraying him or deceiving him or working against him, but of course that was stupid.

Wasn't it?

No. It wasn't. And she knew it wasn't. She knew what he thought about this school, knew his fears, knew that he would want to be apprised of anything that seemed even remotely unusual. Knowledge was power, and if something weird was going on here, he needed all the information he could get.

So why had she kept quiet about the walkway, about the shadows?

Maybe she was keeping quiet because she didn't want him to worry. Or because she didn't want him to nag her again about dropping out of Brea and taking the rest of the semester off.

No.

She didn't know why she hadn't said anything, but she did know that her motives were not that good, not that clean, not that pure.

Which was why she felt guilty.

She had never closed before, and after reviewing the procedures with her, Glenna followed her through the first and third floor, making sure she first warned patrons that the library was going to close before checking the aisles and carrels, the study rooms and bathrooms. After everyone was out, she was to turn off the lights on each floor, starting from the top story and working down.

Glenna was supposed to sign off the computers, lock

the doors, turn off the Xerox machines, and take care of Circulation, so she left Faith alone to handle the fifth floor, traveling up with her in the elevator, then taking the elevator back down alone to the first.

The bathrooms were close to the elevator, and, following the procedure she'd used on the third floor, she started there. She walked into the ladies' room, checked the stalls to make sure they were empty, and turned out the lights as she walked back outside. She knocked loudly on the door of the men's room, waited for a response, then knocked again. "Library's closing!" she announced. When there was no answer or acknowledgment, she pushed the door open to check inside and make sure no one was there.

From the far stall she heard the sound of shoes shuffling on tile, heard toilet paper being unrolled.

"Sorry." She ducked quickly out, embarrassed, her face burning. She walked away from the entire rest room area so she wouldn't have to see the man when he left. The childish thought occurred to her that it hadn't smelled like anyone was in the bathroom.

Maybe his shit didn't stink.

She smiled to herself as she quickly patrolled the perimeter of the fifth floor. Most of the patrons had noticed the dimming of the lights and had already left, but, of course, there were stragglers. She kicked a group of business students out of one of the small study rooms, and stood waiting patiently as a girl walked up and down an aisle, looking for a book that obviously wasn't there.

A young guy carrying an armload of books passed her on his way to the elevator. He looked a little bit like Keith, and she found herself thinking of her brother. He had moved out of the house and was now living in the garage of a friend over on Raitt Street. He had come by when their mom was out, to pick up his stuff, and while she'd questioned him about his plans, she hadn't questioned him too deeply. She wasn't sure if this was a permanent move or if he'd only be gone until he cooled off, but talking with him was like walking on eggshells, and she was careful not to annoy him, not to push him into what he might think was a corner by making him commit to a single plan or course of action.

Her mom had not even seemed to notice that Keith was gone.

Or care.

She wished, again, that the library never closed so she wouldn't have to go home.

She made the rounds once more, quickly, making sure that the floor was cleared, the last student gone, before returning to the men's room, to check it once again before she turned off the lights.

She knocked on the door, waited, knocked again, stepped in.

The toilet flushed, and she heard the sound of coins jingling and a belt buckle rattling as pants were pulled up.

She exited quickly and waited outside, pretending to examine the map of the floor that was mounted next to the elevator door so she wouldn't have to face the guy when he came out.

Only he didn't come out.

She waited.

Two minutes. Three. Four.

Something was definitely wrong here. A chill passed through her, and she realized, in a way that she hadn't a moment ago, that she was alone on the fifth floor.

Except for the guy in the bathroom.

If there was a guy in the bathroom.

She thought of the shadows in the walkway.

She was scared now. All of her instincts were telling her to leave, to go downstairs, to call the campus police or, at the very least, have Rennie come up here and check out the bathroom.

But she chose to ignore her instincts. She was her father's daughter, after all, and she wasn't about to let a little thing like this frighten her away. Especially not after her humiliating retreat the other night.

Humiliating?

That was why she hadn't said anything to Jim, she realized. She'd been embarrassed.

She was still frightened, the chill had not gone away, but as she stared at the closed door of the men's room, stubbornness and resolve temporarily pushed the fear aside. If there was a guy in there, a sicko or a pervert, and he was playing games with her, she'd kick his ass sideways to Monday. And if the bathroom was empty, she'd calmly walk out, turn off the floor's lights, and head down to the third floor to turn off the lights there.

Either way, she refused to be frightened.

She took a deep breath, walked into the men's room. "The library's closed," she announced. "You have to leave."

She headed toward the first stall, looking at the urinals as she passed by.

The lights went out.

In the impenetrable black of the darkness, she heard the sound of toilet paper being unrolled, thought she saw a flash of white movement in the mirror above the sink.

She ran out screaming, not pausing to hit the button and wait for the elevator, but speeding over to the stairwell door and running down, taking the steps two at a time.

She did not slow down until she reached the lighted lobby of the first floor.

TWENTY-ONE

1

It had been several weeks since they'd last seen a movie, and Ian and Eleanor drove down to the Port in Corona del Mar to catch the latest import, a sophisticated French romantic comedy. She liked it, he didn't, and afterward they stopped by a Haagen-Das shop for some frozen yogurt and walked down to the beach, where they sat on a park bench on a cliff overlooking the ocean.

They ate in silence, the only noise the hushed sound of the breaking waves. Here, with her, Brea seemed impossibly distant, the craziness of the past few weeks a memory, relegated to the status of history. Ian ate a bite of yogurt, stared down at the white foam of the waves, dimly phosphorescent against the blackness of the water. Far off, he could see tiny lights—boats—bobbing on the sea.

"So why don't you really want me to take classes?" Eleanor looked over at him. "Do you find it threatening?"

He was caught off guard by the question, and everything returned in a rush of immediacy that tainted the evening, that suddenly placed an overlay of interconnected darkness on things innocent and unrelated. "No," he said. "Of course not."

"I didn't think you were that type. But sometimes it's hard to tell. My ex-husband seemed as modern and liberated as they come when we were first together, but as I started to move up in my company and he stayed where he was in his, he started to resent me for it. He felt threatened by my success and blamed me for his lack of it."

It was the first time she'd brought up the subject of her ex on her own, without prodding, and Ian could not let this opportunity pass. "Is that what led to the breakup?"

"That and the fact that he was fucking a blond bimbo behind my back." She smiled, but there was very little humor in it. "You and I have something in common there."

It was strange to hear her say the word *fucking*, and it sounded harsh and bitter coming out of her mouth.

"Do you ever miss him?"

She looked at him. "Do you ever miss Sylvia?"

"Sometimes," he admitted.

"Well, you two were together longer."

"You don't miss him at all?"

She shook her head.

"Good."

They looked at each other and started to laugh. Ian threw his yogurt container in the trash can next to the bench and drew Eleanor close to him, kissing her. He tasted chocolate on her lips, coconut on her tongue.

She pulled away. "So why then?"

"Why what?"

"What are you so against me taking any classes?"

"I'm not *so* against it."

"You are. You might not realize it, but you are. In your passive-aggressive way, you as much as forbade me to take any night classes."

"I didn't forbid you."

"Not in so many words. But you definitely didn't want me to take any classes, and I want to know why."

"I told you, there've been a lot of incidents—"

"It's more than that, and you know it. There's some other reason."

He looked down at the waves, looked back at her, took a deep breath, and told her. He told her everything, starting with Stevens in his class that first day, through the rapes and riots, to Jim's face on the computer.

It was an effort for him to open up, to explain to her his feelings, his fears, but it was also oddly liberating, and in some strange way it felt like . . . like a victory, as though he had triumphed over something, though he did not know what that something was.

Trust.

That's what it came down to, really. Trust. And after Sylvia—

screaming as the man pumped away between her thighs

—he hadn't been sure he'd be able to trust anyone like that again, to put himself on the line and open up enough to appear foolish and stupid. But he trusted Eleanor, and as he talked and he saw that she wasn't automatically dismissing what he said out of hand, he grew more confident, he stuck less to facts, he relied more on describing feelings and hunches as he explained why he didn't want her to take any classes at Brea.

When he was through, she nodded. "Okay."

He blinked. "Okay? Just like that?"

"I'm not a dolt. You know I don't put much store by superstition. But I'm not willing to automatically dismiss things just because I don't agree with them. I don't think you're lying to me, and if what you say is true, then obviously I shouldn't take any classes at Brea. I'll go to Irvine instead."

"So you believe me?"

"I don't think I buy into your mad scholar's theories, but I think it's unusual for all of those things to be happening at once, and if other people have noticed it too . . ." She looked at him. "I trust your instincts."

"Thank God," he said. He smiled at her. "I didn't know how I was going to keep you from signing up for classes."

"All you had to do was tell me the truth."

He nodded. "I'll remember that next time."

"Make sure you do."

Her yogurt container followed his into the trash, and she put an arm around his shoulder as they stared out to sea.

2

Public liaison representative.

It was a bogus job, a gravy train, a position he'd been given for knowing the right people at the right time, and Cliff Moody knew it. For two years now, he'd hidden himself away in the bowels of the Administration building, issuing press releases when told to do so, fielding softball questions from the press when instructors were hired or retired, publicly stating the party line when the fraternities got out of hand. It should have been a part-time job, really, but who was he to complain? With no direct supervision, no administrative official to whom he had to report on a regular basis, he'd granted himself the privilege of coming to work late, leaving early, taking long lunches.

But now the chickens were coming home to roost.

He looked around the conference room table at Diana Langford, UC Brea's president, at Ralph Lyons, the campus police chief, at Hardison O'Toole, the dean of Student Affairs.

"How many students are missing?" the president asked.

The police chief looked down at the report in front of him. "Officially only three. We have complaints from the friends and roommates of ten others, though. As you're aware, with no official roll sheet each day, like you'd have with, say, a high school, there's no easy way to verify attendance. All we can do is check with the students' instructors to ask if they've noticed any absences."

Cliff straightened in his seat as the president looked in his direction. "The question is," she asked, "how do we contain this? How do we make sure that this information does not get out to the press and the public? We'll be starting our fall fund drive next week, and the last thing we need is for the alumni to hear that students are disappearing. They're probably already spooked from that riot coverage. Nothing closes up pocketbooks faster than crime or scandal."

"I don't think there's any danger," Cliff said. "At least not from a P.R. standpoint." He turned to Lyons. "No complaints have been filed by parents? No one's gone to the Brea P.D.?"

The chief shook his head.

"There you go. It's probably nothing anyway. Kids at this age are flighty to begin with. A lot of them can't handle the freedom of a university environment. They're always skipping class or taking off on road trips or dropping out. My bet is that most of them will show up eventually. These are probably isolated, unconnected occurrences.

I don't think that there's someone out there kidnapping college students."

The president nodded, and Cliff breathed an inward sigh of relief. She bought it. He didn't know if he was right or not, and he didn't really care. All he wanted was to be left alone and not have to deal with the problem, if there was one. Let someone else take care of it. Let Lyons take care of it. It was his job anyway.

"Then we'll leave things as they stand," the president said. "For now." She turned toward Lyons. "Your people will keep this under wraps until we find out if it's a real situation or not?"

"It is real," the police chief said. "As I stated, there are three confirmed missing persons—"

"Your people will keep this under wraps?"

Lyons stared at the president defiantly. "We will not volunteer information because we have no information to volunteer. If someone asks us whether those three students are missing, we will say yes."

"And you will say that the other ten are not."

"We will say that there is no investigation into those disappearances as of yet."

The president stood, smiling sweetly. "Then I guess we're through here today." She nodded at Cliff, at O'Toole, at Lyons. "Gentlemen."

3

"This is the first class I've ditched in the four years I've been here," Jim said. "You're a bad influence on me."

Faith did not even smile as he led her down the dorm hallway to his room.

"Joke," he said.

"I know."

They walked the rest of the way in silence. Faith had been unusually quiet and subdued for the past few days, and though she'd obviously seen or experienced something, and though he was so desperately anxious to find out what it was that he was almost tempted to shake it out of her, he'd forced himself not to ask. As Howie had said when he'd told his friend the situation, Faith would tell him when she was ready; give her time, don't pressure her.

At least Howie hadn't been lying. It really had been the flu, not the M.D., and he was once again as healthy as ever.

Or as healthy as he ever got.

Jim felt a little guilty for not spending more time with his friend. He hadn't really neglected Howie since he and Faith had started going out, but the amount of time they spent together had been drastically cut down, and though Howie professed understanding and claimed that it didn't bother him, Jim knew that it had to hurt.

He'd make it up to Howie. Somehow.

Jim took out his key ring, found the key to his room, and unlocked the door. "This is it," he said. "Home."

They walked inside. He was by no means a messy housekeeper, was in fact what Howie referred to as "far too neat and tidy for a heterosexual male," but he'd still spent the better part of last night dusting, vacuuming, and tidying up the place in preparation for Faith's inaugural visit.

She glanced around the room at his plank-and-cinder-block bookshelves, at his saguaro cactus skeleton, at the chaotic jumble of posters, prints, signs, photos, and ads that decorated the walls. "Impressive," she said.

"Is is what you expected?"

She glanced around the room once more and, for the first time that morning, smiled. "Yeah," she said. "It is."

Jim closed the door behind her, locking it. They'd come up here ostensibly because Faith was curious to see where he lived, but the full-size bed that took up the entire center of the room eloquently symbolized the real reason they'd skipped American Lit today. Faith walked over to the bed, sat down on its edge. "Comfortable."

Jim was suddenly nervous. She'd had her top off in his car, and he'd kissed her breasts. They'd done a little squirming and rubbing. He'd even had his hand inside her panties, a finger inside her.

But this was it.

He couldn't help feeling that it should be different. The mood should be lighter, more upbeat, more happy. She should at least enjoy what they were about to do.

But whatever had been weighing her down the past week or so was still there, between them, and he decided, promise to himself or no promise, that the time had come to find out what was the matter.

He sat down next to her on the bed. "What is it?" he asked. "What's wrong?"

"Nothing."

"Come on."

She seemed unsure of how to respond, and he waited patiently until finally she leaned back on the bed, closed her eyes, and said, "I think it's after me."

He didn't know what "it" was, not exactly, but he knew what she meant, and fear grew within him. His room suddenly seemed dark, and he wished he'd turned on a light or opened the shades. "What happened?" he asked quietly.

"Last week, on Saturday evening, after work, around five—"

"Before we went out?"

"—before we went out, I . . . I saw something. I was parked in the faculty lot, and I thought I'd take a shortcut through the walkway between Performing Arts and Biological Sciences, and . . ."

"And what?" he prodded.

She sat up. "I know this sounds stupid, but the shadows on the sidewalk were moving, the shadows of the plants and bushes and trees. The things themselves weren't moving, just their shadows. Then the shadows started kind of whipping around and blending together, and this big, birdlike shadow flew out and started speeding across the sidewalk toward me, and I turned around and hauled."

"Jesus!" he said. "Why didn't you tell me this when it happened?"

"I don't know!" She matched his angry tone, and they stared at each other until he finally looked away.

"Is that it?" he asked.

"No." She told him about the men's room in the library, about the noises of the man who wasn't there, about the lights going off, about her flight.

"Shit. No wonder you've been spaced." He reached for her hand, held it, squeezed it. "That's all, right? There's nothing else?"

She smiled. "No."

"Your rug hasn't attacked you? Your toilet hasn't turned on you?"

"No."

It was his turn to lie back on the bed. "Jesus. I thought I had it bad. I thought—" He broke off, sat up. "Do you think this kind of stuff is happening to everyone? Do you think everyone's seeing these things?"

She shook her head. "No one in the library seems to've noticed anything weird. I've hinted around about it, but I don't think anyone's seen anything."

"Then the question is, why are we being targeted?"

"I don't know."

He looked at her. She smiled back at him. She obviously felt lighter, but he felt heavier and it was as if the weight of the knowledge had been passed from her to him. No wonder she'd been under such a cloud. He was impressed with her strength. He was not sure he could've borne up as well as she had. He'd seen the face on his computer screen, and he'd run directly to Dr. Emerson. Hell, he'd been half tempted to bail out entirely and hit the road. Yet she had not left school, had not quit her job at the library, had not said anything to anybody. She'd faced it alone and kept it to herself.

Why hadn't she told him?

She had now.

Yes, she had now, and he supposed that was all that mattered. She might have needed some prodding, but prodding or no, she had obviously trusted him enough to confide in him, to share this with him. He felt suddenly close to her, closer than he had ever felt before, and he leaned forward and kissed her. Her lips were soft, tasting lightly of cherry.

She pulled back, looked into his eyes. "I love you," she said.

There was no preface, no possible face-saving equivocation, none of the protective measures he would have taken. There were only the words themselves, stated and left out there to hang.

"I love you too," he responded, and they kissed again. This time it was long, this time there were tongues. He put an arm around her, pulled her closer, but the positioning was awkward, and they leaned back on the bed until they were pressed against each other, arms and legs entwined. He was filled with a deep passion and an even deeper feeling of closeness, and he rolled over, on top of her, and she spread her legs to accommodate him.

And, suddenly, it was gone. Suddenly he wanted to hit her. Her eyes were closed, her mouth open and pressed against his, the softness of her crotch pressed against the hardness of his erection, and he had the urge to just haul off and smack her one upside the head. Her passivity was maddening, the way she just lay there like a rag doll while he climbed onto her, like the fucking airheaded slut that she was—

He pulled away from her, pulled off her, staggering to his feet and stumbling away from the bed.

"What is it?" she asked. "What's wrong?"

He shook his head, trying to catch his breath. What *was* wrong? One minute he was desperately in love with her, and the next minute he wanted to hit her, hurt her. Had this happened a month ago, a week ago even, he would have thought he was going crazy, would have thought he was schizophrenic or something and in desperate need of psychological help. But this impulse toward violence did not come from within him, it came from without. It was in the air, as Howie said, and like an antenna, he had picked it up.

He took a deep breath. Whatever it was, it was gone now. He had fought it off or it had fled, and though he wasn't sure he'd be able to recapture the mood of a few moments before, he lay back down on the bed next to Faith and put his arm around her.

The mood may have been interrupted but it had not disappeared, and they kissed, embraced, and soon her blouse was off and then her bra, his shirt, her pants, his pants, her panties, his underwear. He was not in her yet, but he was on her, and she kissed him softly, rubbed her hands gently over his back, moved beneath him, moaning into his mouth.

He was hard, he was excited, he was ready, but ...

But this was moving too slow. He wanted it faster. He wanted it harder.

He didn't want to make love.

He wanted to fuck.

She ran a hand through his hair, licked his lips.

Tired of the slowness, he pushed himself up, knelt

between her legs, and shoved her thighs roughly apart. She gasped but did not object, and between the folds of her thick vaginal lips, he saw glistening wetness.

He fell on top of her and shoved it in hard.

She bucked against him, and he reached underneath the cheeks of her buttocks as he pumped away, his right middle finger forcing its way into the tightly closed opening of her anus.

His index finger followed.

And she liked it.

4

They did not talk about it afterward, and she wondered if he was as embarrassed as she was.

Or as scared.

She did not know what had come over her. Or over him. But both her vagina and her . . . other opening were aching, sore, and the seam of her jeans chafed against the raw skin as she pulled them on. She had never before thought about doing what they had done. Even in her most far-reaching fantasies, it had not been considered, and she felt humiliated by it now, though she had wanted it at the moment.

Maybe she really was her mother's daughter.

That was scary.

She knew herself fairly well, or at least she thought she did. She considered herself open and uninhibited, and, sexually, there were very few things that she would be unwilling to try. So it was not really the acts themselves that shocked her, it was her own inability to remember making any conscious decisions to perform them. Or submit to them. Passion was great, and in film, in fiction, the surrender to an unthinking animal lust always seemed wonderful—pure and natural and romantic—but in real life it was frightening. It was as though she was merely a puppet, her body acting out the will of another while her own thoughts and feelings remained numb and dormant. The last hour was little more than a fogged blur to her, as though she had been drunk or high, and the loss of control had been anything but wonderful.

She did not know what was scarier: the thought that

her will was weak enough and her lust strong enough to create this sort of split personality, or the idea that whatever was causing all of the other strange things at Brea was making her behave this way.

Brea.

Finally, when it came down to it, that's what she really believed, that's where she placed the blame, and though he said nothing and they had not yet mentioned it, she was sure that was what Jim was thinking too.

Which meant that he was probably just as scared as she was. If it could pick them out like this, manipulate them, force them to do what it wanted, then what hope could they possibly have of fighting it or standing up to it?

None.

They dressed in silence and walked out of the room together, Jim locking the door behind them. She could not help noticing that he seemed to be walking as gingerly as she was.

He was sore too.

There were students in the hallway, though there had not been on their way in. They were neighbors, friends, and acquaintances, and Jim introduced them to her as they passed on their way to the stairs. Though she told herself she was imagining it, she couldn't shake the feeling that the other students had come out of their rooms specifically to see her.

She had been *loud*.

And she knew they'd heard her.

She mumbled a quick hello at each of Jim's introductions and kept her head down, her eyes averted, until they reached the stairway.

They were silent as they walked down the steps and out of the dorm, but as they crossed the parking lot and approached the campus proper, Jim began to talk.

"What was that?" he asked. "What happened back there?" He looked at her. "And don't tell me you didn't notice it, because I know you did."

She shrugged. "You were possessed by a demon, and now I'm carrying Satan's baby."

He stopped next to a tan Toyota, turning on her. "That's not funny. Don't even joke about that."

She held up her hands. "Sorry."

A couple sat up in the backseat of the Toyota, glaring at them, the boy motioning angrily for them to move on.

Faith glanced into the car as she walked past, saw the boy's shirt unbuttoned, the girl's top untucked. Both were scowling at her. She looked over at Jim, and though she tried to keep a straight face, she could not help smiling, and by the time they reached the next aisle of cars, they were both laughing out loud.

"At least some things never change," Jim said.

"Did we look that ridiculous to your dorm mates?"

"You caught on to that, huh?"

"Why else would they have been out there?"

"They had to've heard us."

Now that they were out here, in the open, in the sunshine, talking about it, the incident did not seem so menacing, so ominous. It had been strange, no doubt about that. But it had not ultimately been anything harmful. Painful maybe, but not harmful.

Maybe it was like one of those benign ghosts that haunted houses and coexisted with the people living there.

Maybe, every once in a while, they'd just be overcome with the desire for rough sex.

There were worse things that could happen.

She thought of her botany class, thought of the shadows on the walkway, thought of the fifth-floor men's room.

"So what are you going to do about the library?" Jim asked. "Are you going to quit?"

It was as if he had been reading her mind, and she was caught off guard for a second. "I don't know."

"I don't think you should work there anymore."

"I could try to get another job, but . . . I have to work somewhere. I don't have any money. That's why I'm on work-study."

"Drop out."

"Not that again."

He stopped, turned, held her shoulders. "What's more important? Your classes or your life? I mean, what are you taking this semester that's so important? American lit? You could take that anywhere, anytime."

"That's not the point."

"Then what is the point? You know what's happening.

You've seen it, you've felt it, you've experienced it. You can't be so stupid that—"

She pulled away from him, walked behind the next car.

He hurried around the front of the vehicle to intercept her. "I'm sorry. I didn't mean to call you stupid, but—"

"You know," she said, "I don't need you to tell me what I should do and what I shouldn't do. I'm a grown woman. I can make my own decisions."

"Fine," he said. "Let's not fight."

She glared at him. "Why are you staying, huh? Why don't you drop out?"

That threw him. "Because . . . Because I . . ."

"Because you what?"

"I don't know. Because maybe I can do something. Because I have responsibilities. Because I'm editor of the paper—"

"Oh, and I'm nothing, huh? I have no responsibilities. I'm not important."

He shook his head, exasperated. "I never said that."

"Well—"

"Well, why do you want to stay?"

"I don't want to stay."

"Then why don't you want to go?"

She glared at him. "I. Don't. Know."

"Okay," he said. "Okay, then. Fine. We won't fight about it anymore. I won't even bring it up."

"But you'll be thinking it."

"Shit!" He slammed his hand down on the hood of a red Lexus, and the car's alarm went off, an electronic whooping noise that pierced the mid-morning air. They moved quickly away from the vehicle. "I care about you, I'm concerned about you, I don't want anything to happen to you. That's all. I'm not trying to boss you around or infringe on your rights or anything. I mean, who am I to say? Maybe all this is happening to you for a reason. Maybe you're supposed to stay. I don't know. I don't know how these things work. I've never been involved in a haunting or a possession or whatever the fuck this is."

She took a deep breath, closed her eyes, opened them, exhaled. "I didn't mean to bite your head off. I know you're concerned. It's just . . . I'm under a lot of stress here, and I don't want you to put even more pressure on me, that's all."

He reached forward, took her hand. "I'm not trying to put pressure on you."

"I know."

"Maybe we should talk to Dr. Emerson about this. This is his field, this is his subject. Maybe it'll help somehow. Maybe he'll know what to do."

She smiled wanly. "Tell him what? About our . . . tryst?"

"No, but everything else. Who knows? Maybe this is good. Maybe you have, like, the key to everything, and the evil spirit or whatever it is is trying to drive you away to keep you from using it and solving the problem and living happily ever after."

"Yeah. Sure."

"Isn't that how these things work?"

"It's no crazier than anything else."

They started walking again, moving down the aisle toward the campus proper. "You want to help me on this?" Jim asked.

"Yeah. Sure. I guess. What do you mean?"

"Dr. Emerson wanted me to do a little research, check out all the murders, suicides, deaths, riots, whatever, that have happened here since the school opened."

"I could help you with that."

"We have copies of all of the *Sentinels* since the paper started publishing in 1959. That's a lot of issues, but I figure with both of us going through them, we could get it done a lot faster. We'd only have to look at the front pages. The stuff we're looking for would've been front-page news."

"And we just keep a running tally?"

"Something like that."

"When do we start?"

"You can start whenever. After your classes—" He looked at her. "You don't work today, do you?"

She shook her head.

"I have to put out today's paper, so I probably won't be much help until that's done. But the morgue's yours. I'll get you a chair or something, maybe a tape player so you won't be so lonely."

"The morgue." She shivered. "Appropriate."

A horn honked behind them, and they both jumped. Faith turned around. A ponytailed guy in a beat-up VW van waved at them, his head and arm sticking out of the driver's window. "You leaving?"

She shook her head.

"No," Jim said.

"Shit." He turned off the van's engine.

Jim reached for her hand, held it. She looked over at him, and he grimaced. "What is it?" she asked.

He glanced around, to make sure no one was within earshot. "I'm . . . sore."

She smiled, nodded. "Me too."

"I mean really sore. It might be bleeding."

She gave his hand a small squeeze. "Sorry."

"It's not your fault. But it's going to be . . . awhile. You know? Until we can . . . do it again? Several days at least."

"That's okay," she said. But it wasn't really okay, and an unfamiliar anger coursed through her.

Several days before they could do it again?

Her mother's daughter.

She tried to ignore the anger, tried to make it go away, tried to make her feelings match the understanding expression on her face, but she could not do it.

Several days?

She wasn't sure she could wait that long.

5

Ian stood in the English department office, sorting through the envelopes in his mailbox, half hoping, half dreading that there would be a message from Gifford Stevens.

Nothing.

Invites to conferences, applications for grants, ads for textbooks.

He dropped all of it in the wastebasket.

He turned, smiled at Maria, who was just hanging up the phone. "How goes it?" he said.

The secretary shrugged. "Could be better, could be worse."

"That's life."

"That's what people say."

He chuckled, started out the door.

"Oh, Dr. Emerson?"

"Yes?" He turned back toward her.

"Do you know anything about computers?"

"Not really. But I can fake it. What's the matter?"

She pointed at the screen in front of her, frowning. "Look at this."

Ian walked around her cockpit-like desk and looked over her shoulder at the screen.

His heart began doing a Pancho Sanchez in his chest.

There was a face on the screen.

A horribly distorted three-dimensional line-drawn face that grinned back at him and winked crudely.

The face disappeared, the individual lines of its form detaching from each other, moving around the screen, reforming as pictographs: whirled spirals, spiky triangles, strangely angled animal figures.

"What's wrong with it?" Maria asked, and the puzzled placidity of her voice made him realize that she saw this as merely the latest in a series of ordinary computer problems, nothing to be unduly alarmed about.

His hands were shaking. He practically had to force himself to breathe.

"Turn it off," he said, keeping his voice as calm as possible. "Turn it off and then turn it on again, see if that clears it."

She turned off the power switch.

The pictographs remained.

"That's weird. Maybe the switch is broken." She flipped it on and off.

The screen went blank.

She was about to turn the computer on again when there was a hiss of white static from the monitor, a staccato-rhythmed noise that sounded like the electronic re-creation of a rattlesnake's rattle. She pulled her hand quickly back, and from the blankness of the screen emerged the face again, its befanged mouth opening and closing in time to the noise.

"Dr. Emerson?" She turned toward him, and there was a new note in her voice.

Fear.

"I don't know what it is," he said. He had leaned forward to get a better look, but his hands remained on the back of the secretary's chair. He did not want to touch the computer.

A band of green appeared beneath the face, spanning

the width of the screen, and a series of letters, words, appeared sequentially in negative image, black on green.

He read the words as they formed: "Tell Dr. Emerson to cease and desist."

The movement of the face's mouth and the bursts of hiss were synchronized to correspond with the syllables of the words.

"What's that mean?" Maria asked, and Ian shook his head, indicating that he didn't know.

But he did know.

The words were replaced by others: "Or I will have his head."

Tell Dr. Emerson to cease and desist or I will have his head.

I? Who was "I"?

The university?

The face grinned.

He wanted to pick up the monitor and smash it, throw it down on the ground, break it, kill it, but he knew that Maria would think he was crazy.

Besides, if he did that, the face, the words, would just pop on another screen somewhere else on campus.

Why did he believe Stevens? Why did he think it was the university itself? Why didn't he think it was a demon, a ghost, an outside entity?

Because the groundwork had already been laid in his mind: *Hill House. The House Next Door. Burnt Offerings.*

But what if that had been Stevens' inspiration as well? What if this was all merely a series of bizarre coincidences tangentally tied into a theory by a horror anthologist who'd read a few too many novels.

No.

The face on the computer was real. The violence this semester was real.

"What is that?" Maria asked, staring at the screen. "What does it mean?"

"I don't know," Ian said.

"You think some hacker got in here and did that?"

"Probably," he lied. "I think what you should do is tell Kiefer, have him talk to someone from the Computer Science department and see if they can figure it out. Until then, why don't I just unplug it and put it into the Supply room?"

"But I need it to work on."

"Can't you use someone else's P.C.?"

"No. Everything's on this hard disk. I didn't have time to back anything up."

"Well—"

She turned. "Just leave it here. It worked fine before you came in, maybe it'll fix itself when you leave. Maybe whoever programmed it programmed it to do this when you were in the room."

That's asinine, he wanted to say, but he smiled, nodded, and backed away from her chair, walking around her desk and toward the door. "Sorry I couldn't be more help," he said.

She waved him away. "It's not your fault. Thanks for your help anyway."

He stepped into the hall.

"See?" she called out after him. "Now it works fine!"

He walked back to his office, feeling cold.

"Dr. Emerson?"

Ian looked up. He'd been half dozing, the reality of his office slowly transforming into the bedroom of his childhood beyond his closed eyelids, and the world returned with a snap as he straightened in his chair and focused on the figure in the doorway. "Oh, hi, Jim. Come in."

Jim walked into the office. Behind him came one of the young women from his Creative Writing class.

Jim nodded. "Dr. Emerson? This is my, uh ..." He looked at his companion for help.

"Girlfriend."

He smiled. "My girlfriend, Faith."

"I recognize her." He smiled at Faith. "Hi."

"She's been helping me with the research." He lowered his voice. "She knows."

"Sit down," Ian said, motioning to the chairs in front of his desk. "Both of you."

"You're not going to believe what I found." Jim said, sitting. He glanced toward Faith. "What we found."

"Good," Ian began. "Tell me—"

"Mama's boy!" Buckley swung around the corner of the door frame into the office, stopping short when he saw the two seated students. "Oh. Sorry," he said to Ian. "Didn't know you were busy. I'll come back later."

"No. Get in here. You're in on this too."

"In on what?"

"We've been discussing the university. And what's been happening here."

"What's been happening? You mean—"

"The weird stuff."

Buckley closed the door behind him, pulled a dusty folding chair from its spot against a bookcase, and sat down. "I'm in."

"This is Professor French," Ian explained.

"Buckley, to students who aren't my students."

Jim nodded at him politely. "Jim," he said. "And my girlfriend, Faith."

"Jim and Faith have been researching some of the more sordid details of our school's history," Ian explained. "They've been looking through back issues of the *Sentinel*. I thought if we could get some facts and figures on the violence here, we might be able to establish some sort of pattern."

Jim nodded. "Want to know what we've dug up?"

"Let us have it."

"It's a good thing you're sitting down for this one." He unfolded the sheet of paper in his hand. "Hard statistics: eighty-seven suicides, thirty murders, four hundred and eighteen rapes, sixty-nine missing persons since nineteen eighty. The thing is, the violence has been steadily increasing in both frequency and intensity. It's always been high. Faith used the library's database to compare these numbers with other campuses in the UC system, and there's just no comparison. We're way off the curve. But even for us the past two semesters have been unusual. And this semester ..." He motioned toward the window. "The facts speak for themselves." He handed Ian a sheaf of papers. "I printed it all out here and made a copy for you. There's even a graph on the last page there so you can chart it."

Ian glanced at the papers, shuffling through them. "What about other deaths, natural deaths?"

Jim nodded. "That's on there too." He looked down at his own printouts. "And that's also way off the scale.

Two hundred and six faculty, staff, and students died of so-called 'natural causes' during that time period."

"Shit," Buckley said. "Didn't anyone ever notice this? Somewhere down the line, didn't some bureaucrat pick up a report and note those numbers and say, 'Hey, something's wrong here'?"

Jim paused, looked at Faith, who nodded. "As a matter of fact," he said, "they did. Nineteen eighty-one. A student had just shot to death a teacher who'd given him a bad grade—"

"I remember that," Buckley said. "Paul Norson. Chemistry."

"Yeah. Anyway, the regents issued a letter to the president that said that an investigation was being conducted into the university's disciplinary policies because the rate of violent crime here was way too high. There was a reference to anti-war demonstrations and 'student unrest' and 'outside agitators,' and I gathered that there'd been a study before, in the sixties or early seventies, because even for that time period the turbulence here was way out of proportion to everywhere else. But in this letter the regents seemed to be placing the blame on university policies instead of radical students. The impression I got was that they'd come across some facts they couldn't explain and they were looking to place blame."

"So what happened?" Ian asked.

"I don't know. I found one short article on it, but no follow-up. I have no idea what happened. It might be on a back page somewhere—we basically stuck to front pages. I could check on it."

Buckley looked at Ian. "Hell, we were here then. Why didn't we hear about this?"

Ian shrugged.

Jim smiled wanly. "Maybe you guys should read the *Sentinel* a little more often."

Buckley laughed. "Maybe."

"You know," Jim suggested, "maybe we should talk to the administration, tell them what's going on. Maybe they know something we don't."

Buckley snorted.

"That's not such a bad idea," Ian said. "I don't know where all this is headed or what we can do about it, but the more allies we have on our side, the better. Besides,

Jim might be right. They could be working at this from another angle. We need to pool our resources so we're not at cross-purposes. I'll talk to President Langford."

Jim nodded enthusiastically. "I could start writing a column about this in the *Sentinel*, let people know—"

"But do you want to let *it* know that you know?" Faith said quietly.

They all turned to look at her. She'd spoken softly, but both the fear and sincerity in her voice immediately captured their attention.

She reddened. "Whatever it is," she continued, "whether it's a power or a thing or a creature, it might be better not to tip it off, not to show our hand. If it knows that we're aware of what's happening, it might come up with a course of action. We could use the element of surprise. We might need the element of surprise."

"Good point," Ian said.

Buckley sighed. "Then how do we know who we can trust? I mean, it's obvious that this whatever-it-is has gotten through to some people. If we tell them, then they'll know, then *it* will know."

Ian nodded. "Another good point. What we do is talk to our friends, hint around, feel them out, find out where they stand. As far as I'm concerned, there are two types of people—"

"Those who are with us and those who are against us," Buckley said.

"Not exactly, Joe McCarthy. There are those who, for want of a better word, have been 'corrupted.' The ones who are starting the fights, committing the crimes, killing themselves. Then there are the others, like us, who haven't been corrupted. We need to find the others like us, get together and see if we can come up with some ideas. We have practically every discipline imaginable at this school. Somewhere, from among the scientists and philosophers and sociologists, we should be able to find some people with ideas. I'll talk to everyone I know."

"I will too," Buckley said.

Jim and Faith nodded.

"Then we'll have them talk to everyone they know, and eventually we should hit everybody."

"Pyramid scheme." Buckley grinned. "Good tactic."

"Is that it?" Jim said. "Is that all we can do?"

Ian shook his head, looked from one to the other. "I think it's also time," he said, "for us to talk to the mysterious Gifford Stevens."

Tuesday was his late night. On Tuesday evenings he taught Contemporary Literary Criticism, and although in past semesters that course had been a pleasant one to teach, filled with hip students who were into and up on the latest trends and theories and more than willing to engage in heated discussion, this term the class seemed to be peopled with hard-core math and P.E. majors, students who not only did not understand literature but were actively hostile toward it.

Tonight, once again, it was obvious that almost no one in the class had done the required reading, and although he was tempted to tell them all to go home and not come back until they'd completed all of the to-date assignments listed on the syllabus, a perverse part of him decided to do just the opposite. So he lectured for the entire class period, leaving no room for any discussion, no matter how pertinent, and he made sure that he went over, keeping them until ten, fifteen minutes after the class was scheduled to end.

The creepy thing was that Buckley had told him earlier that the exact same thing was happening to his Chaucer seminar—the same disinterest, the same antagonism—and that worried him. A pattern was developing here.

He did not like patterns.

Evil was so much easier to deal with if it was random.

He kept coming back to that word. Evil. It had gone out of fashion even in contemporary horror fiction, apparently considered too culturally relative in these post-Clive Barker days, but it fit. He was not sure he subscribed to the Judeo-Christian conception of evil, that petty and peculiarly personalized belief that considered trivial foibles like gluttony and pride to be mortal sins. He did not really buy that. But the willful causing of death and suffering, whatever the motive, he definitely considered evil.

And the university was causing both death and suffering.

For its own entertainment, according to Gifford Stevens. Stevens.

He'd tried his damnedest to get in touch with that "psychoprof," as Buckley called him, but with no luck. The number listed at the end of the "dissertation" had been disconnected, and he'd done everything else he could possibly think of, from dialing Information for every city in Orange County to calling the vanity press publisher of *Fighting the Supernatural With Firepower* (which surprisingly, was still in existence), to calling CNN and asking if they'd taken down his number and/ or address after the University of Mexico story in case they needed a demolitions expert in the future.

Nothing.

He wasn't really surprised, but it was frustrating nevertheless. Stevens was the one who'd started this whole ball rolling, and he'd teased them and goaded them and then disappeared. It was highly probable, Ian thought, that he was at one of the other universities mentioned in his paper, trying to drum up support against that school. But it seemed odd that someone as adamant, as militant, as Stevens had been that first day in class would play little games like leaving notes and blueprints and bomb recipes, or ordering rare books from local specialty shops. He'd seemed to think the situation was far too serious and far too critical to spend his time dicking around in such a haphazard way.

Maybe Buckley was right. Maybe he was a psycho.

Ian picked up his briefcase, turned off the lights in the room, closed the door.

Ordinarily at this time of night the hallway was silent. As far as he knew, his was the latest evening class on this floor of the building. But tonight, from the area down toward the elevator, he heard chanting, the deep, rhythmic cadences of what sounded like a ritual. The sound, at this place and this time, particularly under these circumstances, seemed eerie, caused gooseflesh to rise on his arms. The sound grew louder as he walked down the half-lit hallway toward the elevator, and he realized as he strode down the corridor that it was coming from the still-lit room where Elizabeth Somersby held her D. H. Lawrence seminar.

But the seminar was supposed to have ended at nine. *Who was in there now?*

He considered turning around, heading toward the

back of the building, and taking the stairs instead of the elevator. Something was definitely not right here. But his curiosity was as strong as his fear, and he kept walking toward the light. He recognized Elizabeth's voice as he drew closer to the open doorway, and his first thought was that the class had merely been extended and was still going on. But graduate students didn't chant, and he held his breath, tiptoeing quietly toward the room.

He stopped just this side of the door, listening.

"We know now that *The Plumed Serpent* is Lawrence's best work, the clearest expression of his mature theories and philosophy. Lawrence's belief in the authority of the superman, which unifies his political, religious, and sexual theories, is present in its embryonic stages in his earlier works and can be found in a more watered-down form in his later novels, but it is here that his unique vision is given its fullest reign."

"The Morning Star!" the class chanted as one.

"Yes," Elizabeth said, and her voice had dropped an octave. "We are here to worship the Morning Star."

"The Morning Star!"

"In this seminar I am the leader, correct?"

"Correct!" the students shouted in militaristic unison.

Ian heard what sounded like a whip hitting tabletop. "I am the master and you are my slaves. Correct?"

"Correct!"

Another whip crack. "Now close the door. It is time for the sex. It is time to discover, as Lawrence wrote, 'how wonderful sex can be when men keep it powerful and sacred and it fills the world'!"

Could this be Elizabeth? Repressed, prudish, spinsterish Elizabeth?

A young man stepped into the hallway to get the door. He was nude save for a black jockstrap and possessed the heavily muscled body of a weightlifter. Ian stepped back from the door, afraid of being seen, but the student merely smiled mockingly at him as he closed the door.

Once again the sound of chanting could be heard from within the room: "The blood is one blood! The blood is one blood!"

"Now!" Elizabeth screamed. "Let there be sex!"

The cries echoed in the darkened corridor. Cries of pleasure. Cries of pain. He was sweating. He wanted to open the door, wanted to confront Elizabeth and her class, wanted to find out exactly what was going on in that room, but instead he hurried down the hall, careful to keep his footsteps quiet, and when the elevator door opened, he quickly got inside, pressed the button for the first floor, and leaned back against the elevator's metal wall, closing his eyes.

6

Technically, the dorm had a curfew: a time by which everyone had to be in his or her room. Of course, the dorm also had a rule prohibiting sleep-over guests of the opposite sex.

Neither were enforced.

They'd been discussing the latter while flaunting the former. It was nearly midnight, and Jim was camped out in Howie's room, wondering aloud whether he'd be able to successfully sneak Faith into the dorm sometime so she could stay with him overnight.

Dorm officials wouldn't care, Howie said. But Faith's mother might not be too thrilled.

Her mother probably wouldn't care either, Jim told him. But Faith herself might not be willing to do it.

"Then you've got yourself a good one," Howie said.

Jim picked up a napkin from the pizza box on the floor, re-wadded it, and tossed it at his friend. "Victorian."

"Victorian? I'm a hard-core American family values man, I'll have you know."

He still hadn't said what he'd really come over here to say, and Jim looked at the clock. It was five to twelve. "When's Dave supposed to be back?" he asked. Howie's attendant was out on a date and had not yet returned.

Howie shrugged.

Jim took a deep breath, faced his friend. "I think you should get out of here," he said. "I think things are going to get pretty dangerous."

Howie smiled, rocking back and forth in his chair in a futile effort to raise his head. "Danger is my middle name."

"No, Smegma is your middle name." He smiled, but the smile faded far too quickly.

"Don't worry about me," Howie said.

"I do worry about you."

"I'm not helpless." A tone of irritation was starting to creep into his voice.

Jim ran a hand through his hair, exasperated. "I never said you were. But things are getting pretty serious here."

"I know what's going on."

"Do you?"

"No, I'm a poor, retarded defenseless cripple who—"

"Knock that shit off."

Howie forced his head back with one convulsive jerk of his body. He stared at Jim. "I know you're concerned about me, and I'm glad you are, but there's really nothing to worry about."

"I think there is. What if you'd been alone at that concert? What if I hadn't gone with you? What do you think would've happened to you?"

"The same thing that happened to the rest of the people there. Nothing. I might've got hit by a stray bottle or something, but that kind of shit goes on all the time at clubs in L.A. It's nothing new."

"Look, there are people missing, there are people murdered. There was a racist riot, and it's probably only a matter of time before that anti-minority attitude starts including the handicapped."

"Like I said, I appreciate your concern. But let's look at the facts here. The semester's half over—"

"Two-thirds over."

"Okay, two-thirds over. There are probably twenty-five thousand students at this school. Even if the rate of violence continues, that means, what, probably another ten people killed before the semester's end? Ten out of twenty-five thousand? What are the odds that I'll be one of those ten?" He made a motion with his arm that was obviously supposed to mean something but that Jim did not understand. "I'm a senior. After this semester I need only one more class to graduate. I'm not going to just throw this semester away and tack on another year to my schooling no matter how weird things get."

"They might get pretty weird," Jim said.

"I can handle it."

Jim shook his head. "That all sounds logical and reasonable, but what I'm trying to tell you is that things are not logical and reasonable. You can throw logic and reason out the window. This shit that's going down is supernatural. This is real horror movie stuff here."

"I know that," Howie said quietly.

There was a rattle on the door, and Dave came walking into the room, pocketing his keys. He nodded to Jim. "Hey," he said.

"How's it going?"

Dave grinned. "I just got my pipes cleaned out by a thirty-six D with a mouth like a Hoover, now I'm going to take a huge monster dump. What more can a man ask for?" He walked into the bathroom and shut the door.

Jim turned toward Howie. "Charming," he said dryly.

Howie was backing his chair against the bed. "I think you'd better go," he said. "It's getting late."

"Wait a minute. We need to talk here."

Howie was rocking back and forth in his chair agitatedly. "Just go. We'll talk tomorrow."

There was an urgency in his voice that Jim could not recall hearing before, and that put him on alert. "What—" he began.

"He doesn't like you to be here!"

Jim blinked. "Who doesn't?"

"Just go!"

"Hey, lovebirds!" Dave called from inside the bathroom. "Settle down."

Howie instantly grew silent, and he shot Jim a look that told him not to say anything.

Howie was afraid of his attendant.

Jim shook his head. Dave's bulk could definitely be intimidating, but that didn't mean shit. That didn't alter the facts. He was hired by Howie to take care of him. Howie was his employer. His boss, to get crude and technical about it. There was no reason for Howie to put up with anything from that asshole. And if he was getting belligerent with Howie or not doing his job, then Howie should just fire his ass.

Hell, he'd give that fuckwad a piece of his mind himself as soon as he stepped out of the can.

"Please," Howie said. "Go."

Jim looked at his friend. What if Howie was being abused or something? What if this guy was molesting him?

"Is Dave doing anything to you?" Jim asked. "Is he hurting you in any way?"

"No."

"Look, all you have to do is fire him, find someone else—"

"I want you to go," Howie said.

"I—"

"Please."

There was a plaintive note in Howie's voice, a pleading look in his eyes, and something about the way Howie looked at him made him nod his assent. "Okay."

"I'll take care of this," Howie said. "But *I* want to take care of it, okay? I don't want you to do it for me."

"All right, but if you need moral support or a witness or—"

"Just go."

Jim nodded. "Okay."

"I'll call you tomorrow morning."

"I'll stop by."

"Go."

Jim picked up his books and started toward the door. As he walked out of the room, he heard the bathroom door open, the sound of the still-flushing toilet.

"I told you, I don't want him in here," Dave said.

"And I told you, you're not going to tell me what to do," Howie replied.

Jim quietly closed the door. He waited for a moment in the hallway to see if he could hear any raised voices, any signs of an argument, but there was nothing, no sound from the room at all. Staring at the gold doorknob, he considered going back inside and making sure Howie was okay. He had only closed the door, not locked it, and he could easily let himself back in.

But he remembered Howie's voice, remembered Howie's eyes, and he knew that if he did that, his friend would probably never forgive him.

Feeling heavy, feeling guilty, he walked down the hallway and up the stairs to his own room.

TWENTY-TWO

1

Brad McDonald arrived late to school, but for once he didn't care. His Music and Cross-Cultural Anthropology class started at one, and ordinarily he would have pulled into the student parking lot around twelve-fifteen, picked a likely looking row, and sat there, eating his lunch and waiting, one of the countless automotive vultures ready to swoop down on the first available parking space. But today he arrived at half past one and drove blithely up and down the aisles, heedless of the time, radio cranked at full volume. The lot, for some reason, seemed more crowded than usual, several cars lined up for each space, and it was after one-thirty when a blond girl in a mini-truck backed out and Brad swerved in front of a waiting Toyota, snagging the spot. The Toyota driver angrily rolled down his window, sticking out his head and arm. "I was waiting here first, asshole! Get the hell out of there!"

Brad took his keys out of the ignition, locked his door, got out of the car, and cheerfully whistled the theme to *The Brady Bunch* as he opened the trunk and drew forth his silencer-equipped handgun. He pointed the weapon at the Toyota driver, who quickly started his car and sped backward up the row away from Brad. "You're crazy!" the student called out of his open window. "You fucker! I have your license number!"

Brad didn't hear what the driver said and didn't care. He slammed shut the trunk of the car. He had never held a gun in his hand before this morning, but it felt good in his palm, it felt right, it felt natural. He walked across the parking lot toward the center of campus.

For the first time in his life he felt no apprehension about school. Always before, he had dreaded it. As a child he had been short and somewhat chubby, with a permanently out-of-fashion haircut his father had foisted upon him. Other kids, older kids, even some of the boys in his own grade, had made fun of him and tormented him. Once two boys had held him down while another had pulled down his pants. Red-faced and bawling, he had screamed for them to stop, but they had yanked his pants over his shoes and played Keep Away before finally tossing them into a tree, where they'd caught on a branch. He'd had to jump then, a crowd of boys and, most humiliating, girls watching and laughing at his vain attempts to grab his trousers.

Throughout his academic career he had been a natural victim. Several times during his elementary and junior high school days he had been dumped head-first into a trash can, his nose and mouth mashed on top of old banana peels and sandwich crusts and used Kleenex, and each year on the night before school began, he had lain awake in bed, unable to sleep. His family had not been religious—he could not remember ever having set foot in a church—but he had developed his own prayer of self-preservation, and after getting into bed, under the cover of his blanket, he would fold his hands and silently pray, "Dear God, Please don't let anyone beat me up, pants me, or can me. Amen."

He had continued the prayer through his first two semesters of college, though the threat of being beaten up, publicly stripped, or thrown into a trash can had long since passed.

Today, though, he felt good, and last night he had actually looked forward to school for the first time in his life.

Brad walked up the curb and down the sidewalk between the Biological Sciences building and the Performing Arts Center, the gun grasped firmly in his hand. Although the quad was virtually deserted, the four multistory buildings which flanked the center of campus were teeming with people. He could feel them within the walls, squirming in the uncomfortable seats in the classrooms, reading, writing, talking. He looked up toward the top of the Social Sciences building, six floors above, feeling slightly nauseous as he thought of those thousands of bodies within the hidden hives of the school. He quickened his gait. There were a few couples sitting on the grassy knolls, a handful of lone individuals reading on the benches or on the low brick wall, but if any students saw him, they did not notice the pistol he carried at his side, or they assumed perhaps that he was a drama student carrying a prop for a play or a student studying weapons in some obscure history or criminal justice class.

He headed directly for the library at the far end of the quad. It was in the library that he had first heard the voices, that the Master had first spoken to him and told him what must be done, and it was here where his mission lay. He walked through the small stand of trees and across the square of concrete in front of the library, pulling open the tinted glass door and walking inside. Mike Hernandez was behind the front desk, idly shuffling a stack of due-date cards since there was no one else in the lobby. He looked up as the door opened and waved when he saw Brad. "Hey, dude!"

The handgun was already loaded, and Brad lifted his arm, aiming the gun at Mike's head and pulling the trigger. Mike's face barely had time to register confusion, shock, terror, before it imploded, his nose disappearing into a jagged red hole, pulling with it torn pieces of skin and muscle and eye. Blood and bone splattered against the white calendar on the wall in back of him in a firework Rorshach, and his body fell instantly to the floor, his head catching and bouncing off his stool as he fell.

Brad paid no heed to Mike after he pulled the trigger. He walked purposefully through the lobby, past the rows of tables, to the elevator. There were three or four people stationed in front of the OCLC terminals, but none of them looked up as he passed by.

Good.

He heard the voice through ears within his head, a whispery, papery rasp which filled him with awe and terror. He pushed the button for the elevator.

The fourth floor.

The Master's voice echoed in his head. On some visceral level, the voice scared him, but on a more conscious level, it filled him with reverence, and he felt that urgent need within him to please the Master, to do His bidding.

There was a quiet *ding* as the elevator doors opened. Brad stepped in and turned around, facing outward as he pressed the button for the fourth floor.

"Wait!" He heard a female voice and the sound of high heels on the tile as a young woman raced toward the elevator. She was Hispanic, wearing whore's makeup and a short skirt, an armload of books in her arms. He pressed the button again, but it was clear that she was going to reach him before the doors closed, and he lifted the gun and aimed, blowing a hole through her midsection. She fell face first onto the floor, books scattering, blood shooting from the hole in her stomach. In the second before the doors closed, cutting off the screams, he saw other students rushing to her aid as she twitched spastically on the tile.

The slut deserved it.

Yes, she had deserved it. And so had Mike Hernandez. And so did the people on the fourth floor.

The Master had told him about the people in the library—the patrons as well as the workers. They were all degenerates: the girls tramps, the guys perverts. The Master had begun whispering information about individual students to him at the beginning of the semester as he'd sat in one of the study carrels, trying to read. At first he'd thought it was a joke, and he'd searched the area around the carrels, looking for the culprit, but there'd been no one there. He'd moved, but the whispering had moved with him. He looked under the metal desk for hidden speakers but found none. He'd left the library then, but in the lobby on the way out he'd seen a beautiful blond bimbo wearing tight shorts, and the voice had whispered that she liked it best up the ass.

He'd left, but he'd thought about the blonde later and about what she liked, and he found himself returning to the library the next day.

And the next.

And the next.

Gradually, the Master had revealed His true identity. The Master had known things about his life that he had never told anybody, and He had been both sympathetic and understanding. The Master had also told him how the people in the library made fun of him behind his back, and how they deserved to be punished.

The elevator seemed suddenly small. Brad's palms were starting to sweat, but it was from excitement and anticipation rather than fear. He gripped the handgun tightly.

Kill them all.

Yes, he would. His eyes traveled over the panel in front of him, lingering on the braille numerals below the numbered buttons. His gaze moved upward and fixed on the sequence of lighted numbers above the door. Two, three.

His fingers tightened on the gun.

Four.

The elevator door opened.

And he stepped out shooting.

2

In the cage on the sixth floor, Faith pushed her cart forward. The wall of the cage was lined with shelves, arranged by call letter, upon which were stacked books that had either been checked in or had been found in study carrels and needed to be reshelved. She moved over to the section with the art books and grabbed a few of them to load onto her cart. A wave of cold washed over her: a sensation that was both physical and not physical. She quickly put the books down. It felt as though, for a brief second, an air-conditioning duct had been trained directly on her, though she knew that that could not possibly have happened, and she shivered, rubbing her bare arms. Suddenly the cage no longer seemed as safe as it had before. The books were still here—they had not changed—but the atmosphere, the mood, the feeling in the air, had altered. The locked cage no longer seemed like a secure refuge against whatever might be out there, it seemed like a trap, a . . . well, a cage. A cage from which she could not easily escape should something happen.

She was acutely conscious of the fact that she was alone on the sixth floor, that the nearest person was a stair level away.

The sixth floor

Why had she let herself remain up here? She should

have gone downstairs with Glenna when she went on break.

She held onto the sides of the cart, not moving. She was aware for the first time that there were noises here, on this ordinarily deathly silent floor, soft, whispery noises which were very nearly inaudible and which she would not have been able to hear had there been people about. She held her breath, listening. The noises were not rhythmic enough to be mechanical, but were not infrequent enough to be the random sounds caused by bookshelf strain or building contraction/expansion.

The whispery sibilance sounded almost like a voice.

But not a human voice.

She began reaching for books, putting them on the cart, humming an old U2 song to herself. She was scared, but she thought that maybe if she made noise enough to cover the sounds, she would not notice that they were there.

No such luck.

She could hear the whispers in her head, a menacing counterpoint to the upbeat tune she was humming. She threw a book loudly into the cart and told herself that there was nothing to be afraid of.

But she knew there was.

She would have left then and there, would have gone down to another, more populated floor, but the thought of walking between those tall, empty aisles of books unprotected frightened her. She might be trapped in the cage, but at least she could see what she had to deal with in here. Who knew what might be lurking at the end of an aisle, what might be keeping pace with her in another row as she walked, what type of hand or claw might shoot out from between the shelved books to grab her arm?

There was a low chime from the far end of the floor as the elevator opened. Faith's heart caught in her chest. For some bizarre reason the image of John Taylor flashed into her mind. She didn't know why she thought of him, she hadn't given him a second's consideration since that disastrous date nearly a month ago, but her first thought was: Please don't let it be him.

There was the muffled slap of walking tennis shoes.

Gathering her courage, she pressed forward and

peeked between two bookshelves through the wire mesh at the aisle leading toward the cage. She was unaware that she'd been holding her breath, but now she exhaled, an honest-to-God sigh of relief. It was only Glenna, back from her break, striding up the aisle toward her. Faith moved back from her peephole, grateful.

Glenna knocked on the cage door, and Faith hurried over to let her in.

She realized instantly that something was wrong. Glenna's normally unflappable expression was gone, and in its place was a look of confused fear. Her skin was white, her lips pale. "Come on," she said without preamble. "We have to get out of here. They're evacuating the building"

Faith's pulse was racing. "Why?" she asked, though she knew she didn't want to hear the answer.

"Some guy went crazy on the fourth floor about ten minutes ago and started shooting. A whole bunch of people are dead." Glenna turned and started down the aisle toward the elevator without waiting to see if Faith was following.

Faith quickly closed the cage door and hurried after her, keeping her eyes trained directly ahead, looking neither to the left nor to the right, aware that she could now hear the whisperings above the sounds of their footsteps.

The whispering sounded like laughter.

3

FOUR KILLED, SIXTEEN INJURED IN LIBRARY SHOOTING.

Another two-deck banner, 96 point. The photo beneath the banner another award winner: the covered bodies lying on the steps in front of the library, a reflection of the cops and the ambulance visible in the library window.

Once again Richard had gotten some amazing shots. He had somehow bluffed his way past the line of police and before being kicked out had taken two rolls. Jim had seen the proof sheets only once, and only for a few moments, but the images had stayed with him. Rivulets of blood running from a large puddle on the floor, their free-form flow contrasting with the symmetry of the tiles. A shipwreck of fallen bookshelves, scattered piles of

books from which protruded unmoving arms, legs that
were broken at impossible angles. The three old women
who had been working the Reference Desk: one thrown
back over a table, her face covered by a mask of dark
blood; another lying on the floor, arms and legs akimbo,
her dress ripped open by bullets, a sagging breast flopping out from beneath the torn material; the last in a
chair, limbs splayed, dead eyes wide with shock and staring at the camera, a portion of her face peeled away by
a bullet, exposing a skid mark of skull.

Powerful.

Horrifying and frightening and disgusting.

But powerful.

The phone rang, and Jean answered it. "Hello, Production." She listened for a moment, nodding into the
receiver, a list of waxed corrections in her hand. "Jim!"
she called. "It's for you! Dean Jensen!"

Although now in charge of Student Services, Dean
Jensen had at one time been the adviser to the paper,
and, luckily for the *Sentinel* over the intervening semesters, he had never lost those ties. Jim had met him only
once, but he had liked the man immediately. Jensen
alone, out of all the members of the school administration, could be counted on to provide them with both
information and quotes when they needed them, and last
semester he had often called voluntarily with information when he knew they were working on important
stories.

Jim pushed his way through the crowd and walked
over to the desk, taking the phone from the production
manager's hand. "Hello?"

"Is this the editor?"

"Yes. This is Jim Parker."

"Hello, Jim. This is Dean Jensen. I wanted to tell you
that I just received a call from Brea General, and one
of the other students has died. I got the news about five
minutes ago and thought I'd let you guys know. Has
anyone else called?"

"No. We called the hospital about a half hour ago,
but we haven't talked to anyone since."

"Sometimes hospital and police officials don't get
around to telling school newspapers until after they've

hit the TV reporters and the print biggies. I thought I'd give you guys a head start."

"Thanks," Jim said. "Could you tell me who it was?"

"Sorry, but the family hasn't been notified yet. When's your deadline?"

"About an hour ago."

"When's your absolute final deadline?"

"The printer said we have to have everything in by eight."

"Not enough time," Jensen said. "But one of the others has died. I can give you that much. You can do what you want with it. You might try calling the hospital to see if they're giving out any more information."

"Okay. Thanks for letting us know." Jim hung up. "Faruk!" he called. "Call the hospital, find out what happened. We'll rewrite the lead and the headline, and tack on a graph at the end."

"Not again," Jean groaned.

"Yes, again."

"We can't keep up with TV. We can't compete with the real papers. Those guys have their own printers, later deadlines ..." She shook her head. "We do the best we can under the circumstances. What more can you ask for?"

"I want us to do better. And I'm the editor."

"I'm out of here in an hour. Max. Anything later and you're on your own."

"Fine."

Faruk ran in from the newsroom. "They won't talk, won't tell me anything at all, said there won't be any information released until morning. What do you want me to do? I could attribute the info to Dean Jensen."

Jim looked at the production manager, then up at the clock. It was ten to eight already, and the trip to the printer's took fifteen minutes on a good night. He sighed. "All right," he said. "Attribute it to the dean and let's get out of here."

Jean nodded. "That's what I call a good editorial decision."

Fifteen minutes later, the corrections were pasted up, the pages boxed, and Stuart was off to the printers.

Jean remained to clean up the Production office while Faruk, Eddie, and Jim walked into the newsroom. From the hallway Jim heard the hum of Howie's chair, and he turned to greet his friend. "Hey," he said.

"Hey, yourself." The chair slowed. "So how bad was the shooting? I heard three people were injured."

Jim raised his eyebrows. "Three? Try five dead, fifteen injured."

Howie's face went white. "Jesus," he breathed. He licked his lips. "Anyone we know?"

"No one I know, but I'll let you look at the list later."

"It wasn't a vet, was it?"

Jim shook his head. Howie's father had served in Vietnam, and Howie had an almost phobic concern with anything that might further strengthen what he called "the public's conception of the deranged Vietnam vet." "Not that I know," Jim said. "The guy's young, twenty-two, an anthropology major. Apparently, he just went in there shooting, then, after he ran out of bullets, he sat on the floor and waited until the police came for him."

"Jesus."

Jim gathered his books and backpack, waved goodbye to the other editors, and reminded Faruk to lock the door when he closed up.

"Where's Cheryl?" Howie asked, glancing toward the entertainment editor's desk.

Jim sighed. "Fuck knows. I haven't seen her for a week. I've been doing her page, covering for her, but I think I'm going to have to get a new editor."

Howie said nothing.

The two of them took the elevator downstairs.

Outside, a group of six or seven students stood, ganglike, in a silent huddle near the northwest corner of Neilson Hall, cigarettes glowing red-orange in the darkness. They did not speak, but misty wisps of breath hovered in the cold air above their heads. On the sloping lawn in front of them, barely visible in the dim, diffuse light from classroom windows above, two dark figures were furiously copulating. They, too, were silent.

The lack of noise was as creepy as the presence of the people themselves, and Jim strode quickly down the steps of the building while Howie rolled down the handicapped-access ramp. Together they hurried across the walkway, through the quad toward the parking lot.

"Weird shit," Howie said.

Jim nodded, glancing back at the huddled group by the building's edge. "You're telling me."

They were nearly through the small grove of trees in the center of the quad when Howie stopped. "What's that?"

With the cessation of the wheelchair noise, the silence was almost complete. "What's what?" Jim asked. He didn't like stopping here. The spot was dark. Too dark.

"I felt something beneath my wheels. Kind of like a vibration."

"An earthquake?"

"No. Not as definite as an earthquake. It was more like—" His eyes widened. "There it was again! Did you feel it?"

Jim shivered, suddenly cold. He'd felt nothing. "No."

"It felt sort of like being on a waterbed. Or on the ocean. Kind of an up-and-down motion. There!" he exclaimed.

"I don't feel anything. Come on, let's go."

"It's like the ground is . . . breathing. Like it's inhaling and exhaling."

"If you're trying to scare me, you're succeeding."

"I'm serious."

"Let's get the hell out of here." Jim started walking quickly, and after a second's pause Howie followed him, wheelchair humming. There was a definite coldness in the air here at the center of the quad, a sharp drop in temperature that was distinct from the general coolness of the weather, and Jim wondered if his friend felt it too.

He quickened his pace.

Ahead was the library. The building was closed, and three policemen stood behind the yellow-ribboned barricade to make sure no one tried to get in. A patrol car was parked on the wide walkway directly in front of the entrance. The two of them moved past the library on their way to the parking lot, and though Jim forced himself to walk at a normal speed, he had the sudden urge to run from the library like a bat out of hell, until he was far, far away from it. Something about the darkness of the smoked glass windows spooked him.

Had Faith been in there when it happened?

He didn't know. The first thing he'd checked when he'd heard the news was the names of the victims, to make sure she was not among them. She was not, but she had not called or come in after the shooting, and he'd been too busy to leave and try to track her down.

He'd call her when he got back to the dorm, make sure she was okay.

Another group of silent smoking students stood near the corner of the library, just outside the area the police had cordoned off.

"Come on," Jim said to Howie. "Hurry up. Let's get out of here."

They hurried toward the parking lot.

Faith.

She was waiting for him in his room, naked, on her hands and knees on the bed, and though he didn't know how she could've gotten in without a key, he didn't really care.

He, too, was naked by the time he reached the bed.

And hard.

He knew what she wanted, and he wanted it too, and he grabbed her around the midsection and spanked her until his hand hurt, until the cheeks of her buttocks were bright red, before he knelt in back of her on his knees and took her roughly from behind.

TWENTY-THREE

1

Eleanor's car was in the shop again. The mechanics had found another hundred dollars' worth of brake-related problems, and though Ian wasn't at all sure that the problems actually existed, Eleanor's philosophy was Better-Safe-Than-Sorry, and she'd approved the work and agreed to shell out the bucks.

His last class ended at three and she didn't get off until five, so even with the construction and late-afternoon traffic on the Orange freeway, he made it to her office in plenty of time.

The TRW building was a brown brick and mirror-glass structure located in a business park that had been built in the mid-1980s upon the revitalized remains of an eminent-domain-claimed slum. The building was the back end of a trio of high-rises arranged in a U -shape, with a fountain-and-garden courtyard in the center, and Ian pulled into one of the parking lot's green-marked visitors' spaces facing the courtyard. He sat there for a moment. Technically, Eleanor wasn't off for another fifteen minutes, but he didn't feel like sitting here in the car, waiting, and he thought that if she saw him she might take off a little earlier, so he got out of the car, locked the door, and walked through the courtyard to TRW.

In the lobby, he gave his name to the guard at the front desk and told the man that he was here to see Eleanor Matthews in Personnel. The guard picked up an in-house phone, buzzed upstairs, received some sort of confirmation, then gave Ian a plastic-coated visitors' pass and directed him to the elevators.

On the fourth floor, an overweight secretary smiled at him and waved him into Eleanor's office.

She was seated behind her desk, reading through a pile of printouts, and she looked up as he entered. "Hi," she said.

"Hi, yourself."

"You're not kidding about Brea." She sifted through the stack of printouts. "I've been doing a little checking on your school. The place was getting quite a rep even before the murders."

"The latest murders," Ian corrected her.

"Yeah, right, the latest murders." She found what she was looking for and pulled it from the pile. "The state of California regularly ranks its schools in both the CSU and UC systems for insurance purposes. For the past three years Brea has ranked at the bottom of the list of UC schools, and for the past two years it has been at the bottom of the combined UC and CSU schools. It has been flagged as a 'high-risk' institution, and according to this report is almost twice as likely to experience violent crimes that result in injury or death as the next college on the list, which is located in a considerably worse area. By contrast, your next-door neighbors, Fullerton and Irvine, rank near the top, as two of the safer schools."

Ian grinned wryly. "Told you."

"The state also considers it a bad risk, and the monies from bond measures that have been allocated to Brea have been adjusted accordingly." She picked up the entire stack of printouts, dropped it. "And that's just the tip of the iceberg. Your school has a paper trail a mile long. State agencies, financial institutions, everyone seems to have your number. Headhunters and recruiters who do their scouting at colleges and universities have put you on their 'low-priority' list. You're bad news."

"So you believe me?"

"I've always believed you. I just didn't think it would be . . . documented."

"Me either, to tell you the truth." He nodded toward the pile of reports. "Can you get me copies?"

"You know I can't do that."

"Just checking."

Eleanor looked at the clock on the wall, stood, picked up her purse from behind her desk. "Let's get going. Pep Boys called about an hour ago and said that my car's done. You can drop me off on your way home."

"Great. Then we can—"

She held up a hand, shaking her head as she walked around the side of the desk. "We can't do anything. I got sort of carried away with my UC Brea search, and I didn't get around to putting together the spreadsheet I'm supposed to have done by tomorrow."

"All right, then. We'll stay in. I'll cook—"

She smiled at him, took his hand. "I think I'm going to go home tonight. My P.C.'s connected to the main-frame here, and I can pull what I need."

"Or you can download it, copy it on disk, and bring it on over."

She shook her head. "I think I want to stay home tonight."

Home.

He'd almost forgotten that her "home" was a tri-level condo in Anaheim Hills. Over the past week or so, she'd moved what had appeared to be most of her wardrobe over to his house, and though she'd made occasional daytrips to her place in order to water the plants and pick up the mail, for the past two weeks she'd spent every night with him and he'd assumed that they were now living together.

His first instinct was to ask what was the matter, what he'd done wrong. Maybe he'd ticked her off somehow and she was punishing him by going back to her place until he apologized. Or maybe she was just waiting for a formal invitation to move in with him permanently.

Or maybe she was spreading her legs for someone else.

He was being paranoid now. Paranoid and unfair. Eleanor had never given him any indication that she was dissatisfied with their relationship, that she was interested in or even looking for someone else. She loved him.

They're all sluts.

God damn Sylvia. It was his experience with her that was coloring this, that was instilling within him these doubts, making him think things that obviously weren't true, threatening to undermine the trust he and Eleanor had established.

Or was it?

Was there something else giving him a little push, a

little shove in that direction, something that was putting these thoughts in his head?

The university?

He didn't feel as though he was being influenced or manipulated in any way, but, he supposed, no one ever did.

It wasn't an impossibility. It probably wasn't even that unlikely.

"Come on," he said. "Let's go."

He pretended as though nothing was wrong, did not bring it up, talked about other things, and by the time they reached Pep Boys, the subject had been avoided so completely that even though he wanted to talk about it, it would have been awkward to bring it up.

He waited while she paid for the work and made sure that her car would start before leaving.

"I'll call you," she promised.

"I'll be waiting."

"With bated breath?"

"What other kind is there?" He kissed her through the open car window and walked back to his own vehicle.

There were two stalled cars on the freeway, blocking the two left lanes, and the rush-hour traffic was even worse than usual. It was nearly six-thirty by the time he got home.

The house seemed empty and silent, the memories of Sylvia strong, and he immediately turned on the TV, flipping to the news. The light on the answering machine was blinking, and after walking into the kitchen and getting a beer out of the refrigerator, he rewound the tape and played it back.

There was only one call.

It was from Gifford Stevens.

He wanted to meet.

He was seated at the back table in the smoking section of Coco's, lighting up a cigarette, a full ashtray already in front of him. The restaurant was crowded, but he'd somehow commandeered a booth large enough to accommodate six, and he sat in the middle of the curved vinyl bench seat, facing the entrance.

Ian recognized Stevens immediately. He had seen the

man only once, but the impression he'd made had been strong, and he looked exactly as Ian remembered: thick, wild beard, piercing blue eyes, tweed jacket.

"So it's starting," Stevens said as Ian approached the table.

Ian nodded, sat down at the edge of the booth. Stevens slid across the seat, moving opposite him. "The number you gave me," Ian said. "In your dissertation. The one you told me to call. It wasn't yours."

"Can't be too careful. Can't tell friend from foe at first, although I usually start off by approaching English teachers because I trust them. Preferably the ones who are into the fantastique. They're more open-minded. My own personal prejudice."

"So you picked me, out of everyone else at Brea, just because I teach a class on horror fiction?"

"I had to start somewhere. And literature professors are usually good men. Haven't had one fail me yet." He leaned forward across the table. "So you read my dissertation?"

"Two weeks ago."

"What did you think?"

Stevens was staring at him expectantly, and suddenly Ian wasn't sure if the man was looking for an opinion of his theory or a critique of his writing style. He stared back into those bright blue eyes, and the hope he'd had that Stevens might be able to somehow exorcise whatever evil was afflicting the university faded. It was a mistake to have put any trust into such an obvious flake. His first impression of Stevens had been that the guy was a loon, and he was stupid to have ever thought otherwise.

Ian looked away, licked his lips, not sure what was being asked, not sure how to respond.

"Do you believe me?"

Stevens wanted to know about the theory, not the 'dissertation."

Maybe there was still hope.

"Yes," Ian said.

Stevens smiled, revealing brown, tobacco-stained teeth. "Good, good."

"But I don't quite understand how you came to the conclusion that the university is alive."

"You think it's just haunted?"

Ian reddened. "No, I—"

Stevens nodded. "Ah. You're thinking Jackson, Marasco, King?"

"Yes." It was something of a relief talking to someone who spoke the same language, who had the same vocabulary. He wondered if, in another place, another time, under other circumstances, they would have been friends.

"Those were *buildings* that were alive. This is a being that happens to include buildings within its body."

It was strange discussing horror in a literal rather than metaphoric sense, referencing novels as though they were factual reports rather than fictional creations.

"I thought this being had no corporeal body."

"I'm speaking figuratively. No, it's not a physical entity. It's not a Godzilla that's going to go stomping around squishing people. But the campus—the land, the buildings—provides it with the closest thing it has to a body, and as I said, and as you've probably seen for yourself, it can use those physical elements, manipulating them, utilizing them for its own purposes."

"Yes."

Stevens took a long drag on his cigarette. "The real stuff of its substance, though, is people."

"I read where you said it needs bodies, sacrifices."

Stevens waved him away. "I was wrong on that count. I was approaching it from a traditional angle, and I didn't really understand. I've learned since then. It doesn't need lives. It has lives. The students, the faculty, the staff, all of the people at the university make up this . . . organism, for want of a better word. Each individual is analogous to a cell in a living organism. Don't ask me the mechanics of it. I don't know and I don't care. I don't know if people give off a life force or aura or electrical energy or whatever, but something happens when people get together, and in an institution like a university, with such size and concentration of purpose, the created organism is very powerful indeed."

"Then why doesn't this happen everywhere, at all colleges and universities?"

"It does. It's just not noticed. Ordinarily, the character of this organism is variable, in a continuous state of flux.

It changes as the people who teach, work at, and attend the school change. But somehow, for some reason, certain schools remain ... constant. Whether the people it attracts are evil or whether it makes the people who attend it evil, I don't know, but its character remains the same. This is what has happened to Brea.

"Simply put, all universities are alive. But like people, some are good and some are bad."

"And Brea—"

"Is psychotic."

"Psychotic?"

Stevens leaned forward. "It is completely and utterly mad."

A waitress arrived, an ex-student, and though she seemed wary of Stevens, she was effusive with Ian, insisting on telling him the details of her life since she'd taken his class last year, though the truth was that he only vaguely remembered her. Finally, she got around to taking their orders—coffee for Stevens, iced tea for himself. She returned a moment later with the drinks, thanked them, and left.

Ian tore open a packet of Sweet 'n' Low, dumped it in his tea, stirred it with his straw. Stevens was sitting back in the booth, the intensity of a few moments before at least somewhat dissipated. He took a final drag on his cigarette before stubbing it out in the ashtray.

"So if Brea is such an evil place," Ian asked, "filled with evil people, why am I there?"

Stevens shrugged. "No place is all bad. You're one of the healthy cells amongst the cancer, if you will. And you're not the only one. There are other decent people—"

"I know. I'm trying to get us all together."

"Good! There's strength in numbers."

"But why didn't we feel it until this semester? That's what I want to know. Brea didn't just turn bad overnight. If you're right, the school's been rotting from the inside out for years. How come no one noticed it? Tell me why last semester, and the semester before, and the semester before, I felt so damn comfortable there?"

"Did you?" Stevens stared at him.

Ian looked uneasily away. "I don't know," he admitted. "Maybe not. But I didn't really notice anything that unusual or out of the ordinary."

"It was there. You just didn't know what to look for. Now ... Now it would be impossible not to notice."

"So what should I do? What should the rest of us do? Leave? Get out before it's too late?"

"You can't leave. Because you're part of it too. You're a part of the university, you're a part of this organism. It's like your skin. Your skin is a part of your body. Your epidermal cells can't just break off and decide they don't want to be a part of you anymore. It's impossible. Those cells don't have minds of their own."

"But I do. And I can leave if I want."

"Can you?" Stevens looked at him.

"People drop out all the time, add, transfer."

"They're hair, they're fingernails. They're unimportant. They're not the vital organs of the organism."

"And I am."

"Yes! That's your weakness and your strength. You're at the mercy of the university to a certain extent, but you can also act upon it, work to cripple it from within. Maybe the organism analogy isn't a good one, because the people at Brea aren't really divided by function, like organs, but you are a part of this being, and you can attack other parts of it."

"Like corpuscles attacking viruses."

"Exactly!" Stevens swallowed his entire cup of coffee with one gulp. "Tell me, has it talked to you?"

"Talked? You mean—"

"Spoken. Have you heard from it? Has it communicated with you directly, using words?"

Ian nodded slowly and told him about the message on Maria's computer.

"It talks to different people in different ways. Some hear voices. With some it uses radio or video. With you it used a computer." He shook his head. "Bad sign. It knows you. Knows who you are. Anonymity is a key here. Maybe one of your other people will work better."

"Work better at what?"

"I told you before. We have to blow up that motherfucker."

"Like the University of Mexico?"

Stevens grinned, nodded. "Exactly."

The waitress returned with more iced tea for Ian and a coffee refill for Stevens, and though she obviously wanted to hang around and talk, the chilly silence and Stevens' glare quickly sent her away.

"So how did you discover this?" Ian asked.

"And what happened to my wife?"

Ian met his gaze, nodded.

"All the horror teachers ask that one." Again, Stevens finished off the coffee with one huge swallow. He took another cigarette from the inside pocket of his jacket and lit up. "All right," he said, blowing out smoke. "I'll tell you.

"As the dust jacket says, I lived in New Mexico, with my wife, Pat. I was teaching English, I'd just put together my anthology. She taught at the pre-school on campus where our daughter Amy went.

"I'd noticed, over a period of three or four years, a decrease in interest and aptitude among the students I taught. I thought at first that it was just part of the general decline in academic skills that this country's been experiencing over the past several decades. But that year, the year Amy started pre-school, everything shifted into high gear. The students were not just apathetic, they were hostile and downright belligerent. The other teachers also seemed to be acting very oddly."

"Sounds familiar," Ian said.

"It should." Stevens pulled on his cigarette, then pressed it into the ashtray, though it had barely been smoked. "The scariest thing, though, was the change in Pat and Amy. They'd both become very quiet, very withdrawn, and though I constantly tried to find out what was wrong, I was told it was nothing. I started thinking that maybe Amy—or maybe Pat and Amy—had been molested, sexually assaulted. There wasn't really any reason for me to think that. I mean, the pre-school was staffed solely by licensed teachers, like my wife, and child-development majors doing core service, but I asked Pat about it and she went ballistic. We had a huge fight, I ended up sleeping on the couch, but later that night she came out into the living room, crawled onto the couch with me, and told me she was scared. Nothing had happened yet, but other college students, male students, had started helping out at the pre-school, and she said the vibe was weird, the feeling was real uncomfortable. I told her we should take Amy out immediately, but she said that Amy would be okay as long as she was around. She'd make sure nothing happened to her.

"The next day—the very next day—I was scheduled to teach my Beginning Comp class. I'd assigned the students to write a three-to-five-page essay on abortion, pro or con, and they'd all turned their papers in by the time I got to class. Or at least I thought they had. But the papers on my desk were all individual sheets with only one line written on each of them. The same line. 'I fucked your daughter.' "

"Jesus," Ian said.

"I looked up at them, and they were all staring at me and sort of half smiling, and it scared the living shit out of me. I suddenly knew that I had to get Pat and Amy away from the pre-school, away from the campus, that instant, and I ran out of the room and ran out of the building and ran across campus to where the pre-school was." He closed his eyes, breathed deeply, exhaled. "I could see right away that there were way too many people in the little playground. Way too many adults. I ran as fast as I could, and I heard adult laughs and children's screams, and I saw two of our star football players, wearing only their jockstraps, holding a little boy against a cement turtle playground toy while they stripped him.

"Neither Pat nor Amy were in the playground, so I jumped the little chain-link fence and ran inside the building. Pat and two other women were naked and tied up in a corner.

"The men were fucking my daughter."

"Oh, God," Ian breathed.

"And they weren't just using her pussy!" His hand slammed down on the table and his voice rose. "Or her mouth!" Another hand slam. "Or her ass!" Another slam. "They'd cut open her fucking stomach and were doing it through her liver, her bladder, her guts!" He was practically yelling now, and the other customers in the restaurant were all looking at him but trying to appear as though they weren't. "There were three of them on her and another two waiting in line, and a long-dicked motherfucker was spurting in her blood, and I went crazy and grabbed a chair and smashed it over his fucking head, and the two guys in line started attacking me, and I whaled on them." He closed his eyes again, squinting hard as though trying not to see the images running through his mind. "There were other boys and girls on the floor, bloody and dead, but some of them must have gotten away because there weren't that many."

The waitress came over, a worried look on her face. "Dr. Emerson?" she said hesitantly. "Uh, sir?"

"Fuck off!" Stevens screamed at her.

She fled.

"The other three guys took off, and I picked up Amy and put her down on the table and untied Pat, and somehow we carried her to the Health Center.

"She was dead already. I called the cops, and it made the papers and I took a couple weeks off and then I decided I couldn't teach there anymore, and I sent in my resignation, and Pat went with me to go back and clean out my office."

He was suddenly silent, staring off into space. Ian was not sure if he was through talking or if he was planning to continue, but he did not want to push, so he drank his iced tea and said nothing, giving the man space.

"We didn't even make it to my office," Stevens said finally, his voice now quiet. "I could tell right away that things had changed. I could feel the difference. I knew something was wrong, and I should have turned around right there and left everything in my office and gotten back in the car and never looked back. There were broken windows in the buildings; several of the big elm trees that grew in front of the school were leafless and dead, even though it was spring and they'd been fine two weeks ago; there seemed to be very few students on campus.

"But we started walking across the lawn to the Humanities building. We were about halfway there when Pat pushed me. Or at least I thought she pushed me. I fell down, backward, but when I looked up, she was on her ass to my right, looking just as startled as I felt. And then ... and then the grass between us started moving, started pushing upward into a hill. I could see the stalks of the grass squirming, their white roots moving, twining together, until the hill was a shape, until that section of the lawn had formed itself into a creature, a blobby Lovecraftian thing with grass teeth and dirt tentacles and oversized eyes.

"And it ate my wife.

"I watched it, watched it pull apart from the rest of the lawn, swoop over to her and engulf her, and then sort of slide into the ground. She didn't even have time to scream. I didn't even have time to scream. I jumped up and looked where it had disappeared into the earth, and thère was no trace of it, no trace of anything, no hint that anything had happened. There was a rough patch of dirt where it had originally emerged between us, but the spot where Pat had been was clean.

"I started digging, pulling grass up with my hands, and eventually someone must have seen me, because I was taken away. I told everyone what happened, and even though nobody believed me and thought that I was still hysterical because of what had happened to Amy, they dug up the spot anyway.

"They didn't find anything, of course. They dug down ten feet, and there was nothing. The ground had not even been disturbed, although no one could tell me how that dirt patch had gotten there."

Stevens looked up at him. "I blew the place to kingdom come. I got me some fucking dynamite and some timers, and I set everything up in each building, and I blew the place up. What was left, I burned with incendiary devices set up the same way. I left and didn't look back.

"And that's how it started."

Ian cleared his throat. "And that's the only way to combat it?"

Stevens shrugged. "It's the only way I know. And it's proved to be a hundred percent effective."

The waitress returned with a business-suited man who identified himself as the manager. The man favored them with a false smile. "Gentlemen," he said, "your presence here has disturbed some of our other customers. There will be no charge for your meal tonight, but we would appreciate it if you would continue your discussion somewhere else."

Stevens took out another cigarette, ignoring the man.

"That'll be fine," Ian said, waving the manager away. "Just give us a moment, will you?"

"Certainly."

The manager and the waitress retreated.

"Why don't you come over to my house?" Ian said. "We can discuss what has to be done."

"Why don't you come over to my place?" Stevens responded. "I can show you."

Stevens was staying in a rundown apartment complex in La Habra, in a neighborhood marked by gang graffiti and filled with dirty storefronts uniformly protected by wrought iron security gates.

Ian followed the dusty T-Bird into the glass-littered parking lot. Stevens parked in an open space and, not waiting, started up the stairs to his second-floor apartment.

Ian hurried after him.

There were three dead bolts on the door, all recently installed, and Stevens was unlocking the last of them when Ian caught up with him. He looked around the landing, as if to make sure that no one had snuck up behind them, then quickly pushed open the door and beckoned Ian inside.

The interior of the apartment was completely devoid of furniture. Stevens switched on an overhead light. From the doorway Ian could see into the kitchen, living room, and single bedroom, and only a low cot pushed next to one wall indicated that the apartment was anything more than storage space. Boxes of books and manuscripts were piled high against the far wall, effectively blocking the living room's only window.

The carpeted floor was completely covered by spread-open newspaper, atop which sat, at perfectly even intervals, packages of what looked like plastic explosives and elaborately wired gadgets that could only be timers and detonators.

On the back wall of the kitchen were photographs of fires and explosions, arranged in a floor-to-ceiling collage.

"The university is increasing in power even as we speak," Stevens said, turning to face Ian. "It is building up its strength."

"For what?"

"December," Stevens said quietly. "Graduation."

"You mentioned that in your dissertation. What happens then?"

"It graduates too. And if that happens, we'd never be able to stop it. Not without some sort of thermonuclear device that would take out half of Orange County."

"So we have to stop it now."

"Yes." Stevens grinned, and there was something in that grin that made Ian uncomfortable. Stevens walked gingerly across the spread newspapers and picked up one of the wired devices. He stroked the device lovingly. "Let's talk," he said. "Let's talk about fire."

TWENTY-FOUR

From the *Brea Gazette*, November 12:
*Local merchants have joined with homeowners in an effort
to protest what they claim are lax disciplinary policies at
UC Brea and insufficient protection provided by university
police.*

*University and city officials met with the group on Mon-
day to discuss the citizens' concerns. Reading from a
prepared statement, Brett Samuels, chairman of the group,
which is now calling itself Citizens Against Crime (CAC),
stated that over 30 local businessmen have lent their names
and support to a proposal to be presented to the city
council next week that calls for an independent review of
university regulations and police procedures.*

*Samuels said that over a hundred violent crimes have
occurred at the university over the past year and that
simple modifications of UC Brea's entrance requirements
and disciplinary procedures could have prevented up to
half the crimes. He said that most of the crimes were
performed by repeat offenders who would have been
kicked out of the school had the modifications been in place
at the time.*

None of the students, he noted, were Brea residents.

*The CAC spokesperson also placed blame for increased
crime on the university police department, which he described as "a joke." With other members of the citizens'
group cheering him on, Samuels suggested that the Brea
Police Department take over the operation of the now independent university police department in order to "make
it more efficient and more responsive to community needs.*

"We're mad as hell and we're not going to take it any-

more," Samuels said. "If the university cannot do their job, we'll be happy to do it for them."

UC Brea officials listened quietly to the criticism and responded, point by point, to each of the complaints.

In a heated exchange with Samuels, UC Brea Police Chief Ralph Lyons admitted that there had been an increase in crime over the past year, but said that the blame lay not in policies or procedures but in the character of the students.

"They were like that when we got them," he said. "We didn't raise them.

"Maybe if you spent a little more time watching your kids and a little less time forming committees, they wouldn't turn out to be criminals," he added.

Cliff Moody, public liaison representative for UC Brea, was more diplomatic. "I don't want to trivialize the concerns of these people," he said. "But to be honest, all we n~~d are spin doctors, not policy changes. This is simply a matter of public perception. There is no problem with our police or our policies."

CAC is scheduled to present its proposal to the Brea City Council on Monday.

TWENTY-FIVE

1

It had been several weeks since Cheryl had been able to muster enough courage to enter the newsroom, and she wasn't even sure if she was still on the staff. She continued to be listed as the entertainment editor of each issue, but she hadn't really fulfilled that role since . . .

Since the rape.

The rape. She could think about it now, though she hadn't been able to for some time. She'd been like a visitor to her own life, outwardly going through the motions of what she knew "Cheryl Gonzalez" did each day but mentally walking on eggshells, tiptoeing carefully around anything that might in any way remind her of what had occurred. She had not dropped any of her classes, had not been able to go so far as to take any action, but, in a delayed reaction, she had gradually stopped attending all classes that were not on the first floor of one of the buildings.

She did not ever want to find herself having to take a stairway again.

She'd been sleeping a lot lately, had been tired most of the time, even while awake, and she'd lost ten pounds because she just never seemed to be hungry anymore. Nothing tasted good to her.

She'd even lost her interest in music, and that was something she'd never thought could happen.

Today, though . . . Today she felt different. She'd awakened this morning strangely refreshed, filled with the unfamiliar sense that there was something she had to do today, something she had to accomplish. She had no idea what that something was, but she had followed the feeling and it had led her to school, led her here, to the newspaper office.

She hesitated before going in. The newsroom was crowded, filled with the sort of noise and activity she'd been avoiding the past few weeks, and she wasn't sure that she was ready to face it just yet. She hid in the hallway, just outside the door and was debating with herself whether she should go inside or turn tail and run when Stuart got off the elevator and spotted her on his way into the newsroom. "Cheryl!" he called. "Where've you been?"

She was caught now, trapped, and she put on a fake smile and waved back at him as she walked into the newsroom. She was immediately surrounded by the other editors, and for the first few seconds, as they greeted her and welcomed her back, she felt really good. She was wanted here. She was needed.

Then someone touched her arm, and someone else touched her back, and Eddie tried to hug her, and she started to panic. She backed up, pulled away. Was Eddie checking her out? Was Faruk leering at her? She'd put on a baggy blouse and baggy jeans, but maybe they could see anyway, maybe her outlines were visible.

Her breasts.

Her vagina.

She felt warm and she was sweating, and it seemed suddenly hard to breathe. She noticed for the first time that not all of the editors were here. Steve was missing. And Ford. The thought occurred to her that they were in class or busy on an assignment, but somehow she knew that that wasn't the case.

The newsroom itself, she saw, had changed. Gone were the posters she'd hung on the wall behind her desk; gone were the potted plants with which Norton had decorated the room. Gone was Norton. The venetian blinds were off the adviser's office windows, and the interior of the small room was empty, only the bare desk remaining. The rest of the newsroom looked dirtier and dingier than she remembered. There were black scuff marks all over the tiled floor, scratches and nicks in the wood of the desks, a hole in the plaster wall the size of a fist.

She thanked the other editors for welcoming her back, explained to Jim that she'd been sick but was better now and ready to work, and retreated to her desk, dropping into her chair, grateful for the furniture to hide behind.

She glanced through the pile of reviews that had been

left in her in-box. Already she could hear the other editors dropping their voices, talking about her, gossiping behind her back. She pretended not to notice, pretended to be reading one of the reviews, but she kept her ears open, her attention focused on what they were saying. Did Eddie say "crazy bitch"? Did Faruk say "fucked-up twat"?

She suddenly realized that she was the only female editor this semester. Why was that? Because she fulfilled the quota? Maybe Norton and Jim didn't like women. Or maybe they did like her. Maybe they wanted her. Maybe they all wanted her. She thought of the janitor and the stairway, and again it seemed way too warm in here, way too close, way too stuffy.

She forced herself to take a deep breath. That wasn't the reason she was the only female editor this semester. Jim wasn't like that. She knew him better than that.

Didn't she?

Something told her to open the top drawer of her desk. She did so, and inside, lying atop a pad of scratch paper, was a knife. A new, long, sharp, and shiny knife. Tentatively, she reached into the drawer and let her fingers touch the weapon. The metal felt good: cold and strong.

If only she'd had a knife like this when she was in the stairway. She could have cut off that fucker's balls.

Balls.

In her mind she saw the knife in her hand, her fingers wielding it gracefully, using it to slice through skin, through cord, through testicle.

This was why she had come here today. This was the purpose for which she'd been searching. This was what she was supposed to do.

Cut off the fuckers' balls.

Fate. Someone had put this in her desk, and something had led her to it, and everything had clicked together at exactly the right time.

Kismet. Fate.

Jim smiled at her, and she smiled back as she thought of taking her knife and lopping off his gonads.

"Are you sure you're gonna be okay?" he asked.

She nodded at him, continued to smile as she thought of his severed balls. "Fine," she said. "I'm just fine."

2

Ron Gregory sat on the bench in the middle of the quad, trying to concentrate on the open history text in front of him.

Trying.

But not succeeding.

He could not seem to devote his full attention to any sort of schoolwork anymore. Not since the party at Dr. Coulter's.

Not since they'd carved up Miyako.

It still seemed wrong to him. And no matter how much Ruth told him that Miyako had been willing and that it was perfectly normal, perfectly natural, and he'd better grow up if he ever wanted to be anything more than a doltish, unsophisticated rube, he still could not rationalize what they had done. He kept hearing Miyako's screams, kept seeing the expression of panicked comprehension on her face at the end, that look that said she knew she was going to die and did not want to. She might have been willing at first, but she had not been willing at the last, and he was the only one who seemed to have noticed.

And it had haunted him ever since.

Ruth was gone now, and that was probably for the best. It had been her decision. Since the party he had not wanted to go out, had wanted only to stay home, stay in, and she had felt stifled, confined, and had warned him that if he didn't snap out of it, she was going to leave him. A part of him, he supposed, had wanted her to leave, and that was why he had remained entrenched, refused to change his behavior, though he could have easily acquiesced to her wishes in order to keep her.

Jim had taken him off the Greek beat as soon as he'd joined Theta Mu, and he'd sort of unofficially quit the newspaper soon after that. He'd never told Jim, had never filled out a drop form, but he'd stopped going to class and had not turned in the last assignment he'd been given.

Now he wondered if Jim would let him return. He missed being on the staff. He missed the people, he missed the work, he missed the . . . the normalcy. Everything in his life seemed to have turned so damn weird since he'd met the Den Mother—

and the Adversary

—and while a lot of it was great, some of it wasn't, and he often found himself wishing that none of it had ever happened, that he'd been allowed just to go on living his boring, normal life.

He looked up from his textbook to see a lone African-American student, a member of the school's black fraternity, wearing that house's oversized wooden crescent hanging on a string around his neck, cross the open cement at the head of the quad. To his right, underneath the trees, a large group of white students watched him.

"Dick!" one of the white students called out.

The black student kept walking.

"Yo! Jungle bunny! With that fuckin' tree hangin' off your neck!"

The African-American student turned to face them. There was anger in his expression, but it receded a little when he saw the size of the group. Ron stood, picked up his books, the hairs on his arms prickling. The Den Mother had said something like this would happen. Several weeks ago she'd whispered, in her papery voice, that there would be a war, that a member of one fraternity would be killed on campus by the members of another, and that there would be retaliation and escalation that would lead to a full-scale confrontation.

Was that what was happening here?

The white students moved out from underneath the trees, and Ron saw that several of them wore camouflage fatigues. "You want me to shove that moon up your dirty black ass?" one of them yelled.

The black student stopped walking, turned to face them. "You want me to fuck your mama?" He paused. "Again?"

As one, the crowd rushed forward.

There were other students seated around the quad, other students walking to and from classes, but none of them made any effort to help as the mob descended upon the fraternity member and started beating him. Some of them stopped, stared, watched, but they remained passive, like spectators at a sporting event.

This can't be happening, Ron thought. He was reminded of Kitty Genovese, Rodney King, Reginald Denny, all the people who'd been hurt, injured, even killed because people like himself were not brave enough to speak out, speak up, put a stop to it.

Was he brave enough to try to do something about this?

He moved forward, dropping his books. The attackers were yelling, but even through their yells he could hear the screams of the fraternity member: short, gasping cries of agony. From between the khaki and the colored shirts, he caught glimpses of brown skin, white teeth, and red blood. And then the student was down on the ground and they were kicking him.

He was right. This was what the Den Mother had predicted.

His heart was pounding, his palms were sweating, and he was afraid, not just physically but on a much deeper, much more primal level, yet he forced himself to move forward. There was really nothing he could do, no way that one person could stop this entire crowd, but something told him he had to try, and he came up to a screaming army-jacketed student and punched him hard in the back. The student crumpled, caught himself, tried to turn, but Ron hit the side of his head, felt a drop of blood from the student's ear hit his knuckles. Then he was into it, swinging with abandon, hitting, punching, clawing, pulling hair. He could not see who he was fighting, did not really care. It was chaotic, but that was one of the things he liked about it, and though he took a few hits, a few kicks, he did more giving than receiving, and it felt good. He was sweating and bleeding, but he was pumped up, exhilarated, and he never wanted it to stop. At some point he realized that he had joined the attackers, that rather than opposing them, he was one of them, and was whaling away on the black student, but he didn't care, and he brought his foot up and kicked the student in the head, and it felt good to kick him, and he brought his foot back and did it again, feeling the satisfyingly solid feel of bone against his shoe.

Yes, he thought, yes. He was part of the crowd, he was one of them, and there was something wonderful about that, and he screamed "Nigger!" and he continued to kick with the rest of them until the student was dead and his limp, flopping body was unrecognizable.

3

Sit on it

The president dropped the card in the wastebasket. She thought she heard a clicking sound behind her, and she jumped, whirling around, but there was no one else in the office and the door was still closed. She licked her lips, looked into the wastebasket at the small, stiff paper square, which had somehow landed face up.

Sit on it

The card had been lying on her desk when she'd arrived for work.

Next to the ceramic penis.

There was another click. She had not imagined it. She had heard it. This time it seemed as though it had come from one of the recessed air ducts set in the acoustic-tile ceiling. Was someone hiding in the air shaft, watching her, spying on her? Or could someone have installed some sort of hidden camera and hidden speaker in the office?

Yes. Someone could have.

The same person who had left the penis.

Diana walked slowly around the desk, looking at the object, unwilling to give her hidden observer the satisfaction of seeing her react to his taunts. Of course, she had jumped that first time, but it had been a small jump, and her startled reaction probably hadn't even been noticed.

She should call Lyons, she knew, tell him that someone had broken into her office, have him sweep the place for cameras and listening devices, have him find whoever had left this horrible thing and nail the bastard's ass but good.

She stopped to examine the huge penis. Her first thought had been that it was a joke, put here maybe by Harte or Grey, but of course neither of them could have thought up, much less carried out, something so crude and obviously pointless.

She wanted to convince herself that it had been left here by someone she knew, that it was merely a practical joke whose humor escaped her. She found the object more than a little threatening, and the idea that it had been left by a stranger, as some sort of message, frightened her.

A flash of white caught her eye, a flash of white at

the base of the phallus that had not been there a second before.

Another card.

She picked it up, her heart pounding.

Diana

Oh, God. It knew her name! Whatever it was, it knew her name!

It?

Already another card had taken its place on the desk.

Sit on it Diana

She looked again at the object. It was blue-brown, curved slightly to the left, and was approximately half the size of a baseball bat, although neither end was tapered. Thickly sculpted veins wound up from the flat stand at the bottom to the flared head at the top.

Again she read the card: *Sit on it Diana.*

There was something demanding about the declarative sentence, and the absence of punctuation made it seem even more like an order. She angrily tore up the card and dropped it into the wastebasket. No one bossed her around. No one told her what to do. She was the president of this university, for Christ's sake. She wasn't about to be ordered around by some note-writing, cock-sculpting psycho. This had gone far enough. She was going to take that monstrosity off her desk, sit down, and call Lyons right now.

There was another card at the foot of the phallus. She knew she shouldn't pick it up. There was something scary about the way these cards kept appearing, something wrong, and she knew she should get out of the office, tell her secretary to call Lyons, and not come back until the police chief and his men arrived.

But she reached for it anyway, read it.

Sit on it Diana

The request was not so demanding this time. The words had not changed, but somehow the note seemed gentler, like a suggestion, a helpful suggestion rather than an order.

Another card had already appeared, and she picked it up.

Sit on it Diana

Not a suggestion this time. An invitation. An offer. She looked at the giant penis, and she wondered why she had found it so threatening. It wasn't a weapon or anything. It was large, yes, but there was nothing menacing or malevolent about it. It was even sort of inviting, in a way. In fact, she thought, as large as the sculpture was, she could probably accommodate it. She probably *could* sit on it.

Before she fully realized what she was doing, she had kicked off her shoes and was climbing on top of her desk. She stood over the phallus, looking down. From this angle she could see the small slit carved into the tip, and looking at it from this perspective, gave her a feeling of power. How could she have been intimidated by the penis? It could not do anything to her, it was merely something for her to use.

A tool.

Yes, a tool. She smiled as she pulled off her pantyhose and dropped them to the floor. Straddling the penis, she hiked up her skirt, squatted.

It was not cold as she had expected, not hard and unyielding, but warm and pliable, almost as if—

Almost as if it was alive.

There was pain. It was too thick, and she felt a cut around the opening of her vagina where the skin was stretched too tight, but there was also pleasure, and she shuddered as she lowered herself onto the enormous pole. She moved slowly up and down, each time taking more of the phallus's length inside of her.

And then, suddenly, she wasn't moving, she was crouched but still, and she felt *it* moving within her, pulsing, thrusting gently upward, and it was as though she had just awakened from a trance. She saw her shoes and pantyhose on the carpet, next to the last two cards, realized with disgust that she was squatting on top of her desk with a clay cock inside her.

Only it didn't feel like clay anymore, it felt real, felt slimy, felt like muscle, felt like flesh, and somehow that was the most sickening, most disgusting part.

She tried to stand up, but the giant penis was thickening, expanding, still moving, and she could not get off it.

Oh, God. This couldn't be happening. She stood, but the penis came with her, still held tightly within her vagina, and she wanted to scream but knew that if she did,

Nadine would come running in, and she did not want her secretary to see her like this.

The flat base of the penis was dangling just below her knee, and she reached for it, trying to pull the thing out of her, but it turned and twisted in her grasp, seemingly imbued with a will of its own, and it pressed deeper inside her, and she gasped, all trace of pleasure gone now, only pain remaining. Pain and panic.

And fear.

What had happened? How had she let it get this far?

She squatted again and leaned carefully onto her side, using her hands to gently lower herself off the desk.

Was this being filmed or taped? Was this all part of some bizarre, elaborate carnal candid camera?

Something told her no, and she stood in the center of the office and again reached down to grasp the base and try to pull the penis out of her. She yanked with all of her strength, ignoring the strange pulsing tugs of the object, and for a brief second, it seemed, she managed to move it an inch or two out. Then it shoved itself twice as far back in, and she screamed.

That was it. She could not take care of this herself. She needed help. Embarrassment or no embarrassment, she had to get the hell out of this office.

She started waddling toward the door.

Instantly, her desk whipped across the floor, barely missing her, and slammed into the door, blocking it. Underneath her feet, the carpet began moving in undulating ripples, like waves. Her chair rolled warily back and forth, like a bull or a bullfighter, then charged at her. She jumped to the side, landing painfully on one shoulder, and saw the chair hit the wall, bounce off, then spin around on its swivel, as if looking for her.

It found her.

It came speeding toward her across the rippling carpet, and she closed her eyes and screamed as the metal wheels slammed into her head and the ceramic phallus thrust joyously deeper.

The last thing she heard was the clicking noise.

It was the sound of furniture laughing.

TWENTY-SIX

1

Jim awoke with a residual sense of loss from an unremembered dream. Faith was next to him, curled into his back, her arm around his midsection, but even she could not erase the strange feeling of melancholy that seemed to have settled within him during the night. For some reason it made him think of Howie, and he was half tempted to call his friend to make sure that he was all right, but he looked at the clock and knew that Howie wouldn't be up for another hour and decided to let him sleep. He was just being paranoid.

It was impossible not to be paranoid these days.

Faith muttered in her sleep and rolled over, away from him. Carefully, he slipped out of bed. His penis was sore, and when he looked down he saw dried blood on the tip.

What had they done last night?

He couldn't remember.

Breathing deeply, he walked into the bathroom to take a shower.

They met at nine in Ian's office. Jim felt bad about not bringing Howie along, but, despite his protestations to the contrary, his friend was simply not physically able to do everything that he himself could do, and with something like this, where there might be real danger, it was better to be overprotective than underprotective. If that was discrimination, then so be it. He didn't care. He loved Howie and didn't want anything to happen to him.

And if the university knew that Howie was working with them, something would happen to him.

How much *did* the university know? he wondered.

Undoubtedly, it had access to their records, to whatever was filed on paper or computer. But could it read minds or could it only observe actions? He had no idea. None of them did. And that was why they had to assume the worst.

Buckley was the last to arrive. He walked in carrying a box of donuts, and he sat down, the box on his lap, eating and not offering to share.

Ian looked at them, stood, began pacing behind his desk. He cleared his throat. "I met with him," he said. "I met with Stevens." He was silent for a moment.

"And?" Buckley prompted.

He took a deep breath, told them about the meeting, about what the man had said, about the apartment full of explosives.

Buckley whistled. "Heavy shit."

Faith licked her lips. "So—so we're going to be, like, terrorists? We're going to bomb the school?" She shook her head. "I don't know if I'm up for this. What if we're wrong? What if it's not what we think it is? What if we hurt innocent people?"

"I'm not sure this is the way to go either," Ian admitted, sitting down.

"Then, what do we do?" Jim asked.

"I say we stick to the original plan. We recruit, get everyone together, pool our resources and our brainpower."

Buckley grinned. "A ghostbusters think tank."

"In a way. We'll all meet, talk, see what we can figure out. We throw Stevens in with philosophers, scientists, and see what we come up with."

"And if we come up with nothing?"

"There's always firepower."

They were silent.

"Which set of cells make up the brain?" Jim asked.

"What?"

"Which cells did he say made up the brain?"

Buckley looked at him, understanding dawning in his face. "Yes!"

"What?" Faith looked from Buckley to Jim. "Clue me in."

"Kill the brain and the body will die."

"No."

"Yes."

"Do we have to kill the whole brain? Can't we just give it a lobotomy or something? I mean, these are not really cells we're talking about here. These are people."

" 'Kill' is a figure of speech. We'd be killing the brain of this university. That doesn't mean that we'd have to kill any people. As long as we do it right."

"What if we do it wrong?"

Jim shrugged. "Casualties of war."

"But that's exactly what it's doing! Killing people! That's why we're after it!"

"Desperate times call for desperate measures. Things have gotten out of hand here. And we're in it too far to turn back now."

Ian shook his head, held up his hand. "The cell story was just an analogy. He said there weren't actual organs or anything."

"What if he's wrong about that? What if he's only partially right? What if he's got the main idea down, but some of his details are fuzzy?"

"That's why we need to meet with everyone. We don't have enough information one way or another to make an intelligent guess on how to act. We can't fight what we don't know. The only thing we do know is that this school is evil. And that we're the ones who have to try to stop it."

"It's lucky that we all found each other," Faith said. "Isn't it?"

Ian shook his head. "That's how these things work. That's why we have to be extra careful. In horror novels there's usually a small group of people who are brought together by nebulous forces of good in order to do battle with the forces of evil. Only we were brought together by Stevens. He's an English teacher, a horror fan, and he's familiar with those conventions too. For all we know, he's the cause of all this, the one who set all this in motion."

"No," Faith said. "You and Jim were brought together by this guy. But Jim and I got together because of my botany class and because he happened to be in my lit class." She gestured toward Buckley. "And I'm sure this guy didn't bring you two together. You've probably known each other for years."

Buckley grinned. "She has a point."

"Even more reason to worry. We're following the formula. And if it hasn't been artificially imposed by Stevens, then that means it's probably real."

"I thought you and this guy were buds," Buckley said.

"I met with him. And I believe him. Up to a point. But we can't be too careful. And we can't afford to slip."

"What if this is exactly what it wants you to do?" Buckley asked. "What if it's manipulating you to do what it wants? What if we've all been affected? What if we just think we're acting on our own, but it's just pulling our strings?"

Ian shrugged. "Then we're screwed. There's nothing we can do."

"It seems to me," Jim said, "that we're wasting a lot of time with this ... summit or whatever it is. Maybe Stevens is right. Maybe we should just blow the place up."

"I don't think that's our only option. And I agree with Faith—in that case, the cure is as bad as the disease."

"Is it?"

"What if we just leave?" Faith asked. "What if we get everyone to leave? We can get the administration to close the school early this semester. We can all go on vacation. And when we get back—"

"When we get back," Ian said, "everything will pick up where it left off." He paused. "Besides, what makes you think you can leave?"

"I leave every day. I go home after my classes are over, after I'm through working."

"But you come back every day."

Jim nodded. "He's right." He turned toward Ian. "I was worried about her. I asked her to drop out, to transfer to another school, but she wouldn't do it."

"Because I didn't want to," she said angrily.

"Because you couldn't."

"Like Stevens said, we're the good cells of this organism. But we're still cells. Which means that, to a certain extent, we probably are all affected. That's why I want us to be extra careful."

Buckley stood, tossing his empty donut box in the wastebasket. He brushed the crumbs from his shirt. "I have a nine forty-five freshman comp class," he said. "I have to get going."

"Hit up everyone you know," Ian said. "Today. We can't put this off anymore."

Buckley waved. "Gotcha, chief." He nodded to Jim and Faith. "Later."

Ian stood. "I have a class too. Why don't we meet again tomorrow, see what's happened, see what we've come up with?"

Jim nodded. "Okay."

"Maybe we should pray," Faith said, standing.

Ian didn't smile. "It can't hurt," he said.

2

Faith felt cold as they walked out of Dr. Emerson's— Ian's—office. Everything seemed fine, everything seemed okay, when they were in the office together. Sitting there talking, she felt as though she could take on the world, as though she had the strength to overcome any obstacle thrown in her path. But the moment she stepped outside the door, she felt like an unwelcome visitor passing through enemy territory.

No.

Like Pinnochio caught in the whale.

Yes. That was it. She looked down the corridor of the building, and it seemed to her as though she was trapped inside some enemy monster, that she was walking around inside its body, through its veins.

They'd both missed American Lit, and she'd assumed that Jim had to run off to the newspaper, so she was grateful when he said that he had an hour or so to kill, and she immediately took him up on his offer to accompany her to the library so she could tell Phil that she was quitting. She still desperately needed a job, but no amount of money could convince her to stay in the library.

It was back to Burger King.

She paused. Working off campus. Wouldn't that decrease the school's hold on her? She'd still be attending classes, but she wouldn't be employed here anymore, she wouldn't be enrolled in work-study. Extricating herself from a university-sponsored program: wouldn't that give her a little more autonomy?

Maybe it wouldn't let her quit.

She pushed that thought from her mind.

Sue was working the Circulation desk, and she told Faith that Phil was on the fourth floor, covering Reference. The thought of going upstairs, of going anyplace in this building where she did not have instant access to an exit, frightened her, but Jim was with her, holding her hand, and together they took the elevator to the fourth floor.

The bloodstains had been cleaned up, the damaged furniture replaced, but there was still something about the reference desk that made Faith uneasy. The bank of reference librarians, now down to two, Ada Simmons and Phil, faced the elevator and the door to the stairwell across an open expanse which was broken only by the high table atop which sat the periodicals and serials lists. They looked extremely vulnerable here, sitting out in the open, and she found that she was afraid for them.

But she didn't know how to tell them that.

She walked slowly toward the desk, holding tightly onto Jim's hand, the sound of her clicking heels loud in the stillness. Some of the lines between the floor tiles were darker than others, she noticed, but she did not bend down to examine them more carefully. She knew what had caused it, but she did not want confirmation.

"You're quitting," Phil said as she reached the desk, before she'd even opened her mouth.

She nodded. "Yeah." She thought she should explain, but he merely smiled sadly at her.

"I understand," he said.

"I—"

"It's all right," he told her. "You don't have to explain. I'll send the paperwork through this afternoon. You can transfer to another work-study job."

"I'm out of work-study. I'm going to get a job off campus."

He nodded. "That's probably a good idea." His eyes met hers. What was that that she saw in his gaze? Understanding? Comprehension?

Behind the desk, in the small Reference office in back

of him, an unfamiliar alphabet popped up on a computer screen.

Phil looked toward Ada on his left, then leaned forward. "Don't come back," he said. "Go to the public library. Study at Fullerton if you have to. Don't come back here."

It was a warning, not a threat, a word of caution from someone who was on her side, given freely in a spirit of concern, and she nodded. "Thank you," she said.

Phil looked at Jim. "Take care of her."

"She can take care of herself," Jim said, and Faith squeezed his hand.

"I hope so," Phil said. "I hope so."

Outside the library, campus life seemed to be going on as normal. Students were walking from building to building between classes, books in hand, alone or in couples or in small groups. Tables and booths, promoting various organizations or political causes, lined the walkway to the Student Center. A typical day at a typical Southern California university. If she hadn't known better, she would have thought there was nothing unusual, nothing out of the ordinary, nothing wrong here.

Maybe there wasn't.

That's what it wanted them to think. That's why it put on this show of normalcy, to lull people into a false sense of security.

Two young women walked by, chatting amiably. Faith heard the word *blood*.

You didn't have to scratch far below the surface to realize that there was something seriously amiss.

"So what's the plan?" Jim said.

"I guess I'll go look for a job."

"Where?"

"Someplace in Santa Ana, near home. Someplace far away from school."

"Are you staying over tonight?"

She looked away, reddened. "No. I'd better go home tonight. I doubt that my mom gives a shit—she probably didn't even notice that I was gone—but I'd better check in just in case."

He nodded. "It's probably not good to spend too

much time here anyway. My dorm room's still technically on campus. Who knows ..." He trailed off.

She thought of the bruises between her thighs.
"Yeah."

"Besides, it'll give me time to clean the blood off
my sheets."

She looked at him, surprised, and he stared levelly
back. "We have to talk about it sometime. I don't know
about you, but it scares the hell out of me."

Her mouth seemed suddenly dry.

"It's not normal," he said. "It's not right."

"It's not normal," she agreed. "But who says it's not
right? We both ... we both like it."

"Do we? I mean, would we if we were away from
here, if we were someplace else? Or is it making us
like it?"

She was silent.

"You know you've been thinking that too."

"Yes," she admitted.

"Well, maybe it'd be better if we cooled it for a
while."

"Can we?"

"I don't know."

They were walking past the Biological Sciences building, and Faith slowed, looking toward the open door of
the science theater. She looked at her watch, turned to
Jim. "That's my botany class in there."

"Did PETA or anyone ever come out and harass
that guy?"

"I don't know." She continued to look toward the
room.

"Want to take a peek?"

She did and at the same time she didn't, but holding
Jim's hand, she walked up the low steps to the door of
the lecture hall. Inside, the professor was standing at the
lectern on stage, facing the class. She moved to the right,
so the doorjamb would hide her from his view.

"At our next meeting," he was saying, "I will be demonstrating the toxicity of these herbs on some wee young
tykes from our own Children's Center." He chuckled.
"You'll get to see firsthand how the skin burns and peels
when—"

Faith moved away, feeling sick to her stomach.

"Maybe we *should* just bomb this whole fucking place," Jim said as they walked back down the steps.

Faith took a deep breath. "Maybe we should," she said.

2

Chapman Clements.

Buckley stood outside the zoologist's office and wiped his sweaty hands on his pants. He wasn't any good at this shit. Subtlety had never been his strong suit. He knew that about himself and he lived with it. Or, more precisely, he didn't care about it.

But now he was supposed to feel out his friends and acquaintances, engage them in some type of fake conversation, and then try to casually determine where they stood on all the weirdness that was going down?

This wasn't his forté. This wasn't his bag. This wasn't his cup of tea.

And what if his hints were too broad? What if they caught on to him? From the way Ian had been talking, they were as likely as not to whip out a blade and gut him like a fucking fish.

He wasn't cut out for intrigue.

Gathering his courage, Buckley knocked on the door of Clements' office.

"Yeah! Come on in!" the zoologist called.

Buckley opened the door.

So he wasn't crazy.

Chapman stood in the doorway of his office, watching Buckley's retreating figure. He'd thought it was just him, thought maybe he'd been going a little stir crazy from spending too much time in the field and not enough in the classroom.

But Buckley and Emerson had noticed it too.

It should have made him feel good, but it didn't. He would have rather been wrong and crazy than right and sane.

Especially when it came to this.

Buckley had spelled out the examples but not the cause, and he wondered if the English professor knew what was happening. He supposed he did, and he sup-

posed that that was what would be discussed at the
meeting.

He found himself thinking of his Tuesday and Thursday Intro to Mammals class. There was one kid in there,
a strange-looking redheaded guy, who'd given him the
creeps from the very first day. He'd even dreamed about
him once. The kid had turned in none of the assignments
so far, had not taken any of the quizzes, but he had been
in class every day, sitting in the front row, staring up at
him with the most disconcerting look on his face.

The kid had to be part of it.

Chapman checked his watch. Lunchtime. He usually
went out and got something to eat right now, but he
didn't feel very hungry today, and it was more important
for him to find others, like himself, who had not yet
been corrupted. As Buckley said, the more the merrier.
They needed all the support they could muster.

But who to start with?

Jobson. Jobson was cool. If anybody had remained out
of it, if anybody had withstood the pressure, it was the
entymologist. He was the only professor who was even
more disconnected than himself.

Yeah.

Jobson.

Clements. That putz. That walking piece of dogshit.
Who did he think he was fooling with his hey-what's-
happening-I-haven't-seen-you-in-a-while routine?

Asshole.

Ken Jobson locked the door to the lab, bolted it.

The fucker had wanted to spy on him. He'd wanted
to discover his special secret. But no one was going to
find that out. Not until he'd published his findings. When
he was done, when he'd showed the world what he'd
discovered, the face of human relationships—human *sexual* relationships—would be forever changed. A willing
partner of the opposite gender would no longer be required, or even desirable, in order to have a fulfilling
sexual experience.

He removed from his pocket the key to the back
room, and used it to open the door.

Celia was still on the floor, still gagged, still squirming,
still covered with flies.

"Yes," he said. "Oh, yes." The small room was strong with the smell of the honey he'd painted on her body to attract the flies and the musky scent of her arousal.

How many orgasms had she had?

Thirty, he estimated. He wrote down the number on the sheet attached to his clipboard. That would sound good in his article.

But what to call his discovery?

He giggled. Buggery. Maybe he'd call it "buggery."

Celia squirmed. He heard her trying to scream through the gag.

Thirty-one.

He was aroused himself, the stiffness of his erection pressing painfully against his pants, and he pulled the pants down, kicking off his shoes. He removed his underwear and his shirt and, completely naked, stretched out on the floor next to his lab assistant.

He reached into the jar of honey, rubbed it on his penis.

Immediately, the flies swarmed over his member. Hundreds of them. He felt their feet, their wings, moving across his shaft, his head, stimulating the sensitive skin, and his excitement grew to a fever pitch. Gasping, he reached for the beaker of ants. He rolled onto his side, shoved his penis into the beaker, and felt the ants crawl onto him.

He came explosively as the first one bit.

TWENTY-SEVEN

1

Stuart and Eddie, the last two editors in the newsroom, were packing up and getting ready to leave. Howie looked up at the clock. Seven-thirty. If Jim had been planning to come back he would have been here by now.

Straining, Howie lifted his arm, let his hand fall on the toggle switch of his wheelchair. He pinched his thumb and forefinger together and managed to back the chair up, swinging it around. "Eddie?" he called.

The sports editor turned toward him. "Yeah?"

"I can't reach the phone here on this desk. You think you could move it a little closer for me?" He tried to smile, though he wasn't sure if he was successful. "I'll be your friend."

"Weenie."

Howie swung the chair around again and pulled next to Jim's desk as Eddie pulled the phone out. "Thanks."

"So what're your plans for tonight?" Stuart asked.

Howie tried to turn his head to look at the editor, but only managed to twist far enough to see the back handle of his own chair. "Don't have any."

"Eddie and I are going to check out the basketball game. Wanna come?"

"They sent us plenty of press passes," Eddie said.

"That's okay," Howie told them. "But thanks for asking."

Stuart shrugged. "Suit yourself."

Howie turned back to the phone. He could have asked Eddie to take the receiver off the hook for him, could have even asked him to dial, but he felt bad enough having to ask for any help at all, and he did not want to rely on other people any more than necessary.

He leaned forward, until his chest was against the side

of the desk, and threw his arm forward, hooking his wrist over the phone's receiver. He dragged his arm back, the receiver with it, until the mouthpiece was on the edge of the desk next to him. Grunting, he forced his arm forward again, letting his hand land on the rotary dial. Adjusting his arm, he hooked a finger into the 6 hole and moved it clockwise, lifting his hand up when it reached the metal stop at the end and allowing the dial to spin back.

He repeated the process for the other six numbers.

Dave answered the phone on the third ring. "Yeah?"

His attendant sounded angry, the pitch of his voice belligerent, and Howie was suddenly afraid to ask him to bring the van and pick him up.

"Uh, hi," Howie said.

"You little fuck. Where've you been?"

There was no mistaking the belligerence now. "I'm still here, at the *Sentinel*."

"Don't expect me to run over there and pick you up. I have a life to lead, too, you know."

"I wasn't even going to ask."

"Then why did you call?"

Howie's mouth felt very, very dry.

"I thought so. You find your own way home." The line went dead.

Howie was shaking as his hand found the toggle switch again and backed up the chair, only in his arms the shaking was exaggerated, like a parody of someone acting afraid. He did not want to go back to his room. Not tonight. Not with Dave there.

He was scared of the attendant.

Maybe Jim was at the dorm. Or maybe he would be back later—

"We're leaving," Eddie said. "You'd better go too. I need to lock up."

"Is the basketball offer still open?" Howie asked.

Stuart nodded. "Sure. Change your mind?"

"Yeah. I'd like to go."

"All right, then."

Howie pushed the toggle and the wheelchair sped across the floor, through the doorway into the hall. This would give Jim time to get home if he was out with Faith or something. He'd call his friend after the game, see if he was back, see if he'd let him crash at his place. If not, well, he could always call his parents. He dreaded having to explain the situation to them—especially to his mom—but it was better than facing Dave.

Anything was better than facing Dave.

Eddie locked the door, pocketed the key. "Okay," he said. "Let's book."

The gym was crowded, the bleachers nearly filled by the time they arrived, though the tip-off wasn't for another fifteen minutes. The only seats available were at the very top of the bleachers, and though Eddie and Stuart offered to stand next to him on the floor, Howie told them to get their asses up there and snag themselves seats before somebody else stole them.

"All right," Stuart said. "But stay near the exit. We'll find you there at halftime."

"Okay." Howie watched them scramble up the wooden steps, then maneuvered his chair through the crowd, past the scorekeepers' table, toward the exit. There were very few singles here. Most of the spectators seemed to be couples or groups of friends, and though he'd arrived with friends and could probably still see them if he turned to look, it still felt a little strange and uncomfortable to be rolling across the gym alone.

He pulled to a stop at the far end of the bleachers, by the open door, swinging around until he was facing the players warming up on the court. The cool air from the night outside felt good after the heat of bodies in the center of the gym, and he glanced out the door. In the shadows beyond the square of light from the doorway, he could just make out a couple embracing passionately. The man's hand seemed to be shoved down the back of the woman's pants.

He watched them for a moment. Either one could have easily seen that he was looking at them, but they were too absorbed in what they were doing to pay any attention to what was happening here inside the gym.

He sometimes found himself wondering what sex was like. Out of everything that had been denied him, out of all the physical experiences he had not been able to have, it was sex that made him the most curious. Walking? Running? He didn't care if he ever experienced either. He had his own means of locomotion, and while it was sometimes awkward and inconvenient, he was used to it and it served him well. But sex . . . that was a different story. A few years back, as a high schooler, he had devoured all the pornography he could get his hands on—looking at photos, reading stories—and while he'd enjoyed looked at the naked women, and while, intellectually, he had understood the attraction, he had not been able to even imagine the way sex must feel. He had no sensation at all below the waist, could not remember ever experiencing anything physical that he would term "pleasurable," and the understanding of sex remained for him tantalizingly out of reach.

"Hey, you. Handi-man. Watch it."

He looked up. He'd been tinkering with the toggle switch, absently moving it, causing the chair to roll back and forth, and he'd almost run over the feet of a long-haired, leather-jacketed guy heading outside to smoke.

"Sorry," Howie said.

"Dipshit crip."

He watched the man walk outside. He looked familiar, but Howie wasn't sure where he'd seen him before.

The Club, the Jan Anderson concert, a voice inside of him said, and that sounded right.

He stared out the door, at the orange tip of the man's cigarette, bright against the blackness of night, and he remembered the claustrophobic tenseness of the Club concert, the threat of violence in the air, the riot that had almost ensued. He had the sudden urge to leave, to go home, to get away from the gym before the game started. The same thing that had happened in the Club could happen here, only on a much larger scale, and he twisted his body to the right, looking up in the bleachers for Stuart and Eddie, but before he had even spotted them, the buzzer sounded, there was a sudden rush of people across the floor of the gym in front of the bleachers, the cheerleaders came bounding out, and the game was on.

He tried to concentrate on the game, but it was hard. People kept walking in front of him, people who looked like the smoker, who was outside and still had not come in. Leather-clad men, tattooed women; facially pierced people who did not look like the students he ordinarily saw on campus. The game itself seemed to be much rougher than usual. There were not many fouls called, but there should have been. Punchings, trippings, kneeings, and elbowings were the order of the night, and the crowd seemed to love it, cheering lustily when a forward from the opposing team lost a front tooth in a spray of bloody saliva, screaming just as loudly and just as enthusiastically when the Brea center broke his nose.

The side door was still open, but the breeze seemed to have disappeared and the air in the gym was hot and oppressively humid. He wished Jim was here. He felt alone and frightened, and he kept glancing to his left, seeing the crowd of freaks outside grow from one to five to ten. Behind them the couple was still making out, performing for the onlookers.

He should never have come. He'd known it was dangerous to do anything other than to go to class on this campus—Jim had drilled that into his head—but for a brief moment there in the newsroom with Stuart and Eddie, it had seemed normal, natural, a typically harmless way to spend an evening, as far removed from the horrors of recent weeks as anything could be.

And a hell of a lot safer than going back to the dorm and facing Dave.

But in retrospect, it had been a mistake; a big one, and as soon as halftime rolled around, he was going to find Stuart and Eddie, tell them he was leaving, and get as far away from here as possible as quickly as possible.

The crowd roared its approval as one of the Brea guards kneed the opposite team's center in the crotch.

It was nearly forty-five minutes later when the buzzer sounded the end of the half, and before the final shot was halfway to the basket, Howie was rolling. Some people were getting up, walking around, but not nearly as many as he would have expected, and he moved slowly in front of the stands, scanning the top row for Stuart and Eddie. He found the spot where the empty seats had been, but a group of women were there, staring straight ahead, at the bleachers on the opposite side of the court, and there was no sign of either of the editors.

He remained in place, letting his gaze travel down the bleachers, row by row.

Nothing.

They'd disappeared.

A beachball was blown up and sent flying by someone in one of the upper regions. The oversize sphere flew over rows of heads to bounce benignly off a spectator farther down. It was caught by someone else and heaved at the head of a bald man. The crowd cheered.

The bald man stood, looking angrily around, saw a young woman in the row in front of him laughing and clapping, and cocked his arm back, throwing the ball as hard as he could at her face. It hit with an audible smack, then bounced on to someone else. A resounding cheer went up from the audience.

The mood was changing, getting ugly. Howie could feel it, and he suddenly noticed that he was the only one on the floor in front of the bleachers. Everyone else was either outside, getting something to eat or drink, or sitting in their seats. The crowds that had been passing in front of the stands had disappeared. He looked back toward the exit door. The leather crowd had come inside and was blocking the door, staring at him.

Everyone was staring at him, he realized. If any of the spectators was outside eating, drinking, or smoking, they were few and far between. Almost all of the bleacher seats were occupied.

And everyone was looking at him.

If he had not been afraid before, he was now. The implicit threat he had sensed below the surface of the crowd had now been made explicit and was directed specifically at him. He tried to push the toggle switch on his chair, but his arm would not obey his order and panic seemed to have locked up his fingers. Frantically, he once again scanned the staring faces for Stuart or Eddie, spotting neither.

The beachball hit his head.

It was thrown by a girl in one of the middle rows, and it did not really hurt, merely bounced off the top of his head and rolled onto the court, but it was accompanied by a chorus of cruel, wild laughter, laughter that seemed to erupt simultaneously from all sides of the gym, and it was the laughter more than anything else that made him realize what was happening.

He pushed the toggle switch, started toward the entrance.

Another ball was thrown at him.

A basketball.

It hit hard against his chair, knocking the motor behind the back wheels, spinning him to the left. He pressed hard on the toggle switch.

Nothing.

The motor was dead.

Another basketball was thrown at him, hitting him full in the chest, and he rolled backward to the delighted laughter of the crowd. The ball was heavy and had been thrown with force, and it damn near knocked the breath out of him. Sharp pain flared within his chest. He grabbed the ball, curled around it, held it.

"Throw it!" several members of the crowd yelled in unison. "Throw it!"

The cry was taken up by others in the bleachers, spreading until everyone was yelling the same refrain, and he realized that it was directed at him. He straightened his body with considerable effort, thinking for a brief moment that the malevolence he had ascribed to the situation had been all in his head, a result of his and Jim's paranoia over the past weeks. This was merely a halftime crowd game. Someone had thrown a ball to him, he was to throw it himself, pass it on. He couldn't throw, of course, but—

Another basketball hit the back of his head, and he jerked forward with the impact, nearly knocked out of his chair. Tears stung his eyes, but he held his breath and managed to keep from crying out. There was clapping and whooping and loud laughter. The gym echoed with the sound of stomping feet.

The ball he'd been holding rolled down his feet, onto the floor.

Another ball hit the wheel of his chair, turning him again. He was facing the bleachers, and through teary eyes he saw several people standing, orange basketballs in their upraised hands. His heart was pounding so hard that it felt as though it would burst through his chest, and he was filled with an absurd, babyish urge to cry.

He screamed as a ball hit his shoulder, feeling brittle bones break beneath the hard contact. Two other balls, thrown with brutal precision, hit both sides of his head.

He fell from the wheelchair.

There was nothing he could do, no way he could break the fall, and he was still trying to move his arms when they were crushed beneath the weight of his body hitting the floor. His head smacked the boards with a sharp crack, and though it did not hurt as much as the basketballs had, the impact drew blood, and warm, sticky wetness coated his cheeks and forehead.

Now he *was* crying: hurt, humiliated, and frightened, sobbing uncontrollably like a small child. He could not move at all, but he rolled his blurred, wet eyes upward and saw rows of people standing on the bleachers, all of them holding basketballs. Behind him, he heard what sounded like a stampede as the spectators from the other side of the gym ran toward him.

"No!" he screamed at the top of his lungs.

But no one heard him, and he went out in a hail of orange.

2

There was a bust of some kind on the corner of Seventeenth and Grand, three police cars, lights flashing, surrounding what looked like a Volkswagen van at an abandoned gas station. It was her bad luck to be the last one at the intersection when the light changed, and Faith braked to a stop halfway through the crosswalk, keeping her eyes on the light but monitoring the bust with her peripheral vision, preparing to duck should shooting break out.

There was no gunfire during her tenure at the stoplight, and a moment later she was gratefully speeding on her way. She would have thought that the mundane horrors of urban living would have paled, fading into insignificance next to the truly epic evil engulfing UC Brea, but her reaction was exactly the opposite. Her experiences at Brea seemed to have increased her awareness of all danger, of any sort, and she found that she was much more paranoid now than she had been before about car accidents, drive-by shootings, everything.

She had never realized that death was so close.

Always.

There was another police car stopped near the intersection of Main, an officer standing in the street, his drawn gun pointed at the darkened driver's window of a metal-flake crimson Chevy, and though the light was already yellow and turning red before she reached the crosswalk, she floored the gas, speeding through, hearing the angry honking of horns to her right.

She'd rather get a ticket than get shot.

Her mom's car was in the driveway, and she parked in the street in front of the house.

The front door was unlocked, the security gate open, and she walked inside, announcing her presence. "Mom? I'm home!"

"She's not here. I am."

Keith was lying on the couch, watching TV. She walked into the living room, dropped her books on the coffee table. The living room smelled of pot and stale sex.

"You just missed her."

Faith threw her keys on the table, trying to keep it casual. "So you're back?"

"For now."

She sat down in the ragged recliner opposite him. "Does Mom know?"

He shrugged. "Who can tell?"

"But she saw you here?"

"Yeah, but who knows how much of it registered? Her and this week's 'uncle' were pretty far gone by the time I arrived." He sniffed the air. "Does it smell like pussy in here to you? Below the weed, I mean."

She grimaced. "Jesus. You're sickening."

"Oh, yeah?" He sat up. "How do you think I feel? Huh? You think I like coming home and smelling that? My own mom? In the middle of the living room in the middle of the day?"

"It's a wonder you're not gay."

She'd meant it as a joke, but Keith wasn't smiling. "You're not kidding."

She looked at him. "I'm glad you're back," she said. "I missed you."

He leaned back again, embarrassed, pretending to focus on the television. "Yeah. Well."

They sat there for another fifteen minutes, not talking, watching TV. Nick at Night reruns. She wanted to speak to him, but she didn't know what to say, and he seemed perfectly content to just lie there in silence, watching the tube. It was kind of nice, she thought, just sitting around the living room like this, being together.

Like a family.

When the program ended, Keith got up and went into the kitchen to get something to eat. Faith waited a beat, then followed him. On the counter next to the door she saw the pile of books he'd brought home with him: Kafka's *The Trial*, Camus' *The Plague*, Dostoyevsky's *Crime and Punishment*. At least his pretentiousness was now running along the same track his education should have been.

As if picking up her thoughts, he turned away from the open refrigerator, an R.C. can in his hand. He looked at her, almost shyly, she thought. "I've, uh, decided to go back to school," he said.

She smiled at him. "That's great." But the happiness she should have felt was muzzled. She was not as surprised as she should have been, and somehow she knew what was coming next.

"I'm going to go to Brea. Merrick said that Brea's a really happening place."

She looked at him. Her mouth felt dry.

"His brother goes there," Keith continued. "And I know you were really excited to get in there, and I thought, well, maybe I'll go there too."

She didn't know what to say. She did not want her brother anywhere near the school, but she also did not want in any way to discourage him now that he'd made his tentative decision to continue his education.

"Merrick says it's a party school."

She took a deep breath. "Is that what you want? Is that really what you're looking for?"

He would not look at her. "No. Not exactly." He shuffled his feet, staring down at the floor. "I mean, that's not the main reason I'm going."

"Well, actually," Faith said, "it's not a party school. In fact, it's not even a very good school. I'm probably going to be transferring myself after this semester."

"Really?" He was surprised. "Where?"

"Irvine," she said off the top of her head.

"Irvine costs a fortune."

"We could both go there. We could carpool."

"We couldn't even afford the tuition."

She licked her lips. "I don't want you to go to Brea."

Now he was looking at her. Suspiciously. "Why?"

"Because."

"Because why?"

"Because I don't want you to!"

He seemed taken aback by her vehemence. "Have a cow. Jesus."

"I mean it."

"I thought you wanted me to go to school. You're the one who's always on my ass about my not going to college."

She massaged her forehead, exasperated. "I do want you to go. I just don't want you to go to Brea. It's not . . . it's not safe."

"What's that supposed to mean?"

She didn't know what to say. She didn't know how much she could tell him without making it sound like the plot of some Z-grade movie and alienating him entirely. "There's a lot of crime there," she said. "A lot of fighting. Murders. Suicides—"

"Suicides aren't crimes."

"—Rapes."

He grinned. "Like Merrick said: party school."

"I'm not joking!"

"Hey, I'm sorry, I just—"

"I was almost raped in the fucking bathroom of the library! You think that's funny?"

He stepped back, color draining from his face. "No. I . . . didn't know. I'm sorry. I didn't . . . Why didn't you tell me? Did you tell Mom?"

"No. I didn't tell Mom."

"Did you tell, like, the police?"

"Nothing happened."

"You didn't even tell the police?"

"Yes, I did," she lied. "I told the campus police and they caught the guy." She took a deep breath. "The point is, there's a lot of this stuff happening at that school. It's a dangerous place."

"In Orange County?"

"Have you looked around here lately? Do you even notice what kind of neighborhood we're living in?"

"Yeah, but, I mean, this is a university. It's not the same as—"

"It is the same. No. It's worse."

He took a sip of his R.C. "Irvine, huh?"

"There's that new service deal where you can get a student loan and pay it back through community service."

"Yeah. Right. I'm going to waste three years of my life helping gang members plant trees so I can go to school."

"Or you can work as a sales clerk for the rest of your life." She glared at him.

They were silent for a moment.

"You think . . ." Keith cleared his throat. "You think Dad would've wanted me to go to college?"

She nodded, and when she answered him, her voice was quiet, soft, kind. "I know he would've."

"Mom doesn't give a shit."

"No," Faith admitted, "she doesn't." She looked at him. "But I do."

He nodded. "I know."

It was said in his usual bored way, the jaded, unfazed manner of speaking he'd affected for the past three years, but the words were appreciative rather than merely acknowledging, and there was what passed for a look of gratitude on his face. This was the closest he would ever come to admitting that he cared about her, that her opinion was important to him, and it was enough for her. She didn't need anything else.

"*Mr. Ed*'s on," he said.

She nodded, saying nothing, and followed him back out to the living room, where they sat watching television until it was time to go to bed.

3

Chapman Clements stood up from the bench, tilted his watch toward the lamp post, and checked the time. Again.

Eight forty-five.

The class was supposed to have met him here at eighty-thirty, and so far not a single student had shown. He looked to his left, through the open gate of the Arboretum toward the parking lot, but the gravel was empty save for his Toyota truck.

Could he have forgotten to tell them? He'd had a lot on his mind since Buckley had stopped by his office this morning, and he'd been thinking more about what Buckley had referred to as "the situation" then his classes for the rest of the day. It was conceivable that he had been distracted and had simply neglected to tell the class to meet here.

No. He specifically remembered writing the extra assignment on the board as well as passing around a monograph on nocturnal animals native to Southern California.

Apathy.

That was one of the symptoms, Buckley had said, one of the side effects.

Still, Chapman thought that at least a few of them would have shown up.

He'd give them ten more minutes.

He glanced around the empty Arboretum, stared up into the night sky, able to see only a handful of the brighter stars through the light pollution and the haze of smog. What a way to spend his birthday. Appropriate, really. He was thirty-five today, and what had he done with his life, what had he accomplished?

Nothing.

Most of the great scientists had already made their most important discoveries by the time they were his age.

Hell, by the time the Beatles had been his age, they'd been broken up for five years.

The sad thing was that he didn't really have anyone with whom he could share even these self-pitying thoughts. He had no wife, no girlfriend, not even any prospects on the horizon. The colleagues he called friends were little more than acquaintances, and his family and real friends were back home in Ohio.

Thirty-five.

Halfway to seventy.

He might not even live to see seventy. Both of his grandfathers had died in their early sixties. It was quite possible that his life was already more than half over.

God, birthdays were depressing.

Maybe that's why no one had shown. Maybe that's

what had happened to everyone. Maybe they'd found out that it was his birthday and were all waiting, crouched behind bushes, to spring out and surprise him.

He glanced around the dark and empty Arboretum. Who was he kidding? He did not inspire that type of camaraderie. He wished he did, but despite his best attempts to be relaxed and easygoing, he knew he was a rather formal teacher, that he forged no personal relationships with his students, that there was no emotional connection there.

Maybe they were crouched behind bushes, waiting to kill him.

He thought of what Buckley had told him, and in his mind he saw Shaun Diamond and Gene Young and Ed Goleta wearing camouflage fatigues, their faces painted with green greasepaint, clutching long hunting knives as they watched his every move, waiting for the right moment to pounce. He shivered, goose bumps riding a wave down his arms. The imagined scene was not that far-fetched. He was not so paranoid that he believed that members of his class actively wanted to kill him, but still, it was not that hard to imagine them moving stealthily through the bushes, crouching behind the benches, stalking him.

He heard a low rustle in the dried leaves under the tree behind him, and jumped.

That was it. He was through waiting out here. The assignment was over, the entire class had failed. He was going to get his thirty-five-year-old butt safely home, give his parents a quick call, and drink himself to sleep.

The rustle came again, and he picked up his briefcase and hurried down the path toward the exit, toward the parking lot.

On the ground in front of him, a rope sprang taut. He saw it only at the last second, fast enough to recognize what it was but not fast enough to process the information and translate it into avoidance. His ankles hit the rope, and he went sprawling, the briefcase flying out of his hands.

They *had* been waiting for him!

He was scrambling the second he hit the gravel, lurching to his feet, frantically looking for the students who had stretched the rope across the path.

Only it wasn't a rope, he saw now. In the dim light of the lamp post he could see that it was a vine of some kind. A thick green vine.

A vine that was moving.

They were playing a trick on him. They'd tied clear fishing line to the end of the vine and were hiding off to the side someplace, pulling on it, trying to spook him. It was all in good fun.

But tripping him like that hadn't been all in good fun. And there was no way that fishing line tied to a vine could have been pulled that taut across the path. That vine had been . . . muscular.

He looked at it now. It was still moving across the path, like an infinitely long snake, and it was clear that it was on its own. No one was pulling it. No one was controlling it. The back end was lost in the shadows to his left. He could hear the rustle of dead leaves close by and, farther out, what sounded like a sluicing noise, as though it was emerging from the pond. The front end was clearly visible, and it slid along the gravel toward the nearest lamp post. He watched in horror as it slithered over a bench. There was something vaguely obscene, vaguely suggestive at the way it seemed to slow down, to caress the seat of the bench, and he felt his heartbeat accelerate as it stopped for a second, the rounded tip wiggling luridly at him at an angle that made it resemble an absurdly oversized penis.

He started to run. Fuck the briefcase. Someone would turn it in. Or he could come back for it tomorrow. It didn't matter. What did matter was getting the hell away from this garden of evil. Buckley had been right about Brea. But the strange phenomena he'd described was nothing compared to what was going on here at the Arboretum.

In his peripheral vision he saw dead leaves dancing on the ground, bushes shaking, tree branches waving wildly. He glanced to the left as he sprinted the last few yards toward the gate and saw a series of vines speeding next to him along the side of the path.

One of them whipped in front of him and he went flying.

The vines were over him in a second, wrapping around his arms and legs, pressing under his body. He tried to fight them off, tried to roll away, but the grip of the plants grew tighter. His hands held onto the tendril sliding across his neck, fingers digging into the rough plant flesh, trying to keep it from choking him, but the vine was stronger than he was and moved through his hands and under his chin and around the back of his head. Another vine curled around his genitals, and he tried to scream as it squeezed, but his windpipe was cut off and he could get no air.

The plants dragged him off the path and into the bushes.

Leaves fell on top of him, covering him, pressing themselves into his mouth, and he tried to spit them out, tried to bite them, but they were alive and wiggling and pressed themselves down his already clamped-off throat.

The last thing he saw before he blacked out was what appeared to be two bushes dancing happily toward him.

4

Ramon Villanueva had worked as a janitor at a lot of places since coming to the United States: Northrop, McDonnell Douglas, Delco-Remy, the Orange Unified School District.

But he'd never worked anywhere like this.

He stopped, paused, looked around. He thought he'd seen something out of the corner of his eye. Something small and hairy. Running across the corridor from one doorway to another.

As always, there was nothing there.

He continued pushing the broom down the long sixth-floor corridor. That was the problem. There was never anything there, never anything real that he could point to and say, "*That's* why I don't like working here." No, there was only this vague feeling that things were not as they should be, and no matter how many cold spots he encountered in the hallways, no matter how many small creatures he saw scuttling about in his peripheral vision, no matter how many weird encounters he had with other night-shift employees, there was nothing he could tell Angelina that she would buy as a legitimate reason for quitting his job.

Especially with the economy the way it was right now.

"*Ramon.*"

He stopped at the sound of his name, looking around, knowing he would see no one there even before his eyes confirmed the fact. His heart was thumping loudly in his chest, and he wanted to believe that he had imagined the whispered voice, but he knew he hadn't.

It came again: "*Ramon.*"

Angelina or no Angelina, economy or no economy, he was through with this damn job. He was not going to work in a haunted building. No job was worth his life. He'd just tell Angelina there were budget cuts, and he'd start pounding the pavement.

"*Ramon.*"

He threw down the broom and walked quickly toward the elevator. He wanted to run, but there was still a chance that this was part of some practical joke, and if that was true, he didn't want to give the jokesters the satisfaction of seeing him flee.

"Fuck you!" he said loudly.

A skeleton glided out of the darkened doorway in front of him.

He screamed, jumped, nearly fell flat on his ass. The skeleton, propped up on a wheeled stand, bumped gently into the wall.

"*Ramon.*"

He hit the skeleton, swinging sidearm, and the entire display went down—bones and stand and metal fasteners all skidding wildly across the smooth corridor floor.

Out of the corner of his eye he saw movement in the dark doorway, movement too low to be anything human, and he started to run. Behind him, above the sound of his ragged breathing, above the pounding of the blood in his temples, he heard sounds of snapping, cracking, scuttling, heard sounds of wetness and squelching and slapping.

Fuck the elevator. He wasn't going to stand there and wait for the damn thing to show up. He'd haul ass down the stairs—

The lights in the building went out.

"*Mierda!*" He continued running, and almost instantly smacked into a wall. He reeled back, blood pouring from his nose, from his forehead, his cheeks wet with it, his eyes stinging with it, though he could still see nothing in the blackness. Hadn't he been running straight?

The lights flickered back on.

Or some of them did.

He wished to God they'd stayed off.

He was looking back down the corridor the way he'd come. Through the curtain of blood streaming down his face he saw, coming down the corridor toward him, a host of horrors he could not have imagined even in his worst nightmares.

Parts of the broken skeleton were moving, single hand and arm pulling still-connected rib cage, phalanges pulling metacarpals pulling carpus pulling radius pulling ulna, two bony feet working in tandem to transport the grinning skull balanced on top of them. To the sides and behind the animated pieces of skeleton were other, even more disturbing figures: partially dissected frogs not hopping but sliding across the floor on amputated limbs, many of the frogs fused together with gutted worms and surgically altered salamanders; a horde of grotesquely oversize bugs with recognizable composite parts, all connected by what looked like a black tissue umbilical cord; small monkeys with the grafted-on faces of rats; a baby shark with green plant stalk feet.

He tried to breathe, could not. His breath seemed to be stuck in his body, the muscles in his mouth and throat frozen. What were these things? Genetic experiments gone awry, or night creatures created by the building?

Behind him, halfway down the corridor, he heard a loud click.

He whirled around.

The stairwell door had locked itself.

Click. Click. Click. Click.

Doors all along the corridor, locking in sequence.

It was the building. The building had created these monsters from raw materials students and teachers had left in the labs.

As if to confirm this, a new monster emerged from the open lab door, a manlike creature half as tall as himself with a computer screen head atop a body formed from rubber hose and metal clamp and animal organ. Squared eyes, nose and mouth made from clumped sets of numbers on the screen moved jerkily as the creature waddled forward, trailing a long extension-cord tail.

The twin lines of green numbers that formed the mouth separated, met, separated, met.

Talked.

"*Ramon.*"

The remaining lights in the corridor came on, and he could see a scalpel blade glinting in the figure's graceful feminine hands.

The cut on his head was agony, his balance was shaky, his vision was obscured by blood, and he knew that the doors were all locked, but he ran anyway, screaming for help in Spanish and English, trying all the doors as he passed them, until he had reached the walled end of the corridor.

He turned around.

The monster was still waddling toward him, flanked by its smaller brethren.

Madre Dios! He reached into his pocket, found his key ring, clutched it in his fist, keys protruding from between his knuckles. It wasn't much, but it was the closest thing to a weapon he had, and maybe if he was lucky . . .

He took a deep breath and screaming wordlessly, ran full-bore toward the creatures.

It wasn't as bad as he'd feared.

The big monster was slow, and although it slashed open a section of his arm, it could not turn quickly or maneuver, and he punched the keyed fist into its slimy gelatin organ body and was past it, stomping on the frogs and the worms and the salamander things. The bone hand jabbed his ankle, but he was too fast for it also, and then he was past it, reaching down as he ran, trying to yank out the extension cord connected to the big monster's computer screen head.

He ran past the still-open door of the lab from which the creatures had come—

—and into the fist of Johnny McGuane.

The head custodian stood unmoving in the doorway as Ramon staggered backward.

For those first few seconds, despite the fact that the man had punched him in the face, Ramon thought that McGuane was here to save him.

He held his gushing nose. "Thank God," he said. "Those things're—"

The head custodian pulled a scalpel from his overall pocket. "Don't fuck with my experiments," he said.

"What—?" Ramon began, confused.

That was as far as he got before the scalpel was shoved into his face.

TWENTY-EIGHT

1

It seemed unreal, Jim thought, like a staged event or practice for the real thing. His mom wasn't here, and that too felt weird. He'd told her what had happened and she'd been sympathetic, had even offered to fly out and be with him, but she hadn't known Howie and his death hadn't really meant anything to her.

Maybe that's what it meant to be an adult. Having experiences your parents didn't share.

The day was smoggy, the air white and hazy. He'd hoped it would be clear, hoped that blue skies would preside over Howie's burial, but the temperature was unseasonably hot and an inversion layer had trapped a week's worth of smog in the L.A. basin.

At least he had Faith.

He did not know what he would have done without her these past few days. She'd been his confessor, his friend, his support, and he had not only figuratively but literally cried on her shoulder. She had not only been strong for him but unwaveringly understanding.

He looked around the overflowing chapel. He could not help wondering if some of the people who were here today had been at the game when Howie had been killed.

Killed.

It was such a strange word. Familiar, yet distant. It was a word heard on the news or read about in newspapers or magazines or books. It was not a word that applied to the death of a friend.

He'd spent the past few days helping Howie's parents go through his effects. In a dresser drawer, one of the lower drawers Howie had been able to reach on his own, without assistance, they'd found a diary. He'd never known that Howie had kept a diary. In another drawer they'd found a well-worn Bible and an equally worn copy of the *Bhagavad Gita.* He'd never known that Howie had even thought about religion.

He was learning things about his friend, and many of them were surprises, but none of them were bad surprises. The secrets Howie had kept had not hidden a monster, did not now reveal an entirely different person. Rather, they revealed new aspects of the same person, and that made him miss Howie all the more.

It was he who'd gone through Howie's personal phonebook and called all of his friends to tell them what had happened. It had been a strange, surrealistic, and extremely unpleasant experience, and he'd felt dirty afterward, as though he'd been eavesdropping on private lives, spying on people, trespassing on their intimacy. The first few calls had been the worst. He had not prepared any opening line, had not known what to say or how to say it, and had simply blurted out the fact that Howie was dead.

Killed.

No, he had not used the word *killed,* had not been able to bring himself to speak that truth, but stating aloud that Howie was dead was bad enough. Speaking the words brought home to him, more clearly than anything else, the fact that his friend was gone, and that he would never again hear the sound of Howie's voice or the motorized hum of his wheelchair, and in the sudden shocked silence that greeted his crudely announced news he had had to will himself not to cry.

Now he stood in the nave of the chapel, in front of the raised casket that held Howie's body, and that same urge to cry overcame him once again. He looked up at the ceiling, held his breath, tried to think of golf, tried to think of opera, tried to think of boring things with which he had no emotional connection in order to divert the feelings within him, but he was not successful, and the tears overflowed, streaming down his cheeks. He wiped them away with his right hand while Faith held tightly to his left.

He breathed deeply—in, out, in, out—concentrating on the rhythm, and slowly, slowly, the hurt receded, the pain at least temporarily held at bay. He looked gratefully over at Faith, squeezing her hand, and she smiled up at him.

She had never gotten to know Howie, he thought, and suddenly the tears threatened to return.

He thought of Brea, thought of how Howie had died, and let anger take the place of sadness, thankful for its stabilizing presence.

Howie's parents had wanted an open casket, explaining that it was the last chance any of them would have to see their son, and though Jim had not liked the idea, not wanting the image of Howie's corpse to be the last memory he had of his friend, it was not his decision, not his place to comment, and he had not said anything to anyone about it.

The morticians had done a pretty good restoration job, he had to admit. From what he understood, Howie had been beaten severely, had suffered several broken bones and quite a bit of facial damage, but though the restoration efforts were obvious—lipstick on the lips, makeup on the face—they were effective, and the Stepford Howie in the coffin probably looked more like the real Howie than the battered, bloody form that had been found in the gym.

Jim stood above the casket, looking down. Here, in the coffin, surrounded by ruffled white silk, Howie looked small, shrunken, more like a child than a man, and the effects of the M.D. were glaringly obvious. An attempt had been made to straighten his extraordinarily thin arms, to make them lie at his sides, but they bowed out at the elbows and curved in at the hands, and his body looked misshapen, almost freakish, framed by the precise angles of the coffin, ensconced amidst the uniform accoutrements of standardized death rituals.

There were other people behind them, waiting in a line to view the body, and though Jim had been against the idea of an open casket, he felt loath to move forward, to give up his spot. It seemed wrong, somehow, to leave Howie, to get out of the way so that other, less intimate friends and acquaintances could be near him. He told himself that Howie was gone, in heaven or hell or whatever limbo to which souls were confined between reincarnations, but though he tried to make himself believe that what was in the coffin was merely an empty vessel, emotionally he felt as though he were abandoning his friend as he allowed Faith to pull him forward and away.

TWENTY-NINE

1

They were crammed into Ian's office: Buckley, himself, Jim, Faith, and Gifford Stevens. Outside, in the hall, as they'd been waiting for Stevens to arrive, Kiefer had walked back and forth, past Ian's room, pretending to carry papers from his own office to the department office. The department head had obviously been trying to spy on them, to find out what was going on, and the thing that made Ian uncomfortable was the fact that he didn't know if Kiefer was doing so out of curiosity or because something else was making him do it.

Paranoia.

It was getting pretty damn hard to avoid.

The meeting was scheduled for tonight in the University Theatre. Buckley had reserved the theater, writing on the sign-in sheet provided by an officious little bureaucrat that he was intending to use the auditorium to show a film to one of his classes. They had canvassed their friends and acquaintances, had pressured them to recruit others, and they were hoping to have a decent turnout, a broad cross-section of the university community from which some plans and ideas might spring.

Ian was properly supportive, playing to the hilt his role of head cheerleader for the project, but privately he had begun to wonder if it would come off at all. The teachers he'd spoken to, the ones he'd determined that he could trust, had promised to attend, but the importance of it had seemed to escape them. He'd tried to impress upon them the urgent need to do something, and while they had agreed with him, there had been something reserved about their responses, almost as though they hadn't really understood the gravity of the situation.

Or were afraid.

That was more like it. They had behaved as though they were afraid.

He took charge of the meeting in his office, however, reiterated what he needed to reiterate, and pretended as though everything was coming together, as planned.

"Did you ever get to anyone in Administration?" Buckley asked.

"Take a wild guess."

"I know Dean Jensen," Jim offered. "I could call him up."

Buckley waved his arm dismissively. "He's dicksweat, dude. He's nothing."

"I called President Langford," Ian said. "Twice. But she was busy. I stopped by on my way up this morning, and her secretary said she was in a meeting."

"Did you buy it?"

"No."

"Bad sign."

They were all silent for a moment.

Buckley turned toward Faith. "You're a dedicated college student and you work in the library. Did you ever sit down, put your nose to the grindstone, and try to do some serious research on all this?"

"I don't work at the library anymore," Faith said quietly.

"I think we're missing a bet here. I've never known a problem that couldn't be solved by research. Maybe we should put a grad student on it. Maybe there's a hidden storeroom of arcane lore buried deep underneath the building. Maybe there's a bound thesis that addresses our campus's penchant for violence and supernatural activity."

"This isn't something to joke about," Ian said.

"There's nothing to read." It was the first time Stevens had spoken, and all eyes turned toward him. "If there's one thing it knows how to do, it's cover its tracks. It's not about to publicize its weaknesses."

"I just thought that someone might be able to piece something together. You know, like those students who dig around in various sources and figure out how to make an atomic bomb?"

"No," Stevens said bluntly. "You think it's going to

let you discover its Achilles' heel? You think it's going to reward you for your diligence and hard work and resourcefulness? Even if such information was available, the computer storing it would blow up, the book containing it would be stolen." He leaned forward. "You're thinking like a fucking two-year-old. This isn't Nancy Drew. Grow up and get a brain."

"Tonight." Ian said, changing the subject. "Seven o'clock." He went over again what they hoped to accomplish at the meeting, tried to steer the discussion away from anything that might lead to an argument. The last thing they needed was to fight among themselves.

Afterward, when the rest of them were gone, Stevens turned to face him. "I want you to promise me something," he said.

"What?"

"If something happens to me, if it gets me, you'll go back to my place and get my explosives and torch this fucker." He stared levelly at Ian, but there was something frantic in his voice, an unsettling intensity in the way he leaned against the side of the desk, face forward.

"Why?" He tried not to let the worry show in his voice. "What makes you think something's going to happen to you?"

"I heard it. I heard its voice." Stevens' own voice had dropped to a whisper. "It knows me. It *remembers* me."

"Remembers?"

He shook his head. "I don't understand it either."

"I thought all these schools had different personalities and were different entities."

"I thought so too."

"Then what do you mean it—"

"I don't know. All I know is that I was in the basement of the Social Sciences building, making sure the blueprints I had were accurate, and I heard someone call my name and it sounded like my wife."

"Jesus."

"I was alone down there. The maintenance man who'd let me in was still in the supply room up above, and I followed the voice around to the other side of the air-conditioning unit that takes up most of that basement, and I saw what looked like a small leak in one of the pipes, a white jet of Freon or CO_2 shooting into the air.

"The voice was coming out of that leak.

"It was Pat's voice. She said, 'Get out of here, Gif. And don't come back.' Only I knew it wasn't really Pat, because she never called me 'Gif.' I reached up and put my hand over the leak, and the coldness against my palm felt like breath. I waited for a second, then pulled back, and all of a sudden the leak was bigger, a huge spray of cold shooting out, and this deep masculine voice said, 'I'll kill you, Gifford. This time I'll kill you.' "

" 'This time'?"

He nodded. "I wanted to pick up a hammer and pound the hell out of that pipe, but I knew that it was just using that as its mouthpiece. I turned around and left. It was still talking to me, still threatening me, its voice getting louder, but I ignored it and walked back up and thanked the maintenance man who'd let me in and left." He paused. "But it knows about me. It knows my name. It knows who I am. It knew where I was. I don't know what it uses for eyes, but it has them. Everywhere. That's why I'm not sure it's a good idea for us to meet on campus tonight. We're—"

"In the belly of the beast?"

"Exactly. And I think we should watch what we say while we're here on campus, watch what we do."

"But if it knows our every move, hears our every word, then how are we going to fight it?"

Stevens shook his head. "I don't know," he said. "I don't fucking know."

2

It seemed strange pretending that this was a normal day, that there was nothing wrong. Jim wanted to forget about his classes and about the paper and fight the monsters full-time, forsaking his normal life until they were gone. But despite all that was happening, despite all that was going on, the rhythms and routines of school were continuing on the way they always had. It was ironic, but he could stop going to class and devote himself entirely to exorcising the demons of the school, and once he'd saved the world and everything had gone back to normal, he'd still be docked for the tests and assignments he'd missed.

Besides, he was a senior this year. He needed to pass his courses in order to graduate. And he owed it to the other people on the *Sentinel* staff, and to the completeness of his resumé, to continue fulfilling his duties as editor.

But it still seemed strange.

There were a lot of people missing in his classes. And the attitudes of some of those who had remained were decidedly unacademic. But while the content and substance of reality had changed, the structure had not. Papers were collected, assignments graded, lectures given. It was surreal, this melding of everyday routine and the encroaching supernatural, and he felt more than a little disoriented as he pretended that there was nothing out of the ordinary, that he was a typical student at a typical university on a typical day doing typical things.

Faith went home after American Lit to continue her search for an off-campus job, and he made sure she escaped the university safe and sound, watching her car until it disappeared into the white haze of smog somewhere around the second stoplight, before heading back to the newspaper office.

The newsroom was abandoned, and so was Production, and that disturbed him a little. It *was* close to lunchtime, and today's page dummies were laid out, today's articles copyedited and ready for typesetting, so the other editors had been working this morning, but there was still something disconcerting about not seeing anyone around. Last semester the newsroom had been crowded from seven in the morning until nearly nine at eight. And Production had never been unmanned.

He wandered from Production into the darkroom and turned on the red safety light. There was no one in the darkroom either.

But there were photographs hanging on the drying line and taped to the black walls that he had never seen before.

Photographs that he could have gone forever without seeing.

Photographs of mutilation and sexual torture.

He walked slowly into the darkroom, staring at the pictures. The gruesomeness of the shots was disturbing, but that was not what sent chills racing down the back of his neck. It was the fact that these photos looked staged, as though Richard had not merely captured on film events that had occurred but had purposely and deliberately set up the scenes to be photographed.

Richard.

Why had he assumed it was Richard?

Because it *was* Richard. None of the other photographers on the staff had his eye, his ability to compose a shot so that the viewer's attention focused on what he wanted the viewer to see.

And, Jim saw now, several of the photos were of Richard's ex-girlfriend Lucinda.

He stopped to look. The Lucinda photos appeared to have been taken in sequence, and they were posted on the wall to the left of the developer: Lucinda, tied and trussed in the middle of a men's rest room, a booted foot holding down her head, a razor held beneath her chin, screaming, her ordinarily attractive features contorted into ugliness by agony; Lucinda rolled on her side, the toe of the boot shoved into her mouth, forcing her lips against her teeth, drawing blood, the razor slicing flesh, more blood, black against the pale skin of her neck; Lucinda alone, no boot or razor, face unrecognizable, toothless mouth open and screaming, not in a perfect circle but in a wavy-lipped, off-center cry, neck wound bleeding all over the ropes, broken teeth visible in the dark pool on the tile; Lucinda dead.

The final photos in the series were blowups of that last face, that dead face, closely cropped specifics of Lucinda's features impersonally broken down into their compositional elements: long, thin slice of wound; flecks of blood on staring eye; crushed lip; bruised cheek; broken nose.

And the Lucinda photos were the most benign ones displayed in the darkroom.

The others were much, much worse.

"Nice stuff."

Jim turned quickly around to see Richard walking into the darkroom. The photographer looked at the drying pictures, smiling proudly at his work. From one hand dangled his Pentax.

In the other was a hammer.

"You see that babe there?" He said. He pointed to a

photograph of a naked blond girl with the claw end of a hammer embedded in the blood-smeared mound of her vagina. "She got off on it. She liked it. You believe that?"

"No, I don't," Jim said quietly.

"Well, she did."

"Why did you do this?"

"Take pictures? It's my job."

"Why did you . . ."

"Kill the bitches?" Richard laughed. "How else could I get pictures like these? You don't see this stuff everyday. Besides, this way I could control the lighting, the background. . . . Artistic photography is much more satisfying than photojournalism."

Jim said nothing but kept his eyes focused on the hammer in Richard's hand, ready to leap back if he had to, ready to grab the photographer's arm if he could.

Richard looked at him, smiled, raised the hammer—

—and placed it on the counter next to the trays of developing fluid.

"Wait'll you see the shots I got this time," he said. "These are the best yet." He opened his camera and took out a roll of film.

Jim blinked. Richard didn't realize that what he was doing was wrong! He was so far gone that he did not recognize that torturing and killing women in order to photograph their suffering was not normal behavior, was not standard operating procedure for college photo students. He had not noticed Jim's reaction, had not picked up on his fear. He honestly thought that his editor had come into the darkroom to admire his work.

"It's gonna take awhile to develop these," Richard said. "But you can stay if you want. It's worth it."

Jim shook his head, inching toward the door, his attention still on the hammer in case this was all a ruse, an attempt to lull him into complacency before striking.

Richard shrugged, smiled. "That's cool. I'll bring 'em by when I'm done. I guarantee you've never seen anything like 'em."

Jim exited the darkroom.

The door closed behind him.

3

"You take the left side," Phil said. "I'll take the right."

Glenna nodded. "Okay." She cut through the nearest aisle to the study area next to the wall. Around a table several Vietnamese students talked in low voices in their native tongue, engineering books open in front of them. "Library's closing in ten minutes," Glenna announced.

The students nodded, started putting away their books.

She continued on to the line of study carrels. Here, individual students studied in cloistered seclusion. From this angle, all she could see were the tops of heads, mostly blond, mostly male. She kept walking, moving down the line. "Library's closing in ten minutes."

Behind her, she heard books slamming shut.

From the other side of the floor, she heard Phil repeating the message to patrons along the opposite wall, and the sound of his voice made her feel safer. She was glad he was up here with her. She did not feel comfortable being alone in the library anymore. Ever since the shooting, the place had seemed different to her. Something about it had changed. She used to enjoy closing— it got her away from Circ—but now it made her nervous. She didn't like the silence of the upper floors, the long, high aisles of bookshelves.

Shove the handle up her ass!

No, it wasn't just the shooting that had spooked her. The shooting might not even have been the major contributor to her fear.

It was the badminton class, it was Calhoun, it was . . . everything.

Shove it up her cunt.

What if she met someone from her P.E. class here in the library? What if she was walking down one of the aisles and saw the instructor waiting at the far end, a racket in her hands? What if the entire class *and* Calhoun chased her through the sixth floor, turning the rows into a maze from which she could not escape? Those were the questions that occurred to her when she was up here, those were the thoughts that came to her.

She missed Faith. It had been nice working with someone she considered a friend, and although she got along with her other co-workers, the rapport she'd had with Faith was not there, and that just added another layer of tension to an already difficult situation.

Maybe she should quit, too, find a job somewhere else. It couldn't be healthy for her to be alone up here all the time, indulging her paranoid fantasies.

Besides, something *had* changed here. She couldn't put her finger on it, she didn't know what it was, but she knew that it had occurred, and that not only frightened her, it worried her.

She reached the end of the study carrels. "Library's closing in ten minutes," she repeated. There were no students here, but saying the words reassured her, hearing her own voice made her feel a little more confident, and she started down the aisle toward the study rooms.

She could no longer hear Phil from here—perhaps he'd already headed back to the elevator. She could hear nothing but the sound of her own shoes on the tile, and the sudden absence of sound made her quicken her pace. To her left, out of the corner of her eye, she saw graffiti on the concrete wall: thick black Magic Marker letters standing out boldly against the pale yellow wall paint. She turned her head to read what it said, and saw four words, stacked one on top of the other: "We're Having Fun Now."

We're Having Fun Now.

A chill passed through her. The words were innocent enough, or could have been interpreted so, but there was something about the ambiguity of the "We're" and the myriad interpretations that could be applied to the "fun" which she found unsettling. The fact that the sentence was scrawled back here, on the top floor of the library—in the farthest corner of the top floor of the library—made her even more uneasy.

She hurried down the aisle.

The first study room was empty. She knocked, announcing her presence, then pushed open the door, preparing to tell the gathered students that the library was closing, but the room was dark, and when she flipped on the lights, she saw that it was empty. She turned off the lights and closed the door behind her, moving on to the next room. She knocked, pushed open the door and almost screamed.

Huddled around the far side of the conference table, staring wide-eyed at her, was a collection of little people: dwarves, midgets. They were standing shoulder to shoulder, clustered together, and only their heads were visible above the simulated wood-grain finish of the table. What prevented her from screaming was the instant realization that the little people seemed as afraid of her as she was of them. She took a tentative step forward, saw expressions of fear on the petite faces, panic in the small eyes.

"The library's closing," she said.

A thin man with a wispy mustache looked up at her. "Are they gone yet?"

She frowned. "Who?" The startled fear of a few seconds before was already fading, her heart rate decelerating to normal.

"The tossers."

She looked back at the man dumbly.

The little people seemed to be relaxing as well, their own fear of her dissipating. The man with the mustache moved to the side, away from the table, to face her. His small hands kept clasping and unclasping in front of him. "They're grad students mostly," he said. "They like to throw us. 'Dwarf tossing,' they call it. They used to see one of us walking, going to class, and they'd pick us up and throw us in the bushes, or down stairs." He licked his lips. "But now they're tossing us from the top of Neilson Hall. They killed my friend Adam yesterday."

Glenna's fear had returned. "Killed him?"

The little people nodded in unison.

"I didn't see it in the paper. I didn't hear about it . . ."

"No one knows," the mustached man said. "No one cares."

"But the police—"

"Don't care."

Shove it up her cunt.

"Can we stay in here tonight?" an attractive young woman asked. Her manner was poised, her face calm, but there was a tremor in her voice. "It's too late to go home."

"Someone can escort you to—"

"The tossers are out there. They'll toss anyone who helps us."

This was an insane conversation, but she was not

shocked or even particularly surprised by it. She believed what the little people were telling her, and she found herself thinking about all the handicapped students on campus. Out of all of the UC campuses in Southern California, Brea's handicapped-access doors, ramps, and amenities were considered the best, the most state-of-the-art, and as a result the school had an unusually high percentage of handicapped students.

If dwarfs were being tossed, what was happening to physically disabled students?

She didn't want to think about it.

"We won't be any trouble," the man with the mustache said. "We won't leave this room. Just let us stay here tonight."

She shouldn't, she knew. She didn't have the right or authority to do so. But the looks of pleading on the assembled faces spoke to her, made her feel for these students, and she nodded slowly.

"Thank you," the man said, and the words were repeated by the others, who came around the side of the table to show their appreciation.

Glenna looked behind her, down the nearest aisle. Phil would be wondering where she was, what was taking so long. He might come looking for her. She faced the little people again. "I'm going to shut off the light and close the door," she said. "You stay in here and don't make any noise. We'll be coming by once more in about five minutes, to make sure everyone's out of the library. I'll try to make sure I get this side of the floor. But just in case, hide behind the table like you were."

"What's your name?" the mustached man asked.

She smiled. "Glenna."

"Thank you, Glenna. We won't forget this."

She shut off the light. "Stay quiet." She closed the door behind her as she left.

Phil didn't care who took which side of which floor, so after they finished clearing the other levels of the library and returned, Glenna had no problem getting him to let her double-check the study rooms.

She passed the room housing the little people without even opening the door.

Tossers.

She thought about that concept as she and Phil turned

off the lights on each floor. What in God's name was
going on at this school? She hadn't talked to Faith since
she'd quit, but she had the feeling that Faith was somehow afraid of the library. She'd attributed it to the shooting, but she thought now that perhaps Faith knew more
than she'd let on, and Glenna had a sudden urge to talk
to her.

Maybe she'd give her a quick call tonight.

The other library workers had gone home, and the
first floor was empty. Phil told her she could leave as
well. She offered to stay, to help him lock up, but he
said he could handle it himself, and she got her purse
and sweater from Circ and let herself out the far left
front door.

She was grabbed from behind as soon as she walked
outside.

For the first few disjointed seconds she did not understand what was going on. She thought that someone had
tripped or been pushed into her and was grabbing her
around the waist and shoulders in order to regain his
balance. Then a hand shot between her legs from behind, digging into her crotch, and she finally realized
what was happening. Her mind was still slow to react
because it was not really late, classes were still in session,
students were walking through the lighted quad. How
could anyone attack her here, with all these people
around?

She *was* being attacked, though, and she struggled,
trying to escape, shoving her elbows back hard, kicking
her feet up behind her, but nothing connected. The guy
holding her was much stronger than she was. Her frantic
attempts to first pry the one hand off her shoulder, then
to scratch the hell out of it had no effect.

The hand whipped around her mouth before she
started screaming.

She expected to be dragged into the shadows at the
side of the library, but instead her attacker shoved her
forward, onto the wide cement walkway in front of the
library.

He pushed her to the ground.

She fell painfully on her side, but he rolled her onto
her back, and she saw him for the first time. He was
tall, muscular and looked vaguely familiar. She thought

she'd seen him around the gym. He was kneeling over her, and he reached up and roughly pulled down her jogging shorts and panties. He spread her legs apart with his knees, and the panties ripped, the thin cotton material pulling apart.

She was crying now. She couldn't help it. There was pain, terror, and humiliation in her voice, and she hated herself for being so weak. She could feel the cool night air against the exposed flesh of her inner thighs, could feel the cold cement against her buttocks.

"Help!" she cried as loud as she could. "Please! Someone! Help!"

Now other students were stopping, changing course, coming toward her. Students getting out of night classes, students walking to their cars or back to their dorm rooms. She should have felt relieved, should have felt grateful, but there was something about the slow, almost laconic way in which the students walked that chilled her to the bone. The shapes gathering around her were dark and faceless in the night.

They weren't coming to rescue her. They were getting in line.

She saw one of them reach for his belt buckle, unhook it.

Another unsnapped the buttons of his Levi's.

"Noooo!" she screamed.

And then the first one was inside her.

THIRTY

1

Eleanor had called from his house, from his kitchen, on his office hour, and though this was the worst possible timing and probably the least convenient thing he could have done this evening, Ian had agreed to come home and eat the special Mexican dinner she was preparing for him. He'd considered telling her that he couldn't, that he had to take over someone else's class, but this was obviously her way of apologizing for staying at her own place the past few nights, and he didn't want to screw things up by turning her down. Part of him thought that he should tell her the truth, tell her that he had to meet with Stevens and other professors to try to figure out what to do, but he knew that if she found out about the meeting she'd want to come as well and he didn't want her involved. He wanted to keep her as far away from Brea as possible.

So he'd told her he had a department meeting at seven and would have to go back but that he'd be home by four for dinner.

It was hard to avoid the subject when she kept bringing it up. She'd done more checking on the school, discovered a history of financial improprieties involving both individual administrators and the institution itself. She seemed to find it all more fascinating than horrifying, and that worried him. He wanted her to be afraid of the school, not interested in it.

The doorbell rang halfway through the meal, and he got up to see who it was.

The bell seemed to go crazy when he was halfway through the living room, chiming endlessly, but he recognized Buckley's "Iron Man" beat, and he knew instantly that his friend was drunk.

That was the last thing he needed.

Sure enough, Buckley was leaning against the breeze-way wall, smelling strongly of J&B. He lurched through the open doorway into the living room. "I figured it out! I fucking figured it out, man! It's the Republicans! They're behind it all!"

Ian looked furtively back toward the dining room, where Eleanor was getting up out of her chair. "You're drunk," he said. "Why the hell did you do this?"

"I'm telling all of them tonight! It's a fascist plot!"

Eleanor had come up behind them. "You're telling who?" she asked softly. "Where are you two going tonight?"

Buckley looked from Eleanor to Ian, and even in his inebriated state he understood the situation. "Nothing," he said, waving one arm ineffectually. "I'm just ranting and raving."

Eleanor turned to Ian as if he wasn't there. "I'm not a dunce," she said.

"I know you're not."

"And I'm not a child."

"I—"

"If we're going to have any kind of relationship at all, you'd better start treating me with a little more respect."

Ian looked disgustedly at Buckley.

"It's not his fault," Eleanor said, drawing his attention back. "It's yours."

"There's a meeting tonight with us, Stevens, and as many professors as we could get together. We want to see what we can come up with."

"I'm going too."

"The hell you are."

"I don't need you to protect me."

"You have nothing to do with this. This is about Brea. This—"

"I have as much right to be there as anyone. I'm at least as intelligent as the other people who'll be there, and maybe I can help."

He knew he was diving into hot water, but there was no way to avoid it. He'd rather have her hate him than be in danger. "The reason I didn't tell you is because it's none of your business."

She stared at him, blinked.

"You're not invited. We don't want you. We don't need you. You can't go."

"You can't tell me where I can and cannot go."

"I can and I will. I rented the room. I decide who to invite."

Her face hardened. "You made your own bed, buddy. Now you're going to have to lie in it."

She walked off toward the dining room. He watched in silence as she took her plate and water glass from the table and stormed into the kitchen. He heard the sound of glass and porcelain shattering as she threw both into the sink.

Buckley's face was white, and he was rubbing his hands worriedly together. "I'm sorry, man. I wasn't thinking. I was just scared shitless and I broke out a bottle and . . ." He trailed off, shook his head.

"Doesn't matter," Ian said tiredly. "Let me get my shit together and we'll go."

He heard Buckley noisily remove the keys from his pocket.

"And I'm driving."

Two people showed.

It was clear almost immediately that they had failed in their mission, but they sat, waiting. Waited, sitting. An hour passed, and no one else arrived. It was not entirely unexpected, but it was disappointing.

Disappointing?

Devastating.

Ian stared out at the empty theater from his seat at the edge of the stage. He'd had hints that this might happen. Francine had said she had a class to teach tonight, she'd show up if she could. Joachim said his wife was working this evening and he had to watch the kids. But Ian had not expected everyone to bail out on him. There was Buckley, Jim, Faith, Jim's friend Faruk and Nedra Osami, a clerk from the Office of Admissions. Period. Not a single other person had shown. None of them had even bothered to call or leave word, and that's what made the whole thing seem a little suspicious to him. A few of the invitees could legitimately claim that they were unaware of the scope of the problem, but some fifteen faculty members and twenty-five students had been fully informed of the situation, people who were all, theoretically, on "their side."

And none of them had come.

And where was Stevens? He was the guest of honor, the man around whom all the ideas were supposed to be flying, their sounding board. And he was a no-show as well.

That was the most ominous thing of all.

Ian prayed that nothing had happened to him.

Prayed.

Maybe that's what they should be doing. Praying. It couldn't accomplish less than what they were doing right now.

He thought, not for the first time that evening, that maybe he should have allowed Eleanor to come with them.

Allowed?

No wonder she was so pissed off at him.

He looked over at Jim's friend Faruk. He was young, younger than Jim, and had not experienced anything firsthand, but he seemed quick and smart and open-minded, and if they ever did come up with a plan of action, they could use him.

The other newcomer, the admissions clerk, had gotten the word second- or third-hand. No one here knew her, and she had obviously been told about the meeting by someone whom they had told. That was even more disheartening, knowing that the word had been spread so effectively and that still no one had come.

The clerk, Nedra, *had* had personal contact. The tires of her car had been flattened as it sat in the parking lot last week, and while waiting next to it for the tow truck she'd called, she'd been attacked by squirrels. One had jumped onto her head from the tree under which she'd parked her car. Two more had run at her from underneath the vehicle, clawing at and biting her ankles. She'd heard the chittering sounds of more squirrels, many more, and had seen several of the small animals running across the parking lot toward her, and had kicked the two squirrels off her feet, flung the one off her head, and quickly jumped into her car, locking the door. They'd swarmed over the car for a moment, seemingly hundreds of them, and then they were gone.

She had not gotten out of the car until the tow truck arrived.

Ian talked to Jim, Faith, Faruk, and Nedra, and the six of them hashed over what they knew and what they thought, getting nowhere, coming up with nothing new. Buckley was out of it, having fallen asleep shortly after settling into his chair and now snoring loudly.

Maybe Stevens was right, Ian thought. Maybe they should just blow the place up and be done with it.

He glanced at his watch. Eight-fifteen.

"All right," he said tiredly. "Let's call it a day."

Nedra stood, nervously clutching her purse. "Is that it? Are we going to meet again? Are we going to ... do anything?"

"Yes," Ian said. "But I need to talk to Gifford Stevens. I'll keep you informed of what's happening."

"Do you want my home phone number? I don't think it's safe to call me at work."

"We'll meet in my office. Day after tomorrow."

"What time? I get off at five."

"Six, then." Ian looked around at the others. "Is that okay?"

Everyone nodded.

"I guess that's it."

"Could somebody walk me to my car?" Nedra asked. "I don't want to go out there by myself."

"I'll do it," Faruk said.

"Thank you."

Ian woke Buckley, who seemed remarkably sober after his short nap, and they all walked out of the theater together.

They stopped as one, staring at the sight that greeted them outside the door—Kiefer's head, skewered on a sharpened stick embedded in the raised planter in front of the building.

Behind the department chairman's head was yet another sharpened stick, this one sporting the head of a pig.

Nedra suddenly started crying, a strange hiccupping sound that owed more to shock than sadness.

"*Lord of the Flies,*" Buckley said quietly.

Ian nodded, looking around, expecting at any moment

to see a band of half-naked college student savages jump out of the shadows brandishing homemade spears.

Was he Ralph? he wondered.

Who would be Jack?

"Brant Keeler," Buckley said, as if reading his mind. "I bet Brant Keeler's Jack. Although the way that kid's armed, he probably has an arsenal with him instead of some sharpened sticks."

Ian stared at the grotesque tableaux. Kiefer's eyes looked lifelessly back at him. Blood not only covered the ragged flaps of flesh that hung down from the raggedly sliced neck, it dripped from the mouth, nose, and eyes, nearly obscuring the features of the face entirely. A bloody clump of Kiefer's thinning hair stuck up at the top of his head, and Ian knew that this was where the head had been held as it had been carried.

"An English prof is behind this one," Buckley said.

"Or a student who's an English major."

"What are we going to do?" Faith asked. She was comforting the sobbing admissions clerk but was obviously pretty close to crying herself.

"We'll call the cops," Jim said. "The real cops. The city cops, not the school cops."

"Call them from home," Ian said. He gestured toward the heads. "Whoever did this might be back, probably will be back. What we need to do now is get the hel· out of here."

"But we can't just leave the scene of a crime," Faruk said.

"We can and we will. Whoever did this did it for our benefit. They know we're here. We have to get out before it's our heads that are shoved on sticks."

Nedra's crying grew louder.

"And we're leaving together," Ian said. "My car's out this way. I'll drive you all to where your cars are parked."

"I'm at the dorm," Jim said.

"Then I'll drive you to the dorm. No one walks alone."

"But who's going to call?" Faruk asked.

"You call," Ian said tiredly. "Or stop by the station. I'm going home."

"Me too," Buckley said.

"I'll do it," Jim said. "Just give me your names and addresses so I can leave it all with them."

"We're wasting time," Ian told him. "Let's go."

Eleanor was gone when he got home. The dinner dishes were in the sink, half of them broken, the bedroom was a shambles. She'd taken all of her clothes and belongings with her.

He sighed heavily and lay down on the bed, closing his eyes.

The phone rang at that instant and he was half tempted to let it ring, but on the off chance that it was Eleanor, he picked up. "Hello?"

"Emerson?"

He recognized Stevens' East Coast accent, and he immediately sat up. "Where the fuck were you?"

"Wakefield University."

"Wakefield?"

"It's another school I listed as—"

"I know. I read it. But why are you there now?"

"Because they're in contact," Stevens said, and for the first time Ian heard fear in his voice. "They're talking."

"Who's talking?"

"Wakefield," he said. "And Brea."

THIRTY-ONE

1

Cheryl looked at herself in the mirror.

Dressed to kill.

She giggled in spite of herself. A more than apt description. She was wearing a tube top and no bra, and with today's chilly weather, her nipples were erect and pressing against the thin material, clearly visible. She'd inserted a jeweled safety pin into her pierced belly button, and below that her tight shorts hugged her pantyless crotch. The material of the shorts was too thick to show the cleft, but the V was definitely visible and, she made sure, prominent. She wore high heels.

In her hand she held the knife.

She was dressed in a way that men would consider provocative, in a way that the more piggish among them would consider "asking for it." Those so inclined would think that she deserved to be raped. And, if she was lucky, they'd try to do it to her.

And she'd cut off their fucking balls.

She watched herself in the mirror as she pretended to grab a man's genitals with her left hand and then slice through his testicles with the knife in her right.

Damn, she looked good.

Lorena Bobbitt had nothing on her.

Her life had changed completely since she'd found the knife. Gone was the fear, the constant dread that had hung about her like fog every second of every day since the rape. The knife had ... empowered her. Yes, that was it. She was *empowered,* no longer a victim.

She was a victimizer.

Or soon would be—if things worked out the way she hoped.

Even after first finding the knife, she had still remained in that victim mindset, aware at all times of the crime that had been performed against her—

to her, in her

—and of the fact that everyone was treating her gingerly, with kid gloves, as though she were a fragile china doll, easily broken. Every male who looked at her she saw as a potential rapist, and she'd taken to watching their eyes and their crotches—their eyes to determine which parts of her body they were looking at, their crotches to see if what they saw caused any sort of reaction.

All of the other editors looked at her tits.

All of them had telltale bulges.

They couldn't see her tits, of course. She'd worn her baggiest sweaters over the thickest, most constricting bras she could find. But they'd known that her tits were there, and they'd thought about them, imagined them, and they'd been aroused.

Today, she'd really arouse them.

She was not sure what had come over her this morning, but she had awakened feeling not enraged, as she usually did, but calm. She'd been having fantasies of exacting revenge on the pigs ever since she'd discovered the knife, and it was this anger that had kept her going, that had enabled her to go to school and face each day. Today, though, she'd known that the time for fantasies was past, and that knowledge had generated within her a feeling of peace. She did not have to be afraid anymore. She had nothing to fear.

They had something to fear.

She smiled at herself in the mirror as she reached for her handbag on the dresser and slipped in the knife.

Steve had never been her favorite editor. Of course, he was no longer an editor anymore, but that made no difference for her purposes. She still considered him one of the boys.

Cheryl watched him as he leaned against a tree in the center of the quad, talking to two of his friends. They were all talking too loudly, laughing too loudly, checking out the women who walked by and rating their body parts on a scale of one to ten.

This was it. This was her chance.

She felt more than a little nervous as she slowly strutted down the walkway past them, but the nervousness was counterbalanced by an even stronger feeling of anticipation. Blood was pumping through her veins, souped up by adrenaline, and she had to force herself to remain calm.

She looked seductively over at Steve as she sauntered past him.

"Hey, Cheryl," he said admiringly.

She stopped, smiled at him, ran the tip of her tongue over the gloss on her lips. "Hey."

"A ten," the long-haired student on Steve's left said. "For the whole package."

Steve grinned at her. "Haven't seen you around for a while."

She walked toward him, leaning forward, leading with her chest. She pushed aside the guy on his right, grabbing the lowest branch of the tree, acutely conscious of the fact that her freshly shaved underarm was practically touching Steve's ear. "I've been busy," she said.

"Yeah, I heard." Steve chuckled. "I heard you were busy getting raped."

She wanted to smack him upside the head, wanted to whip out her knife and gut him then and there, but she forced herself to smile at him. "I was thinking of you the entire time."

"Whoa!" the long-haired student yelled. "Take her, bud!"

"Feed her some beefstick!" said the one she'd pushed.

She ignored them, looking straight into Steve's eyes. "You want a blow job?" she asked.

He said nothing, merely swallowed audibly, but she glanced toward his crotch and saw the growing bulge in his pants.

"Come on," she said. "I'll do you in the bathroom."

"Men's or women's?"

She smiled slyly. "Your choice."

"Okay." His voice was cracked, tentative, no longer strong and confident, and she was conscious, in a way that she hadn't been even a moment before, of the power she wielded.

"Make her swallow!" said the long-haired student.

She turned, smiling sweetly at him. "I always swallow.

And if you're a good boy and you wait right there, maybe I'll come back for you."

Both of his friends were silent as she took Steve's hand and led him down the walkway toward the Biological Sciences building. His hand was sweaty, nearly limp, and she smiled to herself as she opened the door to the building and stepped inside the lobby. They passed several groups of students before stopping in front of the twin doors that led to the men's and women's rest rooms.

"Which is it?" she asked.

He looked at her, and suddenly his nervousness was gone. He grinned. His grip tightened on hers, and she almost pulled away, almost panicked and ran, but she'd come too far to back out now, and she held tightly to her handbag as he led her into the men's room.

There were three urinals and three stalls, and he pulled her into the last stall, closing and locking the swinging metal door behind them. He pulled her against him, and she felt his erection pressing into her stomach. They swiveled, exchanging places, and she pulled back from him. "Take off your pants," she said. "And sit down."

It was humid in here, and claustrophobic, but she remained in place as he unbuckled his belt, unbuttoned his pants, pulled down his jeans and underwear, and sat on the closed lid of the toilet. He was hard, and she grasped his organ, squeezing it as she knelt before him.

"Ow," he said. "Be careful. That—"

The knife sliced into his cock.

He screamed, jerked, tried to get away, but she had his balls in her hand, and she yanked the knife through the wrinkled skin, ripping his sac, tearing it. Blood was everywhere, and for a brief second she was horrified and disgusted by what she had done, but then she remembered what had been done to her, what Steve had wanted her to do to him right here, right now, and she sawed her way through the rest of his scrotum.

He had passed out by this time, and after the intensity of his screams, the bathroom now seemed unnaturally silent. She let go of his severed genitals, watching them fall into the growing puddle of blood on the tiled floor.

In the stall next to them, someone giggled.

Immediately, her grip on the knife tightened. She looked under the partition, saw black shoes and white socks. "Who's there?" she demanded.

"Me."

"I have a knife!"

One boot slid toward the partition, the tip touching the puddle of blood. The person giggled again. "I know."

"I'll cut yours off too!"

"No, you won't. I'm on your side. Go back and get his friend."

Cheryl sucked in her breath. How could he know . . . ?

"Get both his friends. Bring them back here. I'll wait."

"You'll wait?"

"I'll wait."

"Who are you?"

The person leaned down, sticking a thin white hand underneath the partition. "My name's Brant. Brant Keeler. And I think we're going to be good friends, you and I."

Cheryl shook the awkwardly proffered hand.

"Bring them back. His friends. You do one, and I'll do the other one. Then we'll talk."

Yes, Cheryl thought.

"You won't go anywhere?" she said.

"I'll be right here when you get back."

She stood, nearly slipped on the blood, then opened the stall door and backed out. Still holding the knife, she grabbed a paper towel from the dispenser, wiped off the blood, and dropped it into her handbag.

"Don't go anywhere," she said.

"I won't."

She hurried out of the bathroom.

Behind her, before the door closed, she heard Brant giggle.

2

John Taylor could smell the burgers from across the wide expanse of lawn, and his stomach churned mutinously as the thick, familiar odor of frying grease assaulted his nostrils. He looked up from the grass as he

walked and saw above the heads of the milling students
a thin white cloud of steam spreading upward from the
vent on top of the Hunger Hut.

God, he hated his job.

When he'd first applied for work on campus last
month, after being laid off at Circuit City, he'd been
thrilled to learn there was an opening at the Hunger
Hut. He'd all but resigned himself to working in some
office in Administration as a file clerk, surrounded by
bureaucratic old ladies, and when he'd found out that
he'd be working with junk food at a student hangout,
he'd been ecstatic. He'd been hired to work the window,
taking orders, and had been promised free food as well
as a regular salary. It had sounded like a dream job, but
the novelty had worn off almost immediately. The once
mouth-watering scent of burgers, dogs, fries, and rings
had become cloying in the claustrophobic confines of
the grill, and now he didn't care if he ever ate junk
food again.

The thought of working in an air-conditioned office
with quiet little old ladies had become a dream of paradise to him.

But he stuck with the job, though he was not really
sure why. He hated what he did, he hated the people
he worked with, he hated the people he served. But
he remained.

Often, as he flipped burgers and grilled onions, he
found himself thinking back on his life, on all the dicks
he'd fought with, all the pigs he'd porked. He thought
of the good things too. Sometimes. But it was the bad
stuff he liked to dwell on, his absurdly elaborate revenge
plots he liked to mull over.

He didn't care what happened to the people he liked.

But he wanted the people he didn't like to suffer.

Lately, for some reason, his mind had kept going back
to that ball-breaking bitch Faith Pullen. He'd gone out
with her only the one time, at the beginning of the semester, but he couldn't seem to forget her. He'd reamed
probably dozens of babes he couldn't remember at all—
hell, he'd had relationships with bimbos whose names
he'd forgotten—but for some reason Faith had stayed
with him. It was almost as if something wanted him to
remember her, as if he was purposely being forced not

to forget her. At least once a week he saw her pass the Hunger Hut on the way to some class or other. At least once a week he saw the word *faith* written someplace: in a book, on a wall, in the newspaper.

And every time he got into his car, he was reminded of the way the ungrateful slut had treated him.

He often thought about her as he pressed down on the beef patties, pretending that it was her screaming face he was squishing on the griddle. In the back of his mind was the nagging yet comforting thought—no, not thought, *knowledge*—that sometime, somehow, he would have the opportunity to get back at her, at all the people on his hit list, to punish them the way they deserved to be punished.

And that day was upon them now.

He said nothing as he took over from Javier, as the other student clocked out and left, and he grinned when Bonnie called and said she wouldn't be in today. Everything was working out perfectly, the way he'd known it would when he'd awakened this morning and something within him had told him to stop by the hardware store and pick up a couple of boxes of rat poison before going to school.

For the first time since his first day of work, he was not annoyed with the fact that there was a line in front of the Hut. The line, in fact, cheered him up, made him feel good.

He opened up the first box of rat poison, placed it next to the grill, put a spoon in it, and took orders from the first three customers in line.

He sprinkled a spoonful of poison on each side of the two burgers he fried, sprinkled two spoonfuls in the milkshake he made.

He cheerfully took the customers' money and served them their food.

He felt strangely elated as the line moved forward, toward his window.

He grinned. "Next!" he called out.

3

Patti Seberg almost didn't go to her Comparative Studies of World Religions class. She was halfway there, halfway up the stairs in the Social Sciences building, when a *premonition* came over her. She had never had a premonition before, was not even sure she believed in them, but that was the only way to describe what she felt.

She reached the fourth-floor landing and, as sure as she knew her name, she knew that she would end up eating human flesh if she went to class today.

It made no sense at all, on any level whatsoever, but the knowledge was there in her mind, a certainty, and she could either ignore it or act upon it.

Then it faded, was no longer a certainty but merely a belief, and then was downgraded to the memory of a belief.

She continued walking up the stairs.

Dr. Hart's lecture today was on cannibalism and religion.

She felt a strangely disorienting sense of déjà vu as he began to talk, a dread that seemed intimately familiar, but it was superseded by a far more powerful feeling that was closer to excitement or anticipation. She looked around, at her other classmates in the back row, and they too seemed excited, practically poised on the edge of their seats, as though waiting expectantly for something to happen.

"What all religions have in common," the professor was saying, "is ritual human sacrifice and cannibalism."

A blond, heavyset girl in the front row stood, her face tinged red. "Not Christianity," she said loudly.

"Modern Christianity has tried to downplay that aspect," Dr. Hart agreed. "The single sacrifice of Jesus Christ makes up for the multitude of sacrifices that would have otherwise been required by God, and, with the Eucharist, the eating of flesh has become symbolic rather than literal, but the origins are clearly there. The Bible itself promotes cannibalism. Jesus says, 'This is my body, this is my blood—' "

"This is sacreligious," the girl said. "You're anti-Christian."

"On the contrary," the instructor told her. "I very much approve of the Bible's cannibalistic aspects."

"I will not listen to this any longer." The girl gathered up her books and started toward the door.

"Close it," the professor said quietly.

Another student, a muscle-bound young man to the left of Patti, wearing an athletic department T-shirt, stood, closed the door, and stood in front of it, hands across his chest.

"Sacrifice and cannibalism are the only true ways to communicate with God," the professor said, slowly taking off his jacket.

"Let me out of here!" the girl demanded.

Patti rose with the rest of the class. Knives and forks were already being passed down each row.

" 'So Jesus said to them, "Truly, truly, I say to you, unless you eat the flesh of the Son of Man and drink his blood, you have no life in you." ' "

The girl was sobbing now, obviously terrified. Her books fell to the floor as she tried to push the guard away from the door.

Patti took the knife and fork handed to her and felt a strong sense of revulsion. But the queer exhilaration she felt was even stronger, and she pressed forward with the rest of the class toward the closed door.

The professor grinned. "Eat, drink, and be merry!"

"No!" the girl cried.

And the first fork went into her forearm.

4

Ron was not even sure who had captured him. He assumed that it was another fraternity, but he did not know if it was the black fraternity. They grabbed him as soon as he stepped outside his dorm room, shoving a pillowcase over his head, holding his arms and legs, tying a gag of some sort over the portion of the pillowcase that covered his mouth so he wouldn't be able to scream. There seemed to be a lot of them. He felt several pairs of hands all over his body, and he was not shoved forward and forced to walk but lifted bodily and carried to a car or a van or some type of vehicle.

No one stopped his captors and questioned them about what they were doing, no one said a word to them, and Ron thought that even if someone did see what was happening, they would think it was merely a harmless fraternity prank.

He knew, though, that it was anything but.

This was the latest skirmish in the war.

And he was going to be the next casualty.

He was driven somewhere. And taken out of the vehicle. And carried inside a building. And dropped into a chair to which his arms were tied.

His pants were removed. And his underwear. His feet were tied to the chair legs.

The blindfold was pulled roughly from his head, and he found himself in a low, windowless room filled with red-jacketed fraternity members lined up in identical rows along the dark, cheaply paneled walls. The air was humid and stifling, smelling of sweat and stale beer. The light in the room was dim and diffused, coming not from overhead bulbs but from a source he could not see, and it took him a moment to notice that all of the silently assembled fraternity members were wearing masks.

He was suddenly much more frightened.

He looked from one to another, hoping to spot someone familiar, hoping to recognize a particular tilt of the head, a unique deportment, an unusual size, but all individuality was effectively hidden behind the jackets and the masks.

The masks. They were all the same—Richard Nixon masks—and from behind darkened, sunken holes, he saw glittering eyes staring at him.

Who were these people? He continued to look from one figure to the next. They were too short to be members of the black fraternity.

They were too short to be members of any fraternity.

He looked more carefully and saw the swelling of breasts beneath the red jackets.

He'd been captured by a sorority.

His hopes rose. Maybe there was a chance. Maybe this wasn't anything serious. Maybe this was just part of some elaborate hazing ritual. Maybe they were going to suck him or fuck him and then let him go. He could deal with that.

But as he craned his neck far to the left, his hopes fell. At the front of the room, flanked by the heads of both lines, was a cheap, poorly constructed throne, atop which sat a particularly ugly and belligerent spider monkey. The wall behind the monkey's throne was decorated with blown-up photos of nude men.

Dead nude men.

A figure wearing a Nixon mask but dressed in a green rather than red jacket walked from behind Ron up the aisle to the foot of the throne. The figure knelt. "Oh, Great God Flan," a female voice intoned, "tell us, shall we punish the infidel?"

The monkey leapt to its feet, clapping its hairy palms and chattering noisily.

"So it shall be written," the masked woman said. "So it shall be done."

She stood, turned, and there was a straight razor in her hand.

Ron struggled, squirmed, fought, trying desperately to free himself from his bonds, but the ropes were tied tightly and he could not even make them give. He was suddenly acutely aware of his exposed genitals. The lined sorority members were chanting something, a sound or word he could not make out, and the woman with the razor walked up the aisle toward him.

He started screaming. He didn't want to, but he couldn't help it. He was embarrassed at how feminine his cries sounded, but he did not stop. He could not stop. He continued screaming.

The woman knelt before him. He saw blond hair behind the black plastic of the mask.

Beneath his own screams, as the blade of the razor sliced through the fleshy skin above his left nipple, he finally heard a voice he recognized.

Ruth's.

Laughing.

THIRTY-TWO

1

Ian had called in sick in order to meet Stevens at his apartment at noon, and the English department had been in an uproar when he phoned. Kiefer's death had not yet made the papers, but the entire department was aware of it, and he heard Francine crying in the background as he explained to Maria that he wouldn't be in today.

"Dr. French won't be in either," she said. "He said that you're the ones who found him?"

"Gotta go," Ian said, and hung up.

He didn't feel like talking about it to coworkers.

He'd called Buckley immediately afterward. His friend was suffering from a major hangover and hadn't been in any condition to talk, let alone think, so Ian had not told him what Stevens had said last night. He'd merely said that he'd call back later.

He'd considered phoning Jim and Faith, but they were into it too far already. They were just kids. And he didn't want anything to happen to them.

Several times during the morning he'd tried calling Eleanor, first at her condo, then at her office, but she hadn't answered the calls at home, and her office phone kept going into voice mail. He dialed her secretary, but the secretary told him that Eleanor was in a meeting.

Yeah. Right.

He finally gave it up after the fifth try, telling himself that he'd apologize and make it all up to her after it was over and everything was done with.

Over and done with.

What made him think it *would* be over and done with? Just because these things had resolutions in novels didn't mean that they would in real life. Reality was not structured that way. There didn't have to be a climax and a denouement. The players in this drama, the main characters, of which he considered himself one, did not have to live. By rights, one of them, the strangest one—Stevens—or the most expendable one—which, from a novelistic standpoint, would probably be Buckley, since he had no current romantic attachments—would die. The rest of them would live.

But they could all live.

Or they could all die.

Life did not follow the formulas of fiction.

So why did he keep acting as though it did?

He left the house at a quarter after eleven, but it did not take him as long to get there as he'd expected, and he arrived at Stevens' rundown apartment complex nearly a half hour early.

He was halfway across the small, glass-littered parking lot when he saw Stevens heading toward him, carrying an obviously heavy box approximately the size of an orange crate. "Open the trunk!" Stevens called.

Ian took out his keys and quickly opened the trunk of his car as Stevens put the box down on the trunk floor, where it handed with a heavy thump and some inter-box clanking.

"What's that?" Ian asked.

"Explosives. I want you to take them to your office."

Ian shook his head, his brain already conjuring visions of his car exploding in a fiery ball after a rear-end collision. "I can't."

"You can and you will."

"Why?"

"I think you should have some on hand. Just in case. There's a couple Claymores here and some C4, with detonators. Enough to take out a building if you follow the prints I gave you."

Again Ian shook his head. "I can't store these in my office. What if they fall into the wrong hands—"

"You may not be able to get off campus. *I* may not be able to get off campus."

"What's that supposed to mean?"

"It's never gotten this far before. Everything's accelerated, and I don't think it's going to wait until the end of December. I think it's planning to graduate early, and

I have the feeling that when the shit starts to come down, it's going to come down hard and fast. I don't think we'll have the luxury of being able to drive here, pick up what we need, and drive back—"

"You think we should stay away from Brea?"

Stevens' expression darkened. "Yes, you can do that. If you're a worthless fucking pussy."

"I didn't mean—"

"If something's going to be done, we're the ones who are going to do it. Yeah, it's dangerous. But you knew that when you signed on."

It was macho bullshit. The forced camaraderie of fighting men popularized by pulp fiction and bad war movies, but it worked, it called up the right emotional responses, and Ian nodded, signaling his continued involvement.

"I took out the computers at Wakefield. The schools can't communicate. At least not for a couple days. Not through modems or phone lines. They're pissed off about it, and they know who did it, and that's another reason I want you to have this stuff. In case something happens to me, you're going to have to go through with it." He looked up at Ian. "I forgot to ask you, how many people came to your little shindig?"

"Two."

"That's two more than I expected." He took a deep breath, motioned toward the box in the trunk. "It may not be perfect, but it's the only way I know."

Ian shifted his weight uncomfortably from one foot to the other. "I don't know how to . . . You know . . ."

"That's why I'm going to teach you," Stevens said. "Let's go up to my room."

He left Stevens around four, so he'd have time to drop the box at his office and be off campus before dark. He knew, intellectually, that there was nothing that could happen at night that could not happen in the daytime, but darkness was intrinsically more frightening and, as horror readers, both he and Stevens realized the psychological power of night.

Maybe the university recognized it too.

Maybe it would try to use that to its advantage.

The faculty lot was full, so Ian pulled into one of the

fifteen-minute visitors' spaces near the side of the Administration building. He felt like a criminal, and he glanced furtively around to make sure he was not being watched before opening the trunk and taking out the box.

Felt like a criminal?

He was a criminal. He didn't know the specific laws he was breaking, but he was pretty damn sure that bringing explosives on campus for the express purpose of blowing up one of the buildings was not legal.

The box was heavier than he thought, and he listed badly to the right as he carried it across the lawn to Neilson Hall.

Two days.

That was the latest, Stevens figured, that Brea and Wakefield would remain out of touch. Even assuming that the damage he'd caused could not be repaired, that new equipment had to be purchased and installed, two days was an outside figure.

Which was why he wanted to blow up the school tomorrow.

It had been said so offhandedly, so casually, in the middle of a demonstration of detonator installation, that at first Ian had not reacted to it. The statement had not registered. Then his brain had caught up with his ears, and he'd realized that it was Stevens' intention to blow up as many buildings as he could tomorrow evening. He wanted to object, wanted to be able to say that such an act of terrorism was wrong and morally indefensible, but he could not do so. Instead, he found himself thinking that if they waited until after ten, students and instructors would all be off the campus. There might be a few janitors around, but he and Stevens could probably turn on some fire alarms ahead of time and get them out of the buildings before the explosions. It was conceivable that no one would get hurt.

He'd even wondered why Stevens hadn't decided to do it tonight, but when he asked, Stevens had been vague and elusive, and Ian had gotten the impression that there were other factors to be considered, that there was a reason for the timing, that forces had to be aligned.

He could understand that.

He reached Neilson Hall and rode the back elevator up to the fifth floor. The box was really heavy by now, and he fairly sprinted down the empty hallway before dropping the box in front of his office. Well, not dropping. He wanted to, almost had to, but no matter how much his arms hurt, he was not stupid enough to drop a box of explosives. He placed the box down carefully, then found his key and unlocked the door, flipping on the light. Instead of lifting it again, he bent down and pushed the box inside.

He sensed immediately that something was wrong.

He straightened, looked around. There was nothing amiss, nothing out of order, but he could feel a difference: a thickness in the air, a shift in temperature, an incongruity of acoustics, layers of subtle intangibles that informed him that the university was fully aware of what he was doing.

How could he have been so stupid as to think that it wouldn't know what was going on within its borders? The intercom switched on, and he heard a hiss of white noise that sounded unnervingly like laughter.

It was toying with him, playing with him. It could kill him right now if it wanted to—

Ian blinked.

Or could it?

Wouldn't it make more sense for it to zap him now? Hell, there were only seven of them who were trying to fight it. It could take him out, make his elevator crash, and there'd be one down, six to go. There was no logical reason for it to let him live when it had him in its clutches.

He thought again about Stevens not wanting to detonate his explosives until tomorrow night.

Maybe there was a whole agenda here of which he was unaware.

The sense of wrongness was still there, but it was not quite so frightening, and Ian moved back into the hall, closed and locked the door, and walked to the elevator.

He took the elevator safely down to the first floor.

Outside, it was already getting dark, the sun not yet set but effectively hidden behind a low cloud bank in the west. Ian started across the lawn the way he'd come, heading toward the visitors' lot. To his left he heard a noise, a short, sharp cry, and he stopped walking, turned to look, and saw Lawrence Roget and Midge Connors, naked on the grass, Lawrence's face buried in Midge's crotch, his penis dangling down into her mouth.

Ian said nothing, did not in any way announce his presence, but the two professors looked up simultaneously and fixed him with identically mocking grins.

He turned his head and hurried away, hearing the laughter behind him, and now he noticed other couples—men and women, men and men, women and women—having sex on the periphery of the lawn. Had they been here five minutes ago, on his way in? They had to have been. He'd probably been too busy thinking about the box to notice them.

He heard moans and giggles, cries and screams, and against his will he found himself becoming aroused. He thought of Sylvia, wondered, if they had still been married, if she would have been here now, fucking one of his colleagues.

Probably.

What the hell was wrong with him? Why was he still playing the martyr after all this time? That was over, that was done, that chapter was closed. Sylvia was gone and he was with Eleanor now, and while they might be fighting at the moment, he had no doubt that after all of this was finished, they would kiss and make up. He loved Eleanor, and he knew she loved him, and he knew that the two of them were going to stay together. Eleanor was different. Unlike Sylvia, she had not been a virgin when he'd met her. Hell, she'd been married and divorced. Which meant that she had sown her wild oats, had shopped around, and had decided on him.

The relationship was more complicated than that, of course. But deep down, where it counted, it was the knowledge that she had had other men and had still chosen him that reassured him, that made him feel that she would not abandon him in order to fuck someone else.

He stopped walking, aware for the first time of the direction in which his thoughts were heading. His head felt heavy, his brain slow. It was like a headache without the pain, and he realized that his thoughts were being influenced. He was not thinking what he wanted to think, he was thinking what *it* wanted him to think.

He glanced around the lawn. There seemed to be even more bodies now, though the light was fading fast and he couldn't be sure.

He hurried now, breaking into a trot.

It didn't really matter if Eleanor was different, though, did it? Getting fucked. That's what they wanted. That's what they all wanted. Maybe Eleanor did love him. But if she met some younger guy, some beefed-up, buffed-up stud—

Oh, God!

—she'd do the same thing Sylvia did. He'd come home again, catch them on the floor, hear her screaming with pleasure, see his shiny cock—

No!

He couldn't allow himself to think that way. That was how it wanted him to think.

He reached the parking lot, took out his keys as he sprinted toward the car. Thank God Eleanor had not signed up for classes. Who knew what effect the school might have had on her, who knew what kind of pressure it might have put on her.

But a small, mean part of him wished that Eleanor had signed up for classes. What was happening at the university was horrible, but it *was* a kind of litmus test. If you were good you passed, if you were bad you went down. Would Eleanor have been able to survive, or would she have turned into Sylvia, dropping her panties at the drop of a hat for the first bulge that came looking for her?

This was crazy. Was his own ego really so fragile, his own self-esteem so precarious, that he was willing to expose the woman he loved to this evil?

No. It was affecting him.

Maybe that's why it hadn't tried to kill him. Maybe it thought it could convert him.

Maybe.

Or maybe it was because, as Stevens had said, whether he was with it or against it, he was a part of this university. Killing him would cause damage to itself. It would be like cutting off one of its fingers. Or, at the very least, having its arteries harden a bit. It would cause pain.

He got into the car and turned on the ignition, backing out. Through the windshield he saw that the lighted windows on the east side of the Administration building resembled a face: eyes, nose, mouth. As he watched, the lights began blinking on and off, the lights in other offices doing the same, resulting in a crude sort of animation.

The building was laughing at him.

"Fuck you," he said aloud.

He put the car into Drive and drove out of the parking lot and away from the campus.

2

The dorm seemed lonely with Howie gone.

Even with all the shit going down, even amidst the fear and terror and chaotic activity, Howie's loss was always there, a vacuum in his existence, and though he could not forget it, he could not appreciate it either. He had not had time to truly mourn his friend. He'd experienced his grief in installments, catching a bit of it here and there, when he'd been alone and had the chance, but he had not had the opportunity to be alone with Howie's memory and let himself really feel the loss.

He walked slowly up the dormitory stairs, nearly dead on his feet, and thought of his bed, imagined himself stretching out, closing his eyes—

Cheryl leaped out at him from the shadows on the landing, screaming, knife extended. "I'll have your fucking balls!"

It was clumsiness that saved his life. He tried to speed forward, out of the way, but he tripped in his panic and instead fell back against the railing as she stabbed violently at the spot where he would have been. The miscalculation threw her off balance, her momentum causing her to pitch onto the cement, and then he was on her, stomping her wrist with the heel of his boot until she screamed and let go of the knife. He kicked it away, and then brought the boot down on her hand. He kicked the side of her head and, for a brief second, considered kicking her down the stairs. In his mind he heard the satisfying sound her neck would make as it snapped, saw the way she'd look as her body tumbled to the floor below.

But then reason reasserted itself and he reached down and angrily grabbed her by the wrists, yanking her to her feet. She screamed in agony, and their eyes locked as he drew her forward and brought her face to the level of his. There was a second's hesitation, then a look of complete disorientation crossed her features. She stared at him and burst into tears. "Oh, God!" she cried. "I'm sorry! I didn't ... I ..." The words dissolved into a torrent of sobs.

He let go of her wrists, put his arms around her, and hugged her. She hugged him in return with the hand he hadn't stomped on and cried into his shoulder. He did not know the specific chain of events that had brought the entertainment editor to this pass, but he knew the force behind it. He knew what had led her here.

The spell was broken now, though, and she continued to sob against him for all that she had thought and all that she had done while in its grip.

They remained like that for a full five minutes, while several students passed them, staring openly and curiously. When her cries quieted, he asked her to come to his room, but she shook her head, panicked, and said she had to go home. He offered to drive her, but again she shook her head wildly and said that she'd drive herself. He wasn't sure she should be driving in her condition, but before he could voice his misgivings she was gone, hurrying down the stairs.

He walked over to where he'd kicked the knife and picked it up. His hand was shaking as he looked down at the weapon. What if this was not an isolated occurrence? What if other attackers were waiting to ambush him? What if assassins at this moment were picking off Ian and Stevens and Buckley? What if the university was on to them and was making a systematic effort to kill them all?

What if Faith was being attacked?

That was the important question, the one he was really thinking.

He pushed open the stairwell door and hurried down the hallway to his room. He'd call Faith immediately and make sure she was safe, tell her what happened, make sure she was extra careful—

He opened the door to his room and Faith was there,

sitting on the side of the bed, a white paper sack marked by clear grease stains on the floor next to her feet.

She stood, smiled at him. "I picked up some burgers at the Hunger Hut," she said.

"Thank God you're okay." He rushed over to her, throwing his arms around her, holding her tightly.

She laughed. "What's all this about?"

"Nothing," he said, kissing her ear. "Nothing."

She pulled back, reached down for the sack. "You haven't eaten yet, have you?"

"No," he admitted.

"Then come on. These are getting cold." She opened the sack, took out a wrapped hamburger. "I want you to know, I went through a lot for this. One of the psychos I dated before you was working at the Hut. I was going to bail, but there were a lot of other people around and he didn't seem to recognize me." She turned down the wrapper and offered the burger to him, pressing it against his lips.

"Fuck the food." Jim grabbed the burger and tossed it. It hit the wall and slid down into the wastebasket.

She said she had to go home tonight, and he understood that, but she was here for him now, and he hit her and hurt her and she drew blood in response, and he bit into her vagina as her unlubricated fingers were shoved deep into his anus, and it was good.

3

Faith awoke feeling sore, and she glanced at the alarm clock on Jim's dresser. Eleven o'clock. She should get dressed and go home, but it was so warm and comfortable here in his bed, and it was such a long drive back to Santa Ana, and her mom wouldn't give a shit one way or the other ...

She snuggled deeper into the blankets.

Somewhere within her mind a warning alarm sounded, and for a few brief seconds she was possessed by the need to leave, filled with the certainty that her departure for home was imperative, but she could not locate a reason for the feeling and her mind was too tired to try to think it through, and she drifted off to sleep.

THIRTY-THREE

1

Ian was awakened by Stevens' phone call, and he in turn called Buckley and Jim. Jim said that he would call Faith.

He considered phoning Faruk and Nedra, their two new allies, but he wasn't sure they'd be needed or even be of much help, and he didn't want to involve them unless it was absolutely necessary.

Today was the day.

He'd had a tough time falling asleep last night, and he'd expected to feel anxious or frightened or excited when he awoke. He'd expected to feel *something*. But there was nothing to differentiate today from yesterday or the day before or the day before that.

He didn't know if that was good or bad.

He took a quick shower, poured some orange juice into an old Taco Bell Batman cup, and headed off to Brea. They weren't scheduled to meet for another hour, but he wanted to try one last time to talk to someone in the administration, to attempt once again to get some official support. The body count was racking up, and even President Langford, as isolated as she was from the day-to-day operation of the school, had to have noticed by now what was happening.

Unless she was part of it.

If not her, then one of her flunkies. Someone in power had to have the will and resources to help them.

He had no problem finding a parking spot. The faculty lot was much less crowded than usual, and although that was disconcerting in a way, it also meant that fewer instructors would be on campus today, so there'd be less of a chance that people would be killed or injured when the buildings exploded.

When the buildings exploded.

Jesus.

The lobby of the Administration building was empty, and he did not see a single person as he walked up the stairs to the top floor, where Langford had her office.

The secretary was shaking her head before he even reached her desk. "I'm sorry. The president cannot see you now."

Ian ignored her and continued walking.

The secretary stood. "Dr. Emerson. The president is having a private conference and does not wish to be disturbed."

He strode past the secretary, who moved to block his way, but before she had even cleared her desk, he had already pushed open the door to the inner office.

The president was seated behind her desk.

She was dead.

She had been dead for some time, and Ian whirled to face the secretary. "What the fuck's going on here?"

The woman burst into tears. "I didn't know what to do," she cried. "I thought it would be better to leave her here than to—to . . ."

"To tell anyone?"

The secretary nodded, crying.

She saw nothing wrong with her logic, nothing unusual in her actions, and Ian did not even try to point out how crazy that was.

He turned back toward the president. She was still propped up in her chair, sitting stiffly. Her open eyes were clouded over with white cataracts, and a trickle of dried spittle stained her chin. Her skin was two-toned, white in the forehead, bluish black in the cheeks where the blood had settled. The room was cool and air-conditioned, but even the constant circulation and purification of the air could not mask the sweet, sick smell of decay that emanated from her rotting form.

"How long?" Ian demanded.

The secretary continued to cry.

"How long has she been here like this?"

"A week!"

"She was dead the last time I came by?"

The secretary nodded. "But I couldn't tell you! I couldn't let you know! I couldn't let anyone know!"

"Why?"

She blinked, obviously thrown by the question. "Why?"

"Why couldn't you tell anyone?"

"Because ... because I couldn't."

"You didn't even think to call the police?"

"Oh, Chief Lyons knows. He didn't think I should tell anyone either."

Ian felt suddenly cold. He walked past the secretary and back toward the stairs.

"Don't tell anyone I told you!" she called after him. She was no longer crying. Her voice sounded chipper, almost happy.

He hurried down the stairs.

He hadn't called Faruk or Nedra, but they were here anyway. Jim had called both, and all three of them, along with Stevens and Faith, were waiting for him in the English department conference room. Stevens was at the far end of the table, an array of explosives in front of him.

"Dr. French went to his office to get a coffeepot," Faith said.

"And he has returned!"

Ian stepped aside as Buckley pushed past him, an oversize percolator in his hand.

Buckley placed the coffee pot on the floor and plugged it into a wall socket. "So these are the forces of good, huh? Pretty damn pathetic, if you ask me."

The lights flickered for a second, and the top of the coffeepot came flying up into the air, barely missing Buckley's head. It hit the ceiling and bounced back down, landing on top of the table.

"Fuckah!" Buckley jumped up, looked from Ian to Stevens. "Accident?"

Ian shook his head. "Intentional."

"Dicklip sandwich!" Buckley yanked out the cord and backed quickly away from the percolator.

"An organism will reject those cells which do not fit in, which are different," Stevens said calmly from the head of the table. He continued to tinker with his explosives. "I'm afraid, to the university, *we* are the cancer here."

Nedra licked her lips nervously. "What does that mean?"

"It means it will try to kill us. That's why we have to stick together today."

"Us?" Faruk asked. "Just us?"

"We're the most immediate threat. We're the ones who know. We're the ones who are trying to do something about it. If there are others, they can wait." He looked up. "Was anybody attacked last night?"

Jim glanced at Faith. "I was."

Ian pulled out the chair nearest the door and sat down. "What happened?"

"Cheryl Gonzalez, my entertainment editor. She hid on the stairway of the dorm and tried to stab me."

"Did you kill her?" Stevens asked. There was no emotion in his voice, only a detached interest.

"Of course not!"

"What did you do?"

"We fought, I got the knife away, and she broke down crying." He shrugged. "She left."

"These unstable people," Stevens said, "these 'bad' people, if you will, are like the university's antibodies, attacking perceived threats."

"You mean us?"

He nodded. "Us."

"So other people may try to kill us?" Nedra asked.

"Other people *will* try to kill us. That's why we cannot separate." He reached into his jacket and pulled out a handgun. He placed it on the table in front of him.

From somewhere down the hallway came the sound of men yelling. Ian stood, frowning, and moved over to the doorway, looking out. At the far end of the corridor, Frederickson Eaves, one of the freshman world history instructors, was dressed in a medieval suit of chain mail. Todd Crouse, their own department's resident Civil War buff, was decked out in Confederate regalia.

They were sword fighting.

Ready to jump into the fight was Tom Kashiwa, the Eastern philosophy lecturer, who was stripped down to black tights and affecting a Bruce Lee stance. Behind him was one of the anthropology professors, wearing the garb of some African tribe and brandishing a spear.

"Jesus," Buckley said.

Ian moved aside so the others could stand in the doorway and watch.

"A fight?" Stevens asked from his place at the end of the table.

"Yes," Faith said.

"It'll be to the death," Stevens said calmly. "Close the door. And lock it."

They did not emerge from the conference room until noon. Outside, in the hallway, they heard screams, cries, the sound of things being thrown, the sound of glass breaking, but the heavy, windowless door remained closed and locked, and Stevens explained how to prepare, place, and detonate explosives, and made each of them practice doing it themselves.

When they finally opened the door and walked into the hallway, they saw not the gauntlet of bodies they'd expected, not the litter of debris their ears had led them to expect, but an empty corridor, the white tile smeared here and there with small amounts of blood.

"Sounded like a bigger party," Buckley said.

"Trust nothing," Stevens told them.

They walked down the stairs together, Stevens in the lead, gun drawn. He paused before each landing, but they saw no other people and made it safely to the first floor.

Outside, the campus was a madhouse.

The destruction they'd expected to see in the hallway was clearly visible here. Scientific equipment littered the concrete at the base of the Physical Sciences building; televisions, VCRs, and film projectors were smashed in front of the library. Large areas of sidewalk had cracked open, Jack-and-the-Beanstalk-sized roots having shoved their way through the cement. In the quad, one of the trees had moved, was now growing on a low rise where there had previously been only grass. Everywhere were groups of students and faculty members, many of them dressed for Halloween, almost all of them screaming at one another.

From one of the trees hung the nude and battered body of an eviscerated man who looked to Ian like one of the custodians. Oversize squirrels were furtively eating the bloody entrails beneath his feet.

"Oh, God." Nedra started crying. "Oh, God."

"I'm out of here," Faruk announced. "I'm going home."

"You can't go home."

The voice came from a thin, frightened-looking young woman huddled on the south corner of the building's front steps.

They turned to face her. She looked vaguely familiar, Ian thought. She'd probably been in one of his classes. "Why?" he asked. "What happened?"

The girl licked her lips. "They blocked off the campus. We can't get out."

"Who? Who blocked off the campus?"

"The fraternities. They've barricaded the place. We're trapped here. They won't let anybody out or in."

THIRTY-FOUR

1

The campus was indeed surrounded. The fraternities had barricaded the school, and what appeared to be the combined membership of all seven Greek houses was stationed around the perimeter of the campus, patrolling the sidewalk, carrying automatic weapons.

The good news was that outside authorities were aware of the situation. The bad news was that they did not seem to be able to do anything about it. Two bullet-riddled patrol cars sat, doors open, lights on, in the middle of Thomas Avenue, their murdered occupants lying unattended and uncollected on the asphalt. A crowd of other law enforcement officials huddled behind a makeshift police barricade at the far end of the cordoned-off street.

Jim crept back through the bushes at the side of the Administration building to where the others waited. "She's right," he said. "We're hostages."

"Shit," Buckley said. "I guess that means that our heads'll be on the sticks next."

"Shut up," Faith told him. "We don't want to listen to your doom and gloom while the rest of us are trying to figure a way out of here."

"Really? Well, fuck you, bim. I'm not going to be deprived of my freedom of speech during my last hours on earth. I'll say whatever I damn well please."

"That's enough," Ian said, stepping between them. "The last thing we need right now is to be fighting amongst ourselves. That's exactly what it wants. We're all under pressure here, and what we need to do is stop for a moment, take a deep breath, and calm down."

Jim watched all this with a slight sense of removal, a feeling of detachment. It felt almost as though he was

covering a story, as though he was a reporter assigned
to this event and he was merely recording what was
going on for future reference.

But there might be no future.

He sidled next to Faith, slid an arm around her waist.

"My calculations were off," Stevens said.

"What calculations?" Ian asked.

He ignored the question. "Let's get this show over
with." He motioned toward the toolbox at his feet. "I'm
going to leave this here and try to get the rest of my
stuff. It's in a van parked"—he swiveled around, trying
to get his bearings—"there." He nodded toward the east
parking lot.

"Everything's blocked off," Jim said.

"Are they stationed inside or outside the perimeter of
the parking lots?"

"I don't know," Jim admitted. "I couldn't see that
far."

"I'll check it out. I'll drive the van in on a service road
if I can, smuggle my tools in one by one if I have to."

"I'll go with you," Faruk said. "Two people can carry
more than one."

Buckley looked at him. "You're not going to bail on
us, are you?"

"I don't think that's even an option now."

Jim looked from Stevens to Faruk. There was a
strange feeling in his gut, an unsettling, almost physical
sensation that was not unlike nausea. He was suddenly
filled with the certainty that they were being watched,
that someone—or something—was eavesdropping on
this conversation.

Stevens and Faruk would never make it to the van.

He didn't know where that idea had come from, what
had pressed it onto his consciousness, but he was convinced of its truth, and though he felt a little foolish, he
spoke up. "Don't go," he said.

Stevens turned toward him.

"You won't make it."

"Why?"

"I don't know. I just ... know. I can feel it."

Stevens nodded. "We will be careful."

"You don't understand—"

"I understand. But there's no other choice."

"There is another choice. We wait it out. There's a ton of police out there. And they'll probably call for more. It has to end eventually. The frat rats'll get tired, they'll have to eat, they'll have to go to the bathroom. If we can just stay here until—"

"It's not the fraternities that are doing this," Stevens reminded him. "It's the university."

"But—"

"It can turn that sidewalk to quicksand. It can flip that road up like a cheap carpet. It can make that line of trees walk down the road and crush those cops' skulls. It can create a creature out of our sewage. Do you understand what we're dealing with here?"

"And what makes you think you can fight that?"

"I've done it before. I can do it again."

The words were not said boastfully, were not bragging, but were stated in a calm, matter-of-fact manner, and somehow that made Jim feel a little better. Maybe Stevens did know what he was doing. Maybe he could get them out of this.

"It's been listening in on this conversation," Jim said.

"It's been listening, but hopefully it hasn't been hearing. To it, we're a cough, a cough that's threatening to turn into pneumonia. But it has a lot more on its mind than that one cough right now, and it's distracted." He gestured toward the front of the school, then back toward the quad. "As long as all this is going on, as long as it's not completely focused on us, we have a chance." He looked at Faruk. "You don't have to come," he said.

The news editor nodded. "I'll come."

"Let's do it, then, it's getting late."

"You want us to create some sort of diversion?" Ian asked.

"Do nothing. Wait for us."

"Here?"

"Where would you suggest?"

"I don't like it here. It's too open." Ian thought for a moment. "How about the cafeteria? It's away from the other buildings. The windows'll let us see anything coming—"

"It's too far away," Faruk said. "We'll be coming from the parking lot."

"And we'd have to go through that." Faith motioned toward the quad.

"The Admissions office," Nedra said. She cleared her throat. "It's here in the Administration building, it's on the first floor, and I have the key. There are windows, but there's also a metal sheet that goes down over them. It's to protect the place at night because we keep money there."

"Perfect," Ian said.

"Should we go back and get that girl on the steps?" Buckley asked.

Stevens shook his head. "Fuck her. She's a lost cause. Go to the Admissions office and wait for us there. Don't let anyone else in except us." He turned toward Faruk. "You know where the office is?"

The news editor nodded.

"We're all set, then." He lightly kicked the toolbox. "Take this. If we don't come back, use it."

Ian nodded.

Stevens was off without a word. Faruk waved quickly, then followed him. Jim watched them go. The feeling in his gut was back, and as he saw the two of them hurry away, he was filled with the certainty that he would not see either of them again.

"Come on," Ian said, and the tone of his voice indicated that he'd probably had exactly the same thought. "Let's stake out the Admissions office."

2

"They're not coming back," Jim said.

Buckley snorted. "No shit, Sherlock."

"I knew it. I could feel it. I told him."

Faith glanced up at the clock. Three-fifteen. They'd been here for more than two and a half hours. Her stomach was growling and she had to pee, but she did not say anything. They'd had a bathroom run less than an hour ago, Ian and Jim accompanying her and Nedra to the women's room while Buckley waited in the office, and she wasn't going to ask to go until Nedra said something first.

Faith looked over at Ian. "What are we going to do now? How long are we going to stay here?"

"I don't know," he admitted.

"It'll be dark soon," Buckley said. "I say we either get out now, while it's light, or wait here until tomorrow. I don't think we should go out at night."

"Try the phones again," Jim suggested.

"I just tried them ten minutes ago," Nedra reminded him. Nevertheless, she picked up the receiver. Grimacing, she held it up so they could all hear. Again, faintly, the sound of laughing issued from the earpiece. She put the receiver back in the cradle.

"Attention, shoppers!"

They all jumped at the sound of the voice. It issued from an inset speaker in the ceiling, and they craned their necks upward as though it was the speaker itself that was addressing them.

"The ritual sacrifice of Faruk Jamal, former news editor of the *Daily Sentinel,* and the famous Gifford Stevens, enemy of the university, will take place in fifteen minutes at the stadium! Everyone's invited! Come one, come all! The traitors will be roasted alive in an open-pit barbecue, and fixin's will be served! Bring marshmallows for the wienie roast!"

The voice was exaggeratedly cheerful, possessed of the obnoxious false enthusiasm of a professional announcer, and the juxtaposition of the grisliness of what was being said with the pop shallowness of the way in which it was expressed sent chills down Faith's arms.

"Brant Keeler," Buckley said angrily. "I'd recognize that little pissant's voice anywhere."

"Do you think they're really—" Nedra began.

But before she could complete the sentence, the announcer came on again. "Now, for your dining and listening pleasure, their last words!"

It was Stevens and Faruk, and Faith felt both sickened and frightened as she heard them screaming in incoherent anguish, each of their screams punctuated by canned sitcom laughter.

Faith put her hands over her ears. "Is there any way to shut that off?" she asked.

Nedra turned a knob next to the light switch on the wall with no effect.

"I'll get it." Jim picked up a stapler and hoped on top of the desk beneath the speaker. He started pounding on the perforated metal speaker covering. It caved in, and with two more quick hits the speaker died. He jumped off the desk.

"So why didn't we notice this earlier?" Nedra asked. "How come people had to start dying before we even realized something weird was going on here? It seems like we could have stopped it before it started if we'd, you know, nipped it in the bud."

"Maybe we're not as good and pure and wholesome as we think we are," Jim suggested.

"We did notice earlier." Ian spread his hands lamely. "We just . . . didn't do anything about it until it was too late."

"But why?" Jim shook his head. "Were we too good or not good enough? Were we unwilling to do what needed to be done?" He glanced quickly over at Faith. "Or were we part of it?"

They were silent. Faith found herself thinking of her mom. Maybe Jim was on to something. Stevens had said that the university took its character from the character of the people who attended it. Maybe her negative feelings toward her mother had helped create this . . . monster. Or, at the very least, maybe they had made her vulnerable.

"I hate my mother," she said aloud. "Maybe that's why I didn't notice earlier. Maybe that's why I didn't do anything. Maybe that made me part of it."

"I hate my ex-wife," Ian admitted.

Nedra licked her lips. "I've wished before that my supervisor would die."

"Enough with the pop psychology," Buckley said. "Even if you're right, what does that mean? What are we going to do? Call up everyone's relatives and invite them over for a big reconciliation and love fest?"

"Of course not," Ian said.

"What, then? We tell everyone to get rid of their hostility and negative emotions? Broadcast tranquil messages and New Age music over the intercoms?"

Ian sighed. "If we could get everyone off campus somehow, that might dissipate the power."

"Even if that was feasible, which it obviously isn't under our present circumstances, it would only work temporarily. As soon as everyone returned, it would start up again."

"Do you have any better suggestions?"

Buckley snorted. "Yeah, we hijack the administrations's computer and transfer everyone to different schools."

Jim shook his head. "That's just stupid."

"Wait," Faith said. An idea was forming in her mind. "Maybe it's not that stupid."

"I was joking," Buckley told her.

"But you're right. This ... thing we're fighting, this creature, the school, it's not a separate entity, it's not some outside organism that's taken over our campus. It *is* the campus. And we're part of it. The makeup of the student body determines its personality."

"I wish that was the case," Ian said. "Ordinarily, I guess, it is. But what we have here is a school whose character remains constant no matter who goes to it. That's why it's turned out this way. It isn't born at the beginning of the semester, doesn't die at the end of the semester, and isn't reborn the next term. It's alive, it's always alive, and we just feed it and help it grow."

The idea shifted in her mind. "So the people who go here don't determine the character of the school. The character of the school determines who goes here."

"I couldn't've put it better myself."

"Then what about a transfusion? Like a blood transfusion, only instead it's a transfusion of new students?"

Ian nodded, understanding. "Yes," he said slowly.

"I don't get it," Nedra said.

"It's like when you have a slummy downtown area, and then you pump some money into it to revitalize it," Faith explained. "Or, no, even better, like Garden Grove or Westminster. White trash communities. Then the Chinese and Vietnamese moved in there, built stores and restaurants and shopping areas, redeveloped the place, and the whole character of the city changed."

"And you're saying we do ... what?"

"Well, obviously, there's nothing we can do. If we'd thought of it earlier, we could have gotten new people— good people—to register, to sign up for classes, to become a part of the university, and tip the balance in our favor." She gestured around the office. "It's too bad, too, because we're here in Admissions. We have all the forms we'd need right here."

"You know," Nedra said, "we were working on instituting an 800-number for registration. I don't know how far they got with it, if it's been tied into the computer yet, but they were trying to cut down on the registration lines. I think it was some kind of AQMD thing, to cut down on traffic or the number of people driving here. The computer was supposed to be able to handle something like two hundred calls a second, like those lines for home-shopping networks, and you were going to be able to register for classes over the phone and pay with a credit card."

"Shit," Buckley said. "Just our luck."

"The computers have probably been taken over anyway, and I'm not even sure it's hooked up. Besides, we can't call out. Even if we could set the whole thing up, we wouldn't be able to tell people about it."

There was a sudden barrage of pounding on the door, and they all backed away, moving instinctively toward the rear of the office.

"They found us," Nedra said.

"Let me in!" More pounding. "It's Faruk!"

Faruk? Faith looked toward Jim, and he nodded.

"It was lying to us," Ian said.

"Make him prove it!" Buckley yelled. But Ian was already at the door and opening it. Faruk stumbled in, battered and bruised, his eyes black, his lips bleeding, his shirt off, his pants torn, but alive. Ian slammed the door shut and locked it behind him.

"What happened?" Jim asked.

"We didn't make it. They were waiting for us. He had the gun, though, and he killed a few of them and we escaped."

"Is Stevens . . . ?" Ian didn't finish the sentence.

"He's taking back the communications system: the phone lines and the mainframe computer. I just came from the computer room. He says it should be ready."

Buckley shook his head admiringly. "Is that guy a mind reader or what?"

Nedra picked up the phone next to her. She held it to her ear, listened, grinned, then nodded excitedly. "It's clear," she said. "There's a dial tone."

Jim pumped a fist into the air. "Yes!"

"Let's do it." Ian said.

3

Yes.

Brant Keeler surveyed the campus from atop the library, and a smile spread slowly across his face. Everything was proceeding right on schedule. From this vantage point he could see a group of young women on the walkway between the library and Neilson Hall fighting with senior citizens from the Gerontology Center. The old people were screaming in fear and pain, trying ineffectually to run away as the young women kicked their canes, grabbed their walkers, and beat them. One of the women punched an old lady in the stomach, then grabbed the wig off her bald head. Another kneed an old man in the groin and kicked his head as he went down.

Brant laughed.

He looked to his right. On the other side of the library, the members of the football team were gang-raping a blind freshman. She had stopped screaming and fighting some time ago and was now draped limply over a bench, unmoving, as one of the linebackers assaulted her. Farther back, by the bookstore, one of the campus's Christian clubs was burning books—and bookstore clerks—in a huge bonfire.

Yes.

Brant nodded to himself. Once they finished here, once they whipped the campus into shape, once the University had graduated to Its next level, they could start moving out into the rest of the city.

And beyond.

Beneath his feet he felt the comfortable pulsing of power, that familiar rhythmic vibration he had grown to love as his own.

A shudder passed through the campus, a smooth, fluid movement that rippled over the quad, moving sidewalks, moving earth.

"O Captain, my captain!"

Brant looked down the side of the library to see John Taylor staring up at him. He adjusted the holster on his hip, shifted the machete from his right hand to his left. Putting his right hand on the low-walled ledge at the edge of the roof, he leaned forward. "Yes?" he called.

"We found him!"

"Him?"

"Yes!"

The pulsing grew stronger, and Brant felt a delicious tremor pass through him from the roof beneath his feet. Their work here was almost done.

"Where is he now?" he called.

"We're bringing him out! He killed five of us!"

"Take him to the artists! I'll meet you there!"

Taylor nodded, saluted, and Brant hurried across the top of the library to the roof-access stairwell that led back into the building. He sped down the stairs, past the floors, until he reached ground level, sprinting across the lobby and through the front doors. Once outside, he saw a group of teachers and students dragging a roped and whipped man through the center of the quad.

It was him. The infidel. The walking piece of shit they'd all been warned about. The one who was trying to disrupt the plans of the University and impose his own will on the will of the school.

Well, that was all over now.

A crowd was gathering, lining both sides of the sidewalk down which the infidel was being led. Students spat on him as he passed by, faculty members flung objects at his head. He screamed back at them as they assaulted him, nonsense about how they were all evil, how they were all robotic pawns of the University with no minds or will of their own.

Brant laughed as he strode across the quad.

How naive could you get?

He reached the man just as they were leading him down the foot of the artists' walkway. "Stop!" he ordered.

The captors halted, pulling tight ropes, swinging the infidel around until he faced Brant.

"You are—" the man started to scream.

Brant punched him in the stomach.

The man doubled over—or tried to—gasping for air, and Brant grinned. "It's so nice of you to join us, Gifford." He leaned forward until his face was next to the infidel's. "You *have* joined us, you know. You're part of the University."

"Never!" Stevens managed to croak.

"Oh, yes. You joined us when you killed your wife."

"I didn't—"

"You're right. Technically you didn't kill her. But you brought her to the University as a sacrifice and allowed her to die."

The infidel spat, but he still had not fully regained his breath and the attempt was weak, hitting Brant's shoe instead of his face.

"Which makes you a traitor instead of an enemy," Brant continued. He scowled. "Traitors are so much worse than enemies."

He saw fear in Stevens' eyes, a nervous twitch in the beard-covered mouth.

Brant smiled. "Yes, you're going to die. And you're going to die a slow, painful, humiliating death. The death you deserve." He nodded at the men holding the ropes. "Bring him!"

Brant led the way to the Visual Arts building. The artists were behind a table in front of the entrance, working on the head of Dean Jensen, using their tools and glue and paint to transform it into the head of Groucho Marx.

"We need social relevance," Vance was saying. "Not this post-modernist pop shit!"

"We're making a fucking statement about art in contemporary society!" Godwin screamed. "A serious statement! A big statement! We're not going to play around with your simplistic polemics!"

"Boys," Brant said. "Boys, boys, boys."

Vance, Godwin, and the other art students stopped arguing, stopped talking and stood at attention as Brant walked toward them.

"We have a new acquisition for you." He gestured toward the infidel. "Think you can use it for your project?"

Godwin walked out from behind the table, putting on his glasses. He squinted as he examined the captive man's face.

"Your time is over!" Stevens screamed. "You may kill me, but you will still lose!"

Godwin walked slowly around the man, ducking under the ropes. He nodded at Brant. "Yes," he said. "We can use it."

Brant grinned. "Off with his head."

The other artists moved out from behind the table, their razors and knives and chisels glinting orangely, reflecting the fading glow of the afternoon sun.

"You can kill me!" Stevens screamed. "But you cannot stop me! We are—"

Vance sliced open his neck.

The infidel's screams became a gurgling rasp as blood bubbled out from the hole in the neck. The other artists began working on his body as he struggled, making incisions, cutting off pieces.

Brant stared into Stevens' eyes, a warm contentment washing over him. Beneath his feet he felt a ripple of power.

"But is it the right material?" Vance asked. "Is it good enough quality? What kind of shape is it in?"

Godwin lovingly touched Stevens' bleeding neck. "Pristine," he said, grinning. "Like a virgin."

Brant waited until the head was removed from the body and placed on the table before walking, whistling, back to the library.

4

Jim wanted to call his mother, Faruk his father, Nedra her boyfriend, but the way Ian figured it, they didn't have time to waste. Stevens might have secured the communications system for the moment—although God knew how—but it might not last, and they couldn't afford to waste time explaining that the phone call was real, not a joke, not a prank.

Eleanor knew already what the situation was here, and he immediately dialed her at work. She answered on the third ring.

"Eleanor—!" he began.

She hung up on him.

Fuck! He cursed himself for having let this happen, for not having had the sense to confront and address the problems between them. It was his fault to begin with

for having treated her like a child who needed protection
rather than like a partner, an adult woman—

But there was no time for recriminations or second-
guessing. He quickly dialed the number again, and this
time his call went into her voice mail. Perfect! He could
talk and she wouldn't hang up. Now if she would just
listen to the message . . .

He talked quickly, explaining the situation, telling her
where they were and what had happened. Nedra slid a
piece of paper with the 800 registration number on it,
and he told her to call the number and enroll as a full-
time student and charge it to her Visa.

"I have a lot of friends in Arizona," Jim whispered.
"I can get them to register." He wrote a number down
on a slip of paper. "In case we can't get through, have
her call my mom and tell her what's happening."

"And call the police," Faith suggested. "And community leaders." She wrote a number down. "And my
brother."

The call was well over five minutes long, but the voice
mail did not cut him off and the line remained up.

Nedra called her boyfriend immediately afterward, but
he was not home, and she told him to call her at work
as soon as he got back.

The second she hung up, the phone rang. It was Eleanor, and Nedra handed the receiver to Ian.

"I'm sorry," she said. She was crying. "I love you."

"I love you too. But call in and register. Then call me
back and tell me if it works."

"Okay," she said. Already her crying was abating as
duty took over. "Give me five minutes."

It was the longest five minutes of his life. He kept
wanting to pick up the phone and make sure there was
still a dial tone, make sure that insane laughter had not
started up again, but he did not want the line to be busy
when Eleanor called, and he refrained from temptation.

Five minutes later, exactly, she called again. "It
works," she announced. "I'm registered for twenty-one
units."

"Thank God."

"I'll call these other numbers. I know they're family
members and things, but, Ian?"

"Yeah?"

"There's something else I can try."

"What?"

"It's illegal. And it's unethical."

"Who gives a damn? What is it?"

"This automatic registration system: you can register by phone, but you don't have to. You can register by computer."

"Oh." He understood where she was going.

"I can access the mainframe here at work. There are literally tens of thousands of people on file. I can do a quick and dirty interface program and sign them all up and charge it to their credit cards."

"Do it!"

"Before or after I call police and community leaders?" she said dryly.

"It's a temporary measure. You can correct it after the fact, after it's all over. They'll understand."

"It's going to take me a few hours. Should I make your calls first, get the ball rolling?"

"We'll do that from here."

"I'll get to work, then."

"Thanks," Ian said. "I really do love you."

"If it's any consolation, we wouldn't be able to do this if I was there with you. So I suppose everything worked out for the best."

"Let's hope our luck holds out."

He hung up and explained the plan to the others.

"What if it recruits the wrong people?" Jim asked.

"What choice do we have?"

Faith licked her lips. "Maybe she shouldn't call my brother. I don't know if he's . . . good or bad."

"Good or bad." Ian shook his head. "It's depressing how simplistic this shit always turns out to be. No matter what kind of bells and whistles there are, in the end it always boils down to 'good and bad.' " He looked at her. "What do you really think?"

She looked at him. "Have her call him. I believe in him."

"The phone's free. You can call him yourself."

"But what's this going to do?" Buckley asked. "Really? You think you'll pull this stunt and everything'll automatically be put back to rights?"

"It might weaken it enough to give us some leeway."

"And then?"

"And then we get Stevens' explosives and blow this fucker away."

Eleanor called for the last time just before six, saying that the 800 number was still in service and she was ready to implement her interface program. "I'm going to try something else," she said. "I'm not sure if it'll make any difference, but I've accessed the records from California Christian College. I'm going to transfer all of their students to Brea."

"Brilliant!" Ian said.

"I figure there might be a higher percentage of uncorruptables there than in the general population."

"You're amazing."

"That's what I've been trying to tell you all along. The only thing is, this is all going to happen at once. I know you have other people signing up, but that's just a handful. When I run this program, Brea's student population is going to double. California Christian has ten thousand students. I'll be registering another six thousand credit card holders. If you're right, that'll probably tip the balance in your favor. No matter how strong that school is, it won't be able to maintain its equilibrium under an onslaught like that. But, Ian?"

"Yeah?"

"You should probably act fast. I don't know what's happening there, but it might be able to adjust or adapt. If this works at all, it'll be weakest right after I finish the registration, before it has a chance to absorb all of the new registrants."

"Can't you keep pumping them in?"

"I'll try, but it'll probably catch on and shut me down after that first wave. I suggest you get the hell out of there now."

He looked up at the clock. "Make it five minutes. Six o'clock exactly."

"Will do."

The phone went dead after that, and Ian was not sure if that meant that the computers and the 800 number were down too, but he hoped for the best and told them all to get ready, it was time to venture forth.

There'd been no sign of Stevens, no communication

from him, and they were not sure if he was alive or dead. As long as the phone was up, Ian had assumed that all was well and he was busily doing whatever it was that he needed to do, though he was well aware that Stevens could have merely switched a few wires several hours ago, started back for the office, and been killed along the way while the phone system continued to function automatically. With the death of the phone, however, what little hope he'd had faded away, and he became convinced that Stevens had been murdered.

He said nothing to the others, however, and continued to act as though everything was running smoothly and their plan was proceeding as intended.

He .opened the door at precisely six o'clock.

The hallway was silent. And empty. Moving slowly, ready to rush back instantly to the safety of the office should anything attack, they walked into the building's lobby. Here the scene was not quite so placid. Chairs, tables, and potted plants had been overturned, thrown through windows, thrown over counters. Paper, dirt, and dead leaves littered the floor. On the stairs leading up to the second story, the body of a secretary lay nude and spread-eagled, her wide eyes white against the deep redness of the drying blood on her face, the stump of a severed arm protruding from her distended vagina.

"Maybe we should go back," Nedra suggested.

"Whatever happened here already happened," Ian said. "It's over. I'm hoping it's the same outside. If everything went off right, there's a lull now, the school's stunned. This is when we need to strike." He turned toward Faruk. "We should find Stevens first. Where is he?"

"The computer room in the second basement of the Physical Sciences building."

"We'll go there first."

They walked outside.

The entire landscape of the school had changed.

It was night out, the sun had set more than an hour ago, but every light on campus had been turned on. All of the windows in all of the buildings were brightly illuminated, and the quad and the walkways were lined with lamps turned to full power. Only the walkways now went in different directions. The one that had led from Ad-

386   **Bentley Little**

ministration to Biological Sciences now sloped over a
hill that had somehow been created during the afternoon. The one leading to Neilson Hall now descended
into what looked like a train tunnel in the center of the
lawn. In the buildings, shadows flitted past the windows,
black against the light, strange shapes that were half seen
and impossible to recognize. On a bench across the
stretch of concrete in front of them, a bench that had
been refashioned to look like a throne, sat a man covered from head to toe with crawling insects. They could
not see his features, but every so often his body would
jerk spasmodically and he would let out a low-muffled
moan.

"How come we didn't feel any of this?" Buckley wondered, looking at the hill. "You'd think we would've
heard some noises or felt some vibrations or something."

"I don't know," Ian admitted. "But I don't like it."

"Was all this here when you left?" Jim asked Faruk.

"Sort of," Faruk said. "But it's changed."

The one thing that hadn't changed was the standoff
between the fraternities and the police around the perimeter of the campus. They could see the situation
clearly from this angle. There were more police now,
they'd brought searchlights of seemingly every shape and
size and there were two helicopters flying noisily overhead, but the fraternities were holding their own, and
what appeared to be the body of a policeman was hanging head-down from the flagpole in front of the school.

Elsewhere, however, the campus appeared to be deserted. The warring groups they'd seen earlier, the wild
crowds, were all gone.

They moved forward cautiously, following Ian's lead.

He walked slowly, acutely conscious of the fact that
he was responsible for the group of individuals behind
him. With Stevens missing, he was the de facto leader,
and it was a position he did not like one bit.

Beneath his feet the ground seemed to pulse, a rhythmic thumping that reminded him of the beating of a
heart. He was not sure if the others had noticed it or
not, but he didn't want to ask.

They walked deeper into the campus.

Despite the lights, it seemed darker here, and when

he breathed, the air seemed harsh, burning, as though filled with petrochemicals.

Here there were people. Atop Neilson Hall a large group of students and instructors were holding what a computer-generated banner strung across the ninth floor referred to as "The First Annual Dwarf-Tossing Contest."

"Free! Fun! Free!" the sign proclaimed.

Ian looked up at the top of the building. He heard cheers and shouts, then a scream, as a midget was thrown over the side of the building to the concrete below.

The cement was already littered with five or six bloody, crumpled, broken bodies that had been thrown from the rooftop.

The midget hit the ground, broke open, and splattered, and a huge cheer went up.

"What's next?" someone screamed.

"Spic tossing!"

"No, niggers!"

Ian turned away. There were other people in the quad and on the steps of the buildings, but they seemed quiet, subdued, almost sedated. Many of them were sitting down, and those that weren't seemed loath to move. His spirit rose. It had worked! Eleanor had gotten through, and their guess had been right and it had worked.

Then he saw it.

Stevens' head.

He suddenly felt as though he'd been punched in the stomach.

It was speared on a brass spike, and it was one of a series of impaled heads that lined a new walkway leading toward the Visual Arts building. The heads had all been decorated, adorned with hats and hair, defaced with sculpted additions, made to look like media icons. There was Hitler and Groucho Marx and Michael Jackson and Ronald Reagan. Stevens' head had been altered to resemble Madonna, his beard shaved, his hair scalped and replaced with a blond wig, his nose broken and remade, a gap cut into his upper teeth, his lips sliced off and replaced with thicker, redder lips that had been glued into place and formed into an irregular smile that very nearly resembled a grimace. The illusion was close to perfect, marred only by the dead eyes and the dried trickles of blood that ran irregularly down the face from beneath the hairline of the wig and from the nostrils.

The frightening thing was that Ian understood what the artist was trying to say here. He comprehended the metaphoric meaning of this walkway of heads. The materials that had been used were abhorrent, sickening, unforgivable, but the result was Art, with a capital A, and something about the paradox was profoundly disturbing.

"What did they do with his body?" Buckley asked quietly.

"I don't know," Ian answered, and he was surprised to hear that his voice was clear, steady, totally unlike the way he felt.

He found himself focusing all of his attention on Stevens' desecrated face, mentally trying to reconstruct the true features of the man, as though concentrating on this, to the exclusion of everything else, would somehow grant him a reprieve from all that was happening around him and give him the time he so desperately needed in order to think clearly and sort everything out.

"What do we do now?" Faith asked.

I don't know! he wanted to say. *HE knew! But now he's dead and we're all screwed*! But he forced himself to look away from the head and took a deep breath. "We do exactly what we planned to do." He glanced over at Faruk. "Do you know which car's his?"

Faruk shook his head. "No. But it's a van, and I know the area that it's parked in. I assume it's stacked with boxes. It shouldn't be hard to find."

"We go there, then."

"But the guards—"

"Shit!" He mentally kicked himself. He was rattled, not thinking clearly. If he didn't straighten up and fly right, his muddleheadedness might end up getting them all killed. He hadn't realized until now how much he'd been relying on Stevens to steer them out of this.

"I don't know if this means anything," Faruk said, "but he told me that if something happened to him, I was to tell you that the library's the brain."

"What?"

"He said, 'The library's the brain.' Whatever that means."

Ian looked at Jim. "Kill the brain and the body will die."

Buckley snorted. "So much for there not being any specific organs." He laughed harshly. "Why don't we lop off its cock? Castrate the fucker."

"Shut up," Ian said. "We have something here." He looked around at the others. "It won't be easy, but I think we have a fighting chance. We may be able to bring this university down."

"We should have guessed it," Faith said. "When I was researching the history of this place, a large percentage of the rapes and attacks happened in the library. And the place is full of evil collections. Child pornography. Serial killer letters. Nazi stuff. Satanic cult memorabilia. Even during the good years, the years where not very much happened, the library was still gathering all this, collecting it, storing it." She paused. "And you can feel it there. The power. I didn't like the place the first time I set foot in there."

"The sixth floor," Faruk said.

She nodded excitedly. "Yes!"

"And it's in the exact center of the campus," Nedra said.

"We go to my office." Ian suddenly felt stronger, excited, filled with adrenaline, his hope returned. "We get the explosives and we . . ." He trailed off, squinting. A figure was running toward them from the dark-hearted center of the quad, a black, blurred shape that probably would have blended into the background of foliage had it not been traveling so incredibly fast. Behind it, two white forms that looked like ghosts were fluttering in pursuit.

All three figures passed into the illuminated area directly in front of them, and Ian saw what looked like two lab-coated professors chasing a hairy, brutish creature that resembled a cross between a caveman and a bear. The creature screamed, a high, wild cry of raw animal anger.

"What—" Jim began.

And then it was upon them. They scattered, yelling, trying to move out of its way, but with one swiftly coordinated motion it grabbed Nedra and ran, carrying her under one oversize arm as though she weighed nothing.

She was screaming and it was screaming as it ran toward that huge hole in the ground, using its free arm to push along the broken cement and assist in locomotion.

"Nedra!" Faith cried.

Ian was too shocked, too slow to react, but Jim and Faruk both took off after the monster, running as fast as they could.

The two professors followed close behind, one writing furiously on his clipboard, the other talking into a portable tape recorder.

"He's not only atypically aggressive when threatened, but when unprovoked and in the presence of a menstruating female, his response is exactly the same," the writer said excitedly.

"If he is indeed, as expected, following a genetically determined pattern of behavior," the other one said into his microphone, "his next act will be to remove and eat the eyes of the victim before—"

Buckley punched the man in the stomach as he ran by.

The professor doubled instantly over, falling flat on the ground, his tape recorder flying. The other man kept on running, oblivious.

"What. The. Fuck. Are. You. Doing?" Buckley demanded through gritted teeth.

The man ignored him, still talking to a tape recorder that was no longer there. He scrambled along the ground, stood, and hurried after his colleague.

Buckley looked at Ian. His face was white, strained.

Jim and Faruk returned, out of breath but still running. Their faces, too, were white with shock, and Ian did not want to know what they had seen. "Let's go," he announced before they could say a word. "We need to get the blueprints and my explosives. We need to take out the library."

"What if it's not really the brain?" Faith asked. "What if we're wrong?"

"Then hopefully it'll cause enough of a disturbance that the fraternities will scatter and the police'll come in. The school's weakened already. Maybe this'll push it over the edge."

"What if the fraternities don't budge?"

"The police will come in anyway. They'll have to, with an explosion like that. There may be some shooting, but they'll get here. And once they see what's going on, this place'll be swarming with law enforcement."

"What if that doesn't happen? What if it doesn't work?"

"We'll cross that bridge when we come to it," he said.

5

It was like a nightmare, Jim thought, only it was less scary. The horror was there, and the surrealism, but things were moving too fast, there was no time for thought or reflection, no chance to really absorb what was happening, and the emotional luxury of being frightened simply wasn't available. Friends were here, then they were gone, monsters appeared, disappeared, and no matter what happened they had to keep going, they had to move on.

This is what it's like in battle, he thought, in a war.

They'd probably all suffer from post-traumatic stress syndrome when it was all over.

If they lived.

If it ended.

It was easier than he expected to return to Ian's office. They passed a toga-clad student viciously throwing textbooks at the prone bodies of two dead professors, but they ignored the student and the student ignored them, and they continued on. The other people they passed were leaning against tree trunks or sitting on the ground, tired and dazed, and the five of them quickly reached the steps of Neilson Hall, where the same girl was sitting in the same spot in which they'd left her. She was naked now, and she spread her bruised legs and grinned slyly up at them as they passed, but they ignored her and walked inside.

They took the stairs up, seeing no one along the way, seeing no metamorphic changes to the stairwell.

The fifth floor was a different story. Grass grew here now, out of the tile, and the walls were bent out of shape to an unrecognizable degree, looking not angular and Expressionistic but soft, rounded, rubbery. The entire ceiling glowed, giving off a cold white light.

In some spots the walls had grown over the doors of offices, spongy protuberances sealing over entrances, but though Ian's doorway was partially blocked, it was accessible, and Jim and Ian crawled inside to get the blueprints and explosives. They placed the blueprints on top of the explosives box and pushed everything back out onto the grass of the corridor.

The amplified sound of breathing echoed through the building, and rhythmic bursts of harsh chemical air were sucked simultaneously in and out of the air-conditioning ducts, but they purposely ignored the show the school was putting on for them as Ian spread out the plans of the building.

The glowing ceiling faded, throwing the corridor into total darkness.

Beneath the breathing, mixed far down on the sound scale, there was giggling.

"Wait a sec," Ian said.

Jim heard him going back into the office, and a moment later the beam of a flashlight shone through the obstructed doorway.

"Earthquake kit," Ian explained. "It pays to be prepared."

The locations within the library that Stevens had marked as points at which the explosives were to be planted were all easily accessible. There was a basement in the building, but the stress points were all on the first and third floors.

"Who's going to set them?" Faith asked.

"I will," Jim said.

"No." Faith shook her head.

"Who, then?" He motioned toward Buckley and Ian. "I'm younger than those two and, no offense, Faruk, but I'm in better shape than you. I'm probably the fastest runner here. In case I need to get out quickly, I can handle it."

"I'll do it," Ian said.

Jim picked up the box. "No you won't. Now, let's go. We're wasting time. It's probably heard every word we said and is sealing off the library right now." He started walking.

"You can't go in there alone," Ian said. "Something might happen to you. This is too important. We need a backup. I'm going too."

"What about the rest of us?" Buckley asked.

"Wait for us in the quad. Stay out of the open, in the trees, but get as far away from the library as possible. Stay near Social Sciences."

"I'm going with you," Faith announced.

Jim looked at her. "I don't want—"

"There's safety in numbers."

"I'm going too," Buckley said.

Faruk cleared his throat. "I'm not staying out there by myself."

"Then let's hit it. We knocked the fucker out with that registration trick, but I don't know how long it's going to hold. We probably don't have that much time."

They hurried down the hall and down the stairs.

The quad was still quiet and virtually empty, what few students remained wandering dazedly about, and the five of them faced no obstacles as they ran across the concrete walkway to the library.

"Stay close together," Ian ordered.

They pushed the doors open, walked inside.

The interior of the library was hot, hellishly so, and the air was moist and heavy. The walls were wet, as was the floor, and water dripped from the ceiling. The catalog terminals were on and going crazy, strange shapes and unknown characters flickering rapid-fire across the screens. There was no noise here, no sound, and even their own voices seemed muffled, tinny, one-dimensional, as though they were coming from a cheap television speaker.

The box was getting heavy, and Jim shifted it in his arms.

There were students here, at the tables, in the study carrels against the far wall, but they seemed frozen, caught between moments. One nude young woman knelt before a dead man, holding a paintbrush dipped into his open body cavity. On the floor beside her was a partially completed blood painting. Several old men knelt before a poster of Adolf Hitler, right hands upraised in a Nazi salute.

If the library really was the brain of the university, Jim had thought, it would still be active. If any place on campus remained unaffected by the registration of new students, he figured it would be the library, and he'd prepared himself for the worst, expecting they'd have to fight their way through the building. But this area seemed to be even more drained of power than the campus outside. He didn't entirely believe it, but he was grateful for it.

"Third floor," he said.

Faith nodded. "We'll take the stairs." She led the way to a side door, and they walked up slippery steps coated with a pink material that was simultaneously slimy and fuzzy and that stuck to their shoes.

"What is this shit?" Buckley said.

"Come," Faith said.

Buckley roared with laughter, a response entirely out of proportion to the effectiveness of the joke, and in a second they were all laughing. It hadn't been that funny, but they'd been more tense than they'd all realized, and the release felt good. They continued up the steps moving much more quickly.

They stopped cold in the third-floor doorway.

There was nothing left of the library on the third floor. It did indeed look like the inside of a brain, and the pink fuzzy slimy material that coated the stairs covered everything here. Where there had once been chairs and tables and desks and shelves, there were now wormy twists of pink tube the circumference of culvert pipes that wound from pink floor to pink ceiling and intertwined with one another in between. The walls, the floor, the tubes, the ceiling, everything pulsed rhythmically.

"Where do we put the explosives?" Jim asked. "I don't recognize anything from the blueprint."

SHOVE THEM UP YOUR ASS.

He looked around wildly. The voice had been in his head, but it had been so loud and powerful that the others had to have heard it.

They had.

Faith was holding her head, Buckley was squinting, Faruk and Ian were glancing furtively around.

"It's waking up," Ian said. "We have to move quick."

"But where do we put it?"

Faith moved next to Ian. "Let me see the plans."

He spread out the sheet of paper with the library's third floor, and pointed at the wall and pillar at which the explosives were to be set. Faith glanced around the metamorphosed floor. "There," she said. She pointed straight ahead.

"Where?"

"See that space between those two tubes? That sort of bump beyond it? That's where that pillar was. The wall"—she looked again at the plans—"that's about twenty feet to the left of the bump."

"It's too small for all of us," Jim said. "I'm going in."

"Fine by me." Buckley's voice was unusually subdued.

"Use the mines," Ian said. "They're faster. We'll use the explosives on the first floor."

"Gotcha." Jim put down the box and removed the two heavy metal mines.

"Anything happens, yell," Ian said. "I'll come after you."

YOU WON'T MAKE IT.

"The fuck 1 won't," Jim said aloud. He started forward. He was much more frightened than he let on, and what he really wanted to do was turn tail and run, but he forced himself to walk across the wet, squishy floor. The pulsing was coming faster now, as though it was a heartbeat that had suddenly started racing, and he crawled between the two tubes that Faith had identified and placed the mine on top of the rounded hump. He hoped Faith was right.

He walked to his left, through a tangle of smaller tubes that squirmed against his face as he pushed his way through them. He reached a pink, fleshy wall, and though he wasn't sure if this was the wall indicated on Stevens' plans as the other stress point on this floor, he dropped the mine and hurried back.

I'LL KILL YOU ALL.

"Then why haven't you done it already, you impotent cocksucker?"

Jim followed the sound of Buckley's voice and reached the stairwell door in less than a minute.

He picked up the box, hefted it, and though the stairs were slippery, they took the steps two at a time until they reached the first floor.

The people here had moved. They were still, not currently in motion, but the painter's brush was now out of the body cavity and in the middle of a stroke on the floor. The Nazis were now standing.

"Where here?" Jim demanded.

Ian pointed to the left. "That study area and the women's rest room."

"You guys go out. I'll finish it." He grabbed the blueprints from Ian, shoved them in the box.

"We—" Faith began.

"Go!"

He did not look to see if they had heeded his command but sprinted across the floor to the study area. Here racist epithets had been scrawled in colored chalk on the rear wall, chairs and tables had all been piled in the center of the room, and that same throat-scorching chemical that he'd smelled in Neilson Hall was being inhaled and exhaled through the air-conditioning ducts. Jim ignored all of it and strode directly to the pillar on the right side of the room.

He put down the box and quickly spread the materials out before him. The components were ready to go and needed only to be connected in order to create what Stevens had referred to as a "prefab bomb."

Stevens had made the procedure so simple that even a moron could do it, and he had drilled the steps into all of their heads so often this morning that each of them could probably do it blindfolded.

Had it only been this morning?

It seemed so much longer than that.

Jim packed the malleable clay-like explosive against the base of the pillar, inserted the two wire ends, spooled out the wire, and clamped on the small black timer.

He ran out of the study area and repeated the procedure in the middle of the floor of the women's rest room.

He hoped Stevens had been right about the placement.

He left the box behind, grabbing only the tools—flashlight, vicegrips, screwdriver—and quickly ran out the door.

The second he emerged from the rest room, everything suddenly came to life. The students started moving, orders were shouted over the library's ceiling speakers: "KILL! KILL! KILL! KILL!"

All heads turned toward him.

"Shit!"

He ran across the lobby, dodging the arms that reached out to grab him, knocking over an old lady who whirled on him and started screeching. Luckily, the people still seemed to be stunned, not moving as quickly or clearly as they ordinarily would, and he was almost to the door before a skinny guy approximately his own age, draped in gun belts and wielding a machete, stepped out from behind a pillar to block his way.

"Not so fast," the young man said, grinning.

Jim glanced quickly to the left and to the right, at the other doors, but he realized instantly that there was no way he could get to them without passing this psycho.

"Psycho?" the young man said, raising an eyebrow. "I'm no psycho. I'm just a friend of the library." His grin became wider. "Name's Brant."

Jim started at the name. "Brant Keeler?"

"The one and only."

Oh, God, Jim thought.

"Yes," Brant said. "Oh, God."

The fucker could read his mind!

"No shit, Sherlock."

Jim looked at the other student. "Then you know this building's going to blow in about two minutes."

Brant smiled. "Death is not the end."

"It'll be the end of you."

"No, it won't. I'll be one with the University." His smile became almost beatific. "It's all I've ever wanted."

Jim dropped the flashlight and the vice grips and held tightly onto the screwdriver, holding it outward like a knife. There was no time to fuck around here, no time to face off and trade witticisms.

Brant laughed, waved the machete in front of him. "Mine's bigger," he teased.

Jim rushed him.

The decision was made and acted upon at the same instant, and apparently whatever

the university

was translating for Brant could not communicate with him that quickly. The attack took the other student completely by surprise.

Jim intended to slide past Brant, hitting the slippery floor as though he was playing baseball and sliding into home, and speed under the swinging machete and into the doorway, but he was afraid that Brant would know his plan if he thought about it, so he imagined and concentrated upon a different scenario, one in which he leaped on Brant and stabbed him in the eye with the screwdriver.

All of this went through his mind in the three seconds that it took him to cross the floor between them, and though he dared not think about it directly, dared not concentrate on it, Jim prayed that his mental misdirection would fool the other student long enough to allow him to escape.

He feinted, raised his arm, pretended as though he was going to aim high, then slid, feet first, under Brant's swinging arm, feeling but not hearing the slash of the machete through the air above his head. He thrust the screwdriver hard into Brant's leg, heard him scream, heard him fall, but kept moving, not looking back, scrambling to his feet, pushing open the door and running out.

He'd made it! He jumped off the front steps and hauled ass toward the center of the quad, catching up with the others in front of what looked like a dead rat the size of a German shepherd.

He looked over his shoulder, breathing hard, but neither Brant nor any of his other pursuers had left the library. He could not see Brant, who was probably still writhing on the floor, but he could see the others, pressed against the dark glass windows and doors, mouths open, screaming, and they were making no effort to follow him outside.

"Did you do it?" Faith asked.

"Yes," he said, and he realized that he felt good about it. Not good because he was being noble and this was the right thing to do, but good because he was excited, because he wanted to hear the explosions, because he wanted to see the fire.

He hoped that *all* of the psychos in the library would all be killed in the explosion.

He pushed that thought out of his mind.

Behind Faith, in the darkness, he saw movement, heard sound, but before he could say anything they were surrounded by a group of eight or nine professors who emerged as one from behind the trees and foliage. All were dressed identically in strangely designed black robes. He recognized Dr. Yanks, his old philosophy professor, and Dr. Hickman, the communications department's Comm Law instructor.

"The faculty council," Faruk whispered in his ear.

"What the fuck do you think you're doing?" Dr. Yanks demanded. He was addressing Ian, but it was Buckley who answered.

"Exactly the same thing you'd be doing if you weren't a traitorous piece of fascist dogshit."

"I wasn't talking to you, you fucking commie."

"Exactly the same thing you'd be doing if you weren't a traitorous piece of fascist dogshit," Ian said.

As if on cue, the members of the faculty council each folded their arms identically over their chest.

"You're part of this university too," Yanks said. "You'll only be hurting yourself."

"Eat shit and die," Buckley told him.

Yanks whirled on him. "I'm not *talking* to you."

Buckley shoved him. "But I'm talking to you."

All lights winked off as the first explosion hit. The ground-floor windows of the library blew outward, sparkling shards of glass flying out in front of a bright orange fire cloud. Throughout the campus, simultaneously, the lights in all of the other buildings, as well as the lamps lining the walkways, went out. There was a tremor in the earth, a jolt, and the deafening sound of an impossibly loud scream, the anguished cry of a wounded beast, issuing from the library, from Neilson Hall, from the Physical and Biological Sciences buildings, from that huge hole in the ground, and coalescing into one mighty roar.

Jim felt a weird spasm of pain in his chest as the explosives went off, and the pain spiraled upward in intensity as the mines on the third floor exploded and the building began collapsing in on itself.

They were still too close, the flying debris was probably going to bury them, and he grabbed Faith and pulled her deeper into the quad, away from the library, trying to ignore the pain in his chest. Faith, too, was holding her chest, and Faruk, Ian, and Buckley, limping after them, also seemed to be in serious pain, their faces contorted by grimaces. The black-robed faculty council had fallen to the ground, screaming, their high-pitched cries sounding in harmony with that deeper, louder roar.

All of them *were* part of the school, Jim realized, as much as they wanted to deny that they were not, as independent and autonomous as they believed themselves to be. The faculty council was right. By hurting the university, they were hurting themselves.

So what was going to happen if they succeeded in killing the school?

The pain in his chest twisted hard, causing him to stop running and cry out, his muscles feeling as though they were going to tear, and then the pressure suddenly lessened. The cry of the university faded, the sound of that monstrous scream metamorphosing into the sound of metal, glass, and concrete smashing onto the ground.

The pain in his chest continued to subside in intensity. He felt short of breath, and he breathed in as deeply as he dared. He glanced toward Ian. The professor was looking back at the fallen faculty council members.

"Let's get away from here," Ian said. He started walking toward the front of the school. Buckley and Faruk, moving slowly, trailed after him. Jim squeezed Faith's hand and the two of them followed.

Around them, in front of them, people were screaming, but the screams sounded refreshingly normal, the ordinary sounds of panic and terror, and the cries were welcome to Jim's ears. The air of alien unreality that had existed since they'd emerged from the English department conference room at noon had been rent, the spell shattered, and while everything was still confused and chaotic and crazy, it was now recognizably so.

Was it over?

Faruk stopped, looked back at the burning ruin that had been the library, and whistled. "Wow," he said. "That Stevens really knew his stuff."

Jim nodded.

"Is that it?" Buckley asked.

Ian shook his head grimly. "Now we find the van, get the rest of the explosives, and take out the other buildings."

They were silent for a moment, looking at one another.

"What'll happen when they all go?" Buckley asked. "I assume you felt the same thing I did." He patted his chest.

Ian nodded.

"Those peckerheads were right. We hurt it and we felt it. So what happens if we put a stop to it? If it dies, do we die? After all, cells can't continue to live after an organism's dead."

"I don't know," Ian admitted.

Faith was looking toward the street. "Maybe it is over," she said. "Maybe we don't have to do anything."

"What?"

She pointed.

Jim followed her finger, blinked. He swallowed thickly, and suddenly there were tears in his eyes. He didn't know why, he didn't know how, but the tears were there and there were too many of them to blink away. He wiped his eyes with the back of a finger. He looked toward Ian, and the professor looked like he was about to cry too.

"Maybe it's over," Faith repeated.

Ian nodded slowly. "Maybe you're right."

6

It was a miracle.

Faith watched as what looked like a platoon of police cars and National Guard vehicles rolled over the curb and onto the campus, a parade of firetrucks following behind. In back of the vehicles, on the sidewalk, and in the street, uniformed officers, National Guardsmen and other law enforcement officials, nearly all of them wearing riot gear, were subduing suddenly unarmed fraternity members and handcuffing them.

And following the cops came the cavalry.

Civilians, seemingly hundreds of them, swarmed onto the campus from Thomas Avenue. The people who'd registered for classes. The transfusion that had turned the tide. It was so dark and there were so many people that it was nearly impossible to pick out individual faces, but she thought she recognized Bill from the burger stand and the attendant from the Texaco station near the school. Several other business-suited men looked almost familiar, and she thought they were probably community leaders whose faces she'd seen in the newspaper.

Then a truly familiar face detached itself from the crowd.

Keith.

Her brother came running toward her, and for once the expression on his face was not one of hip apathy but of genuine relief. He stopped in front of her, smiled, and then she moved forward and threw her arms around him and hugged him. He was stiff at first, obviously not expecting the hug, but then he loosened and put his own arms around her, squeezing her back.

"Thank God you're safe," he said.

She hugged him tighter.

There was another jolt, another shifting in the earth, but it felt more like a settling than a disturbance, and there was something wonderfully final about it.

"I guess you're right," Keith said. "I guess this isn't a party school."

She laughed. She laughed so hard that tears came to her eyes. And then she was crying and her brother was holding her. Another pair of hands touched her shoulders, and then her brother moved away and Jim had his arms around her.

She took a deep breath, wiped her eyes. An attractive middle-aged woman was talking to Ian, and she assumed that this was the famous Eleanor, the one who had brought all these people together. She approached the woman, hand outstretched. "Thank you," she said.

Eleanor took the hand, shook it, smiling slightly. "I'm probably no longer employed, but you're welcome."

"Are you kidding?" Keith said. "You're a hero." He looked at Faith. "She was all over the news. She's the one who got everyone here."

Faith looked around admiringly. She saw students being embraced by parents, husbands reunited with wives. "But how did they all get here so fast?"

Eleanor frowned. "Fast? It's been three days."

Faith looked questioningly toward her brother, who nodded.

"No." She shook her head.

"That's not possible," Jim said.

Ian blinked. "It's only been a few hours."

"A few hours?" Eleanor said. "A few hours since what?"

"A few hours since—since it all started. I came to school this morning—"

"Which morning was that?" Eleanor asked.

"Wednesday."

"It's Saturday."

"But the days didn't change," Jim said. "It was morning, then it was afternoon, then it was night..." He looked down at his watch. "My watch still says it's Wednesday, nearly midnight."

"It's eight o'clock. Saturday."

"You've been in the news for three days," Keith said.

Ian shook his head dumbly. "How long has it been since I called you? Since you registered all those people?"

"That was Thursday morning."

"It couldn't be!"

"It was."

They looked at each other.

Buckley nodded sagely. "Elasticity of time," he said. "Read your Gabriel Garcia Márquez."

"Shut up," Ian told him.

"Just trying to show the importance of literature."

"So is that it?" Faith asked. "Are we free to go?" She was disappointed. It all seemed so anticlimactic. It felt like there should be some sort of closure, some sort of resolution, something definite, not merely this confused dispersion.

They should have killed some people.

No. That wasn't it.

Yes, it was. There should have been a fight. A battle. They should have been able to shoot or stab their enemies—"

She felt suddenly cold.

"No!" she said.

They all looked over at her.

"It's not over."

Jim frowned. "What are you talking about? We killed it. We killed the brain."

"I feel ..." she began. She licked her lips. "I feel violent. I want to ... hurt something."

"But—"

"I don't usually feel that way."

"I feel it too," Faruk admitted.

Ian nodded. "It's the school."

"So what," Buckley said, "it's functioning without a brain?"

"I don't know," Ian said. "But it's still here."

And then they heard the chanting.

7

It was the scariest moment of all, Ian thought. Of everything that had happened, this was the scariest. It had been terrifying to be trapped in the Admissions office, it had been frightening to see what had happened to the school, but to hear that chanting, to know that the school was still alive, still fighting, still pushing forward toward whatever purpose it had, despite the fact that twenty thousand new students had been registered by computer, despite the fact that its brain had been destroyed, despite the fact that police and firemen and National Guardsmen were swarming onto its campus.

That was part of it too. The juxtaposition of the supernatural with the material. Horror was much, much less scary when kept in its place, when confined to graveyards and haunted houses and eldritch ruins. But when it invaded the realm of the rational, when it coexisted with tanks and firetrucks, when matter-of-fact people in solidly grounded occupations were forced to deal with unseen powers and metamorphosing matter, its impact was much more frightening.

The boundaries had been crossed.

It could not be stopped.

That was the big fear. That's what scared him the most. The idea that the school could not be stopped, that this would grow and spread, that all the king's horses and all the king's men couldn't put Brea back together again, terrified him more than he would have thought possible.

The chanting was coming from the hole, the huge tunnel that had appeared in the lawn to the north of the Administration building. He didn't want to, but he turned and walked toward the lawn, forcing himself to move forward. He looked toward the opening.

Students, scores of them, were marching out of the tunnel entrance. They were lined up in rows, in columns, like soldiers, five abreast. There were boys in football jerseys and ROTC uniforms, girls in cheerleader outfits, students in lab coats and graduation gowns. They were clutching what looked like spears, and they shouted in unison as they marched. "Queens and fairies and dykes, oh, my! Niggers and gooks and chinks, oh, my!"

He'd wondered where all the people had gone, although he hadn't wanted to say anything or even admit it to himself. There were some twenty-five thousand students who attended Brea, and they'd seen only a couple hundred on the campus itself. Obviously, the others were not sitting in classrooms. And he supposed that in the back of his mind he'd known that they hadn't left and gone home.

Now here they were.

"Wops and kikes and chollos, oh, my!"

Ian ran back toward the parade of rescuers swarming onto the campus. "Get out the hoses!" he yelled at the firemen. "Turn the hoses on them!"

He expected to have to argue, expected there to be resistance, expected that he'd have to recite a litany of unbelievable horrors in order to make his point, but to his surprise, two of the firetrucks had stopped and the firemen were already preparing to do just that. They were hooking up hoses, turning on pumps. Policemen were lining up with shields and batons.

The faces of the front line were visible now, and Ian saw Buckley's old pal Brant Keeler at the head of the marchers. Brant was battered and bloody, barefoot and limping, the skin on his face and arms burned and blackened, but he was grinning, holding high his spear.

"Out of the way!" one of the cops yelled at him, and Ian hurried back to where Eleanor and the others were standing.

A moment later the hoses were turned on, and the students went down like toys beneath the onslaught of the water, their spears flying into the air. A thrill of excitement, almost of ecstasy, coursed through him as he saw a powerful stream hit Brant Keeler's midsection and send him flying backward into the girl behind him, and he wanted the fireman to adjust the hose and hit Brant in the face, wanted to see the boy's eyes forced into his skull, his burnt skin split open.

He forced himself to close his eyes, take a deep breath, turn away.

When he looked back a moment later, the police and firemen had moved forward. The firemen, ten or twelve of them, with five or six hoses, were approaching the tunnel entrance, and behind the wall of water figures were fleeing, running back into the darkness of the hole. The policemen were picking up wet, stunned students off the grass, passing them, in a relay, toward the vans and wagons at the front of the school.

"It's still not over," Faith said, moving next to him.

He nodded. "Stevens was right. The university isn't just the people. It's the buildings, the land, everything." He nodded grimly toward the side parking lot. "We have to get the explosives out of his van. We have to take out the other buildings."

"Maybe we can plant the explosives down there," Faruk pointed toward the tunnel, where firemen were now walking inside. "That's probably the heart of it—"

"There is no heart," Ian said tiredly. "It's all the same. We'll just do what Stevens said. We'll get the buildings."

"What about us?" Jim asked. He pounded a fist against his chest. "What's going to happen to us when it goes?"

Ian still felt a residue of pain in his own chest. "I don't know," he said. "And I don't really care. Right now I'm more afraid of what the school can do to me if it lives than if it dies."

Buckley nodded. "You're right. I'm with you a hundred percent, and if any of you are too pussy to tough it out, then get out of here now and don't look back, because this place is going down."

Ian looked from Faith to Jim to Keith to Faruk to Eleanor.

"I think we're all in," Eleanor said, smiling slightly. "Although I would have said 'chickenshit' rather than 'pussy.' "

"Semantics," Buckley said.

They didn't okay the plan with anyone. They just did it, retrieving the explosives, planting them, setting timers for the hour maximum, then telling the on-site authorities what they'd done. There was no time for recriminations, barely even enough time for a panicked evacuation of the campus before the Performing Arts Center exploded in a glorious burst of sound and fury. They were standing on the far side of Thomas Avenue, behind a barricade of National Guard vehicles, tensed for pain that never came. Ian was holding tightly to Eleanor's hand, looking at Jim, at Buckley, at Faith, at Faruk, wondering if any of them were going to survive or if their heads or hearts would explode, and . . .

Nothing.

Whatever it was that had made them a part of the university, that had tied them to the school, had been severed, and they watched, physically unaffected, as one building after another exploded in perfect sequence. Beneath the noise of the explosions Ian heard screaming. It sounded like many screams, then it sounded like one scream, then it sounded human, then it sounded inhuman, and he knew it was the university itself crying out. There were shapes as well in the smoke and flames, lights and shadows, hints of figures both familiar and unfamiliar, known and unknown, but though he saw them, he did not acknowledge them, and he was not sure if anyone else noticed their existence.

Then there was a . . . a whoosh, a spontaneous wave of powerful cold that passed over him, under him, around him, through him, and then the shapes and sounds were gone. There were only normal explosions, normal fires, normal destruction.

From far away came the sounds of sirens, additional help.

Thomas Avenue was crowded with people, as were the adjacent side streets, but a lot of them were probably gawkers, and even with the gawkers there was nowhere close to twenty-five thousand individuals here.

What had happened to the rest of the students? And the faculty? And the staff?

Were they gone? Had they gotten out? Had they gone home earlier?

He didn't know, but he didn't think so.

He *hoped* so.

But he didn't think so.

He wondered what the eventual body count would be.

Thomas Avenue itself had been seriously damaged.

The road had folded and buckled, and the destruction had extended to many of the adjacent buildings.

The university had already been spreading.

They stood there for what seemed like hours, staring at the burning campus. Perhaps it was hours. He had lost all sense of time. But Eleanor was with him, and the others, and even if people had died in there, he felt good. The people who had died were the right people. They had deserved to be—

He stopped himself, feeling cold. Maybe it wasn't over.

No. It was over. He knew it. He could feel it. The university was dead. And the thoughts he was having were normal thoughts. Not pure thoughts, not good thoughts, but normal thoughts.

He wanted more than anything else to go home, to lie down in his own bed, stretch out and sleep for the next two days. He was suddenly tired, painfully so, and it was all he could do to remain standing. He had been up for—what? Three days?—and it was as though it had all caught up to him this minute. He leaned against Eleanor's shoulder. "Let's go," he said. "Let's go home."

"Can we go?" Faith asked. "Don't we have to . . . ask permission?"

"They know who we are. They know where we live. They're too busy to bother with us right now. Give them a couple days."

"Are we going to be arrested?" Faruk asked.

He didn't know, Ian realized. In horror novels the story usually ended here, with the defeat of the evil. The aftermath—practical situations, real-world problems— was never addressed. He assumed that they were free and clear. Everyone else had seen the same things they had—and a lot of other horrors would probably be uncovered during the next few days. But, technically, they had committed arson and acts of terrorism, and he supposed they could be held responsible for the physical damage they had caused.

He smiled as he thought of the trial that would be held if the city or the state tried to prosecute them.

That could be a novel in itself.

"Don't worry," he told Faruk. "You won't be arrested. You'll be fine. Go home. Go to bed."

"I need a ride," Buckley told Eleanor. "My car's in there somewhere. You think you could drive me home?"

"Sure. Anyone else need a ride?"

"I'll drive everyone else," Keith said.

Ian yawned, nodded, forced his aching legs to walk. "Keep in touch, gang. It's been real."

He and Buckley followed Eleanor past a news van and camera crew onto the sidewalk. To their right was a crowd of manacled prisoners, all lying flat on the ground, screaming, convulsing, obviously having felt physically the effects of the university's death. Lying closest to them, blackened, bloody, in pain, but still attempting to sit up, was Brant Keeler.

He saw them, grinned.

"Brant," Buckley said.

Ian nodded.

He looked at the student. The kid wasn't just a victim, he was part of the problem. The school had fed his hatred and prejudices, but it had drawn strength from him as well. It had been a symbiotic relationship, but whether the school had attracted him because of what he was or he had been attracted to the school because of what it was, Brea had not made him turn out this way. He would have been the same person no matter where he'd gone.

Brant got to his knees, stood shakily. He pointed with one burnt, manacled hand toward Eleanor. "I wish I could've fucked your wife there," he said.

Ian walked up to the student and punched him hard in the stomach. The boy went down, and Ian stepped aside, while Buckley kicked him hard in the crotch.

Buckley grinned. "You were a poor student anyway, you worthless piece of shit. I was going to give you an F." He looked at Ian, took a deep breath, looked across the street toward the school. "I feel good," he said. "I feel really good."

"Me too," Ian admitted.

Arms around each other's shoulders, they followed Eleanor to her car.

THIRTY-FIVE

1

Eleanor's clothes were back in his closet. He noticed that the next morning, or rather the next afternoon, when he awoke. He said nothing about it, but the presence of her clothes did more than anything else to make him feel that the world was back on track, that life was normal once again.

"I love you," he said when he found her, watching TV in the living room.

She stood, hugged him, kissed him. "I love you too."

The next three days were filled with questioning. By police, FBI, psychologists, lawyers. He was questioned alone; with Eleanor; with other professors; with Jim and Faith and Buckley and Faruk. In the newspaper, on TV, theories were bandied about; mass hysteria, exposure to toxic chemicals, even gang violence.

Gang violence?

Gangs had caused the walls in Neilson Hall to melt? Had caused hundreds, perhaps thousands of students to become psychotic? Had killed the president and propped her up in her office? Had ... had done everything?

But of course that evidence was gone, blown up, burned. Nearly all material evidence had been burned, and there was only eyewitness testimony to describe what had occurred.

The psychologists kept describing to him the symptoms of shock and trauma, explaining the tricks they could play on memory.

The police knew the truth, as did other governmental authorities, but they were not talking to the press. They were keeping it quiet, low-profile, and he thought about all those other old conspiracy theories.

UFO's.

JFK.

He had never dismissed those theories out of hand, but from now on he would probably listen to their arguments more carefully. The powers-that-be were more capable than he'd realized of presenting facts and tailoring approaches in such a way that the truth was buried or shunted off to the side. Not from any brilliantly conceived, comprehensive cover-up but simply by adhering to a mainstream, middle-of-the-road line of thought that invalidated anything that did not conform to prevailing wisdom.

Nedra.

He had not given her much thought, either while it was all happening or after. She, more than anyone else, had probably saved their lives—and much, much more—with her automatic registration suggestion, yet he had not really known her, had hardly spoken to her, and even now found it hard to conjure her image in his mind. He had half hoped that she'd be found alive. Hurt, perhaps, but still living, able to be saved. But survivors, almost all of them, had been discovered by the second day, and after a week had passed and she had still not turned up, he assumed that she was dead.

They still had not found all of the bodies.

He hoped her death had been quick, but he thought of the creature that had carried her off, of the two professors and what they'd been saying, and he knew that she had died painfully.

He had been allowed by the police to view the video taken from the choppers. In its last moments, from above, the campus had indeed looked like a beast, a stereotypical monster, the squarish Administration building its head, the parking lots its arms, the football and baseball fields its feet. The explosions had caused shudders to pass through the ground of the campus, and the gyrations of the earth made the school look like a creature writhing in torment. Stevens had been right about the school being a living creature, but maybe he'd been even more correct than he'd thought. Ian had paused the video. The hole in the ground, that enormous tunnel, looked from this angle like a mouth.

A mouth growing out of the creature's neck.

If they had struck early, as Jim had suggested, could all this have been avoided?

He felt some of the impotent powerlessness Stevens must have felt after the murders of his daughter and wife.

Although it was only partially visible in the video, tendrils of destruction had spread outward through the city at the death of the university. A strip mall north of the campus had gone up in flames, storeowners claiming that the fire had erupted from the earth beneath the floors of their businesses. A sinkhole had claimed a section of Imperial Highway. Brea Mall suffered a savage earthquake that was not felt even across the street and did not register at all on Cal Tech instruments. Within a five-mile radius there'd been a sudden, unexplainable, and specifically timed rise in violent crime. During a half-hour period four people had killed their spouses and six rapes had taken place.

The most ominous development, to Ian, was the fact that the phone lines between Brea and Wakefield University had been fried. Wakefield itself had suffered serious damage. Two buildings had spontaneously combusted, and a hole had been blown in the center of the football field. He wanted to believe that it was some sort of delayed explosive that Stevens had set, but he had the unsettling feeling that the spirit, the soul, the whatever-it-was that had animated Brea had attempted to escape to Wakefield through the telephone lines.

He remembered that whoosh.

But had it died there? Or had it escaped elsewhere? Had two personalities attempted for that brief time to cohabit the same body? Had either survived, and, if so, which one?

He did not know.

He supposed he would never know.

He hoped he would never have to know.

Stevens was gone. He didn't exactly feel sad, but he felt ... something, an uneasy sense of loss. Had the mantle been passed? he wondered. Was it now his responsibility to monitor the level of violence at all colleges and universities, to run around warning people when their schools were about to blow? He knew the situation, he'd lived through it, he knew how to combat it. Was he now obligated to devote the rest of his life to this cause?

No.

He would do what he could. But he would not follow in Stevens' footsteps, madly dashing from school to school, desperately attempting to blow up institutions of higher learning. Hell, there were a lot of evils in this world. Poverty, famine, murder. But because he was aware of their existence, he was not automatically obligated to spend the rest of his life working to combat them. There were such people, self-sacrificing saints willing to devote their lives to a crusade, but he was not one of them. That was not his talent, that was not why he had been put on this earth. He was a teacher, and it was his responsibility to teach, to try to inspire others the way he himself had been inspired. That was his niche, that was his duty.

But would he be able to ignore the violence at other universities?

No. He supposed he wouldn't. Whether he wanted to or not, he would be hyper-aware of sociological campus trends from here on out, his antennae constantly on the lookout for telltale signs. And if another situation came up he would be there.

But he was not Stevens. It could not be the sole reason for his existence.

Maybe the government would be monitoring everything from here on in. There was obviously a real version of events floating around because Eleanor had not been fired. Someone from somewhere had talked to a higher-up in TRW, and it had been decided that her registration of tens of thousands of credit card customers as Brea students had been "an error."

Despite the fact that she'd had to write a specific program to do it.

She was given the opportunity to "correct" her mistake.

At least one of them was employed. There was no more UC Brea, so he no longer had a job. But he'd sent out his resumé to all of the other Southern California schools, in both the UC and CSU systems, and he was confident he'd get a job somewhere.

Besides, the semester off would give him a chance to beef up his list of publications.

He could write a paper on the ability of horror fiction to emotionally prepare readers for death, loss, and disaster. Or something along those lines.

He'd considered putting together his own anthology, but he'd decided that it was better to let Stevens' work stand as the definitive example of its kind. He owed the man that much.

Maybe he'd try to write a novel.

Often, as he sat at his desk, in front of his blank word processor, he found himself thinking of the epilogue to *The Shining,* with Wendy, Danny, and Hallorann peacefully fishing by the shore of a lake in a backcountry paradise, and he thought that maybe that's what he should do, just fine some rural area, far away from the hustle and bustle of city life, and live out the rest of his days in the country, fishing, hiking, living with nature.

Then he'd think about Eleanor and he'd realize that, no matter how inviting that might sound in a novel, it would never work out for him.

They were city folk.

Always had been, always would be.

Eleanor moved in with him permanently two weeks after.

In mid-December he received an offer to teach at Cal State Fullerton.

On Christmas Eve he asked Eleanor to marry him, and she accepted.

2

They'd discussed it after everything was over.

"I guess I still have another semester to go," Jim said. He looked at Faith. "Want to go to Fullerton?"

She shook her had. "That place sucks."

"Where, then? You do want us to go to the same school?"

She smiled, nodded, held him. "Of course."

The rest of this semester was shot, so they sent applications out to several schools in both California and Arizona, and Jim took her back to Williams with him, though they slept in separate beds and bedrooms for his mom's sake.

They did it where they could, when they could—in the car at night, on hiking trails in the daytime, in the house when his mom was gone—but though he loved Faith, and she loved him, it was not the same as it was, there was something missing.

He knew what it was, but he did not want to admit it even to himself, and to Faith he pretended that everything was fine, everything was great, he was blissfully happy.

By the third week of December he had received responses from all of the schools to which he'd applied. He'd been accepted to NAU, UCLA, and Wakefield University. He told Faith and his mom about NAU and UCLA, showing them the letters, but he said nothing of Wakefield and hid the letter from that school outside in the storage shed, on a shelf behind the fertilizer. In his gut was that same feeling of dread he'd experienced during the summer, before returning to Brea, but there was something familiar and almost comforting about the feeling.

That night, after Faith and his mom were asleep, he snuck out of the house and into the storage shed.

He held the letter in one hand and masturbated.

Faith's brother, Keith, called the next day and said that she had been accepted to NAU, UC Irvine, Cal State Northridge, and Wakefield. She'd received financial aid offers from NAU and Wakefield.

"Wakefield?" Jim said.

She nodded, looked away.

"I didn't even know you'd applied there," he said.

She looked at him, looked at his mom, did not respond.

His mom was making lunch when he took Faith out to the storage shed and showed her his own letter of acceptance. He took a deep breath. "So what are we going to do?" he asked.

"I don't think we should go there," she admitted.

"Then why did you apply?"

"Why did *you* apply?"

She shook her head. "It's dangerous."

"But you miss it, don't you?"

She licked her lips, nodded slowly.

He took her there, on the floor of the shed, roughly. A trowel fell, glanced off the side of her head, and that made it even better. She reached for the trowel, slapped it hard against his buttocks.

Afterward, they lay there, hurt and spent, breathing heavily.

"We're infected," he said.

"But it's contained."

"So what do we do?"

"We go to NAU."

"Are you sure?"

She nodded. She sat up, stood, reached for the acceptance letter. "But we keep this."

Yes. That sounded good, that seemed right. He smiled, reached for his letter, took it, held it.

"Jim!" his mom called from the house. "Faith! Time for lunch!"

"Be there in a minute!" Jim yelled back.

The door slammed, and he took his letter as well and threw it back up on the shelf. He dragged her down, slapped her breasts. She grabbed his penis, squeezed, nails drawing blood.

And it was good.

11/15/23